GODSVERSE PLANETS

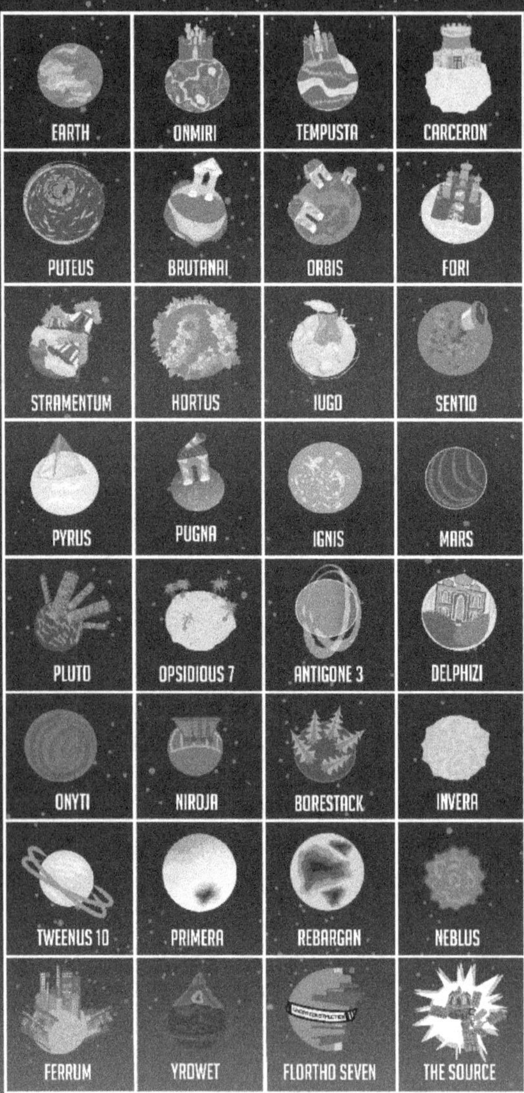

1000 BC – BETRAYED (HELL PT 1)
/PIXIE DUST
500 BC – FALLEN (HELL PT 2)
200 BC – HELLFIRE (HELL PT 3)
1974 AD – MYSTERY SPOT (RUIN PT 1)
1976 AD – INTO HELL (RUIN PT 2)
1984 AD – LAST STAND (RUIN PT 3)
1985 AD – CHANGE
1985 AD – MAGIC/BLACK MARKET HEROINE
1985 AD – EVIL
1989 AD – DEATH'S KISS
(DARKNESS PT 1)
2000 AD – TIME
2015 AD – HEAVEN
2018 AD – DEATH'S RETURN (DARKNESS PT 2)
2020 AD – KATRINA HATES THE DEAD
(DEATH PT 1)
2176 AD – CONQUEST
2177 AD – DEATH'S KISS
(DARKNESS PT 3)
12,018 AD – KATRINA HATES THE GODS
(DEATH PT 2)
12,028 AD – KATRINA HATES THE UNIVERSE
(DEATH PT 3)
12,046 AD – EVERY PLANET HAS A GODSCHURCH
(DOOM PT 1)
12,047 AD – THERE'S EVERY REASON TO FEAR
(DOOM PT. 2)
12,049 AD – THE END TASTES LIKE PANCAKES
(DOOM PT 3)
12,176 AD – CHAOS

ALSO BY RUSSELL NOHELTY

NOVELS
My Father Didn't Kill Himself
Sorry for Existing
Gumshoes: The Case of Madison's Father
Invasion
The Vessel
The Void Calls Us Home
Worst Thing in the Universe
Anna and the Dark Place
The Marked Ones
The Dragon Scourge
The Dragon Champion
The Dragon Goddess
The Obsidian Spindle Saga

COMICS and OTHER ILLUSTRATED WORK
The Little Bird and the Little Worm
Ichabod Jones: Monster Hunter
Gherkin Boy
How NOT to Invade Earth

www.russellnohelty.com

TIME

Book 3 of The Godsverse Chronicles

By:
Russell Nohelty

Edited by:
Leah Lederman

Proofread by:
Katrina Roets & Toni Cox

Cover by:
Psycat Covers

Planet chart and timeline design by:
Andrea Rosales

BOOK 1

CHAPTER 1

In the ashes of her past, she will rise, and her death will save us all.

My mom thought getting a psychic reading would be a good birthday present. After all, I was constantly worried about the future ever since my adopted sister disappeared through a portal into another world and never returned. Even though the pixie Kimberly came back and told me that Anjelica was just fine on whatever planet she'd ended up on, that didn't make me feel much better. I mean, I was happy she wasn't dead but—well, I didn't even know being whisked across the universe was a possible future for somebody. I was only twelve and hyper-impressionable, so I became rather obsessed with the idea that something I couldn't even fathom would come out of left field and suck out my soul, or vaporize me, or turn me into a toadstool for the rest of my life.

No matter how many times my mom, Junebug, told me, "Lizzie, you're being a drama queen," I had one irrefutable piece of evidence that proved my worries were warranted. After all, it happened to my sister, or at least the closest thing to a sister I ever had. We weren't blood, and I only knew her for a week, but Junebug and Carl adopted her all the same, just like they had me, and that made us family. They never made that mistake again, unfortunately, which made me an only child, at least on this planet, what with Angelica living her life somewhere across the galaxy.

The town we lived in—Bronard, Missouri—had a lot of weird people in it. Some might even call them monsters. I don't know what drew so much fairy folk and monsters to our little piece of America, but Mom liked to boast that we had the most fairy folk per capita anywhere in the contiguous United States. I didn't know if that was true. It's one of those unverifiable pieces of Americana, like the world's biggest ball of wax or the biggest ham sandwich. Sure, maybe even Guinness would back us, but there's no saying somebody didn't make a bigger sandwich just for laughs. It was a big sandwich we had in Bronard though, and fairy folk were the meat inside of it, that much I knew. We weren't cannibals or anything, I'm just bad at metaphors.

One of the most unique of all the fairy folk that lived in Bronard was the Oracle, just like the ones that used to reside in Delphi. They said this one was a descendant of theirs, but that was just hearsay—little towns ran on gossip, and Bronard was no different. Nobody really knew the truth about the Oracle for sure. Most people kept clear of her since she rarely gave good news. The best you could hope was that her prophecy had nothing useful in it at all and just said you were gonna be a boring sod plowing sod for the rest of your life. That's what I was hoping for, at least, when I'd gotten my reading.

Mom had thought it would be a good idea to get me one, even with all the warning signs, if for no other reason than to prove that I was destined to live a simple, old life, helping her with the bakery and helping Dad with the farm. Might seem like a boring life to some people, but that's all I wanted. I didn't need to become a space pope. I just wanted a little piece of Earth and a little peace of mind.

That's not how things worked out, though.

I remembered every moment, every aching syllable, of our interaction. It stuck to me like a wet shirt.

Mom brought me to Starr Wolfsong—what a name for an Oracle— a couple of days after my sixteenth birthday in 1990, back before cell phones or AOL, when we still had to play phone tag to catch somebody instead of checking their away message. It was a simpler time, though maybe it was just simpler for me.

The Oracle lived in a trailer park, in a double-wide that sunk as we stepped up to it, creaking at us to stay away. We didn't listen. It was double for Mom to sit and listen to the fortune, and when she asked if I wanted her to stay, I shook my head. I was a brave girl. I could handle it, or so I thought.

"Would you like half my grilled cheese?" Starr asked with a hoarse voice, her gray-skinned hand wobbling as she held out her bony arm to me.

"No, thanks," I said.

Starr looked unhealthily gaunt, skin hanging off little more than bones as if the muscles underneath had melted away. She lit a cigarette and took a deep inhale, and then blew it out the open window next to her. The whole of the trailer reeked of smoke and misery which, even without the woman looking like she would keel over any moment, was enough to make me lose my appetite.

"I sense apprehension in you," she said through her thin lips. "If I may offer you a piece of advice. You will not like what you hear, so I suggest you leave now."

"How do you know?"

She ran her bony fingers through strands of thinning hair. "I have lived too many years and performed too many readings. Were I a charlatan, I could pretend that I don't see the death of every soul that walks through my trailer. If I were a better showman, I might be able to imbue my prophesies with an ounce of hope." She coughed a wet cough into her hand for a long moment before catching my eyes again. "People do not want the truth. If they did, I would be as rich as Miss Cleo or any of them who prey on the insecure. People pay for comforting lies, not harsh truths."

"My mother seems to think it will help me."

Starr flicked the cigarette out of her hand, and it landed in a puddle of muddy water. She turned to me, setting her hands face up in the middle of the table. "Place your hands in mine, and your fate will be known—though I warn you: None get out of this world alive."

"Are you saying you will see my death?"

She took a shallow breath, wheezing as she let it out. "I do not know what I will see. That is the nature of my power. I am a slave to it."

I nodded and slowly, gingerly placed my hands inside hers. The moment I did, a shock jolted through my body as if my fingers were touching an electrical wire. I opened my mouth, trying to scream, but before I could, the sensation passed, and my body relaxed.

Starr was still, her eyeballs rolled back into her head so that only the bloodshot whites were visible. She muttered under her breath for a long moment, her voice barely audible. With every loop of her circuitous words, I made them more clearly until they filled my soul with dread.

"In the ashes of her past, she will rise, and her death will save us all," the Oracle gurgled like her mouth was filled with water. "In the ashes of her past, she will rise, and her death will save us all."

She continued in that manner until her words boomed against the walls, echoing off every surface. I tried to pull my hands from her clutches, but her weak arms held me tightly, no matter how hard I pulled back.

"Stop!" I shouted. "STOP! MOM!"

The door slammed open, and my mother saw what horror she wrought on me as she heard Starr's screaming words. "In the ashes of her past, she will rise, and her death will save us all!"

Seeing the dread in my face, Mom reached forward to pry me free from the Oracle's fingers. When her hands weren't strong enough by themselves, she ran to the kitchen and pulled a butter knife out of the drawer. She wedged it under the woman's knuckles and wrenched me away, one finger at a time.

When I was finally free, Starr's shrieking stopped, and she fell onto the table, limp. She wasn't dead, but she had been knocked unconscious.

"Should we call an ambulance?" I asked.

"Don't bother." A woman stepped out from the hallway. She had big red hair like Reba McEntire and a gruff, gritty voice like she gargled with rocks. "Happens three times a week, and she couldn't afford the ambulance ride even if you did call." She brushed past me. "Just go. I'll take care of her." She turned back to me and narrowed her eyes. "I hope it was worth it."

It wasn't, but I didn't say that. Instead, I looked over at Mom, who made her way out of the trailer. There was a deep shame in her eyes like she'd known what would happen. Or maybe she knew what I would do next.

In the ashes of her past, she will rise, and her death will save us all.

I spent the next week thinking, ruminating over those words. I went back to the trailer park, looking for the Oracle, but she had packed up and left town. I was the straw that broke her back, apparently, and I didn't quite know how to feel about my prophecy causing such a reaction in her that she had no recourse but to flee town.

The only thing I knew for sure was that Carl and Junebug, my parents, were in trouble. They were my past and they were my present. I did not want them to turn to ash so that I could rise. I didn't want any of it, and I especially didn't want to be a savior.

I did the only thing that I could think of to save my parents. I ran away and didn't stop running. Maybe it was a rash decision, but it was the right one. I was sure of it. It was hard at first, moving from town to town the minute I caught feeling for something or someone, desperate not to have a past, so there would be nothing to burn.

Over the next ten years, it got easier, at least that's what I told myself. Nothing like a comforting lie to help you sleep at night.

CHAPTER 2

My latest home was a small town called Oakmont, California, far from the hustle and bustle of places like Los Angeles and San Francisco. Most people think that the Golden State is all glitz and glamour, full of coastal liberal elites, movie stars, and beaches. Really, most of California was farm country, filled with farmers, truckers, and people who worked with their hands.

Sure, Los Angeles had an outmoded influence in the state, but even at a million square miles, it was a fraction of the total land in the state. Oakmont rested above San Francisco and east of Napa Valley, up where the slanted coastline turned straight for Oregon. I had worked up in Oregon as a waitress for three months before somebody caught feelings for me, and I left.

There were a few keys to being able to leave a place in the dead of night at the drop of a hat. First, you needed a crappy job that paid you in cash at regular intervals. You couldn't spend two weeks waiting for that last paycheck. It also helped to have a job you hated. It was another bonus if they didn't ask questions about your work history. Any job that needed a resume was out. Waitressing fit all those things at once. Almost all my wages were made in tips that I pocketed at the end of the night, and it was terrible work that I absolutely hated.

Nothing against the profession. I knew there were people who liked waitressing and were much better at it than me. I didn't have the personality for it. Getting yelled at for getting an order wrong, standing on your feet for twelve hours, and smelling like greasy, sweaty, swamp ass after a long shift was not my idea of a good time, not to mention the pay was crap, even in bigger cities—though I almost never stopped in those since they were too expensive.

So that's the first and second key to life on the road, I guess. The third, final, and most important, was that you could never form an attachment to anyone, no matter what. My rule was that I couldn't stay in a place more than six months even if I liked it because just being around people enough made me like them, and liking somebody was a good way to build a past with them, and I didn't want anyone to burn because of me.

I would never admit it to his face, but that's the reason I left the last town. I liked a boy too much. His name was Tom, and I liked him enough that I was already considering leaving before he admitted the attraction was mutual, and it pushed me over the edge. If I was honest with myself, I probably stayed too long even before Tom confessed his love for me, all because of a serious bout of lonely, and he was the treatment. A stout, gentle, country boy, who always said "please" and "thank you" after ordering, and called me ma'am, no matter how many times I told him to call me Lizzie.

There were Toms all over the country, ghosts of lives I might have had if I stayed in Bronard, if I'd had the simple future I wanted. It seemed like at least twice a year, I fell for somebody in one town or another along the road, and it was happening more frequently with each passing season. It was a lonely life, and I was still a warm-blooded woman at the end of the day. It was all I could do not to act on my impulses…but I never did. I hadn't even kissed anyone since my boyfriend, Pete, in high school.

He had been the hardest one to leave. We were together since middle school—since Anjelica taught me how to flirt so, I could get his attention. He would have graduated college already. I often wondered about what he was doing, but he was my past—a past I was trying to protect by being on the run. I wasn't doing him any favors by keeping him in my thoughts.

I was in Oakmont now, and the present was where I needed to focus my attention. I had been working at Murray's for four weeks since blowing into town and was just getting the hang of the regulars who came in for their morning breakfast before work and the ones that caught me on the way home after their shift.

It always amazed me how every town was the same. They all had their little diners, at least one that had the best pancakes in town and another that made its money by being open later than the others, even though their food was average.

Murray's was the former. I had worked in dozens, maybe hundreds at this point, and every one of them had their own little customer base, and they always tipped better if you remembered their orders by heart.

"Short stack, over easy, with a cup of joe?" I asked a bearded man with long, black hair and olive skin. His name was Jeff, and I appreciated that his order was simple and consistent. There were bigger orders than Jeff's, and bigger tippers, too, but Jeff was quiet and polite, with dark brown eyes that you could get lost in forever. Yes, I certainly had a type.

"That's right, ma'am," he said, and I bit the inside of my lip to stop from letting out a little moan. It got harder and harder to deny my body's needs. We were pack animals, after all, and forced celibacy was driving me nutty. "And could you bring some sugar and cream, too?"

"Of course, sugar," I said with a playful smile that oozed with unintentional flirtation. "Be right back."

I wrote down the order and slid it into the queue on the kitchen counter. A big, gruff bull named Oscar spun the orders around the belt until he grabbed it, grunted, and then went to work.

"What are you waiting for?" Victoria, one of the other waitresses, the nosey one who's always up in everyone's business—every workplace I've ever been at had one like her—said to me. "He is Heaven on a stick."

I shook my head. "He's not my type."

"Pardon my French," Victoria said. "But that's a load of bull. I see the way he looks at you, and I hear the lilt in your voice when you chat with him. Not to mention the bounce in your step when you walk away from his table."

"There is no bounce!" I replied, indignant.

"You're lying to yourself, kiddo." Victoria shook her head. "That's the worst kind of lying."

The bell rang behind me, and an order came up. "Comforting lies are all I have."

I grabbed the order and brought two plates to a couple of truckers in the corner that I didn't recognize. Since it was a small town, ninety percent or so of the customers were regulars, and if I didn't recognize them by now, it meant they were probably just passing through. The diner wasn't far from the freeway, which made it convenient for long haulers to stop off for a meal while they were on the road. Once I served the truckers, I went to fill up water glasses for a family of four on a road trip, and a woman eating alone, drinking coffee like it was going out of style.

The whole time, I kept the side of my eye on Jeff, thinking about what Victoria had said. Maybe it would be okay to have a one-night stand with—no, that's how it started. One night became ten, and before long, you had a past and a future, and then you were dead.

I spent a lot of time thinking about not risking anybody's life, but I would be lying if I didn't admit the biggest reason I was avoiding my prophecy was to prevent my own death. Yes, the past would burn, but when it did, I would die…and I didn't want to die.

"Order up!"

I picked up Jeff's order from the window and brought it over to him.

"Looks delicious," he replied with a smile. "Oscar's talents are lost in a place like this."

"Yeah, they're really lucky to have him, I guess." I turned around. "I'll be right back with your coffee."

I rushed behind the counter; my breath hurried with teenage adrenaline just from being near Jeff. I needed to calm down. This wasn't like me. I was cool, controlled, and focused. He was only a guy—one of a hundred guys I'd crushed on over the years, who vanished out of my brain the moment I was a hundred miles away.

I brought the coffee and set it down next to Jeff. He took it with a smile, and when I turned away, he cleared his throat.

"Yes?" I said, turning back to him but trying to avoid his fiery eyes.

"You forgot the sugar, sugar," he said with a carefree smile.

"Dang it! Right." I grabbed a handful of sugar packets from another table and brought them over to him. "Here you go."

When I set them down, he slid his hand over mine, just for a moment. A flash of electricity flowed through me. I turned to look into his eyes and saw my entire life flash between us. I saw a wedding and children, and happiness…but I also saw a fire, and finally, my death.

I yanked my hand away quickly. I gave him a small smile and turned, taking a big gulp of air. Well, this town was nice while it lasted, but it was time to move on before beautiful Jeff became a casualty of my prophecy, and then, inevitably, I did, too.

CHAPTER 3

I learned very early in my travels that if you wanted to leave at a moment's notice, you had to travel light. Over the years, I only accumulated enough stuff to fill my old purple Jansport from before I dropped out of high school, and a small rolling suitcase where I kept two pairs of jeans, a black pleated skirt, and a black dress, along with enough underwear to last a week, plus two pairs of heels that needed to be repaired or replaced, a pair of slippers, and an extra pair of tennis shoes, along with a puffy coat and a light jacket. In my backpack, I kept a lockpicking kit, toiletries, a small make-up kit, a CD player, whatever books I was reading at the time— I'd just finished Anne Rice's *Interview with a Vampire,* and now it was Dan Brown's *Angels and Demons*—and a first aid kit. For a while, I kept old aprons and nametags from all the places I worked, but I packed in a hurry some years ago and lost them somewhere around Nebraska.

It was for the best because they linked me to my past and the memories I made along the way. As it stood, I tried my best not to keep any clothing for more than a year if I could help it. The only thing I kept from my childhood was a black opal necklace that my mother once gave me for protection.

There was nothing else to bind me to the past, not even my name, which I made sure to change at least once a season whenever I could find a good counterfeiter. Usually, I worked with some high school or college kid who could connect me with somebody that made fake IDs, but they were of dubious quality. I needed them to fool even the police. In a pinch, I could make one, but good equipment wasn't cheap, and I rarely had extra money lying around.

After cleaning out my motel room, I walked to the front desk. There wasn't a fancy name for it or anything. It just said "motel" in big, neon letters that buzzed through the night. Bugz kept the place clean enough, and the price was right. Apropos of the owner's name, the place was littered with cockroaches, but they scattered when the lights were on. I almost always stayed in motels wherever I traveled. I didn't even want to commit to a month-to-month lease.

"Evening, Niobe," Bugz said to me, giving me a smile that showed all four of his chipped front teeth. "What can I do ya for?"

"Checking out, Bugz," I replied.

His face dropped, and he scratched the stubble on his chin. "That's a shame. You were a good tenant. Never made no trouble for me." He leaned in. "Not like some people who come here for all sorts of illicit activities."

"I've heard 'em here and there," I said. "I just try to keep my head down and stay out of trouble."

His face scrunched. "Seems like trouble found you, though, didn't it?"

He pointed past me to a shadow that stood next to my Civic hatchback. I recognized Kimberly's outline immediately, even in the dark. She had a way of standing out when she wanted to look tough, and she had tracked me down enough times that I knew the way she leaned against my car.

I grumbled to myself and put down a wad of money. "Looks that way. This should be enough since I paid up last Friday."

Bugz flipped quickly through the wad of fives and ones, and then nodded. "Seems like it's all there. Take care of yourself, Niobe, ya hear?"

I pushed open the glass door of the office. "I'm trying, but some people aren't making it easy."

I felt like stomping across the parking lot and having it out with Kimberly, but that's exactly what she wanted—to get under my skin—and I wasn't about to give her the satisfaction. Instead, I smiled brightly at her, putting on my best "aggrieved waitress trying desperately to stay sane face", and walked toward her.

"I thought I finally lost you," I said. "How did you find me? This town isn't even on the map."

Kimberly had bangs that cut across her face like Aaliyah, and her black hair was just as shiny. I had no idea how she fought when she could only see out of one eye, but she managed somehow because she was still alive. In her line of work, that meant something. It wasn't just anybody who could track down demons and slaughter them. I was deeply scared of Kimberly the first time she tracked me down but had since numbed to her incredible powers.

"You're getting sloppy," Kimberly said. "You used to drive for days, zig-zagging across the country before you stopped. This one was less than a day's drive, and it seems like you took the 5 all the way down here. You didn't even switch cars. That's amateur." She pushed off the car. "Plus, I got a look at the stash of IDs you keep in the glove box last time, and there are surprisingly few Niobe's in California."

I sighed. "Yeah, I knew I was going to have trouble with those weird names I bought last time. Then again, I figured you would just go away."

"It's been a decade, kiddo. When will you learn I'm never going away?"

"When will you appreciate what I'm trying to do here? Oh right, you don't fear death because you're immortal."

She held up her hands. "I am as the gods made me."

"As Thanatos made you if I remember correctly." I shook my head. "What do you want?"

She sighed. "Junebug is sick. Doctors don't think she's going to make it through the month. She wants to see you before the end."

My fists clenched. I felt my heart thump faster in my chest and the tears well in my eyes, but I did everything in my power to appear calm. "So?"

Kimberly's brow furrowed. "You've been trying to outrun your past—to decouple your emotions from everything you were for over a decade, and one mention of your mom sends you to tears. Maybe that's a good indication running isn't a good idea anymore."

"Goddamn it!" I threw my hands in the air. "I'm doing this to save them."

Kimberly had found me a dozen times before in a dozen cities around the country, and every time she did, she tried to convince me to return home to be with my parents—that I could have a normal life, even knowing what I knew. She tried to tell me that my past wouldn't burn and I wouldn't die. Every time, I sent her back to my parents empty-handed, but now with my mom dying…*how could I not go?*

"That's garbage!" Kimberly screamed. "You're doing this to save yourself. That's fine, honestly, but why don't you think of somebody other than yourself for a change and go see your mother before she dies?"

"All I do is think of other people!" I shouted back. Before the words even left my mouth, the tears began to fall. Big, heaping tears like I hadn't cried in years—like I don't know if I had ever cried, at least not in the past decade. It was as if every emotion I'd siphoned away flooded out of me at once. I collapsed on the ground, right there in that motel parking lot, and curled up in a ball.

"What's going on out here?" Bugz shouted as the door to the motel office flung open. "You okay, Niobe?"

I don't know what I said to him, but whatever I pushed out of my mouth seemed to be enough to satisfy him, and he went back into his office, though when my eyes found the window, I saw him watching me as Kimberly rubbed my back.

Eventually, the tears were gone, and there was nothing left to do but clean myself up. I walked back into the lobby and asked if I could use his bathroom. Graciously, Bugz gave me the key to my old room.

"You still technically have it 'til morning." He smiled at me as I left him.

I didn't notice that Kimberly had followed me inside until I came out of the bathroom and yelped in surprise at her standing there. I thought about saying something vicious but choked it back and sat on the bed, alone, as she sat on the chair across from me.

"What does she have?" I asked.

"Cancer," Kimberly replied.

"What kind?" I whispered, barely able to keep it together.

"One of the bad ones. Pancreas, or at least it metastasized there, and her lungs, and her—the last set of x-rays lit up like Rockefeller Center on Christmas, Lizzie. I think it would be easier to tell you where she doesn't have cancer right now."

"What about chemo? Radiation? Whatever other stuff they have to fight this stuff?"

"She's been sick for a long time," Kimberly said. "She swore me to secrecy. Didn't want me to guilt you into coming home. Now there's nothing left but to wait for the end."

"Why are you telling me?"

"Cuz I want you to see your mom before she dies. She's earned that much. Even if she doesn't want it, she needs it. I think now she's just holding on…she's just holding on to the hope that you'll come home—"

I had never seen Kimberly waver in all my years, but the tears came, even for her. I walked into the bathroom and brought her a roll of toilet paper. She took a few squares and dabbed her eyes, taking a moment.

"Junebug would kill me if she knew I told you this." Kimberly sighed. "Or she would if she wasn't bed— bedridden." She barely choked out the last words, and I felt for her. She was family to my mother, and vice versa.

"If waiting for me to come home is the only thing that's keeping her alive, then I can't go back. I can't be the reason she dies—I can't."

Kimberly nodded, more to herself than me. "I figured you would say that. I hoped maybe this time would be different, but deep down, I knew it wouldn't." She pushed herself off the chair. "You're the most selfish being I've ever met in my whole stupid existence…and I'm including demons into that equation."

"How am I selfish? I'm staying away to save her!"

"No," Kimberly replied. "You're staying away to save yourself. It's okay, like I said. I don't know why I expected this time to be any different."

She reached into a pouch on her belt and pulled out a pinch of pink powder. Without another word, she threw it on the ground and disappeared into a puff of pink smoke. With the lingering smell of burnt ember from Kimberly's smoke, I threw myself on the bed and began to cry again.

CHAPTER 4

Every turn of the tires crashed like a wave of guilt on my heart, but I knew I was making the right decision…didn't I? If I went to see my mother, I would be putting her in danger, both from the prophecy and from her own will to live. If I wanted her to live, I had to stay away and live with the guilt.

It wasn't like I hadn't come to terms with guilt. Hell, I'd worn it like an old shawl since I ran away. That first night I left home, I could barely close the door on Dad's pickup truck, and I had to fight against my own body to put the key to the ignition. It was like I got punched in the gut when the engine turned over, but I was determined to leave, to protect those that I loved, and never to love anything or anyone ever again. Once I found a new car, I called and told Carl where to find the truck. I couldn't have that on my conscience, too.

It was a lonely, solitary life, and through the last decade, the one thing I could count on was the guilt. It sat with me every day. Sometimes, it squeezed my stomach so tight I could barely move, but usually, it was a light din, like something ringing in my ear. It just needed somebody like Kimberly to turn the volume up.

She wasn't wrong, either. She was just a dick about it. She saw things from her side and from Mom and Dad's side, but she never tried to see things my way. Imagine being sixteen years old and told that you must die to save the world, and that your past must burn along with you. Yes, Kimberly had had a tough row, too. As a baby, she'd been kidnapped and brought to Hell as a sacrifice to the Devil. Later, she had to watch as the mentor who saved her from that terrible fate was slaughtered in front of her eyes.

But Kimberly had agency to fight against that fate. She became a monster hunter, a savior of fairy folk. She didn't have to die to fulfill her destiny. She didn't have to burn her past to live her life.

I did.

I wished I'd never known my fate. I could have gone on in ignorant bliss. But now, a nagging thought pushed its way to the surface—could anyone really outrun their fate? I had built my life on the idea that you could. Deep in the back of my brain, the part of my brain that only spoke in the deepest silence, I knew I was on a fool's errand; if the fickle finger of fate wanted me to die, it would find a way to make it so.

Hell, it was nudging me right now, pushing me back to my past, the past that I'd done everything in my power to avoid. If my past died before I showed up, then it couldn't burn, could it?

Ah, there you have it, Lizzie, the crux of the matter. You can't kill the past if it dies without you, and if you can fight against that part of the prophecy, then perhaps you didn't have to die at all, at least not for a very long time—as an old woman, maybe. Peacefully, in your sleep. *That's what you want, after all, in the end, right?* You don't care that your mother will die without seeing you for a decade—that your father will die alone, without his wife to help him pass into the darkness. What matters is that you'll be alive.

I clutched the steering wheel and turned off the road at the next town I saw. Any town would do. I wasn't picky. I often fought against my guilt by swerving into whatever truck stop town came up on the map. I couldn't take the voices pounding in the back of my head. One of the best tactics against guilt was to fill it with work, and lots of it.

I had no idea how long I had been driving or where I was exactly, just that the name on the exit said Edgemont Rd, and it was somewhere along the 80 past Reno. Everywhere in Nevada looked kinda the same: Large swaths of desert speckled with lush forests and small towns nestled by the bits of water that popped up along the way.

It was the middle of the night, but I passed a couple of motels with vacancy signs. There was no point in going to bed. My brain wouldn't shut up until morning. Better to find an open diner, get some food, and check out the classifieds for a job. I had acquired enough skills over the last decade that I could do most entry-level jobs well enough. I had experience working at call centers, logging companies, answering phones, telemarketing for vitamin companies, selling cars, and, of course, waitressing. That was the one I kept coming back to, even though it was the one I liked least—except for telemarketing. There was nothing worse than calling people, interrupting their dinner, and getting them to scream at you for five minutes, or hanging up on you in the middle of a sentence.

It didn't take me long to find the little diner with the lights on. Several semis were parked outside, which was how I judged a good diner. Truckers talked, and you could always rely on them for recommendations on good, fast, cheap eats along the interstates. I often peppered them with questions about their favorite towns along their routes, and more than once used their recommendations when I moved further down the line.

Sometimes, I would get a trucker who became a regular at more than one place I had worked, even if they were hundreds of miles apart. Maybe that should have been a cue to move on, but there was never any fear of developing more than a passing connection with them. They never stayed around one place for more than a meal, anyway. However, now that I thought about it, maybe that's how

Kimberly tracked me across the country, by using the same truckers I did to rebuild my path.

Very sneaky. I would be sure to take side streets and country roads next time. Although if Junebug died, I doubt she'd be looking for me anymore. Kimberly liked my father enough, but she would kill for my mother. Watching Junebug suffer couldn't have been easy, and it likely drove the pixie to check up on me more often than she otherwise would have—to beg me to come home. Once Junebug was gone and the constant pain was off her heart, Kimberly would forget about me, and that would be for the best.

The bell over the glass door dinged when I opened it, and a smiling waitress, way too perky for the middle of the night, walked over to me wearing a pink apron and red shoes, accented with a red headband to pull back her brown hair. Her nametag read Becky in glittering letters.

"What can I do ya for, hon?" she said.

"Table for one, please."

"Follow me," she replied, snaking through the empty tables to a red vinyl booth by a window looking out at the main road. "Here you go."

She handed me the menu, and I smiled at her. "You don't have to do that, Becky."

She cocked her head. "Do what?"

"I'm a waitress, too," I said. "I know that customer voice anywhere, and it's exhausting, so you don't have to, but if you want to drop the act around me, it's okay."

Becky took a deep breath, and the smile dropped from her face. When she spoke again, her voice had dropped half an octave. "Thank Christ. I'm at the second half of a double, and I don't think I could pretend to give a care about one more person. No offense."

"Girl, I have been there." I looked at the menu. "What's good here?"

"People like the burger, but what greasy spoon doesn't have a good burger, right?"

"What kind of fries?"

"Real crispy ones," she said.

I pointed at her. "That's what I want. And do you have a vanilla milkshake?"

"We do, but the strawberry is better, in my opinion."

"I'll have that, then. I know better than to go against a waitress's recommendation."

The thing I liked most about greasy spoons was that they didn't care about presentation. They were much more worried about taste, the good ones at least, which was where I tried to end up. Becky wasn't wrong; the burger was dynamite. Though, if you couldn't get a burger right, you had no business being in the diner business.

As I savored my meal, the few truckers in the diner funneled out until it was just Becky and me. She smiled at me as she cleaned the tables around me, and when that was done, hopped from one foot to another, trying to maintain the energy to stand on her aching feet.

"How much time do you have left on the clock?" I asked her.

She looked up to the glittering wall clock above the counter. "Two hours."

"Busy this time of night?"

She shook her head. "Not too bad. Could be a couple more people or a couple dozen before I get to go home. All of 'em will be crap tippers, though. That's for sure."

I swirled a fry into my milkshake and popped it into my mouth. "Want some help? I'm a pretty good waitress if I do say so."

"Uhm…I don't know how to answer that."

I pushed the basket of fries over to her. "If you're anything like me, you haven't eaten since you started shift. So, how about you eat some fries, take a load off, and I'll handle the next customer." She looked at me funny, trying to size me up. "You keep the tips, too."

"What's in it for you?"

I popped another fry. "I'm new in town, and I need a job, so you might consider it a tryout, and well…I really don't want to be alone right now. Doing work will stop the voices in my head from driving me crazy."

She stepped over to my table, and I handed her a fry. "I am real hungry."

I slipped out of the chair. "What can I get you? My treat."

She lost the last of her resolve and slid into the booth across from where I had just been sitting. "You wouldn't believe it, but Bryan back there makes a real mean Cajun chicken pasta."

"Weird, but I like it."

CHAPTER 5

Turned out that Becky didn't have the power to hire any new waitresses, though she did put in a good word to Celeste, the owner of the restaurant, who ran me through my paces before agreeing to hire me.

"Lots of people just want a job here cuz they think it'll be easy," Celeste said during my interview. "When they realize it's hard, harder than hell, they decide it's not for them. That sound like you, Jude M—"

"Absolutely not," I cut in before she could finish saying my new assumed identity. "I've worked waitressing jobs before, and I know just how hard they are. If people got paid based on how hard a job was, we'd all be making Bill Gate's salary, is what I say."

"Amen, sister." I didn't actually ever say that, but it seemed to appease Celeste. She looked me up and down for a long time, furrowing her brow. "Are you a size six?"

"Depends on the cut."

"Bryan!" Celeste hollered. "Bring me a six."

A tall man with a mustache came into the office carrying the same pink apron I'd seen Becky wear the previous night. I didn't realize that the apron was sewn into the dress itself, making it all the more hideous.

"Here you go, my little waterfall," he said, twitching his mustache as he gingerly handed it to Celeste. "Anything else?"

"Not right now, sweet thing." Bryan left, and Celeste handed the dress-apron combo to me. "The customers like it. It cinches in all the right places."

"You don't have to convince me to wear a demeaning dress, ma'am. I have been in this game for a long time. Whatever brings in tips, right?"

"And keeps people coming back. The more you flirt, well…you know."

Nobody wanted to say that the job was as much pretending to flirt with the customers as anything else. I didn't have any reservations about that part of it. I'm sure there were some waitressing jobs where that wasn't true, but truckers had simple pleasures. After being stuck in a truck for a dozen hours, having a lady be nice for a couple of minutes as they ate their food made them feel good, and that went a long way to getting a nice tip. We were all whores in some way. Maybe we didn't have sex for money, but we sold our souls for it. The way I figured it, if you were going to prostitute yourself, it helped to understand the rules of the game and how to exploit them to your advantage. I didn't have many things going for me, but I was always charming.

I was supposed to be on probation for the first couple of weeks, learning the ropes from Becky's expert guidance, but I already knew the lingo and had excellent customer service skills. After three days, they took off the training wheels and let me work on my own. I found a motel up the road, close enough that I could walk, and worked as many hours as they would give me.

It always surprised me how quickly I acclimated to a new place. Within a week, my new life felt like normal. The town of Edgewater, Nevada, became my new home, and the customers soon became regulars. Becky and I became friends, or as close to it as I would let myself get to the idea.

I never let our friendship leave the diner. Once I stepped out into the parking lot, she didn't exist, as far as I was concerned. On the clock, we were inseparable. It was amazing how you could work a hundred jobs not connecting to a single person, and then step into a place where you feel an instant bond like you were sisters, separated at birth. She told me about her life, her ex-husband, and her little girl, Veronica, a precocious six-year-old too smart for her own good.

Sometimes, Veronica would come into the diner after school and do her homework. She was dark-skinned with a puffy afro that her mother kept meticulously quaffed. She didn't talk much, but one day I showed her how delicious dipping fries into milkshakes could be, and she fell in love with me. Every time she came into the diner, she begged her mother for fries and a shake, and Becky always relented. That girl had her mother wrapped around her finger.

I actually legitimately liked both of them, which was vexing for me, but it kept the guilt of my mother at bay. I decided to use Becky and Veronica's happiness like a drug to anesthetize me to my failed relationship with my parents. I should have left, but I just…couldn't get the courage to do so…not yet. Turned out I was just as big a hypocrite as anyone else.

I grew very protective over them in short order, partially because the kid was nearly impossible not to love, but also because Becky had terrible taste in men—or specifically, one man—Rick.

"You seen Becky?" He came in the restaurant at all hours, asking the same question, bothering her at work, and, more than once, nearly getting her fired. This particular day he looked worse than usual. His pale skin was moist with sweat, and the bags under his eyes were more pronounced.

"She hasn't come in yet, today, Rick," I replied as I slid behind the counter to place an order. "Stack of Vermont, frog sticks, fry two, let the sun shine, and a 50/50." When I turned back around, Rick was still there. Usually, he rushed out as quickly as he came in, but today, he wasn't leaving. "Why are you still here?"

"I have to find her, Jude." It had been almost a month, and the new name still didn't sit right with me. "Now."

"Maybe she left you." I pressed my hands into the counter. "I've been pushing her pretty hard to dump your ass."

"She would never do that." He shook his head fervently. "I protect her."

My eyes narrowed. "That's what all abusers say."

"I'm NOT—!" He cleared his throat as all eyes in the diner turned to him. "I'm not abusing her." He reached into his shirt and squeezed a necklace under it. "I protect her. We protect each other."

"I've heard that before."

"Listen to me!" He screamed, slapping the counter loudly. The movement jostled his clothing and set the necklace free. My eyes went wide. It was a black opal, just like the type my mother gave fairies to protect them from something terrible coming to find them. "We have to stay together."

"Where did you get that?" I asked, pointing to the necklace.

He suddenly realized the necklace was out and stuffed it back into his shirt. "Nothing. Nowhere. Don't—please. She talks to you. Have you—"

Behind him, the glass door swung open, and four men, bulky, tall, hulking even, entered, each uglier and meaner than the last.

"It's over," the man in front said, the folds of his neck creasing his bald head. "Give us the girl."

Rick knocked his hands together and shot fire from the tips of his fingers toward the men, who walked forward as if the fire was a harmless breeze. The other people in the diner weren't so calm and began to rush from their booths toward the other door.

"You're a fae," I said.

"Don't be crazy," Rick replied. "You're talking foolish."

One of the men, this one with a demon tattooed on his cheek, swung at Rick. He ducked it and knocked the tattooed man in the face before kicking him backward, crashing through the glass door. The other three advanced, and I did something stupid. Something I hadn't done since I was a child.

"*Frigus tempestas*!" I shouted, and ice shot from the tips of my fingernails, coating the men in a thick layer of ice. I slid over the counter and grabbed Rick by the hand. "Come on!"

"You're a fae, too?"

"DUH!" I screamed. "I try not to use my powers in public, though, and now I gotta leave another town because I did. Thanks a lot, Rick!"

We slammed through the front door. "This isn't my fault!"

"Well, it's definitely not mine! So, if not mine and not yours, whose fault is it? And don't you dare say Becky or

Veronica." I looked around the parking lot. "Where's your car?"

He pointed to a piece of crap brown Buick Century from the 80s, big as a boat and twice as slow. We rushed toward it and got in. Rick peeled away just as the men smashed through their ice prisons and ran outside.

They fired at us on our way onto the street. I ducked the bullets, but then the horn blared as the car began to turn toward the sidewalk. I spun around to see Rick lying on the steering wheel, his head bleeding from a bullet wound.

"Shit." I reached over and pulled the driver's seat door open before kicking Rick out onto the road. It was an inauspicious end for a man I had completely misjudged, but the shooters were rushing forward, and I didn't have time to be delicate.

I slid over into the driver's seat and kicked my foot onto the gas, the door flapping open as I gunned it. I yanked it shut as the bullets fired into the car, barely missing me. I tore off down the street and couldn't help but laugh through my fear. *The fickle finger of fate was a fucker.*

CHAPTER 6

I racked my brain to try to remember where Becky lived. We chatted so much that she must have told me before, but I couldn't think—in a flood of adrenaline, I passed an intersection where the street sign triggered a memory. I'd driven her home once after Rick stood her up.

Though, she wasn't a human at all, was she? She was probably fae, like Rick, and they were on the run, just like all those poor little fairies that came into our house when I was a kid. They were scared—petrified, really—and alone. The world was tough enough for humans, but fairy folk had been hunted down for centuries.

We could blend in with humans, sure, but our magic left a mark. Anybody that knew what to look for could find us. That was why Rick's necklace was so important. The black opal had special properties allowing magic to bind to it, specifically a very powerful protection spell that kept fae hidden from all but the most powerful magical forces. However, you needed runes to keep it charged, or else it was useless.

I parked on the street across from Becky's house. She drove a rusty Dodge Charger that barely turned over most days, which I didn't see in the driveway. If I had a heart, I would have offered her my car, or at least to give her a ride, but I was protective of my wheels in case I needed to leave town at a moment's notice.

That made me wonder why I was still there. I'd run away from so much less. Normally I would already be on the road, halfway across the state by now. And yet, I couldn't will myself to leave Becky. How had she made such an impression in such a short time? Why were some people so good at burrowing themselves into your heart?

It was probably the magic. Of course. Becky might not even be aware of her power, but it was the only explanation. I was far too rational to let her win me over any other way. Even with the possibility that she might have cast a spell on me, I couldn't put the car back into drive and speed off into the horizon.

I was sitting there wrestling with my desire to leave when the beat-up Dodge Charger pulled around the corner and into the driveway. Becky removed two brown bags from the backseat and walked toward the house.

I stepped out of the car and walked toward her. "Becky!"

She turned to me. "Jesus, Jude. You almost gave me a heart attack."

"We have to go. Come on."

"What are you ta—" She looked past me toward the car behind her and instantly made the connection. "Where's Rick?"

I dropped my eyes. "He's dead. Four men came looking for you. We tried to escape. I made it. He didn't. Where's Veronica?"

She started trembling. She tried to control her crying, stay in control, but the emotions were winning. "She— how—Are you one of them?"

"Who are them?"

"They're—they're after Veronica," she said. "Because of what she is. Because of what we all are."

"No, I'm not one of them." I looked back to the street. They would be coming any minute. "Let's go inside. Do you have a go-bag?"

She opened the front door. "We've had one since we moved in, just in case." She set the food down on the counter. "Guess I don't need these. I was gonna make lasagna." She walked toward the stairs. "Wait here for me."

"Where's Veronica?" I yelled down the hall.

"Still at school. I was just about to pick her up."

I peered out of the window. A long black car slid to a stop in front of the house. "We have to go, now!"

When I turned back, Becky had a duffel strapped to her side and was holding a tiny backpack just the right size for a little girl. "I'm ready."

"Who are these guys?" I asked, watching them walk out of the car.

"Demons," she replied.

"Why are they after Veronica?"

"We didn't know for a long time. They have been after us since she was born. Finally, we went to an Oracle."

"Let me guess," I said, pushing a chair to the lock as they stormed up the stairs. "She's a prophecy girl?"

"Well, she is a girl, and she has a prophecy, so yeah, I guess so. The Oracle said she would save the world. Then, she told us to get some black opal and lay low, and we've been doing that ever since." She pulled the necklace from her blouse. "See?"

"Did you charge it?"

"Nobody said anything about charging it."

Someone pounded loudly against the door. "Of course they didn't. Is there a back door to this place?"

"Yes," Becky replied, turning around. We heard glass smashing, and two demons rushed inside, guns drawn.

They began to fire their weapons. Bullets tore through the front of the house as I rushed up the stairs, pulling Becky along behind me. She cried out and fell to her knees, a thick red streak on the wall behind her. She looked up at me with glassy eyes, pressing her fingers against her stomach.

"I'm fine. Keep going."

I dragged her along with me to the master bedroom at the end of the hallway and pushed a heavy dresser in front of the door. Becky stumbled to the edge of the bed. Her breathing was labored and wet.

"Let me see." I ripped open her shirt to find the bullet hole that had punctured her stomach. It spurted blood with every heave of her chest.

"Listen to me," Becky whispered as the door slammed. "Protect my daughter, please."

I shook my head. "You're going to protect her just fine. Don't worry."

She squeezed my hand. "Don't lie to me. Promise me you'll protect her."

My eyes filled with tears as I nodded. "I promise. I promise, but you're going to—"

"Millard Fillmore. Mister Matt's class. She's a panda…" She slumped over, white as a sheet.

There wasn't any more time to say my goodbyes. Heavy footsteps thundered down the hall. I ripped the necklace off Becky's neck, grabbed the bags, and smashed through the window out onto the roof. The moment the demons banged open the door, I slid down the roof and landed in some bushes.

By the time they fired at me, I was already halfway down the block in Rick's Buick. *Just leave, Lizzie. Just leave. You* don't owe her anything. You've only known her a month. Just a single stupid month. You don't owe her your life.

Even as I said the words to myself, my hands turned the wheel away from the main road as if I was being guided by an invisible force. At the end of the block, I took a right, and in four blocks, I ended up in front of Millard Fillmore elementary school.

I ducked inside and headed to the bathroom to wash the blood from my hands in the tiny sinks much too small for my body. I did my best to scrub at my pants, but I didn't have much time. I had to hope people would assume it was paint. It wouldn't take long for the demons to realize Veronica wasn't at the house and come to the school looking for her.

The building wasn't very big, and I followed the pandas down the colorfully decorated hallways. There was a jolly one painted on Mister Matt's door.

"Excuse me?" I said, knocking on the crepe paper taped to the door.

Mister Matt was in the center of the room reading a book to the kids, and he turned to me with kind eyes before his smile dropped from the sight of me. "Can I…help you?"

I nodded. "I'm sorry to be a bother, but I need to see Veronica."

"Are you a parent, or—"

"Her mother is very sick, and her father rushed her to the hospital. They sent me here. All I have is this?" I pulled the black opal necklace out of my pocket. "Do you recognize this, Veronica?"

She looked at it for a moment and then pulled an identical one out of her shirt. "That's Mommy's. I have one just like it!"

"I know this is irregular," I said.

He shook his head. "I simply can't—"

"There's no time for this!" I didn't blame him, but right now, he was an obstacle to Veronica's safety, and he had to get out of my way or suffer the consequences.

I stormed into the room and picked Veronica up. By the time I turned around, Mister Matt was on top of me, lumbering over me with his lanky frame.

"Let her go!" he screamed.

I pushed him hard as he rushed toward me. He stumbled backward and fell into the tiny tables the children used. The children screamed bloody murder and rushed to him.

"I'm sorry you had to see that," I called out to the class, then turned to Veronica. "Are you ready to go?"

"Are we really going to see Mommy?" She was strangely calm, given the situation.

I nodded. "Of course. She's very excited to see you." The lie sent pangs through my body. There was only one place safe enough for an orphaned fairy kid. Looks like I would be headed back to Bronard after all. *Mom will be so excited.*

CHAPTER 7

We drove through the night. Veronica repeatedly asked me where her mother was, but I just couldn't—every time I tried to tell her the truth, a lump lodged in my throat and forced me mute. Eventually, Veronica must have realized that her mother wasn't coming with us. Perhaps she recognized the blood on my pants, or the fear in my eyes, or the pain on my face at the mention of Becky. Whatever the reason, she settled down once we reached Utah and let the car lull her into a fitful sleep.

What the hell was I doing? By any metric, I was kidnapping Veronica, and now I had taken her across state lines, making myself a felon. If a police officer pulled me over, they would see a girl that wasn't related to me and the residuals of her mother's blood on my hands. They would arrest me, and Veronica would tell them where she lived. The murder would be all over the news by now.

This was why you're not supposed to make connections, Lizzie. I was supposed to keep my head low and leave a place before I caught feelings. That had been my motto and kept me safe for the past decade, and now, in one day, I'd abandoned everything I believed, all for a little girl and her fae mother.

I didn't know for sure Veronica was fae. Rick was fae, and all three of them had the necklace, but there's all manner of reasons why somebody would want a little girl like that—a prophecy girl who was supposed to save the world.

It wasn't lost on me that our fates were similar, and I didn't believe in coincidence. Maybe Veronica's destiny was intrinsically linked to mine, and every mile I drove toward Bronard was one step closer to a rendezvous with the inevitable conclusion of my story and hers.

You should just leave her on the side of the road or drop her at a fire station. They would find a home for her. She's adorable, after all. Who wouldn't love her?

I shook off the thought. No, she would tell them where she's from, and then they would bring her back and—there was only one person who could keep her safe, and it sure as shit wasn't me. And I didn't know how to contact Kimberly except through my mother.

Kimberly had saved hundreds of fae over the years. She would know what to do. Junebug would know what to do. Papa Carl would know what to do. I bit my lip to avoid crying, but deep tremors fiercely shook through my body and tugged on the steering wheel until I had no choice except to turn off the road into a rest area. It wasn't much more than a bathroom with a couple of vending machines.

I wiped the last of my tears from my face, then shook Veronica awake. "Hey," I said in a whisper. "Do you have to pee?"

"Mommy?" she replied, bleary-eyed. When her eyes focused on me, her face dropped into a scowl. "You're not Mommy."

I shook my head. "No, I'm not. Do you need to use the bathroom?"

She yawned. "Yes."

I unbuckled her and pulled her out of the car. She didn't try to tug away from me.

"I'm not kidnapping you," I said as we washed our hands in the bathroom sink. "I want you to know that."

"That sounds like the kind of thing a kidnapper would say," she replied, looking up at me as I handed her a brown paper towel.

"You're not wrong," I said. "Your mother—she taught you well, but I'm not kidnapping you. I'm trying to protect you."

"Protect me from what?"

"From bad people."

"Do the bad people have Mommy?"

I sighed. It was time to tell her the truth. It wouldn't be any better hiding it from her only to hear it from somebody else. I needed to stop being a chicken and bite the bullet, whatever the cliché was.

I sat her on a bench outside after buying her a bunch of sugary candy to help ease the pain. I turned on the lights to the car, so we could have some illumination. The night was bitterly cold. I hated deserts. They didn't retain heat during the night, and yet they sweltered in the day.

After Veronica had eaten half a bag of Skittles, I spoke. "Your mother loves you very much. Did you know that?"

She nodded. "I know. She tells me all the time."

She would never tell her again.

"The bad men. The ones chasing you. They…they hurt your mommy, Veronica. I tried to help her—to save her—but—but—your mother died."

It started slow. She cocked her head to the left, then to the right, before blinking several times, trying to process what she just heard. The realization of my words seemed to hit her in waves, lightly at first and then crashing upon her with greater and greater force until the flood of tears was so great that I thought she might drown under them. I was ill-equipped to deal with children, let alone grieving children. I had survived by bottling up my emotions about everything and everyone I met. In the face of strong feelings, I turned the other way.

There was no turning away from this—Veronica's poor life had been changed forever. The two people who had protected her were dead, and all she had left was me.

When she stopped heaving tears, she slid her arms around me, hugging my stomach. She didn't speak for a long while, and neither did I. She simply cried into my shirt, and I rubbed her back, trying to comfort her.

"I'm going to take you somewhere you can be safe," I said, finally.

"I want my mommy."

"I know, sweetheart. I know, but—well—you know you can't see her again, right?"

She sniffled. "I'll see her in Heaven."

Maybe. "Not for a very long time, sweetheart, but I'm sure she'll be waiting to welcome you when you die—which won't be for a very, very long time."

She squeezed me tighter. "Because you'll protect me."

"I'll take you somewhere where you'll be safe," I replied, correcting her. "My friend will know what to do to protect you. She's a real badass."

"A…badass?"

"That's right," I said with a smile. "She'll know exactly what to do because she's done it so many times before with so many other kids just like you."

"How do you know?"

I pulled the black opal necklace that I kept around my neck. It was the only thing I'd kept from the past I worked so hard to distance myself from because I was a hypocrite. "Because she helped me."

Veronica pulled her necklace out from beneath her shirt. "Just like mine!"

"That's right, and my friend is going to help you, just like she helped me."

"She sounds nice." She nodded with determination. "Not mommy nice, but nice."

"She's something, all right." I chuckled. "And you know what else? I'm going to introduce you to a woman who's gonna love you so much."

"How can you know that?"

"Because you are totally loveable." I gave her a little squeeze. "And for another thing, she's my mom, so I have some experience with her."

"That sounds nice, I guess."

"I know it's not perfect, kiddo, and it's not your mom, but it's still gonna be great, I promise."

"Pinky promise?" She held out her left pinky.

I hooked it into my finger and closed it tight. "Pinky promise."

CHAPTER 8

I turned down the streets of Bronard using muscle memory, surprised that so little had changed in the decade I'd been away. The Johnsons were still selling corn on the side of the road, and a few farms down, you could get berries from the Clacksons. The road down the middle of town toward my parent's farm was filled with food stands with all manner of fruit and veggies in them. As we passed the homemade signs, I took note of the children I'd grown up with, now adults with their own children in tow as they worked their family farms.

That was supposed to be my lot in life, to help Dad and Mom till the fields, to care for them in their old age, to carry on their legacy. There was no doubt I would come back to the farm after college and work it until I died. Some people might not have thought that appealing, but it was my dream—a dream shattered by the prophecy that loomed over my head.

"It smells funny," Veronica said as we drove through.

"That's good, good country air, Veronica," I said.

"Smells like poop," she observed.

"It sure does. I've missed it."

"Weirdo."

Papa's truck was still in front of the white farmhouse. His tools, now rusted and in disrepair, hung on the shed on the right of the driveway. It was like stepping back in time to a past I never thought I'd return to.

"We're here," I said.

"Thank god," Veronica said. "That was a long ride."

I had tried to get her some coloring books and games to play, but Veronica wasn't interested in any of that. She just wanted to get where we were going and focused on the road. When I unbuckled her seat belt, she hopped out of the car and latched onto my hand on our way to the door.

We hadn't even reached the steps before the creaky screen swung open, and my father, Carl, shuffled out, hunched over a cane. His dark skin was cut with deep grooves. He wasn't a young man when I was a child, but now he looked like the world had sucked the last of his life out of him. When he saw me, his face lit up, and the old Dad came through the thick wrinkles for a moment.

"L-Lizzie? My gods, is that you?"

I grinned. "Hi, Dad!"

He stood straight up then and scooted toward me as I made my way to him. We embraced in a long hug filled with tears and laughter.

"I never thought I would see you again, kiddo."

"I never thought I'd see you again either, Dad." I thought it would be awkward, after all this time, to see my father, but it felt like old times, like we hadn't been estranged for a decade. I smelled his scent as I hugged him tightly and knew I was home. It was the thing I'd spent a decade running from, and it was the only thing I never knew I always wanted—to see my parents again. I lied to myself into believing I didn't crave this moment, but there was no more lying now. The truth rushed at me in a torrent.

After a long while, Carl's eyes moved from me to Veronica. "And who is your friend?"

I unlatched from his embrace and turned to her. "This is Veronica. She's—I think—one of us, and she's in a bad way. That's why I came back."

He nodded. "I thought maybe you just wanted to see your old man and your mother before she…I'm just glad to see you." He hobbled over to Veronica and held out his hand. "It's nice to meet you, little one."

She shook his hand. "It's nice to meet you, too, sir."

"Carl," he said. "You can call me Carl."

"Nice to meet you, Carl."

He smiled a weak smile. "How would you like some cocoa?"

"I'd like that very much, Carl."

He placed his hand on her back. "Then how about we have some hot chocolate while Lizzie here goes to say hello to her mother."

"Who's Lizzie?"

"I am, Veronica," I replied.

"Oh." She looked at me, confused. "I thought your name was Jude."

"I've had a lot of names, but my real name is Elizabeth—Lizzie."

"I like Jude better."

"Noted." I touched Dad's shoulder as they passed. "Where is she?"

"Our room. Upstairs." He helped Veronica into the house. "I think you know the way."

CHAPTER 9

It was exactly the same as when I left it, down to the coats on the hooks to the left of the door. I used to rush through the door after a day at school and throw my backpack—the same one I would abandon in Edgemont when I left with Veronica—on the ground next to my muddy shoes and flop on the couch to watch television before chores.

The same laughing sounds that Veronica was making from the kitchen were the ones I once made, too, as Dad made hot chocolate, or soup, or any number of snacks for me. And if Mom was home, she would pull one of her famous eclairs or donuts out of the oven and stuff them in my belly. God, what it was like to have a fast metabolism in my younger years.

The television was blaring classic TCM when I passed by on my way to the stairs. The television had been replaced since my youth, but the rest of the room was glaringly the same, though the thick coating of fuzz made it seem grayer than I remembered. A floorboard under me moaned, exactly five steps into the house, just like always. I hopped over it the night I left to avoid being caught.

As I placed my hand on the banister, Veronica rushed out from the kitchen door and into the dining room, where she sat on the same chair that I had once claimed. Children were incredibly resilient, and it was amazing to see her smiling at Carl as he hobbled back into the room.

"Do you want marshmallows, too?" Dad asked.

She nodded. "Course I do. I'm not a savage."

"A girl after my own heart," he said with a chuckle, disappearing back behind the door.

I took the stairs one at a time, in no rush to see my mother's failing condition. The stairs squeaked and cracked in chorus as if the house was greeting me. The banister, like the rest of the house, was coated in a thin layer of dust. It hung in the air above where I'd placed my fingers for a moment before floating down to the floor.

There was a heaviness in my feet as I stepped onto the second floor of my childhood home. The door to my room sat on the far end of the hall, and on the near end was the one they gave to guests that had been occupied for a short time by my estranged, world-hopping sister. On the other side was my parent's office and on the far end, across from the door to my room, was my parent's bedroom. That's where Mom was.

I needed another moment to gather my courage. Instead of opening Mom's door, I pushed open the door to my childhood bedroom. I wasn't surprised to see that it hadn't been touched since I left, except that the bed had been made and the schoolbooks I'd left spread across my desk were nowhere to be found.

I thought I was edgy, putting up pictures of the Cure and the Smyths and painting my walls black "to match the color of my soul." I cringed a little. If only I knew what real pain was, perhaps I would have been able to see the joy in this home, in my innocent childhood.

That was the problem with youth. It was impossible to understand just how long life would be or how dark things could get when you hadn't lived much of your life. A year seemed to last a century when I was younger. Imagining that there would be four to five times as many days to live—well, that was an impossible task.

I knew I shouldn't blame myself for believing that I had reached the zenith of my misery back then. If, when I was a child, I had been given even a fraction of the weight that my life now carried, I would have buckled under the pressure. I had to grow and mature into the idea that living with the misery was possible, that every single person in the whole of the world deals with so much misery that it's hard to believe the world keeps turning. And yet, not only does it keep turning, some people even find joy in it.

Dust plumed into the air when I sat down on the bed, causing me to hack a few times. I stood immediately and made my way out of the room to grab some air, closing the door behind me to lock in the dust particles. When I stopped coughing, I was in front of Mom's door, my hand resting on the doorknob.

"Carl?" a weak voice said. "Is that you? It doesn't sound like your clodhopper footsteps."

I entered the room where Mom lay in bed, shriveled and weak. Her skin was gray, and her eyes sunken. A heart monitor beeped next to her, and even the stress of moving her head to look at me was too much for her to manage. She fell back with a painful moan. I wanted to wail at the sight of my strong mother degraded like this, but I choked back my emotions, hid them like I had so often in my past.

"No, Mom. It's me. It's your Lizzie. Do you remember me?" I took a few steps through the musk that permeated the room.

Her voice shook when she talked. "Lizzie?" This time she fought through the exhaustion and turned to see me. "My gods, is it really you?"

I grabbed her hand. "Yes, Mom. It's really me."

She gave a wobbly smile and squeezed my hand tightly. "I never thought I would see you again."

I nodded. "It's so good to see you, Mom."

"It's good to see you too, baby. Now, come and give your mom a hug."

She opened up her arms, and I collapsed into them like I had when I was a child. Listening to her heart beating in her chest made me feel safe in a way I hadn't felt in a long time. I let my eyes fall closed.

CHAPTER 10

I didn't know how long I slept, but when I woke up, the sun was ready to set again, and Mom still slumbered beside me. I slipped out of her gentle embrace and made my way down the stairs. Dad was sitting on the couch, watching *White Christmas* even though it was nowhere near, as Veronica lay curled up on the couch next to him.

I intentionally stepped on the creaky floorboard in the middle of the hardwood, and he turned to me with a smile. He eased himself out of his chair and hobbled into the dining room.

"Coffee?"

I nodded. "As much as you can spare."

"A woman after my own heart." He quietly disappeared into the kitchen. Junebug and Carl always had coffee brewing, no matter the time in the day or night, because there was always work to be done. I had long been convinced they were immune to the effects of caffeine.

A few minutes later, he came back into the dining room holding two cups of coffee in tremoring hands. I jumped up and took my cup from him before easing him into the chair.

"This isn't anything fancy, so if you like that kind of French vanilla crap or mocha choco blast, you're not gonna find anything like that here." He grunted. "We drink our coffee black in this house, in case you don't remember."

I took a sip. "I remember. It hasn't been that long."

Dad placed the cup down, looking down at his liver-spotted hands. "Feels like a lifetime. Last time you were here, I could pick you up in my hands and lift you straight over my head."

I rolled my eyes. "I wasn't a baby when I left. I was sixteen, Dad. Exaggerating much?"

"That's how I remember it—you running away—barely up to my waist."

"Delusion is a great gift, old man." I took another sip of coffee and saw that my innocently jestful tone didn't come across. "That was a joke."

"I know it was a joke, but it wasn't funny. I never humored you as a kid, and I'm not gonna start now. Besides, you were telling the truth. I am old. Feel like I aged a hundred years since you left."

"You look great, Dad."

"Don't you lie to me, dang it. Not in my own house." He looked down at the coffee in his cup. "I can barely get out to do chores anymore. Yields are down, so I can't hire staff. Most days, I think the only thing I'm good for is dying."

Thoughts of the prophecy danced through my head. I spent so much time away to save my parents from death, but it had come for them anyway.

"I thought pixies lived for a long time, Dad. You're not that old. Mom either."

He squeezed his hands together. "I don't know how magic works, kiddo. Nobody does, and anyone who tells you otherwise is duping you, duping themselves, or both. It was like one day I was fit as a fiddle, and the next I could barely lift a shovel."

"I don't know much about magic, but I know that's a load of horse manure." I brought my eyes to his. "How long ago did you try curing her yourself?"

He sighed. "Don't even remember now, and it doesn't matter. It didn't work. Kimberly tried to tell me there would be side effects, but I didn't care—I don't care. Life's not worth a lick without her, so maybe it's a blessing that it backfired and took so much from me." He took another sip of coffee. "How is your mother?"

"You know how she is."

"I do, but I want to hear you say it."

My head dropped. "I've spent the last decade stuffing every emotion I've ever had deep down in the dregs of my soul. The last day has cracked all that open, and now every feeling I've suppressed for ten years is hitting me at once. And none of that was as bad as seeing her in that bed."

He nodded solemnly. "It's hard to watch my little Junebug waste away like that. Sometimes—sometimes she looks at me like she used to, with love and hope in her eyes. Those are the worst moments because I know there is no hope left."

I slid my hand across the table and touched his. "There is hope left, Pop. I'm here now."

"Then you'll go again."

"Maybe," I replied. "But I'm going to help until then, and I'm going to take care of you both while I'm still here, okay?"

There was something he wanted to say, and it danced across his face for a moment, but it was replaced by a simple, sad smile. "How bad is it with the girl?"

"She lost the only two people that cared about her today. She didn't watch them die, at least, so there's hope there."

"That's the blessing in this curse, I suppose." He sipped his coffee again. "She's welcome here. We still have your bed made upstairs."

"It needs a good cleaning. I'll bring down the sheets when I go back up."

"Bring the ones from the guest room, too." He stopped for a moment. "You know, had you told us you were coming, we would've made the bed up for you."

"I didn't know I was coming until I walked through the door." I hesitated. "I know you don't believe this, but I was trying to protect you both. That's why I left."

His face was stone. "I know you think that, but it wasn't your job to protect us. It was our job to protect you, and we failed." His lip quivered. "Your mama never forgave herself for that."

I opened my mouth to say something but couldn't. I knew my appearing out of nowhere picked open some wounds that had long since been scabbed over. It was selfish to come back here, but as Kimberly had made all too clear, I was a selfish girl.

"Let me get the linens." I pushed my chair out. "Do I need to pull them off Mom's bed, too?"

He shook his head. "No, Johnny will be here soon to look after her."

"Johnny?"

"He's the fella we hired to look after Mom in her last days. He does a crack-up job, too. Makes sure she comfortable."

"That's nice, Dad."

He took a long sip of coffee, staring at the floor. "It's something. That's for sure."

CHAPTER 11

Even with coffee running through my system, I had no trouble falling asleep after finishing with the sheets and carrying Veronica to bed. The last couple of days had been exhausting, mentally, physically, and emotionally, and the farmhouse was the only place I ever truly felt safe.

I never slept well on the road, which made me a good worker because I was always up for a shift, but as I laid in the four-poster bed in the guest room, Veronica asleep in the next room, I felt a decade of exhaustion smash into me at once. I didn't have to worry that some meth-head would burst in on me or listen to a prostitute and her john in the next room. Instead, there was just quiet, quiet for miles. In that quiet, I found peace.

When I woke up, the sun stung my eyes, and I heard a rooster crow. The stairs creaked outside my room, and I rolled out of bed to find Dad wobbling down the hallway holding Mom's breakfast on a tray.

"Let me help you with that," I said, pushing open the door to Mom's bedroom.

"Come on, then," he said, placing the breakfast on Junebug's lap. It wasn't much, a half a bagel with cream cheese, some milk, and a few cut-up grapes, but she beamed when she saw it.

"Looks delicious," she said, taking one of the grapes.

"I'm no chef, not like you, my dear." Dad kissed Mom on the forehead. "But I make due. Betsy says hello. Sends her love."

"Did you already go into town this morning?" I asked.

"Of course. I go every morning. Only fresh bagels are good enough for my Junebug."

"You spoil me, love," Mom said slowly as she took a tiny bite. "Poppy seed. Yummy as ever."

"Well, I would love to waste the day with you, my dear, but chores call," Carl said with a smile. "Until we meet again."

"No, don't worry about all that right now," I butted in. "Rest, both of you. I'm back home. I'll do the chores."

"Sure you can handle it?" Dad said, but he didn't need to be told twice. He slid off his shoes and then into bed next to my mother.

"Any of it changed in a decade?"

He shook his head. "That's the beauty of this place. Nothing changes 'cept the seasons."

I rushed down the stairs to see a middle-aged man with a shiny, jolly face wearing a set of blue scrubs. "I'll be off now, Car—" He caught sight of me. "Oh, hello. You must be Lizzie, right? Carl talked about you…a lot."

I nodded. "And you're Johnny?"

He held out his hand, and I shook it. "I am."

"Thanks for taking such good care of my mom."

"Happy to do it." He smiled. "Junebug is a real special woman. I'm glad I got to know her."

I choked on my emotions, and I turned to the back door. "Me too."

Choring was like riding a bike. Once you learned the ropes, your muscles never forgot the motion. I started with milking the cows before feeding the chickens, then walked the lines, spraying the corn and looking for defects until the morning watering started, then I leaped back to fill the straw for the cows and pluck the eggs from the chicken coup.

By the time I went back inside, I smelled like a foot, but a sweaty, accomplished foot. Dad must have heard me come in because not long after, he crept down the stairs just as I finished placing the basket of eggs on the dining room table for inspection.

"Nice haul this morning," he said, ambling over. "Put them in the fridge. I'll bring them to Betsy tomorrow morning."

"I can do it," I said. "How much do you get for them?"

He shrugged. "We keep a tab for pastries at this point. Money's not much good on the farm these days, and with your mother sick, I get more out of the pastries anyway."

"Daaad—" I started to lecture him about in-kind bartering but cut myself off. Who was I to judge? They made it to old age and deserved their eccentricities. "I need to go into town anyway, so I can bring them when I pick up new clothes for the kid and me."

"What kind of person doesn't bring clothing when they travel?"

"I had clothes and a wad of cash waiting for me in the motel when I saved the girl, but since then, we've just been traveling." I looked out the front window at the Buick that sat in the yard. "Speaking of, you know anyone who needs a car and will be real discrete about chain of title?"

He nodded. "I'll give you a number. He'll chop it up and use it for parts. Meanwhile, there's plenty of clothing in your closet upstairs if you wanna look at it. We haven't thrown anything away."

I chuckled. "I appreciate that, but I'm through my Goth phase, I think, and Veronica's too small for them just yet."

"Well, bring them into town anyway. Dana's kid has been after us for years to sell that stuff. Says it's vintage. Might be able to get some coin for it." He sighed, taking in a good, long look at me. "I know you're adopted, but you really do look just like your mother."

I chuckled. "She's white. I'm Black. You're losing it, old man."

"Maybe that's it. Anyway, I think she might have some clothes that would fit you. That way, you don't smell like a cow going into town." He reached into his pocket and pulled a credit card from his wallet. "You can put the clothes on this card. They shouldn't give you any guff about it once they figure out who you are."

"You don't have to—" I started before Dad held up his hand.

"Least I can do." Tears welled in his eyes. "Please, let me do this for my daughter."

I took the card. "Thanks, Dad."

The center of town was about twenty minutes from our farm if you drove with a lead foot, thirty if you respected the speed limit. There was a time when I could tear around bends at full-tilt boogie speed, but I didn't have the same feel for the roads anymore, so Veronica and I made it in a little closer to a half-hour. My dad might have made it in fifteen, especially in his prime.

My mom's old store, Dessertations, sat at the end of a quaint strip of town that also held Dana's Dress Barn, a sheriff station annex, and a smoked meats bar-b-que. It made me smile that it was still standing even if my mother couldn't. It was her legacy.

"Let's go," I said to Veronica, who was already out of the car. I grabbed her hand in mine, holding the eggs with the other, and walked into the store. I was expecting to see Betsy but instead found a baby-faced man whose nose was covered in dough.

"Morning, ladies. Welcome to Dessertations! What can I do for you?" he said, then peered closer at us. "My, you two must be from out of town because I don't recognize you at all."

"It's been a decade, Ed, but I haven't changed that much, have I?" I replied. "How's your mother? She in?"

"She only comes in the early morning these days." Ed smiled at me and squinted closely. "Oh my goshness, is that little Lizzie back from the dead?"

"I was never dead, Ed," I replied. "And this is Veronica."

He spun from around the counter and hugged me tightly, pluming flour between us. "So good to see you again." He shook Veronica's hand. "And nice to meet you, little one. Your mom is a bit of a legend around here."

"She's not my mother," Veronica said flatly. "My mom's dead."

"Oh." His face dropped. "I'm sorry to hear that."

"We all are." I slid in front of Veronica and held up the basket of eggs. "Carl says you have an arrangement for these?"

Ed took the basket. "Your family really does have the best eggs. I don't know how you do it, but yes." He walked behind the counter. "Meanwhile, pick anything you want, on the house."

"What do you think, Veronica?" I said, brushing flour from my mom's hideous pink flannel shirt. "My mother's favorite used to be eclairs."

"What's that?"

"It's like a long donut with gooey cream inside, topped with chocolate."

Her eyes got big. "I want that."

"Make that two." I smiled. "I love that you have kept this place the same even after all these years."

Ed dipped down into the glass counter. "Well, your mother was an institution. When she sold the shop to my mom, Mom promised to keep that tradition alive, and then when I took over last year, it had already been standing for two decades and—well, let's just say if I tried to change it now, there would be an uprising."

I took the eclairs from Ed and gave one to Veronica. "Thanks, Ed. I guess I'll see you around."

"I sure do hope so."

We sat outside and ate our eclairs. They were just as delicious as I remembered. I've had a thousand eclairs in a hundred towns, and Mom's recipe was still the best. Veronica must have thought so, too, because even with her small frame, she finished the whole éclair, then licked her fingers clean of all the sticky goodness.

After finishing our sweets, we had enough sugar to tackle Dana's Dress Barn. Dana never liked my mother, but I got along fine with her daughter Jennifer when we were in school, which gave me hope that she wouldn't be a heartless shrew like her mother.

"Are you serious?" Jennifer said as we slammed the clothes on the counter. She dug through my old clothes with relish. "This is like the mother lode. I've been dying to get Junebug to sell this to me forev—" That's the moment she saw my face behind the mountain of clothing. "Oh my god! Is that really you, Lizzie?"

I nodded. "It's me."

"It's so good to see you!" She shouted before pointing at Veronica. "And who's your little helper here?"

"This is Veronica. She's not mine. I'm just babysitting right now."

"Hey!" Veronica protested. "I'm not a baby."

I nodded. "You're right. I'm sorry. I'm watching her right now, is what I meant."

Jennifer shook her head at both of us. "Well, the two of you look a fright. Luckily, I have a cure for what ails ya. Best selection of threads in three counties."

I glanced around the store and had to admit that it had promise. Gone were the gaudy styles of the old dress barn, replaced with modern looks and sleek aesthetics. "Thank god you got rid of the mom jeans."

"Oh god, hon," Jennifer said. "They were the first thing to go. Well, go pick out whatever you want, and then I'll square up what's left over when you're done."

I picked out enough clothes for a week before turning my attention to Veronica. She was harder to shop for, but after an hour, we had a selection of shirts, pants, shoes, and underwear enough to get her wherever Kimberly was going to take her. I wanted her to have something from me since after she left my care. I would likely never see her again.

I felt a little guilty putting so much on Dad's credit card, but if he wanted to buy us clothes, who was I to argue. Once the new clothes were purchased, Jennifer reached into her drawer and handed me $100 for the clothes I brought in.

"This is too much, Jennifer," I said when she put it in my hands and closed it around me. "No way my clothes are worth that much."

She shook her hands. "I owed you from back in high school. Consider this my repayment, with interest."

Why was everybody being so nice to me today? *Was it because I had a little kid with me?* I needed the money, so I didn't argue. I'd lost the rest of my rainy-day fund back in Nevada and used almost all my tips from my last day of work just getting to Bronard. It was nice to have some extra money in my pocket.

The last stop was offloading the car. Dad's connection was in Maynard, three towns from Bronard, and past the site where the Oracle gave her prophetic vision of my future. When I passed the trailer park, I stopped dead, slamming the brakes on the old car until it skidded to a stop.

Right there, in the middle of the park, walking like she hadn't destroyed my whole life, was the Oracle, Starr Wolfsong, without a care in the world. She looked a little worse for wear, but it was definitely her. Then a thought flashed across my brain: Maybe she could help me figure out how to help Veronica.

No, she *would* help me figure out how to help Veronica. It was the least she could do after… And if she wouldn't, well, part of me hoped she wouldn't so that I could make her pay for the last decade of my life.

CHAPTER 12

"This place is gross," Veronica said as we pulled into the trailer park.

She wasn't wrong. I had lived in my fair share of trailer parks in the past ten years. On the whole, they were clean, if rudimentary, but this place was dingy and sad. Every person we passed looked like the hope had drifted from their eyes long ago. Some of the faces I recognized from my last trip to the park over ten years ago, or from school and around town. All of them relics of a bygone age, hollowed with time and drained of all signs of life. They stared at my boat of a car as we slid through the dirt road littered with plastic and glass bottles.

Crumpled bits of paper rolled across the ground like tumbleweeds. I followed Starr back to her unit, staying far enough behind that she wouldn't recognize me. She was in the same derelict unit she occupied so long ago, even more dilapidated now, just like her.

The last time we met, I remember thinking the woman seemed like she was at death's door. Somehow the years had taken even more from her, thinning her out until there was little more than a skeleton, in a suit made of skin, shambling up the stairs of her unit and struggling against gravity to make her way inside.

"Stay here," I said to Veronica as I put the car in park and locked the doors behind me.

"Shouldn't leave your kid like that," a gruff voice called from behind me. I turned to see a pot-bellied man with a five o'clock shadow going on nine if he didn't find a razor soon. His jagged teeth caught me by surprise as he moved toward me, yellowed, with several having given way to rot and others fallen out completely. "Not safe, that."

"I don't want any trouble, mister."

"Jake. They call me Jake. You can call me 'honey' though, love. You're a delicious-looking one, ain't ya?" He licked his lips, accentuating his jagged teeth. "Yeah, yer a tasty one."

"I don't want any trouble, Jake."

He stepped forward, grabbing at the belt on his waist as he went. "And what if I want trouble?"

"Leave her be, Jake!" a woman screamed behind us. I turned to see the red-haired woman who tended to the Oracle. "Don't be an animal. It's not even a full moon tonight."

"Come now, Charlie," Jake said. "I ain't causing trouble."

"Yeah, yeah," Charlie said, scampering up to us. Unlike the woman she served, she was as spry as ever, though she had packed on a couple of pounds in the face and more in the stomach. The extra heft suited her. "Go watch your stories and leave the girl be."

Jake threw up his hands and turned away, ambling back to a frayed lawn chair and picking up a beer bottle with the label mostly peeled off.

"Thank you," I said to Charlie.

She dipped her head in acknowledgment. "You look like a girl looking for answers, and if my associate and I know anything, it's how to find those answers for people."

"That's what I'm hoping for," I said.

"You here for a reading?"

"I'm not sure, but I am looking for answers." I pointed to the car. "The girl—she's in a bad way, and I need to figure out how I can help her."

"We usually don't do readings for people that young. Never works out well for us. Had some bad experiences in the past."

"I—I get that. She's already had a reading, though, but her mom—well, she's my responsibility now, and her mom didn't get a chance to tell me about her prophecy before she—before the girl was left in my care."

"So, she's got a prophecy on her, then?" Charlie thought for a long moment, ping-ponging her eyes between Veronica and me as she stroked her chin. Finally, she gave a nod. "Bring her in."

I unlocked the door and eyed Jake warily as I pulled Veronica out of the car. We followed Charlie toward the double-wide and up the rotten wooden stairs to the door. As it creaked open, the distinct smell of stale smoke smacked into me. My stomach leaped into my throat, and a memory flashed through my brain, the memory of a scared little girl, trembling with fear, watching the Oracle thrash across the table, telling her she was going to die and take everything she loved down with her.

"Starr," Charlie sang sweetly as we made our way into the trailer. "We have a customer."

Starr moaned, rousing from a couch next to the door. She stared at me with sunken eyes, and the hatred I had for her melted away. Time had taken more from her than I ever could. She destroyed my life, but life destroyed her just the same. All that was left in me toward her was pity and shame that I carried such hatred for her for so long.

"It's fifty," she said. "If you wanna stay in the room, then it's a hundred."

I reached into my pocket and pulled out the money I had just gotten from Jennifer at the Dress Barn and handed it to her. *This better be worth it. Otherwise, I had just wasted my nut chasing phantoms.*

Charlie pocketed the money and helped Starr to her feet. They shambled together across the trailer into the same little booth where I had sat once before. I brought Veronica over and sat with her on the other side of the booth.

"Veronica," I said as tenderly as possible. "This is my friend Starr. A long time ago, she helped me find my place in the world, and now she's going to help you."

"N-nice to meet you," Veronica said, her voice trembling.

"It's nice to meet you too, child." Starr's voice was raspy, and her feral eyes moved from Veronica to me. Her eyes seemed to look through me, not at me, as she pondered me for a moment. "And you, yes, I remember you. Evil things I saw in your future. If this child has something to do with your fate, then I want nothing to do with her." She turned to Charlie. "Give this woman back her money and send her away."

"No!" I shouted. "Please. I have to know if this child has something to do with my prophecy. I have to know what to do with her. You owe me that much after what you did to me. I've been on the run for ten years." The anger bubbled back into my stomach, and I clenched my jaw, trying to fight it off. "Please."

Starr Wolfsong shuddered visibly. "I traveled across this whole country, trying to unsee the things I saw in your future—trying to escape the feeling of hopelessness that your vision brought to me, but everywhere I traveled, you followed me."

"And after your prophecy, I ran away from home trying to avoid my future, only to be forced back here and to this trailer park, where I found you, again. Whether you believe in fate or not, that's too big a coincidence to discount, don't you think?"

"The fates are fickle mistresses, but yes, I admit I have felt compelled to return here as if every move I made to turn away from this place led me here again. I have often wondered why the universe kept me alive so long, in so much pain. Perhaps it is to be here, now, in this moment." She swallowed, a painful grimace settling over her face. "I'm sorry for what happened to you and for what you must sacrifice—what you have already sacrificed."

"Thank you for that, but right now, I just want to find out what this girl's part is in this whole plan and how to help her."

Starr reached her arms toward Veronica. "My sight has been blocked since that day with you, but I have other ways of telling the future." She managed a smile. "Place your hands in mine, girl, palms up."

Veronica looked over at me, and when I nodded, did as she was told. Starr leaned forward and stared at the little girl's palms for a long moment before shaking her head slowly. "Your lifeline is broken so early…yet, it continues. I have never in all my years seen anything like this, and your fate line—" She turned to me. "Let me see your palms." I turned them over for her. "Identical. I thought as much." She closed both of our palms. "Your fates, I fear, are intrinsically linked, and they are both bound to the fate of us all."

"What did you see that night?" I said. "When you gave me my vision?"

Starr looked at me for several long moments before she spoke with a trembling voice. "I saw the Earth, overrun with demons and all manner of Hellbeasts…and then I saw your death. In your eyes, there was a new beginning, as the past burned." She pressed her hands tightly into mine. "It is not fair, but life is not fair. Not for any of us." She sighed and looked over at Charlie. "Give them back their money. They will need it more than me."

I slid out of the booth and took the money Charlie held out. "Thank you."

Starr dropped her head into her chest. "No, thank you. I feel a great weight has been lifted off my chest. I only wish I did not have to place it on you instead."

I smiled sadly. "You didn't do anything. Fate did that."

CHAPTER 13

After I left the Oracle, we headed to the lot Dad recommended and sold the car with no problem. It was an old junker, so I didn't expect much for it, and I didn't get much for it. When Dad came to pick us up, he asked me about my day, but I could only answer that it was "fine." Any more depth than that, and I'd have to give the awful truth: I was going to have to leave them again. I didn't want to. The longer I spent in my childhood home, the more I realized how unmoored I had been in the past decade, traveling from town to town, searching for a modicum of peace.

Humans have an innate ability to acclimate to their surroundings, and I'd grown to believe the hollowness inside of me was normal, but now I knew that was a lie. The hollowness came from being away from my home and the people I loved, quarantining my heart from the rest of the world. It had all come flooding back to me now. Like a numb hand regaining feeling after a long sleep, the pinpricks of pain meant I was feeling something, and I liked it.

I don't know what I had hoped the Oracle would say. Maybe that she was wrong, and it was all a big misunderstanding. "Whoopsie, I made a mistake" would have been really nice. My intellectual brain knew that would never happen, of course. And my emotional brain was an idiot that couldn't find its way out of a paper bag.

When we got home, I decided to do chores to clear my head and figure out my next steps. If I had to leave my parents again, I wanted to remember the feel of the soil on my fingers before I fled like a thief in the night.

"What are you doing?" Veronica's voice said from the end of a row of tomatoes.

I turned to her, stunned to find that dusk had settled on the farm. I had been in my own head for hours. I wiped the sweat from my brow and gave a deep exhale, looking down at my basket of rotten tomatoes.

"You can't let the rotten fruit stay on the tree. It corrupts the whole crop." I held up one of the bruised tomatoes. "See?"

She leaned forward to look at the rotted and bug-eaten tomatoes I'd pulled from the vines. "Gross."

"Have you ever heard the expression 'a few bad apples spoil the bunch'?"

"Mommy used to say it."

I smiled at her. "She's a very smart lady, but it's not just an expression. This is where it comes from. If we let these bad ones grow, they'll attract all kinds of nasty bugs, and if we don't pick these rotten ones, they can destroy a whole season's crop. So, I'm going through and picking them."

"Can I help?"

I pushed the bucket over to her, and we looked for rotten tomatoes until it was too dark to see anything but our noses. I remembered back to my own father teaching me how to tend the crops, and now here I was, passing the knowledge to a new generation. Part of me wished we could stay on that farm forever, tilling the fields and watching them grow, but the rest of me knew that was impossible.

If we stayed together, all of us—Mom, Dad, Veronica, and I—would be in danger. Starr told us that our fates were intertwined, and if that was true, then perhaps this little girl would die with me, and I couldn't let that happen. The only thing that would protect us was to separate from each other, as far as possible, with no way to contact each other.

"Supper's ready!" Pop yelled at us from his spot at the back door. "Don't let it get cold!"

I picked up the basket of rotten tomatoes and walked hand in hand with Veronica to the compost bin, where I tossed the rotten fruit so at least they could do some good. A few bad apples can spoil the bunch, but just because they've gone rotten doesn't mean they can't still be useful.

"What are we having?" I asked as I took off my shoes inside the house. "I'm starved."

"Meatloaf," Dad called from the kitchen. "Thought we'd have a nice, family dinner together."

That did sound nice, at least until I walked into the dining room and saw Kimberly sitting at the end of the table. My heart sank. Instinctively, I knew that she had found a place for Veronica. I squeezed that little girl's hand so tight, and I never wanted to let go, even though I knew it was the right thing—the only thing.

"Nice to see you had a change of heart," Kimberly said. "And that you're back where you belong."

I didn't respond. I took Veronica into the bathroom, where we washed our hands together. Desperation swirled in my stomach. I couldn't acknowledge that this would be the last night I spent with Veronica, the last meal I shared with her. *You barely know this little girl, Lizzie. Screw your head on straight.* We finished cleaning our hands and took our seats just as Dad slid the meatloaf onto the table.

"Eat up," he said.

"It smells delicious, doesn't it, Veronica?" I asked.

She nodded. "Totally."

"And hello to you, Veronica," Kimberly said. "Since Lizzie won't do it, I'll introduce myself. My name is Kimberly. We're going to have so much fun together tonight."

Veronica cocked her head to the side. "What kind of fun?"

"We'll talk more after dinner, but I was hoping you would come with me on an adventure." Her voice was whispered but excited. "Do you like adventures?"

Veronica looked down at her lap. "I used to like adventures, but then—" She didn't have to finish. "Now, I just like farming. Did you know that a few bad tomatoes can spoil a whole crop?"

Kimberly took a bite of her meatloaf. "I heard something about that. It's nice you're learning something. I have a friend who is an excellent teacher. If you like learning, you should really meet him."

"I don't want to meet new people for a little while." Veronica looked over at me, but I focused on swirling barbecue sauce in my mashed potatoes. "You're here to take me away, aren't you?"

That took us all by surprise, but Kimberly recovered properly. "You're very smart. How did you know that?"

"You used the same voice Lizzie did when she brought me here. With adults, the worse the news, the higher their voice." She took a bite of meatloaf. "I don't have a choice, do I?"

"It's for the best," I said, half trying to convince myself.

"How do you know?" Veronica asked. "What if I'm supposed to be here with you?"

"I'm no guardian, kid," I replied. "You need to be in a loving home, with parents who—who can take care of you better than me."

"What about Carl and Junebug? You said you'd take care of them. Why can't you take care of me, too?"

"Because I can't. If you stay around me—I'm trying to keep you safe, okay?"

"You promised to look out for me, and now you're just going to give me away? And I don't even have a say in it? That's not fair!" She slammed her fork on the table. "Why didn't you just leave me with my mom if you're just going to abandon me?"

She pushed out her chair and rushed upstairs. I started to go after her but felt the tug of my father's arm on mine before I could stand.

"You stay here. I don't think she wants to see you right now."

I nodded and watched him leave the table. Kimberly waited until he was up the stairs and out of sight before she spoke. "I suppose you'll be leaving too, before long."

"I came to make sure Veronica's taken care of and say goodbye to my mom. I've done both of those things, so the best thing for me to do is move on."

Kimberly chuckled. "You really are an idiot."

"Excuse me?" I scoffed. "I mean, I know I'm an idiot, but to what specific reason are you referring?"

"Even after all this time…" She shook her head. "Don't you think your parents would rather have you here, even if it puts them in danger?"

"That's not their choice to make."

She stared at me, unblinking. Kimberly's steely demeanor always unnerved me, and more so at that moment. "Maybe not, but you should let them make that choice."

I shook my head. "I couldn't live with myself if something happened to them."

"And that's why you're an idiot, a selfish idiot. Your parents are good people, and they're dying. Whether they burn in a fire or die in their bed, they will be gone soon, and I don't think it matters to them how. What matters to them is that you're here with them for the end, not off on some stupid noble quest." She shrugged. "But then, it's not about what they want, just what you want, right?"

"That's not fair."

Kimberly took her plate to the sink. "It's the fairest thing I could possibly say about you."

Footsteps creaked on the stairs. Dad walked into the dining room just as Kimberly came back from the kitchen.

"She's packing now," Carl said with a deep sigh. "She doesn't like it, but she's doing it. That girl is hard-headed like a mule. Reminds me of somebody else I know." He turned to me. "Are you sure this is the best idea?"

"That doesn't matter, Carl," Kimberly said. "It's the best thing for her, and that's all that matters."

Low blow, Kimberly. Low blow. I calmed myself before I spoke. "No matter what either of you thinks of me, I've only tried to do what's right for the people I care about."

"I know," Dad said, squeezing my shoulder. "It's just funny how trying to do the right thing can lead you to so many wrong decisions."

Low blow, Dad. Low blow.

CHAPTER 14

My feet stepped heavily on the way up to Veronica's room as if concrete had filled my boots and hardened. With great difficulty, I reached the top of the steps and inched open the door to her room. She had ripped all the posters off the wall and capsized the corner desk chair in a fit of anger, but now sat patiently on her bed next to the leather suitcase Dad had given her.

She acknowledged my presence by folding her hands in front of her and turning toward the wall. "Go away." Her voice was measured and calm, but there was a weariness to it. Her eyes were red and puffy, and the glistening of her cheeks belied her tears.

"It's time," I said, trying to give my words an air of finality.

She snapped her head toward me. "Why did you even save me if all you were going to do was send me away?"

I sat down next to her. "Saving somebody and caring for them are two different things. I'm not much of a hero, but I'm even less of a mother. I thought maybe—maybe Mom and Dad could—but they are both old and sick. This is your best option for a happy life. Kimberly's done this before, and she knows what she's doing. I trust her."

"I hate her," Veronica scowled.

"I don't like her, either."

"I hate you, too."

"Join the club, kid." I held out my hand. "That's not going to change anything. Hate me all you want right now, but soon enough, you'll forget all about me."

She wiped her cheek. "How do you know?"

"Cuz I've watched it happen a thousand times before."

She grabbed my hand and pulled herself to stand. "I don't think so, Lizzie. I think I'm going to remember this forever."

There was nothing else to say, so I guided her toward the door, carrying the heavy leather suitcase that held the clothes and things I'd bought her—everything that she owned in the world. As we walked down the stairs, I realized that in our haste to leave Nevada, I hadn't even grabbed a picture of Becky for Veronica to hold on to in her sadness.

That would not do.

The girl at least needed one memento of her mother. When we reached the bottom of the stairs, Carl and Kimberly stood in front of the door, waiting.

"Dad," I said. "Can you watch Veronica for a moment? There's something I need to do with Kimberly."

"Oh, this should be lovely," Kimberly replied. "One more thing to hold us up. You know I do have other things to do than wait at your beck and call."

I pulled Kimberly into the other room, and after telling her what I needed, she begrudgingly agreed it was a good idea.

"Close your eyes and imagine the house, every detail that you can," Kimberly said. "Make it real in your mind, down to the smallest detail."

I did what she asked, filling in everything I remembered. When I had a clear picture of the house, my stomach fell out from me, and a cold shiver blew through me. For a moment, all hope drained from my body, and then, like a rubber band, my stomach snapped back into my throat with a jerk, and I opened my eyes to see Becky's house in front of me, just as I remembered it.

"Let's make this quick," Kimberly said.

My steps toward the house were measured, made cautious by the memories of the death I'd witnessed there. Kimberly opened the door with her elbow and walked inside through rows of yellow police tape. Bullet holes riddled the walls of the living room and up the stairs, where a streak of blood led us up to the second floor.

"Take your pick," Kimberly said to the pictures that lined the walls. Some of them were cracked with bullets or were only of Veronica, but at the top, I found a nice big one of the three of them—Veronica, Becky, and Rick, smiling in the grass, as if they would never have another care for the rest of their days.

"This is the one," I said, grabbing it.

"Good," she replied. "This place gives me the creeps."

I stepped past her, led somehow by the bloodstains on the floor in the master bedroom—where Becky had bled out like a stuck pig. Anger rose in my throat when I thought about what monsters could take a mother from her daughter—and that they were still hunting Veronica.

I slammed my hand into the floorboards once, twice, three times, as the tears of rage and grief came, and then I felt Kimberly's hand slip over my shoulder.

"How could they do this—" I blubbered. "She was such a good one—she didn't deserve—"

"Monsters don't care, Lizzie. Not if you're a saint, or a nun, or a mother. I've seen it so many times before that sometimes I forget that most people don't know that." She knelt next to me. "I envy that you thought you could avoid your destiny. Even though it was a fool's errand, you really thought that the gods would allow you peace in a world filled with monsters."

"She's not going to be okay, is she?" I asked through more tears.

"I don't know. I found her a nice family and warded it, so she's protected, but the rest of it is on her. If she's like Anjelica, stubborn and foolhardy, they'll find her in a minute, but if she's careful—if she takes her protection seriously—maybe she can outrun it. It's possible."

"You've never seen it before, though, have you?" I asked.

"For the time being, she'll be okay, but if demons are after her…they are relentless."

I clenched my fists together. "We have to kill them."

"I'm working on that. I have to find them first, though, and while I'm doing that, Veronica will be safest away from you, somewhere your prophecies can't come true, either of them."

I nodded. "I want to be there when you kill them. I want to watch them banished back to Hell where they belong."

"I can make that happen." She stood up. "But one thing at a time. For now, let's get that picture back to Veronica, okay?"

I placed my hand in Kimberly's, and we vanished again. For a moment, I was surrounded by black ichor as far as I could see in every direction. My stomach dropped to my knees, and then we were back in my old house, a plume of purple and pink smoke surrounding us.

Veronica jumped back with a stifled scream. It wasn't every day you saw a pixie materialize in front of you, after all. She calmed after a moment, and I held the picture out for her.

"I wanted you to have something happy that you could look back on, so you don't forget them."

Veronica touched the picture, sliding her hand up to her mother's laughing face. "This—we—I—" She broke down and fell to the floor, sobbing for a long while, while we all tried to comfort her. After a long while before she was calm, she clutched the picture tightly to her chest. "Thank you."

"I wish I could do more."

She smiled a sad smile at me. "Maybe you will."

She held her hand out to me, and I wrapped my fingers around hers. She was so small. She needed protection, but from somebody else. I wasn't equipped to give her what she needed, no matter how much I wanted to be that person for her.

"We should go," Kimberly said. softly

I let go of Veronica's hand, and she took Kimberly's. "Maybe you'll come visit," Veronica said.

I smiled. "Maybe."

I knew it wasn't to be. Once she vanished, Kimberly would carry the secret of Veronica's location to her grave and beyond. In a puff of smoke, they were gone, and a piece of my heart broke.

"Come on," Dad said. "I have an aged bourbon that would be very appropriate for a shit situation like this."

CHAPTER 15

Dad wasn't wrong. The bourbon burned going down, but it burned so good. After taking a swig from my glass, I pushed it over to Dad to fill me up again, which he did without so much as a raised eyebrow.

"Ben Coleman up the road makes this himself. If it isn't the smoothest bourbon I've ever had, I don't know what is." He finished his own glass and refilled it. "I've been his best customer since your mom got sick."

I swirled the drink in my glass. "I should have been here, Dad. I'm sorry I wasn't here."

He chuckled lightly to himself. "You don't owe us anything, kid. That's not how parenting works. You don't have a kid so they'll take care of you. It was an honor to bring you up and watch you make your own decisions." He took a long drink. "Wish you made different ones, mind you, and could've used your help, 'specially in the last couple of years, but you don't owe us anything. I just hoped you lived your best life out there on the road. Did you?"

I shook my head. "I didn't live much of a life, Dad. I saw a lot of the country, though. I don't think there's a sight or attraction I haven't seen, in fact. I made it to every national park in the contiguous and just about every roadside attraction I could find."

He smiled. "Which was your favorite?"

"They were all pretty cool, but the Billy the Kid museum—the one in New Mexico, not the one in Texas— that one's gotta be the weirdest. They have a whole exhibit dedicated to a woman that went to Sunday school every week for over fifty years."

"Was she Billy the Kid's ancestor or something?"

"Not that I know. She was just a woman. Plus, they have cars, and trucks, and dolls, and other stuff that definitely did not exist in the 1800s. Charming, though. I bought a pin, but I lost it. I lost so much on the road, Pop."

"Sounds like you lost yourself out there," he said.

I nodded. "Yeah. This is the first time I feel like myself in a long time."

"And you're still determined to leave, then?"

I looked at him for a long moment. We both knew the answer. I didn't get a chance to say it because as I sat there, footsteps banged down the stairs. Johnny, harried and flustered, rushed into the dining room.

"What is it, Johnny?" Dad asked, confused.

"Sorry to disturb you, Carl, but I think it's time."

Dad went first into the room, and I followed close behind. Mom's breathing was so shallow it barely looked as if her chest was moving at all.

"Junebug?" Dad choked out, taking Mom's hand into his. "I'm here, baby. I love you so much, Junie. You made me happier than I thought possible, for longer than I ever imagined…but I'll be okay, Junebug. I want you to know that. I know you could never leave if you didn't know I was going to be okay." He patted her hand with his, shaking with every word he said. "I'll see you soon, baby."

He couldn't continue through his tears and beckoned me over to him. I sat down beside him. "He's right, Mom. I'm here. I'm going to take care of him. I promise."

I didn't know why I said that. Just moments ago, I was ready to disappear again. But looking at the two of them, I couldn't leave. I couldn't just abandon the farm and everything I ever knew—the only place I'd ever been happy—not until I knew that Dad was going to be okay. By the look on his face, he was never going to be okay again. Not until he could join his wife in the great beyond.

"I love you, Mom. I'm sorry I was gone for so long. I'm sorry…I wish I had this past decade with you. I wish I'd called—I wish…there are so many things I wish. But I'm here now, just like you wanted. You can go, now, Mom, because I'm here, and I'm not going anywhere—"

The tears took me over, and I couldn't say another word. I believed she had heard me. As I wept, the heart monitor flatlined. She let out one final breath, and she was gone.

CHAPTER 16

I laid crumpled on the floor until the coroner came and collected the body, and then I helped Dad strip the bed down to the mattress. He'd had a long time to prepare for this moment. He carried out the plans he'd made beforehand in rote detail. I didn't have the same luxury. Even though Kimberly had told me that my mother was sick, it never actually registered that she was going to die.

When I came home and saw her enfeebled and bedridden, her death imminent, some part of me still believed that she would live for years and years. Perhaps because she had been alive my entire life, and she was indomitable, a larger-than-life force of nature that nothing could topple.

But time toppled her, didn't it? The great equalizer. Death.

I wasn't ready to be without a mother. Then again, Veronica wasn't ready to be without a mother, either, and I expected her to be strong. I had to be strong, too.

Most of the arrangements had already been made. They'd picked a church for the service and a burial plot. Dessertations, mom's old shop, catered the wake. Betsy and Ed baked up a spread of bagel sandwiches, donuts, and eclairs for the occasion. The lox was a nice touch.

The wake took place three days after her death, in a small funeral parlor that I used to pass on my way to school when I was younger—when I had all the hope in the world. The funeral director's son, Brian, had gone to school with me, though he was a few years older.

"It's nice to see you again," he said to me softly when Dad and I arrived at the funeral parlor for the wake. "You look lovely."

I didn't. I had been crying for the last three days and had only realized I didn't have the clothes for a funeral a couple of hours before. Luckily, Mom had plenty of dresses. I picked one that was too big on me, but black even if it had fat white polka dots on it, and cinched it with a belt. I said a polite "thank you" and accepted his hand.

"Come this way. We have her set up in the viewing area."

Mom had wasted away over the last year of being stuck on the bed, but Dad managed to find a dress that fit her perfectly, a simple black number with a white, frilly collar. She wore her favorite dark red lipstick, and they made her up to look nearly alive.

We had an hour alone with her before the people started funneling into the viewing area. First was Ben, the man who made the bourbon we drank the night of her death.

"I'm so sorry for your loss," he said to us both, taking our hands in turn. "I made a special case for you, old friend."

He reached into his coat and pulled out a bottle of bourbon, and Dad started crying when he saw that Ben had labeled it Junebug, with a little cartoon June bug as the mascot on the label. I took the bottle, as Dad's hands shook with sadness.

"That's very sweet," I said. "He loves your bourbon."

"We all loved Junebug." Ben placed his hand on Dad's shoulder. "And we love you. I'll deliver that case tomorrow and check on you. Louisa's gonna make a casserole, too."

The rest of the wake was a bevy of faces, hands, and names, some I recognized from years ago and others that were new to me. We must have shaken hands with over a hundred people during the three hours of the wake, and I heard stories from so many people that filled my heart with joy. It had been years since I heard about my mother saving the neighbor's dog from getting run over by a tiller or how she used to make the best eclairs in the whole state—so good that the governor had asked her to cater his daughter's wedding.

But there were also stories from the years I missed, and they ripped my heart in half, little by little. I was nearly a puddle on the floor by the time the last of them fell on my ears. That night at home, we ate a dinner of bagels and donuts, taking turns swigging from the bottle.

The next morning, I woke early with a splitting headache and realized we'd finished over half of the bourbon Ben gave us. I popped some Advil and rode into town to pick out a new dress from Dana's, landing on a spaghetti strap, knee-length black dress with a cardigan to cover my shoulders.

I returned to the house just in time to pick Dad up for the funeral. He was looking over a set of cards and mumbling to himself.

"I forgot to mention this last night," he said, pulling on his coat. "But you are going to need to say something at the funeral today."

"Me?" I said. "I haven't prepared—I have no idea what to say. I'm not good at public speaking."

"Just speak from the heart—and remember, it doesn't matter if everyone hates it. The only thing that matters is that your mother asked for it, and we need to follow her last" —he choked back tears— "her last wishes, okay?"

I nodded. "Okay, Dad."

He was in no condition to operate a vehicle, so I drove us to the church. I hadn't been to a church since I was baptized, and the fact that Mom wanted to have a funeral in one struck me as odd.

"She came to it late in life," Dad answered the question on my mind as we pulled up to the white-washed church. "When she could still get out, they had support groups in the church, and they were kind to her."

There were already a dozen cars at the church when we arrived, and more streamed in behind us. By the time the service started and the pastor called for his first blessing, the church pews were nearly filled. My mother was quite a woman, it seemed, and touched so many people in the town.

After the pastor delivered his remarks, Dad walked up to the pulpit and cleared his throat. "Thank you for coming. If you knew my wife, you know that she loved telling stories. I loved listening to them. I'm afraid I'm not much of a talker. That was Junebug—my wife's job. She was the one everyone loved, and I was the one who made friends simply by being in her presence. After all, how bad could I be if Junie chose to love me, right?"

He laughed sadly. "She put out so much good into the world. It was her fuel. There was never a school fundraiser or bake sale she wasn't willing to donate her time and her baking expertise to help—and god, could that woman bake." There was a murmur of agreement and light laughter throughout the church. He continued, "It's not often that a person finds something they were better suited for than Junie and baking. If you ever had something she baked, you know those hands were blessed by God—and now they have returned to his grace." He cleared his throat. "I love you, Junebug. You were a light in the darkness, and the world has become colder without you in it. And now, I believe my daughter has something to say.”

He rushed off the stage and sat down as I stood and walked to the pulpit. “Wow. I was just thinking that I pitied the person who followed that—and um, I guess that’s me. I was only told I had to say something a couple of minutes ago, so I am just winging it—can you tell?” I sighed and collected myself, gathering the words. “My mom was one of the two greatest humans I’ve ever known, and I’ve been all over this country, met all sorts of people. Mom was one of a kind. She took me in, even though I’m not her blood, and gave me a home. She didn’t have to do that. She didn’t have to do any of the amazing things she did, but she did them anyway, no matter the cost. I’ve been gone for a decade, and I know there wasn’t a day she didn’t talk about me because at least once a day, my ears would start ringing—that was just one of the many things I learned from my mom. ‘If your ears are ringing, then somebody’s talking about you.’ What if you have tinnitus, though? She never answered that one. The minute I came home and felt the love both Mom and Dad imbued in the house I grew up, I knew I had made a mistake leaving all those years ago. I have never felt that kind of love before, or since, except in that house. Mom loved, recklessly and often, even when people didn’t deserve it—especially when people didn’t deserve it.”

I stood there for a minute, stifling tears before I sat down. When Dad squeezed my arm and looked at me with pride, I knew I had not embarrassed myself or my mother’s memory.

After the funeral, we led the procession to the burial plot and threw flowers into the grave as her body was lowered into the ground. And then it was over. The people dispersed, heading back to where they were from—and left behind two broken people grieving alone over Mom's grave.

CHAPTER 17

Exhaustion didn't begin to describe how tired I was. When Dad and I returned to the house that night, not only were we physically drained from standing on our feet all day, but we were emotionally shattered from repeatedly rubbing the rawness of our loss.

"I'm going to bed," I said, trudging up the stairs.

"Can you take your old room, kiddo? I'd like to sleep in the guest room." Dad asked. "I can't be in my room right now."

I nodded. "Of course."

The bed in my old room was more comfortable than most of the motels I'd stayed in over the past few years, but it was hard as a rock compared to the guest room's. Still, how could I complain? We would probably have to change mom's mattress, if not the whole bed, before he could get on with sleeping in there again, but we would cross that bridge tomorrow, maybe later. Mom's death was too fresh to imagine doing anything functional except close my eyes.

Tomorrow, I thought to myself as I closed my eyes and drifted off to sleep. Or, I would have liked to drift off, except that as I did, a bright blue light filled the room. I opened my eyes to see a glowing blue man, unbound from his body, projecting something like the aura of himself at the edge of the bed.

"Elizabeth, you have been chosen by the great powers beyond and have turned from your quest. It is now the time to turn back toward it, for fate had finally aligned fo—"

"Shut up," I growled, throwing the blanket over my head.

"Excuse me?" the voice said, indignant. "I am Saint Nari, herald of the archangel Gabriel, and you will—"

"I said shut up," I grumbled, turning from him. "Can't you hear? I am not interested."

"Wha—in all my years I have neve—" The angel stammered. "I have a message to deliver, and I will have you listen to it."

I rolled back to him and sat up in bed. "If I listen, will you go away and leave me alone?"

"That is the nature of a messenger. Now, if you will allow me to herald for a moment, it would be preferable to the alternative."

A chorus of angels chimed behind him in song, making Nari's appearance even more insufferable.

"Which is?"

He held up a finger. "Me boring the message into your skull with my index finger."

"That doesn't sound pleasant."

"It is not."

"And there is no scenario where you just…go away? I don't want any of what you're selling."

"I hear that a lot, actually."

"That's not surprising. I have never heard of anybody that was visited by an angel and had a good time afterward."

"How—how did you know I was an angel?"

"Do you not hear the choir behind you?" I shook my head, exasperated. "Seriously, I need you to take about 40 percent off whatever is going on right now."

The angel tried to hide his irritation, but it was written all over his face. "I come from a long tradition of—"

"Just get on with it then. I'm trying to sleep."

"Excuse me?"

"I don't need your life story. The longer you are here, the more annoying you get. Since I can't get rid of you until you make your speech, get on with it."

"Well—uuhh—" He scratched his head. "I forget what I was supposed to say."

I sighed again. "Let me help. I have a great destiny. I'm supposed to save the world. It's almost time to get started, for the fate of the universe is at stake. Or something like that, right?"

"Uhh—yeah—that's kind of exactly—how did you know that?"

"I got my prophecy when I was twelve. I've known all this for a long time, but now that you're here, it means that I was right to stay away from this place."

"Are you thinking of foregoing your destiny? That would be disastrous to the world. I can't even begin to th—"

"Let me stop you right there," I growled. "Why do I care what happens to the world? I'll be dead. I won't even be able to enjoy this world I'm saving. So, I'll ask again, why should I give a care?"

Nari floated toward me. "You are part of this world. Those you love are part of this world. Would you not want to save it for them?"

"There's only one person I care about in this world, and he's old as dirt."

"And what about the girl? Do you not care about her?"

I leaped out of bed and stomped over to the angel. "You leave her out of this."

"I'm sorry. She is very much in this, and if you wish her to stay safe, I suggest you change your attitude."

"Is—that a threat? Is an angel threatening me?"

Nari shook his head. "No, not threatening. Just stating facts. We cannot make you choose your fate, but the sooner you accept it, the better it will be for everyone and the higher chance you have to save this world you claim to hate." The angel floated back toward the wall. "But the choice is yours, jerk."

The angel snapped his fingers and vanished. It might not have been a direct threat by an angel, but he confirmed there was a threat to Veronica's life. I needed to protect her, no matter the cost. *You promised to protect her, Lizzie, but what if running toward her was exactly what the stupid angels wanted in the first place? What if that put her in more danger?*

Even if that might be true, I couldn't just stand around and do nothing. I snuck out of my room and downstairs to the kitchen. Dad kept Kimberly's number on a Post-It note in our junk drawer when I was younger, and I was happy to see he hadn't moved it in the decade since I left.

I pounded the number into the phone and waited for her to pick up. Unfortunately, all I got was her voicemail.

"Kimberly, I need to talk to you right now. She's in trouble. Do you hear me? Get here now. I'll be out back so as not to wake Dad."

I slammed the phone down, put on a coat, and made my way to the backyard, a hundred yards from the house so that I couldn't be heard through the windows. There, I waited in the cold for Kimberly to come.

Please come, Kimberly. I can't save the girl without you.

It was thirty minutes in the frigid cold before the flash of purple smoke popped in front of me. I waved my hands, and Kimberly trudged over, yawning and stretching her arms.

"This better be good. You roused me from a great dream about eatin—"

"An angel just came to me, said that the prophecy was about to come tru—you know what, that part doesn't matter. He said that Veronica is in trouble, and I have to save her."

"That sounds like angel bologna to me. Trying to manipulate you into playing their game, the one you've been ducking for a decade."

"And what if it's not?"

"Then I—"

Cars screeched in front of our house. As they came to a stop, three red flashes popped in the front yard.

"Shit, shit, shit," Kimberly said. "This is not good."

"Who are they?"

"Demons, I'm guessing. I was worried this would happen. The wards on your house were bound to your mother. I had made a second set bound to your father, but when Carl decided to play hero and try to save his wife— well, he doesn't have magic anymore…I'll bet when that angel came, it was like a beacon for demons."

"Dad!" I screamed. It didn't matter if I was okay. The idea of his burning in that house flashed through my brain.

I smashed through the back door just as a fireball exploded through the living room. Five demons rushed inside, each uglier and more grotesque than the last, with red horns atop their heads and faces contorted in fury.

"*Crepitus glacies!*" I shouted. Ice shot out of my hands and exploded in the faces of the demons, sending them flying backward. "*Vento tempestas!*"

A galeforce wind blew from my fingers and spun two of the demons out of the door. One of the remaining demons rushed forward, a fiery sword burning in his hand. As he raised it into the air and charged, a pink plume of smoke appeared in front of him, and Kimberly stuck two daggers into the demon's throat. He dropped the sword, which set fire to the floor and the alcove next to the stairs.

Another demon charged just as an explosion rocked above us. The demon flew backward, and I looked up to see Dad ambling down the stairs with a shotgun.

"Get her out of here!" He fired another round as a demon rushed through the door and threw a fireball at him. Dad fired one more round before he went up in flames.

"Dad!" I went to help him, but Kimberly grabbed me and pulled me toward the back of the house. "Let go of me!"

"If we stay here, we die!" A tinge of sadness rose in her voice. She had spent almost as much time in that house during my childhood as I had. "We have to go."

The demons were closing in on us, and I knew we had no choice. With one last look at my father as he laid limp on the landing above us, I let Kimberly drag me away. Behind us, the fire consumed the whole house, except the demons that chased after us.

My past, and everything I had ever loved, was gone in an instant.

CHAPTER 18

It had begun. For a decade, I tried to outrun my prophecy, but as I watched the fire consume my childhood home with my father's charred body inside of it, I knew for a fact that the last decade of my life had been folly. I could have stayed put, in my cozy room, with my loving family. I didn't have to abandon them. I didn't have to run for ten years. I didn't have to blow up my life—my prophecy came for me anyway.

I could have graduated high school, gone to college, worked the land with my parents while they were still young and healthy enough to do so, and taken the load off them when they grew enfeebled. If I had been home, maybe my mother would have fought harder, and my father wouldn't have given up so much of himself to save her.

But I left to protect them and took on the burden of a hard, horrible life, to make sure they didn't suffer…and yet, they did suffer. And in the end, my prophecy caught up with me.

"We have to go," Kimberly said, pulling me through the fields.

"The fire," I said, stunned. "We have to stop the fire."

Even as I said it, I knew that was impossible. Flames had consumed the walls and the roof already. If a fire truck arrived right then, it still would have been hard to contain, and the nearest station was ten minutes away.

Kimberly was an expert at fighting monsters, but I saw the fear in her eyes as red flashes blinked all around the house, and more demons appeared to give chase. Despite all of that, my instinct was to run inside, back to my father.

"Don't be an idiot," Kimberly grumbled, stopping to catch her breath. "He's dead. Mourn him, but don't join him."

"Fine," I said, watching the demons charge toward us. "You're right. Let's go, then!"

"I need a minute. If I don't focus perfectly, we could be lost in the ether, and I'm not in the best state right now." Red lights flashed around us, and three more demons appeared in the cornfields. "Guess I don't have a choice."

Kimberly pulled me toward her and tossed a pinch of pixie dust from her pouch to the ground. We evaporated, and I fell through the inky blackness. It didn't suck the hope from me this time because I had no hope left. I had only the knowledge that I was fate's pawn. Everything I had ever heard about having agency and free will was a load of garbage.

My stomach sank and then expanded as we popped back into the universe, and I fell to the ground onto cold concrete. We were in an empty building. Plastic covered the exposed walls and the office equipment that speckled the floor.

"Catch your breath," Kimberly said, rubbing my back. "If you want to cry—"

I threw off her hand and stood. "I don't want to cry. I want to punch something!"

She shrugged. "Well, this place is being renovated, and all these walls are scheduled for demo, so go for it."

I looked back at her, trying to judge if she was messing with me, but she just gave a small nod. I had spent a decade bottling up my emotions, and at that moment, I didn't want to contain them anymore. They came out like a geyser.

I picked the closest wall to me and slammed my hand hard into it. The drywall buckled but didn't cave, and the impact stung. It felt right. The ripples of pain that shot through my body when I punched the wall again masked the pain erupting from my broken heart. Everything I knew had been ripped away from me.

No mother. No father. No place to call home.

I beat my fists against the wall until the tears overtook me, and I crumbled to the floor, streaks of blood trailing from my knuckles.

"Are you done?"

"NO!" I shouted. I punched the wall again, but my strength had left me.

"Okay." Kimberly crossed her legs and watched me. "Take your time."

I turned from her gaze. "Stop looking at me."

"I can't do that, kid. I promised your parents I'd look out for you, and you're in a fragile state. I have to make sure you don't hurt yourself…well, hurt yourself more." She stopped for a moment. "Did you break anything?"

I looked at the blood-stained wall. I had managed to knock a big hole in it, and a piece of drywall dangled above me. "Just the wall, I think."

"Didn't hit a stud, did you? Those things hurt like the dickens."

"No." I looked down at my hands, flexing them in alternating pulses. "Aside from being bruised and bloody, they don't feel broken."

"Good," Kimberly replied. "Last thing we need is to take you to the hospital with a broken knuckle."

"Yes. That would take this night to another level of suck."

"I know that's a joke," Kimberly said. "But please trust me, there are so many additional levels of suck here that you couldn't even imagine."

"Name one."

She slid closer. "Well, you're not in Hell right now, so that's one right there." She scooted closer still. "You didn't have an arm ripped off by a demon; there's another one."

"No, just everything I've ever known was taken from me. I guess that's just a jolly stroll in the park to you."

Kimberly slid next to me. "No, Lizzie, this sucks really bad. Almost nobody in the history of the world had had a crappier day than you, but it could always be worse."

"Cheery," I croaked through my tears. "You always were a ray of sunshine."

She placed her hand on my leg. "Nobody has ever accused me of being chipper, just effective. Part of that includes being able to put terrible situations in context and keeping my head." She sighed. "It's a skill I don't wish on my worst enemy."

I rested my head against the wall behind me and looked at her. "Seems to be working out okay for you."

She chuckled. "Yeah, people call me resilient. They say because I've seen so much, I can bounce back from anything, but no one…we shouldn't have to be resilient. No one should have to see the things I've seen. I only hope that everyone I ever save can grow up to be soft. But that's not the way of the world now, is it?"

"It's a nice dream."

She squeezed my shoulder. "Unfortunately, you're going to have to be resilient today, Lizzie."

"Why? Can't I just crumble?"

"Two reasons. First, the prophecy said that once you have lost everything, you'll rise, and I have faith that's true, as much as I hate it. You may not believe this, but I was hoping that prophecy was garbage as much as you were— maybe more."

I wiped the tears from my eyes. "And what's the second reason."

"There's a little girl out there whose prophecy is intertwined with yours, and there's no doubt in my mind they're after her, too. If they haven't found her already, they will soon."

Veronica. She was in trouble. The moment the words crossed my mind, every bit of sadness crusted over, replaced by a determination to save her. The demons would not win. They would not get Veronica…even if it cost me everything, I would make sure that little girl was safe.

I pushed myself up. "Then we have to go…now."

CHAPTER 19

I expected the worst when we flashed in front of an unassuming house in a humble suburb somewhere on Earth, supposedly. Kimberly had journeyed to other planets, but I figured even she couldn't teleport between planets, at least not easily. The last time took a blood sacrifice and a god interceding on her behalf.

"Where are we?" I asked as we walked to the door.

"Toronto."

"So it *is* Earth," I muttered to myself.

"What?"

"Nothing," I said quickly.

There was nothing that would have distinguished this house in Toronto from any other suburban sprawl. It was a clean, two-story house with a tented room and big, shuttered windows on either end of both levels. The bottom floor was wrapped by a wooden porch, complete with a rocking chair and trellis of vines that laid dormant and brown in the cold winter air. Nothing seemed amiss in the quaint neighborhood, which was a welcome surprise. I half-expected demons to be rushing down the streets, looting and burning the place for fun.

The house was dark when Kimberly pulled open the screen door and rapped loudly on it three times. "Nolan! Open up!"

The lights flickered on as footsteps thundered down the stairs. A squat man with thick, blond hair and thin glasses flung open the door hurriedly, dragging a long robe behind him. "My goodness, Kimberly. It's half past midnight. Are you trying to give us a heart attack?"

She pushed past Nolan and walked in. "I'm sorry, but there has been an attack, and we needed to make sure you guys and Veronica were okay."

Nolan adjusted his glasses and gestured me inside. "Veronica is perfectly fine. She's asleep, or at least she was until you made a fuss."

"Everything all right down there, sweetie?" a booming voice called from upstairs.

"It's fine, Zachary," Nolan said. "Just Kimberly."

A few seconds later, a tall, thin Black man wearing a lavender robe sauntered down the stairs. "Oh, hi, Kimmy!"

"Nice to see you again, Zach," she said. "I wish it was under better circumstances."

"Oh please, you know I can't sleep with Nolan sawing logs. I was just finishing a lovely book, and I was about to come down for some tea anyway. Can I get you anything?"

Kimberly and I both shook our heads. "No, thanks."

Zachary caught my eye. "And who are you? My, you look a fright."

I nodded. "Sorry, yeah. Both my parents died this week. I'm Elizabeth, but everybody calls me Lizzie."

Zachary smiled. "I had a friend in school named Elizabeth. We used to call her lizard breath. She hated it."

"I haven't heard that one in a long time, but I don't like it much either."

Zachary held his hand out, and I shook it. "Nice to meet you. Sorry about your parents. Sure I can't get you any tea? It really helps you sleep."

"I don't think we'll be sleeping much tonight," I replied.

"I have something that can help that, too."

"Is that Lizzie?" Veronica exclaimed from the stairs. She rushed down in the dinosaur pajamas I'd bought, her hair pulled back in two big, bushy pigtails. "It is you!" She leaped off of the last stair and wrapped me in a big hug.

I gripped her tightly. "It's good to see you, kiddo."

I never thought I would see her again, and feeling her pressed close to me made me nearly burst out crying yet again, except that there was nothing left inside of me.

"Well, this has been lovely," Nolan said. "But I'm very sure that you aren't here for a family reunion. You said Veronica's in trouble?"

"We think she might be."

"I mean, isn't that why she's here in the first place?" Nolan said. "We haven't taken down the wards or anything, and they've held so far every other time yo—"

"I know," Kimberly said. "But demons just recently tracked us down at the safest house I've ever warded, which means they're determined."

"To do what, love?" Zachary asked as the teakettle boiled in the kitchen. "Do I need to get my gun?"

I chuckled. I didn't know Nolan or Zachary, yet I liked them immediately and felt completely comfortable in their home. I lifted Veronica into my arms. "Hey, do you want some tea? Or hot chocolate?"

"Hot chocolate!"

"It's late, dear," Nolan said. "No chocolate."

"Oh hush, Nolan. You're such a fuddy-duddy," Zachary said. "Come here, girl. I'll get you some hot chocolate."

"She's gonna be up peeing all night!" Nolan said through gritted teeth.

"Honey, I don't think we're going to be sleeping much tonight anyway unless I completely misread this situation." Zachary furrowed his brows. "In fact, I think I'm going to switch to some oolong."

"How about coffee?" Kimberly said.

"Nasty," Zachary said. "But if you want that bitter garbage, I'll make you a pot."

Nolan relented, and ten minutes later, we were gathered around the kitchen table, enraptured by the drinks in front of us. I agreed to a cup of coffee and had to admit that it was more than a little better than the swill I normally drank.

"Ancho chile powder," Zachary said, watching me take a sip. "Gives it a little zip, don't you think?"

I offered an appreciative smile as he disappeared back into his oolong, then turned my attention to Veronica, who had a dollop of chocolate on her nose as she tried to suck up the marshmallows with her tongue.

I winked at her. "You should try getting some in your mouth."

"It's better this way," she replied, wiping the chocolate off her nose with her finger and then licking it.

Kimberly hadn't spoken much since we sat down. "I think we should move her," she said, finally.

"And then what?" Zachary said. "Keep moving her again and again and again for the rest of her life?"

"Maybe," Kimberly said. "Or at least until I figure out what's happening and how to stop it."

"Are you sure you can stop it?" I asked. "Cuz I ran for ten years, and my prophecy still caught up with me, and trust me, those ten years sucked."

"So, what? We should just let her stay here, waiting for her destiny to catch up to her, too? Waiting for the demons to come to find her?"

I shook my head. "It's funny because for the past decade, you've been telling me I made the wrong choice, and yet, here you are, making the same one."

"That's when I thought the prophecy was hogwash. We've since had new information to prove that it's very much real."

"And that you can't avoid it."

"No, only that you can't avoid it," Kimberly said, tapping her fingers on the table. "Now that we know what we're dealing with, maybe I can figure something—"

Red flashes illuminated the side of Kimberly's face, and by the time I turned to the door, an explosion had rocked it off its hinges. It flipped over the living room, crashing into the TV. In its wake, three demons rushed into the house. I jumped up, ready to fight…for me, for Veronica, and to tell destiny it can screw itself. Neither of us was going to die in this twisted game.

CHAPTER 20

Nolan rushed toward the curio cabinet on the far side of the room and ripped it open, but before he could reach inside one of the demons punched clean through his sternum and out his back on the other side, splattering his blood across the wall behind us. Veronica screamed.

"NOLAN!" Zachary shouted, red fire filling his eyes. "That's it!"

He slammed his hands down on the table and wailed in pain. The muscles on his back and arms bulged and grew until he was so big that the top of his hairy, elongated head touched the ceiling. Great claws protruded where his hands had been, and they flung the heavy oak table toward the demons. He howled as he charged forward, having transformed from a kindly, little man to a monstrous werewolf.

"Let go—" Kimberly started, but before she could finish, a fireball exploded at her feet and shot her into the kitchen, slamming her against the wall.

"*Glacies fracta*!" I screamed. I scooped Veronica up into my arms with one arm, with the other, I shot a ball of ice toward the center of the room. When I opened my palm, the ice ball shattered, blasting the demons and sending them flying. I sprinted toward the hole in the front door and leaped down the stairs out into the front lawn.

"*Glacies murum*!" An ice wall rose from the ground and covered the porch with a thick layer of ice.

"Where are we going?" Veronica asked.

I covered her head and brought it close to my chest. She was heavier than she looked. *Come on, Lizzie, dig deep.*

We weren't halfway down the street before the ice shattered behind us. A demon flew through the air and slammed into a white truck parked across the street, causing its alarm to blare loudly into the still, night air.

Zachary leaped out after him and drilled the demon deeper into the dented side of the car. Lights began to flick on all over the street, and I turned down one of the driveways, rushing into the backyard.

Two red flashes popped behind me. Instinctively, I ducked into the darkness of the tree line behind the house, desperate to lose myself in the canopy. The dead leaves crunched under my feet, giving me away, and soon enough, the demons had rushed into the woods after me.

I zig-zagged through the woods as long as I could, but I wasn't a strong woman, and I had no experience carrying children, only trays of food. It wasn't long before my arms began to shake and gave out under me. I toppled to the ground, and Veronica fell to the earth next to me.

"Are you okay?" I said, huffing and puffing.

She held her knee. "I think so."

"Let me see," I said quietly. I pushed up her dinosaur pajamas to reveal a shallow cut on her leg. "You'll live."

"It hurts."

"I know, kid," I replied. "I need you to be brave, though. And quiet."

I tried to keep my breathing shallow and slow, but I was gassed and couldn't help sucking wind hard. It didn't take long for the demons to track me to the gnarled tree doing its best to hide us.

"*Aqua effusorium!*" I screamed, shooting a geyser of water from my outstretched arms. They were ready for it this time and countered my attack with a fire spell of their own, resulting in a fog of steam between us. They had inadvertently given me a perfect distraction to escape.

I grabbed Veronica's hand and pulled her through the steam toward the edge of the woods, where we came upon a road. We didn't have time to beg for help. I needed drastic action, so I ran into the road as a car approached, hoping it would slow for me.

It skidded to a stop right in front of me, and I ran around to the passenger's side. "Please, please. Help us." I slammed against the window. "Somebody is chasing us!"

The door unlatched, and I slid into the passenger's seat and slammed the door. A young woman with wild hair and a vacant expression looked at me with glassy eyes. "Who are you?"

"Does that matter?" I screamed. "Just drive!"

The girl put the car in gear and drove off. "Whatever, man. I'm Rhel, by the way. I was just trying to be polite. Who is chasing you?"

"You wouldn't believe me if I told you," I replied, buckling Veronica and myself into the seat. "Thank you for stopping."

"I mean, you gotta help people, right? Isn't that what it's all about?" Rhel said as she shifted gear. "That's what I say."

She turned the corner, and two flashes of red light appeared in front of the car. Rhel didn't brake in time, and she slammed into the demons, sending them flying backward while we lurched forward into the dashboard.

"Are you—?" I turned to Rhel, only to see her head slumped against the steering wheel, bleeding and unconscious.

I tried to help her, but another demon appeared on the side of the car and ripped off the passenger door. They reached inside and yanked a bleeding Veronica from my hands.

"No, please. Stop," I croaked. I could barely see straight for the world spinning around me, and I certainly couldn't fight the demon that threw me aside like a ragdoll.

This was the end. I didn't die for some great cause. I didn't save the world. If anything, I helped end it. I closed my eyes and waited for death, but it didn't come. Instead, I heard a yell, and when I opened my eyes, Kimberly stood in front of the car, the demon's outstretched arm lying on the ground, seeping green ooze into the dirt. It was standing in the car's high beams, holding Veronica in its remaining arm.

The demon screeched as it stumbled backward. Kimberly took a step closer. For a moment, the demon looked like it was going to attack, but it must have thought better of the situation. Instead, it screamed to its friends, who gathered closer. All three of them vanished from sight with Veronica in tow.

And then, everything went fuzzy as I collapsed onto the dashboard.

CHAPTER 21

I swirled in the darkness, enveloped by it, drifting in the nothingness. When I entered the void previously, I had felt cold, hopeless, and desolate, but this was nothing like those times. Now, the darkness enveloped me like an old friend, and in it, I found the comfort I had been seeking for almost half my life.

It is not your time, yet, a soft voice said, and then a sudden jerk pulled me back into the light. I opened my eyes with a moan, and when I tried to move, a piteous whine followed a deep whimper.

"Don't move," Kimberly's voice said, and so, of course, like a petulant child, I moved a second time, and it hurt even worse.

"Take these," Zachary whispered, placing some pills in my hand.

I popped the pills into my mouth. My eyes focused on the glass of water he held toward me, and I downed it all before sitting up. My head was bandaged, and I felt dried blood still on my cheek.

"What ha—" I started, but then it hit me all at once: the attack, the escape, the crash, Veronica being ripped from my arms, and the demons—*they have her*. I bolted upright like a rocket, my face immediately contorting in a painful grimace. A pained sob escaped my lips.

"You're going to hurt yourself—more," Kimberly said.

"We have to find her."

We were in the office building where Kimberly had shepherded me after the attack on my parent's house. They had taken the plastic off one of the couches and used it as a makeshift bed.

"We're going to, honey," Zachary said. "Don't you worry about that."

"He's right," Kimberly replied. "I already made contact with a source in the demon world. Once you're feeling up to it—"

"I'm fine," I snapped, cutting her off. "Let's go, right now." She had something to say, but she stopped herself. "I know I'm in no condition to fight, Kimberly, but this is happening one way or another, and that little girl is not dying while I still draw breath. Do you understand?"

Kimberly nodded solemnly. She knew it meant sending me to my death. We both knew that, but that was always how it was going to end. We both knew that, too. She wrapped me up in a hug.

"I promised your parents I would look out for you, but even before that, when I brought you to them, do you remember what I told you?"

"I haven't thought about it in a long time." I looked at her while I probed my memory. "You told me that you were bringing me somewhere I would be safe—that I could be happy."

"I wish you were happier longer, Lizzie. I feel like I failed you."

I placed my hand on her shoulder. "You didn't fail me, Kimberly. You saved me. You've always tried to save me. It's okay. Really, if this is the way I'm going to go, then…well, at least I'll go out in a blaze of glory, and maybe even take some of those demon nut sacks with me."

"Heck yeah, honey," Zachary said. "And you know what to do when you find out where they are, cuz I want a piece of those sum bitches, too."

"You'll have your chance," Kimberly said. "Something tells me we'll need all the help we can get."

She swallowed the rest of her tears, then grabbed my hands, and together, the three of us vanished into the abyss. I had always seen it as a scary place, devoid of hope, but now, I knew that it was also a place of peace, of quiet, and of comfort, where you could be alone in your sadness without judgment.

We appeared again in the lobby of a beautiful hotel. I felt completely out of place. It didn't help that several of the guests, each dressed in their finest, turned up their noses at us when we passed. Kimberly was unfazed, and I was too pained to care.

She led us toward an oak bar in the lobby, where a single figure, dressed in a red sequin dress with flowing, silky, black hair, sat, swirling an olive in a martini glass.

"Darling," she said, without turning to us. "You must think highly of my skills to think I would have an answer already."

Kimberly sat down next to her. "Cut the shit, Lilith. You already knew where they were when you sent me away. I saw it in your eyes."

"Ooh, girl," Zachary growled. "If that's too—"

"Quiet, mutt." She ate the olive from the toothpick before carefully turning to address Kimberly. "Another of your strays? I expect no less from your mannerless urchins."

"Enough!" I hissed. "Where is Veronica?"

She furrowed her brows. "Excuse me now, little girl, it's rude to interrup—"

Kimberly sighed. "Do you know where she is, Lilith?"

Lilith nodded. "I do. I'm afraid I don't have good news for you. The girl…well, she is destined to end the Apocalypse, to be the last death in a great battle between Heaven and Hell. The demons in Hell—one, specifically—don't want that to happen, obviously, and so, they want her to die now."

"If she's destined to end the Apocalypse," I asked, threats be damned, "then how can they stop it? I mean, isn't destiny, destiny?"

Lilith scoffed. "You know so little of the universe. It has its machinations, but we, each of us, have ours. If we couldn't fight against our destiny, then your friend here would be dead a hundred times over."

"So, it is possible to change your fate?" I asked excitedly.

Lilith looked me over, staring for a long moment. "Tough, but possible. Not for you, I'm afraid. Not this time, at least."

"Says you," I replied. The idea that I could change my fate brought a smile to my face and a shudder of exhilaration through my body. "If there's a way to save Veronica, I'm going to do it."

"We're running out of time, Lilith," Kimberly said. "Give me an address."

Lilith reached into her bra and pulled out a card with an address written on it in beautiful calligraphy. "Be careful. There are dangerous games afoot."

Kimberly snatched the card out of her hand. "There always are."

CHAPTER 22

The address Lilith gave us led to a meat packing plant in the heart of Prague. Demons didn't like the daylight and tended to hop around the world following the night across the time zones. Kimberly told me that when I was young—probably to convince me not to go out at night, but that didn't make it any less true. Even fairy tales held a grain of truth, after all. Kimberly didn't know Prague very well, so the closest she could get us was the Sedlec Ossuary, a church decorated in bone, an hour outside of the city.

"Why couldn't you get us closer?" I growled as the cab driver turned off the highway into the city proper.

"I have to remember a place perfectly to teleport to it, or I'll get lost in the void. Is that what you want, to be lost in the void forever?"

"No," I said, though I wasn't sure of my answer. The last time I was knocked unconscious, I felt a comfort in the darkness; it wrapped me like a comfortable blanket. "Of course not."

It had been three hours since the girl had been kidnapped, and my heart raced as the cab made its way into the city. When the driver finally let us out in front of the brick warehouses, there was an air of confusion about him. I doubted that many tourists made a habit of seeing nondescript buildings outside of the city center.

"You stay here," Kimberly said to me. "I'm going to scout the perimeter."

Before I could protest, her wings glowed on her back, and she flew up into the air, landing on the edge of a nearby roof. She glanced back at us before she disappeared from view.

"I don't like waiting," Zachary said.

I pulled my coat tighter around my chest. "Me either. I'm amped up now and ready to fight. Every minute we stay here is a minute that we risk them killing the girl."

"I am so angry I could take down a hundred demons with my bare hands." He pressed his fists together. "Plus, it's frigging freezing out here, and that's not helping my mood."

He was right. It was absolutely frigid, even in my coat, and by the time we had waited for ten minutes, Zachary's nose was red, and his teeth chattered loudly. I was just about to give up and find shelter when Kimberly appeared above us and she floated down to the ground.

"They're inside. They have Veronica tied up on a conveyor belt. There is no good way to save her without causing a scene."

"So what? We just go in, guns blazing?"

She nodded. "Seems like it. There's a skylight above the building. I think we smash through it, Batman-style, and use the element of surprise to snatch her up and escape before they get wise."

Zachary smiled. "That sounds good to me, except I'm not leaving until I send at least a couple of those assholes back down to Hell."

"Then you can be the muscle. Go in first, and the two of us will use the distraction."

"Sounds like a plan," I said.

"Then grab on."

Zachary and I latched onto Kimberly's shoulders, and she flew us up to the roof. It wasn't graceful—she clearly wasn't used to carrying so much weight with her. As we made our way across the roofs, dead demons lined our path, victims of Kimberly's stealthy attacks.

Two more demons laid dead on the roof of the meat packing plant where they held Veronica, making six bodies, but there must have been three dozen more below us. As I peered through the skylight, the demons parted, revealing Veronica bound to the end of a long conveyor belt. On the other end was a collection of mechanical saws, still bloody from cutting through bone and viscera.

"They're going to chop her up," I said. "That's disgusting."

"They want to be sure nothing or nobody can bring her back together again," Kimberly replied. "They must be very afraid of this girl."

"Enough talk," Zachary said. "Are we doing this or not?"

"We're doing this," Kimberly said. "It's a very, very stupid thing, but we're doing it."

Zachary howled as he transformed into a werewolf under the light of the moon. When the transformation was complete, he leaped into the air and crashed through the skylight, sending broken shards of glass raining onto the floor below and drawing the attention of the guards.

"Ready to kick some ass?" Kimberly asked me.

"Oh, hell yeah."

She pulled out a switchblade from her boot and passed it to me. "In case you get to her before me."

She grabbed my hand, and we leaped through the skylight as demon guts and green blood flew across the room from the carnage Zachary wrought among the demons.

"*Crepitus glacies*!" I screamed, releasing a ball of light from my fists, opening my palm. I watched it explode on the demons below us. "*Grandinis*!"

As we landed, a hailstorm grew above us, showering hail on the waiting demons. They stumbled backward. Kimberly didn't wait to attack once she landed. She moved forward like lightning, stabbing and slicing one demon after another.

"Get the girl!" she shouted.

The demons must have heard her because the conveyor belt whizzed to life, and Veronica let out a scream as she started moving toward the rotating buzzsaw.

"*Glacies spica*!" I screamed at one of the demons guarding the conveyor belt, and it fell, bleeding a thick green ooze from the ice spike embedded in its forehead. "I'm coming, Veronica!"

An orange-tinged demon swung a scimitar at me, and I dropped to my knees to avoid it. However, I realized too late that it wasn't slicing toward me, but Kimberly. I heard a scream and turned back to see Kimberly falter, a gash across her back. I went to help, but before I could muster a spell, she turned and drilled a dagger into the demon's eye.

"Go!" she screamed, though her voice was less steady than before. She leapt into the air as two demons made their way toward her, and she kicked the demon she'd just killed.

"*Glacies spica!*" I shouted again to the demon at the controls. The spike fired, but the demon was too fast. It dodged my attack, and the spike went into the controls for the machine, causing it to fritz out of control and speed up the belt. Veronica careened even faster to her gruesome end.

"NO!" I screamed. There was no way to turn off the controls in time, so I rushed toward her. A demon came after me, but Zachary hurtled a mangled demon toward it, and both of their bodies crashed into the belt.

"Thank you!" I shouted.

I sent an ice spike into another demon before I reached Veronica. I pulled out the switchblade and cut her free from her thick ropes as she looked at me with wild, scared eyes.

"It's going to be okay," I said as I frayed the rope. We were getting precariously close to the spinning blades, but finally, I cut her free and pulled her from the conveyor belt, wrapping her in a hug as we cried in each other's arms.

"I knew you would come for me," she said, grabbing me tightly.

"I always will," I replied. "Now, let's get you home, okay?"

"Yes, please."

I pulled her into my arms and rushed toward the door. "Let's get out of here!"

"Go!" Kimberly shouted.

"We'll be right behind you," Zachary growled, ripping a demon in half.

Zachary and Kimberly were still engaged with demons, so I needed to take charge and bring Veronica to freedom. I dodged a razor-sharp demon's claws and spun away from another before I had a clear shot at the door.

It was right there, and my steps grew faster as I neared it, ready to—

—I let out a gasp as a sharp pain shot through me. I looked down to see a thick metal rod had pierced through my chest and straight into Veronica's neck. Blood oozed onto my chest as the life left her eyes.

"No, no, no, no, no. Please don—"

That was all I had the energy to say as the last of my breath left my body, and I fell down, dead.

BOOK 2

CHAPTER 23

Screams filled my ears as my eyes fluttered open to a mix of black, orange, and red dancing along the craggy rock above me. My body no longer ached, and when my hands found my chest, there was no rebar sticking out of it. There were, however, hundreds of other shuffling cadavers, moaning and shambling. They filed around me like a school of fish.

There were corpses, thousands, tens of thousands, hundreds of thousands, maybe millions, queueing in a line that extended as far as the eye could see in any direction. The sea of people did not end at the horizon, either. Great towers of souls swayed high in the caverns, causing the orange and red that lit the cave to flicker against my face with great waves of shadow, the light seeking slivers of space between the wobbling masses.

Behind me was only a flat nothingness. There was nowhere to go but forward, except that was impossible, too. The throngs of people stood shoulder to shoulder, preventing any egress or ingress from the line. Crows and vulture screams cut through the air as their shadowy figures flew overhead.

I was dead, right? And somehow, I made it to the underworld. Kimberly had told me about Hell when I was a child but said nothing about how many people crowded every inch of it. There was no doubt I was in Hell, either. Heaven would not smell of charred remains or be filled with screams of suffering.

Veronica! The thought hit me like a ton of bricks. Where was she? Had she somehow lived? No, it was impossible. I had watched the light leave her eyes and felt the last gasp of her life.

"Veronica!" I screamed, trying to push through the masses of bodies. "Veronica!" I turned to the person next to me, a glassy-eyed man with a shabby beard and shabbier clothes. "Excuse me, please." I tried to push past him, but he didn't move. "I have to find—move!"

He looked over. "Wait your turn."

"I'm not waiting for—Are you crazy? I have to find my friend."

He sighed but still didn't move. "I had a friend. Promised we would find each other in the hereafter." He chuckled. "God, I hated that guy. If I never see him again, it would be too soon."

"Not much of a friend, then."

"He was the best friend I ever had," he said as I ducked down to burrow my way past him. "If you're gonna touch my unmentionables, at least introduce yourself. My name is Simon. Simon Albert."

"I don't care," I snapped, looking for a way past him.

"That's the problem with people these days. Don't care about the niceties."

It was impossible. There was no way to dig through the bodies—but if I couldn't go through them. Maybe I could go over them.

I smirked to myself as I thought of the idea. I turned back to Simon. "I'm sorry. You're right. The worst part of Hell is the unpleasantness of the other people."

"Oh my," he replied. "Do you really think we're in Hell? I did everything right, though, and now…now…" He dropped to his knees. "Oh god, what have I done to deserve this?"

I didn't answer. Instead, I stepped on the crook of his back, using him as a springboard to the arms of the person next to him, and then leaped forward along the shoulders and necks of the souls all around me.

"VERONICA!" I screamed as I made my way across the undulating masses. "Veronica! Where are you?"

"I'm Veronica!" I heard somebody shout out.

"My name is Veronica, too," another echoed.

"I'm Veronica, too!" This time it was a man's voice, and I growled because none of them sounded like my Veronica.

"I'm not talking to any of you! I'm looking for a Veronica who was killed in Prague. She's a little girl, just six years old. Please, she's probably alone and scared."

A warbling female voice shouted, "I'm alone and scared!"

I was getting nowhere, but I couldn't give up. Most of the people were packed in so tight that even through their consternation, they could not lift their arms to swat me away as I walked over them. Instead, they had to suffer my weight until I moved off of them, and then they'd give out a relieved moan.

"You should get down!" a man's voice shouted at me.

"Shut up, Ronald!" the woman next to him snapped. "Let the demons sort it out."

"What do you mean?" I said. "What are the demons going to sort out?"

"You think you're the first person who tried to cut the line?" Ronald called out. "Happens all the time, and that's when the demons circling above swoop down. Send you to the back of the line is what they do."

I considered this. "That doesn't sound so bad. Especially since we're all waiting to get into Hell."

"They rough you up," a shrill voice added. "Leave you bloody, with your entrails hanging out, 'til you reach the front in a million years or so. Happened to a buddy of mine."

"It did not!" Ronald shouted back.

"Enough!" I screamed. "I'm not trying to cut the line. I'm looking for a little girl. Can you help me or no—"

"There you are," a voice boomed.

I was scooped up by the arm and dragged into the air. "Let me go!" I kicked and screamed. "I am not trying to cut the line!"

"I know. You're looking for Veronica."

"Yes, I am," I said, straining my neck to get a look at my savior. The light of the cavern blinded me. "Do you know where she is?"

"I do, but I don't think this is the right place to discuss it. Do you mind if we go somewhere else? I really shouldn't be here. It's drying out my skin."

"Where are you taking me?"

"Heaven, of course," the voice said, and then my skin glowed a bright blue, and we vanished. When we disappeared, I could swear I tasted strawberry lip balm.

CHAPTER 24

A cool breeze washed over me when we reappeared. It wasn't like the frigid cold of the abyss or even the type that came from my hands when I cast spells. This was like a crisp fall day, right when the leaves change colors, and you have to dig into your winter clothes to find your scarf so you can head into town and pick up a Pumpkin Spice from Starbucks.

The fluffy cloud I was dropped into cocooned me like a swaddled newborn for a moment, then released me back to its surface. I rose to my feet just in time to see a tall, blond man brushing the soot off his smoldering toga.

"I hate Hell," he grumbled. "Not even supposed to go there, but desperate times, you know?"

A shimmering golden gate glowed in the middle distance. Its bright light gave everything an ethereal glow. Just before the gate, a podium separated a bearded, old man from a line of people.

The man turned to me after brushing more ash from his toga and extended a pair of white wings behind him. "Tell me, do I have anything on my wings?"

I examined them for a moment. I leaned in and brushed some soot off his left wing, and he jumped back slightly.

"Sorry, you just had something on your wing. You didn't ask me to brush it off, though, so I apologize."

"No, it's fine," he replied. "I just…don't remember the last time somebody touched me."

"Must be lonely," I said. "What's your name?"

"They call me Gabriel."

I chuckled. "Like the archangel."

"Yeah." He beamed. "It's kind of exactly like that."

"Oh—" I started before the realization hit me. "Oooooh! Well, it's a pleasure to meet you."

"And you. I've heard a lot about you. I always hoped we would meet in better circumstances."

"Wait. You…know about me?"

"We keep track of every prophecy relating to the Apocalypse that we can find," he replied. "and you—well, we should go."

I brushed the last of the ashes from his wings. "There you go."

"Thank you." He flew into the air and looked back at me. "It's easier if you bounce, like a trampoline."

I didn't know what he was talking about at first, but when I took a step, my legs wobbled under me like jelly, and I understood what I needed to do. I pressed my legs into the cloud and hopped into the air after Gabriel.

"Open up, Peter," he grumbled to the old man sitting behind the podium.

"Hold your horses," the old man said, turning from a dark-faced man with a thin goatee. "I'm sorry, Mr. Tony Carson, but you have been judged and found wanting."

"No, but I—I know I deserve to enter the kingdom of Heaven. I did everything right!" As he pleaded, a hole opened in the floor of the clouds, and the man plummeted toward the earth below.

"Obviously not." The old man looked back at us and snapped his fingers. The gates creaked open, and the people waiting in line gasped with amazement.

"You called him Peter," I said, following Gabriel through the gates. "Like Saint Peter?"

"Please don't call him that." Gabriel took one last look at the man on the podium. "He has a big enough head as it is."

"Not as big as yours, *Saint* Gabriel, " Peter called after us.

It was certainly not how I expected saints to behave, snickering and mocking each other, but I simply shrugged. *Not my monkeys, not my circus.* I bounced behind Gabriel as we made our way across the planes of Heaven. It was so different than Hell, not only in temperature but density. While every inch of Hell was teeming with people, there was almost nobody in Heaven. In fact, aside from the line of people waiting to be judged, I barely saw anyone.

"Where are we going?" I asked Gabriel.

He pointed at a small hill with several unanchored pillars dotting its tip. "God rests atop the mount, and he has called for you."

"God?" I could barely contain my disbelief. "He called for me?"

Gabriel nodded, stone-faced. "Verily."

"I've had a weird few weeks, but this is the weirdest thing that has ever happened to me by a long shot." I bounced toward Gabriel, overtaking his position. "Why would God have any reason to speak to me?"

"I already told you," he said, without a speck of irritation or irony. "We keep a close watch on every possibly Apocalyptic situation. Really, I think it would be better if you heard it from him. I know this must be frustrating to hear, but God doesn't have much to look forward to these days, and he has anticipated this meeting for a long time."

I had so many questions, but I bit my lip. It was clear Gabriel wouldn't answer them. I hoped God would be more forthcoming. *Wow, there was a phrase I never thought I would say—er, think.*

As we neared the hill, a tall, strongly-built woman wearing a tight bun walked toward us, having no problem navigating the clouds. Clearly, this wasn't her first day.

"You're thirty-seven seconds late, Gabriel," she growled. "You know how much God detests tardiness."

"Easy, Moana," Gabriel said. "I know you like to micromanage every second of his day but bring it down a little bit. He hasn't had an urgent meeting since the Dark Ages."

"All meetings with his royal grace are important," Moana sneered. "By the simple fact that they are meetings with him."

Gabriel sighed. He had clearly had this argument before and lost. His face turned from annoyance to forced contentment, and a smile rose on his face. "You're right, Moana. How could I be so inconsiderate? I will put a word into Lucifer and ask him to improve his file systems…in Hell."

"Yes, well, I suppose you can be forgiven, given the circumstances." Moana turned to me. "Good afternoon, I'm the…hm, how do I explain this? I'm the chief operating officer, I suppose—to put it in a way you'd understand—of Heaven. God is more a visionary, and I make sure it's all running smoothly."

"Well, I think you're doing a great job," I said. "Bang on, compared to Hell. Lucifer could use your help, I think."

A smile cracked on Moana's face. "Yes, well. I do what I can." She turned toward the mount. "Well, go on up then. He's waiting for you. This is a very exciting day for him."

Gabriel and I continued to the hill. A set of stairs, disconnected from anything, hovered in the sky and gave slightly when I stepped onto them. We trod step by step to the top, where I was reminded of the ruins of Rome or Athens. The pillars around the hill seemed to have been built to house some sort of structure, but now they hung free, the roof broken off at some point. Above me, I saw every star in the galaxy, and in the middle of the room, a sword hilt lay buried into a metal casing. On the far end, a man with a white beard and long, flowing, white robe sat watching an old television, eating a bowl of popcorn.

"Excuse me, sir," Gabriel said. "I have brought Elizabeth, the prophecized girl of legend."

"Oh, I don't know if I'm all tha—" I sputtered.

Gabriel held up his hand.

The man stood. His eyes glowed white as he stood to his full glory. In fact, all of him glowed, brighter and brighter as he made his way toward me.

"It's a pleasure," his voice boomed with grandeur and oozed with opulence. "I have looked forward to this moment, though I do wish it was under better circumstances."

"As do I, sir, and yes—yes, it's nice to meet you, too— an honor, really."

He brushed off the popcorn kernels that had collected on the front of his toga. "Christ on a cracker. That is not very godly of me. Please, forgive me."

"Oh no, it's fine. It's kind of charming, in a way."

God smiled. "Lovely. And you are certainly quite charming too, aren't you? Yes, I think you will do nicely. Fate has shone its countenance on you, and, as with most things, Ananke was right again."

"Ananke?"

"The goddess of fate. She set all of this in motion at the beginning."

I scratched my head. "Beg your pardon, sir, but didn't *you* set all this in motion?"

"Well, I…it's not important. What is important is that you are here, and just as prophecized, you have died and have risen, which means you might still be able to fix this mess."

"What mess?"

"Surely you saw Hell, yes? Horrible. There are bodies stacked on top of each other down there, and I mean literally."

"I did, sir. It wasn't pleasant."

God bit his lip. "There will be a reckoning, and it will happen soon. There doesn't seem to be any way out of it, unfortunately. I believe in Lucifer, but now I think he's in quite over his head. Soon, there will be no way to contain the pressure built up and Hell…Hell will consume us all like—um," he turned to Gabriel. "How did we describe it the other day?"

"Like shaking up a soda can."

"Yes, that's right," God said. "Quite."

"And what does any of that have to do with me?"

"I'm getting to that! You see, you happen to be destined to save the world, and this is the moment when your service to me begins. The girl, Veronica—she cannot die."

I furrowed my brow. "She's already dead, though."

He nodded. "Yes, we know. Unfortunately, the scrolls we interpret these prophecies from are not very good, and we believed it would just…all work out without our involvement, as it always has. However, that is not the case, in this case, so we must intercede."

"Intercede in what? She's flipping dead…and I can't curse here, it seems."

"Correct," Gabriel said. "God detests a potty mouth."

"Back to the matter at hand," God said. "We would like to send you back in time to reset this mistake and make sure Veronica lives."

"Okay, we'll do that, then. I'm game."

God's eyes darted to Gabriel and then back to me. "Yes, well, that is where the problem comes in. While I am very powerful, I do not have the power to rewind time. That power rests with one being, who is tasked with keeping all timelines in congruity."

"We call her the Time Being," Gabriel said. "She's a real stickler about this kind of thing."

"Now, Gabriel, that's not fair. She is just very particular about her job." God scrunched his mouth. "And she hates gods almost as much as she loathes angels."

"Which is where you come in," Gabriel said.

"Oh goodie, I was wondering when this would come around to me again."

"We need you to find the Time Being and negotiate with her to let you go back in time. She will only allow this request from mortals, and only once in a generation."

"Well, that sucks because I'm dead."

Gabriel held up a finger. "Right now, you're only mostly dead, which means you're also slightly alive."

"In the void between living and dead, we can send you back to your body, which you can use to find the Time Being."

"If you can save me, why can't you save Veronica, too?"

God sighed. "Your body is irreparably broken, and hers is even worse. If we brought Veronica back from the dead, I'm afraid she will never live to play her part in all of this."

"And what is her part in all this? To die at the right time?"

God and Gabriel looked at each other, then God held out his hands with a shrug. "Yes, to die at the right time, for the noblest of all causes—to save the planet and the universe."

"I'm not going to let you raise her for slaughter."

"If she dies now, she will live in Hell and suffer, as will the world. But if she lives and fulfills her purpose, I will bring her to my kingdom as a reward for her service."

"That's a pretty good reward," I said. "What do I get?"

"I offer the same to you and more. If you go to the Time Being, you can not only rewind all of this, but you can go back even further. You could have a life with your parents and save the girl at the same time. You can have it all, and then, when you die, you will come here."

"You should take him up on it," Gabriel said. "We haven't let somebody into the gates of Heaven in a long time."

"You mean I can have the last decade of my life back?"

"Yes," God said. "That is the power the Time Being possesses."

Time with my parents? The ability to save them from their mistakes? To have a real life and till the land, not having to run from my destiny for a decade? That sounded like a good deal to me. "I will help you if you grant my parents the same chance to enter your kingdom as well at their death."

God thought for a moment. "Very well. Consider it done."

"Then you have yourself a deal."

"Lovely," God said with a smile. "Good luck to you."

CHAPTER 25

A heaving breath brought me back to consciousness. Pain rippled through my body, excruciating pain in every joint of every limb. I didn't know what I expected when I opened my eyes, but it wasn't hanging in a freezer surrounded by slabs of meat. A cursory look around the room, and I counted three other demon bodies swinging between the carcasses of cows and pigs.

Mostly dead, my ass. I was half blue, and my chest burned like it was on fire.

I swung myself up and grabbed onto the hook that held my legs. I kicked my feet as hard as I could, and my legs fell free…and then I plummeted to the riveted metal floor with a clatter. I reached into the pocket of my jeans and pulled out the switchblade, scooting myself into a corner to wait for the other demons to enter the room. When they didn't come, I slid up the back wall, trying desperately to catch my breath. Every inhale sent cold air into my lungs that cut like tiny needles in my chest.

Veronica. If I was here, then so was she. I wouldn't let her become feed for voracious demons. When I finally found her in the far end of the room, I choked on my tears. My body was so frozen that they wouldn't fall from my eyes. There was no light in the little girl's dead eyes as they stared out at me, and when I pulled her off the meat hook, she didn't give or shift her weight. Truly, there was nothing left of her except for the flesh sack her soul once inhabited.

She would not be a meal for demons. I wrapped her arms tightly around me, struggling with her uneven weight, and moved to the door. It clicked open for me, and I slid out into the warmth of the factory.

I expected to see dozens of demons, but instead found a bustling factory of humans, going about their work as if they didn't know there had been a huge battle there. They were at best ignorant to the comings and goings of the factory at night, but I suspected they were sympathizers— or worse, active worshippers of the demons. There were plenty that worshipped demons as gods, and the tiny "miracles" that demons could perform spread to the enfeebled and pathetic, those that had no other choices— and those that chose to believe the half-truths and worship false gods.

Angels were bound in some way to the truth, as were gods, in another way, but Kimberly had explained to me that demons held no such standards. They would promise anything to escape Hell and roam the earth again, and the easiest way was to convince poor suckers that they could get ahead by summoning the demonkind. Of course, it never worked out well for those humans in the end. Either they were mauled as fuel for the demons, hunted for sport, or abandoned with nothing except the knowledge of the depths of their depravity.

I hugged the walls of the factory on my way to the door and into the alley behind the meat packing plant. I shuffled into an alcove and pushed Veronica's face away from me. She was cold and blue, with vacant eyes.

"Please don't collect trash today," I whispered to myself as I hid Veronica's body underneath a pile of trash bags and slinked out onto the street.

I was stuck in Prague. I needed to contact Kimberly or Zachary—yes, maybe if I could find a phone, I could make an international collect call. It took me thirty minutes of wandering before I found a phone booth, but when I went to punch in Kimberly's number, I realized that I had never memorized it, and no amount of staring blankly at the receiver would change that. When a middle-aged woman tapped on the door after waiting for several minutes, I ceded the booth to her and wandered some more, hoping to find a library with an internet connection.

Luckily, Prague was a tourist city with plenty of maps in English, and helpful sorts who sent me in the right direction of a library a couple of miles away. When I arrived, the sliding doors opened, and I was met by a warm blast of welcome heat. I must have looked quite a sight as I ambled to the information desk. The young man looking up from his computer couldn't hide the look of horror on his face.

"*Jak vám mohu pomoci?*" he said. The plaque on his desk said Robert Williams on it.

"I know this is very American of me, but do you speak English, Robert?"

He frowned and then spoke in a thick accent. "Of course. How may I help you?"

"I seem to have lost my friend. We went out last night, and she didn't come back to our flat. I need to use your computer to see if she sent me an email or anything that shows where she might be."

Robert's expression turned from confusion to concern. "Of course, right this way. Do I need to call the constable?"

I shook my head. "I've already spoken to them, but I can't just sit around waiting for her to call." He pulled out a chair so that I could sit. "Thank you so much."

He leaned over and typed something onto the keyboard, and the language turned from Czech to English. "There you go. Let me know if you need anything."

I thanked him, and he left. Kimberly was well-known for not being online in any form, but Zachary owned a house and lived in a nice neighborhood with a man named Nolan. He was my best bet to finding Kimberly, and since I hadn't seen his dead body in the meat locker, there was a good chance he was still alive.

It took some time to search through public records, but eventually, I found an announcement that a Zachary and Nolan Nycz had traveled to Barcelona to get married in a civil ceremony. The house was held jointly by both of them, and soon enough, I had a phone number. I ran back into the street after thanking Robert and back to the phone booth.

I pressed in the number to call collect, dialed, and when the message to identify myself came up, I took a breath and waited for the beep. When it came, I spat out as quickly as possible. "I'm alive. Meat packing plant. Now."

I barely got the words out before the beep, and my chest tightened. What if they weren't home? What if Zachary never went home? What if he's in the hospital? What if this was all for nothing?

I would have to find somewhere nice to bury Veronica and then move on with my life. No, I couldn't think like that. I had to believe that miracles could happen because one had just happened to me. I was alive, something that I hadn't fully appreciated until now. My bones hurt, and my body ached, but I was alive. I could smell the air and feel it filling my lungs.

That was something to celebrate. Even if the task I agreed to felt impossible, I was going to take it one moment at a time, and now, all I had to do was return to the meat packing plant and wait for Kimberly to find me.

CHAPTER 26

I dragged Veronica from the trash pile and brought her to the other side of the meat packing plant. I laid her against the wall so it looked like she was sleeping and tucked her as tightly as I could into the clothes she was wearing when she died. Luckily, the day was brisk to prevent her decay, but I kept a cold touch on her throughout the morning as we—I— waited for help.

As day turned to night, I began to doubt whether Kimberly would come. Soon, I would have to make other arrangements with Veronica. It wasn't possible to stay outdoors for the whole evening in the blistering cold of Prague. Perhaps I could leave the girl in front of a coroner's office or funeral home. *They would surely take pity on her, wouldn't they?* Maybe they would even start an investigation, and if I planted enough clues, they could even find their way to the meat packing plant and the horrible things within its walls.

Just as I was about to give up hope, a cab pulled up in front of the square, and Kimberly stepped out. I had never been so happy to see somebody in my whole life, not even my parents after a decade away from them. I rushed forward and wrapped her in a hug before she even had a chance to pay the cab driver.

"How did you—how are you—I saw you die," she said, stammering as she gripped me tightly. "How is this possible?"

"I'll tell you all about it," I said without letting her go. "But first, we have matters to attend to."

"Can I pay the cabbie, though?"

I nodded and let go of her. She gave the cabbie a generous tip, and I showed her over to Veronica. Kimberly let out an audible gasp. It took a lot for her to get emotional, but the sight of the dead little girl forced a small squeal from her lips, and she had to bite her finger to prevent crying.

"She needs to be buried," I said.

Kimberly nodded. "I know a person who can help."

"Of course you do."

She picked up Veronica in her arms and then grabbed onto my shoulder. In an instant, we were gone from the mortal realm, floating through the darkness, before a familiar feeling tugged at my stomach, dragging me forward, and we ended up in front of the Bishop and Rook Funeral Home. It was a tall Gothic building with high arches. Dying trees crisscrossed in a creepy canopy above us. Even in the dead of night, the lights in the house were bright.

Kimberly knocked on the door before she swung it open, more a courtesy than a request for permission to enter. Candles burned throughout the house, and it smelled overwhelmingly of juniper and lilac. In the antechamber to our left, a casket laid open. We approached slowly. The old man laid there was pale white, even after the mortician got done with him, and wore a bright red suit with a blue pocket square.

A whistle came from the other room moments before a dapper-looking man turned the corner. Even in a white apron, it was impossible to deny the elegant stride with which he carried himself. When he saw us, he jumped backward before adjusting his glasses and realizing Kimberly was one of the intruders.

"Jesus Christ, you scared me, Kimberly," he said.

"Sorry, Michael," she replied. "But…" she held out Veronica for him to see.

"Horrible." Michael adjusted his glasses again. "What happened to her?"

"Demons," Kimberly said, matter of fact. "We need her buried quietly, as quickly as possible."

He held out his arms. "May I?"

Kimberly slid the girl's body into his hands expertly, as if she had done it a hundred times before. Heck, she probably had, and the thought gave me a deeper appreciation for Kimberly's demeanor and why she hid herself behind an impenetrable façade.

"Young children are always the saddest," he said. "I'll get to work on her right away."

"If you can have her ready to bury today, I'll pay you triple."

He thought for a moment. "I don't have a viewing until later tonight, so I can make that happen. Mrs. Michelson can wait for her beauty treatment. It's not like the dead are going anywhere."

We said our goodbyes, and Kimberly took me to an all-night diner with overly bitter coffee and soggy pancakes. I couldn't remember the last time I ate, so I scarfed it down without a second thought.

"Tell me what happened," Kimberly said after she could see I was satiated. I told her about my trip to Hell, then Heaven. I explained my mission with the Time Being and how I needed to find them somewhere in the universe. She listened intently to it all, and when I was finished, her face was covered in measured deliberation.

"So, if I have this right, Veronica's death can be reversed."

"Only if I can somehow find this Time Being and plead my case to her. God has no idea where to even look, so I figure I'm at best one or two notches from being completely screwed."

"From what I hear, God is clueless," Kimberly said, poking at her pancakes thoughtfully. "I mean, he would have to be to let all this terrible stuff happen, right?"

I shrugged. "I guess that makes sense. It doesn't feel like there's much of a plan involved in any of it."

"If there was, Veronica wouldn't be dead, and you wouldn't have to go to literally even God doesn't know where to fix it." She took a sip of orange juice. "Still, it's nice to know that there's a way that you both don't have to die."

I felt a pang in my chest. Somehow the seeping wound had closed over, but it still ached when I breathed. It was best not to think about how I was alive and just enjoy it while it lasted.

"How is Zachary?" I asked after a long pause.

"Recovering. The house is—I think I ruined his life." She sighed. "I mean, he knew the risks and all, but it's a very different thing knowing you are doing a dangerous thing than being presented with the ramifications of it."

Sadness hung in the air for the rest of the meal. We headed to the funeral home when we were done, where Michael slid a tiny coffin into the back of a hearse and drove us to a cemetery several miles away.

"I chose a grave on a hill, where she could look out over Portland. I thought you would approve." Michael looked at Kimberly. "I assumed money was no object, as always."

"Thank you," I said. "I'm sure she would love it."

There was no ceremony or fanfare as we laid her in the ground, just solemn acknowledgment that this all sucked so badly it wasn't even worth talking about. Kimberly grabbed my hand as the gravediggers lowered Veronica into the ground, and for the first time in my life, I saw her cry, which caused me to cry. We continued as the gravediggers worked to cover the plot and well past. We were alone on the hill, looking out over Portland as the sun rose high into the sky.

Staring out over the morning, I tried to hold tightly to the idea that this wasn't the end, not really. Veronica still had a chance to live—all I had to do was the impossible, which didn't seem so hard at that moment. I would do anything to make sure that Veronica didn't suffer a moment of pain, even if that meant spinning the universe back on its axis to bring her back from the dead.

"Are you ready to do this?" Kimberly asked as she wiped the tears from her eyes.

"Absolutely not," I replied. "But now is as good a time as any to get started."

CHAPTER 27

I had no idea how to track down an elusive god that didn't want to be found, but Kimberly—well, Kimberly lived for this type of thing. Once we left the cemetery, it was like a feeling of peace washed over her, calm and determination in equal measure. This was her comfort zone, and her confidence was contagious. I took her hand, and we disappeared into the ether.

When we reappeared, it was inside an apartment with floor-to-ceiling windows that looked out onto a vast body of water. Outside, a large deck had enough room for two sun chairs and a small table. The apartment was sparsely decorated, but everything was meticulously chosen to complement the minimalist aesthetic of white with hints of red on accent walls and paintings hanging throughout the rooms.

"Welcome to my home," Kimberly said. "Can I get you a juice or anything?"

"No thanks," I replied. "You have a nice place. It's…sparse. Don't you have money?"

"More than I know what to do with," she said, grabbing a bottle of orange juice from the fridge. "Molly doesn't like stuff, though, except books. Don't tell her, but I kind of hate that uncomfortable couch. It kills my back."

"Oh, I know you hate it," a woman said behind us. I turned to see a middle-aged Black woman drying her hair with a towel. "But since you're always gone anyway, what do I care if you like it?"

"Hi, honey." Kimberly smiled, giving her a kiss as they met in the kitchen. It was odd to see her give anyone affection, let alone have somebody return it so freely. "Miss me?"

Molly sighed. "You know I did. I was hoping to have some alone time with you, but I see you've brought a stray." She smiled at me. "She has quite a collection."

"Oh, I know," I said.

"Sorry," she said. "I'm not usually a dick. It's just been a while since I've seen Kimmy."

I let out a snort. "Kimmy."

"Don't you dare," Kimberly growled, pointing a finger at me.

"Yes, yes," Molly sighed, walking to the kitchen. "You're very tough. Now, will you be around for food, or are you off again on another mission to save the world?"

"We already ate," Kimberly said.

"Of course you did. Guess it's too much to think you stayed on diet."

"Definitely did not stay on diet," I said. "Unless fried cheese and syrup is on diet."

"Lizzie!" Kimberly threw her hands in the air. "I thought you were on my team."

"I don't know what makes you think that," I said. "I much prefer your girlfriend, even though I barely know her."

"Yeah," Kimberly said. "That's a common reaction, and I can't blame you." She walked to the stove where Molly was standing and wrapped her arms around her waist. "I missed you."

"Of course you did, darling. I'm lovely, but I know that voice, so out with it. What do you need?"

"Know anything about the Time Being?"

"Like, 'I don't think you're going to get any for the time being' kind of time being?" Molly said. "I know the expression, but otherwise, no."

"It's apparently an ancient being that controls the flow of time or something like that. We need to find it to save the world."

Molly took Kimberly's hands. "It's very hard to stay mad at you when you say you're saving the world. How many times is that now?"

"I lost count at fifty," Kimberly said.

Molly kissed Kimberly sweetly. "Nothing is coming to mind right now, except for the expression, I mean, and that would be a stupid coincidence."

"What if it's not?" I asked. "Do you know where that expression came from?"

"I—" Molly started. "I suppose I have heard dumber connections before." She unwrapped herself from Kimberly and walked down a long hallway, gesturing for us to join her. She turned into a room lined with books from floor to ceiling. They were all leatherbound and smelled of the musk that only came from old tomes. She bent down in the middle of the room and pulled a dusty volume off the wall. She flipped through it until she came to a passage and placed her finger on it.

"Ah, yes. Well, unfortunately, that word looks to have its origins in literature in the 1500s, but it could have been around much longer, I suppose." She scooted herself along the floor and picked up a pink ledger from the wall filled with her own handwriting. "No, I don't have record of any cults relating to a Time Being, either, so, for the time being, I think there's only one course of action." She grinned. "See what I did there?"

"You're very clever, my dear." A shadow passed over Kimberly's face. "I really don't want to talk to her again. Last time I nearly punched her in the face for playing games while we were chasing down a little girl."

Molly stood. "I understand, my love. Lilith is, objectively, the worst, and you know I love everyone. I have no love in me for her, but she's older than these books, and in the absence of angels or gods, she's the oldest being in the world who doesn't want you dead."

"I'm not sure she doesn't want me dead," Kimberly mused.

"I don't want you dead," I offered with a smile.

"Present company excluded."

"I never said I didn't want you dead," Molly said. "There would be so much less agitation, and I would have so much more time to read without you always asking me to work for you." She cocked her head and smiled. "I'm kidding, of course. Please be careful, will you?"

Kimberly bent down and wrapped Molly in a hug. "I love you."

Molly kissed Kimberly. "I love you, too."

They were sweet together, sickeningly so. It was amazing to see another side of Kimberly, one that didn't have her barking at me or saving me from one thing or another. She had a life with somebody she loved—which was more than I could say about myself. I had thought that at least I had one person in my life who had cut themselves off from the outside world, happy to be a hermit, but that wasn't Kimberly at all. Even she had let love into her life, and knowing that made me feel very much alone.

When they were done saying goodbye, Kimberly walked back into the kitchen and made a phone call. When the receiver picked up, the voice was so loud that I could hear it even from a few feet away.

"Lilith, I need your help," Kimberly said.

"Hello to you as well. My, my, my, it's incredible how somebody could have so much money, and none of it can buy you manners."

"The advantage of having money is not having to worry about what other people think of my manners, Lilith."

"And yet, it is still you that needs my help, so humor me."

Kimberly plastered a big, fake smile on her face and spoke slowly. "Hello, Lilith. How are you today?"

"Just marvelous, my love. Just marvelous. And you?"

"I've been worse, but I've certainly been better."

"Lovely to hear it, and now, you need my help with something, I hear. How may I be of service?"

"We're looking for the Time Being," Kimberly said. "Do you know anything about how we can find them?"

Lilith's voice changed to a growl. "This isn't something to discuss over the phone. I'm staying in Chateau Marmont. Ask the concierge to ring Mistress Westcott in the penthouse, and I'll tell you what I know." There was silence on the phone. "And bring a swimsuit. It's lovely here. You're gonna hate it."

CHAPTER 28

From the death of John Belushi to the wild parties of Hollywood stars and starlets, Chateau Marmont was famous, and yet, walking through its entrance was anything but austere. Yes, it did rise over a hill that made the French-style building stick out against the others nearby, but that's mostly because the rest of the strip around the hotel was grimy and dirty. The lobby was filled with plush carpet and even plusher chairs, but there was something…fake about it all, like if I chipped the veneer, there would be rotten wood, fake walls, and stairs that led to nothing.

Kimberly walked up to the front desk and asked to ring Mistress Westcott as instructed and, after a brief conversation, led us around to the sparkling blue pool offset from the lobby. She headed to a chair covered by a large umbrella, where Lilith laid in a red one-piece swimsuit nibbling a piece of apple from a sangria goblet.

"Ah, there you are," Lilith said, placing her glass down next to three others. "I thought I would have to stay out here all day, not that I'm complaining, mind you. Is there anything better than the weather in Los Angeles?"

"It's just fine, I guess," Kimberly said. "I like seasons, though."

"L.A. has the best season all year long." Lilith sighed. "Philistine." She leaned forward to acknowledge me. "And I see you here again. I assume this has something to do with the girl."

"She's dead," I replied. "We need to find the Time Being to get her back."

"Well, you don't need the Time Being for that, love," Lilith said. "Just a good necromancer. I promise it will be much less of a headache."

"Then you know of the Time Being?" I asked.

"Somewhat, by reputation at least. She is a severe and stern woman who takes her job very seriously—just so, so, so, so seriously, and she hates gods, really any immortals." She eyed Kimberly. "Which means you and I are right out when it comes to finding her."

"Why is it always a song and dance with you?" Kimberly said. "Do you know how we can get in touch with the Time Being or not?"

"Well, it's a little of both, I guess. I've never met her myself, but there was one human who got a wish from her several decades ago. She went mad as a hatter afterward, though. Imagine going through all of that to get a wish, only to go loopy. What a waste."

"How can we find her?" Kimberly asked.

"So, she's like dead then," I said.

"Oh, very much so, which makes talking to her complicated." She again turned to Kimberly. "You'll have to go into Hell."

Kimberly went white as a sheet. "I—I—I can't do that."

"Are you scared?" I said. "I've never seen you scared before."

"You've never seen what I've seen." She shook violently. "I can't—I won't go back there. If you had seen—if you'd seen it, you would never go back, either."

"Um, I have seen it. I was in Hell, remember? I died."

"Well, for a dead woman, you look wonderful," Lilith said.

"Thank you," I replied, touching the wound on my chest. "God brought me back to life, so—I guess he's pretty good at it or whatever."

"Of course. I suppose that old codger is who put you on this fool's errand, too?"

"He is."

"Figures. Gods forbid he handle his own mess." She sighed. "Is your constitution as weak as your friend here"—she pointed to Kimberly— "or do you think you can survive a trip to Hell? Because that's the only way to find the Time Being. Of course, you could just give up now and enjoy a nice drink with me. That sounds lovely, too." She sniffed the air. "You smell like death. Did you know that?"

"Yeah, probably because I died and all." I shook my head. "But no, I'm not giving up."

Kimberly squeezed my arm. "You don't have to do this. There are things in Hell…I can't—I can't do it. I can't even think about it without—don't do it."

I ripped free of her. "Pull yourself together. There's nobody up here I love, not like you. If this is the little thing I can do to help make the world a better place, then I'm stuck doing it."

"Stuck," Lilith said. "Now, that is an interesting word. I've met many others like you, stuck to your fate. I myself am stuck in this body due to the vengeance of the same god that glued you to your path." Her brows furrowed, and she pulled a pad of paper from the table. She grabbed a pen and wrote something on it. "I sympathize with you, doll, so I will do you this courtesy. I have a son who owes me a favor—many, in fact. He can shepherd you into Hell, straight into Dis. You have to find your way from there, but it shouldn't be hard for somebody with your qualities."

I didn't trust this. "What do you want from me in return?"

She handed me the paper. "When you find this Time Being, remember that you have agency, my dear. You might be stuck, but just because it's your fate doesn't mean you have to do what you're told, either. If you get to the Time Being, just remember that. You have agency here, even though it doesn't feel like it."

I grabbed the paper. "No offense, but this seems nicer a favor than I believed you capable of."

She smiled. "Oh, don't you worry. I very much enjoy adding favors to Kimberly's account, and this one is a doozie. Now, run along before my charity runs out."

I turned with Kimberly, but something stopped Kimberly from moving. When I looked back, I saw that Lilith was holding her back. "Not you, precious. I think I might use some of that good will I've banked up right now, if I may."

"Do I have a choice?" Kimberly asked.

"Not if you want your little friend to live, no."

She let out a groan of resignation and turned to Lilith. "Then, I would love to help you."

I said goodbye to Kimberly, wondering if we would ever see each other again. She'd always been a friend to me, and I wouldn't forget that, even if I ended up in the chasm of space-time, drifting for eternity. *God, that was bleak.*

I figured there was at least a slim chance I'd succeed, so I might as well get on with it. It was time for me to become the hero Kimberly had always hoped I would never have to be.

CHAPTER 29

The address Lilith gave me led to a run-down, derelict house in Hollywood, not far from the Chateau Marmont. The view was lovely looking out across the city, but the house itself needed some TLC and maybe a couple of support beams to prevent it from listing too much to the left and tumbling down into the street.

I knocked lightly at first, fearful that the sudden vibration might cause the structural integrity to give way. I tapped harder with each successive attempt until I found myself banging heavily on the creaking door. Finally, a cranky, groggy lump of a man answered.

"What do you want?"

"Are you," I glanced at the name on the paper Lilith gave me. "Xavier?"

"What's it to you?"

"Your mother sent me. She says you owe her about a billion favors and sent me to collect one on her behalf."

He sniffed the air. "You a human?"

"Something like that. I mean, I'm at least part water nymph, but I'm mostly human."

"You're a mortal, though, right? God, you smell even more like death than the others. Why does my mother choose to hang out with you ruddy lot? It's embarrassing."

"I can't speak to her choices, just that she sent me here. Maybe she figures it's better to work with humans than rip them apart. It's a refreshing change of pace, compared to the rest of you demons."

"Yeah, well, I'm assuming you deal with your fair share of humans. Are you really telling me you don't want to rip their stupid heads off every minute of the day?"

I thought for a second. "Touché."

Xavier kicked a crushed can sitting in his doorway and turned from the door. "Come in, I guess."

The smell of stale beer and regret hung in the air as I followed him past the bevy of beer cans that littered the house. I followed him up to the main floor, where more crushed cans mixed with half-empty food containers. He brushed a collection of trash off a recliner and sat down.

After rattling several beer cans, he found one that wasn't quite empty and took a swig. His face turned slightly, but then he swallowed it down. "What can I do for you?"

"I need to get into Hell and find somebody that's been in contact with the Time Being."

Xavier's face twitched, and then he let out a deep belly laugh as if I had just said the funniest thing in the history of the universe. When he finally calmed down, he took one more look at me and busted out laughing again. After ten whole minutes, he let out a deep sigh and shook his head.

"Did Lilith put you up to this? What did you do to get on her bad side?"

"I'm not—I don't understand what's going on here."

"Well, for one thing, everything. The woman you're looking for, her name is Rosalie Louey. As far as I know, she's the only person who's ever been within a thousand miles of the Time Being in—well, if not every galaxy, at least this one. She's kept in a heavily guarded facility made specially to contain her."

"Contain her?"

Xavier nodded. "Her experience with the Time Being left her soul unstuck in time. It was real tricky to contain her, and Lucifer—well, he's a bit obsessed with keeping her close. He's been trying to find the Time Being for eons. That old man has plenty of regrets. So, what you're asking me to do is to get you, a human, into Hell, through a heavily guarded facility, to meet with the single most important prisoner in the history of Hell."

I looked at him, deadpan and brimming with determination. "Are you saying you can't do it? Because if that's the case, just say it. No need to make a big thing about it."

He stared back at me quizzically. "Do you really not understand how stupid this is, or do you simply not care?"

I shrugged. "Why not both?"

He let out a deep rumble of a laugh. "I can see why she likes you. Then again, maybe she hates you, and this is how she's chosen to punish you."

"It doesn't matter which it is. If Rosalie Louey is the only person who can help me find the Time Being, then she's who I need to see. If that means breaking into a secure facility, so be it. I really don't care because I don't have another choice."

"Oof, well, I can't imagine old Lilith liked that one bit. She always thinks you have a choice, even if it's a bad one."

"The other choice is untenable," I replied. "Now, are you going to help me or not? Because I'm not getting any younger."

"You have spunk, kid," Xavier said. "All right, I'll send you to Hell, past the gates, and right to Dis proper. I'll even give you a contact that can help you plan the mission, but you can't bring your body. It's just too dangerous. I'll keep you here, safe and sound, while I send your soul into the great beyond. I'll buy you as much time as I can up here, but it won't be forever. Your body will decay and wither without your soul, and after enough time, you can't come back. Even if you could, you wouldn't want to because your body would be nothing worth using. I have a feeling yours won't last very long at all."

"I can hear the 'yeah, but' coming any second."

"It's not so much a yeah, but, as…except that."

"Well, get on with it then."

Xavier gestured around his slovenly, unkempt house. "As you can see, I don't keep the cleanest shop, and there are ingredients I need to complete the ritual that I just don't keep on hand. It's not every day an idiot comes to me asking to enter Hell." He narrowed his eyes. "You get me the ingredients I need, and I'll get you into Hell."

A shiver ran through my spine. "This sounds like a terrible idea, but what other choice do I have?"

He shrugged. "You could forget about it, which is what I recommend you do. Forget about it and walk away."

"I can't do that," I said. "Give me the list."

CHAPTER 30

I was getting really tired of being sent places to fetch things for other people. I wasn't an errand girl. The one thing about life on the road—I had agency about where I went and when. The first few years were tough, but once I understood the "life", jobs came easier, especially after I'd mastered the lingo. Since I paid by the night at motels, I could come and go at a moment's notice. Even if destiny had been hurtling toward me, I was able to ignore it. Now that the fog had been lifted, it felt like I was on the rails of a rollercoaster, moving mechanically from one place to another on the whim of some unseen force.

I didn't like it, but it no longer mattered what I wanted. This wasn't about me. It was about saving Veronica—about saving the whole blasted universe, so I had no choice but to play the game, even if all I wanted to do was make a hard left turn on the 10 and take it east until it led me far off into the distance.

But I didn't. Instead, I continued toward the water, and Santa Monica—Venice, to be specific. I parked the cheap rental Kimberly got for me and headed up the canals to a tiny bungalow resting on the nape of the man-made river cutting between the homes.

I rapped on the blindless glass door of the house and heard a dog barking inside. A couple of seconds later, a woman stretched from the couch and put on a pair of aviator glasses. She walked toward the door and slid it open, wearing only a T-shirt and black underwear. Her skin was so pale as to nearly be translucent, and her jaw was hard and chiseled.

"What do you want?" she growled.

"Are you Oleander?"

"Don't call me that. Everybody calls me Ollie."

"Sorry."

Her lip curled into a snarl. "It's a mistake I don't let people make twice. Now, you have seven words before I slam this door on your face."

"It's a sliding door."

She didn't seem amused by my attempt at a joke. "That's four."

I didn't like her, but I swallowed my pride. "Xavier sent me."

"Which Xavier?" she asked.

"The demon."

She popped her hip and softened her shoulders as if she led down her guard slightly. Or maybe her interest had been piqued. "Which one?"

I cocked my head to the side. "You hang out with a lot of demons?"

"Depends on your definition of 'a lot.' Enough that I know multiple demons named Xavier."

"Slovenly one, lives in the Hills. Very punchable."

She gave a small smile like she knew all too well. "They're all very punchable, but I know which one you mean. What did he need from me?"

"He said you could help me track down some ingredients for a job."

"Sounds like something I could do," she replied. There was no hesitation or emotion to her voice like my request was something she heard every day, instead of one of the most ludicrous things to ever come out of my mouth. "You have a list?"

I dug into my pocket and pulled out a receipt, on the back of which Xavier had written the ingredients he needed. Ollie snatched it from my hand and tilted her glasses down. One of her eyes swirled a vibrant blue, like arctic ice, while the other burned red like fire. I only glimpsed them for a second before she slid her glasses back, but it was hypnotizing.

"Most of these are easy enough," she said. "A couple of them might take a couple of days."

I shook my head. "That's not going to work. I need them now." I remembered something that Kimberly said to the funeral director a few days back—or was that just earlier today? "If you can get them by tonight, I'll pay you triple."

"You don't even know my price," she said.

"It doesn't matter. I'll pay it." I reached into my pocket and pulled out whatever money I had left. A few hundred dollars, maybe. It was every dollar I had in the world, but I wouldn't need it. Not after this, anyway. "Here's a down payment."

She looked down at the money. "It's two thousand under normal circumstances, but since I like the cut of your jib, I'll give you a deal on expedited service. Five thousand, in cash, upon delivery."

I nodded. "Done."

"All right, then," she said. "Meet me back here at midnight, and I'll have it for you. Meanwhile"—she looked me up and down— "I hope you can pull together that money. I don't like being stiffed." She slid the door closed.

Five thousand dollars was almost three months of tips, and I had to find a way to get it in a day. Luckily, I knew somebody who was rich and had a vested interest in saving Veronica. I just hoped that Lilith hadn't sent Kimberly too far away.

Chateau Marmont was all the way across town, and in Los Angeles, that meant an hour's drive in light traffic. I parked the car across the street at a meter because I wasn't about to pay their valet prices. I walked through the lobby to the pool, and when I didn't see her there, I headed toward the front desk.

"Can I help you?" a kind-looking man with a big smile asked. The nametag pinned to his shirt said Jonathan.

"Yes, Jonathan. Can you please ring up Mistress Westcott for me?"

"Sure, I ju—" His face scrunched into a little ball. "Oh, poop. She has a 'Do Not Disturb' on her phone. I'm afraid, in the interest of privacy, I can't disturb her. I mean, it's right there in the name."

"I understand, Jonathan." I slammed my hands down on the counter. "What will it take for you to break that rule, just this one, for old times' sake?"

"Old times' sake?"

My hands tented, and as they did, ice spread from my hands, covering the counter. "Sure, Jonathan. We're old friends, Mistress Westcott and me. I wouldn't want anything to come between the two of us. That would be bad for everyone…me, her, you." I leaned forward. "Maybe you can get me her room number."

"S-s-s-s-she's in the penthouse."

The ice receded from the counter, and I smiled at him. "Of course she is. Now, how about you give me a room key, and I'll be on my way."

I didn't like intimidating the poor boy, but time was of the essence, and I was done mucking around. Jonathan would never say anything to anyone about my ice powers unless he wanted to be thought of as a loon.

I slid the key into the door once the elevator had taken me to the top floor and made my way inside the penthouse. A golden lantern hung from the entranceway to the suite, and a checkered black and white tiled floor led down a hallway lined with portraits of beautiful women. I hated it.

"Is that you, Penny?" Lilith said from the other room. "You really are the quickest woman in the—" She turned into the hallway and sneered when she saw me. "Oh, it's you. I see you take after Kimberly's stable boy manners. I suppose you've spoken with my dreadful son, then."

I nodded. "He sent me to get ingredients for him, and the person I hired wants five thousand for them."

"Well, that's—" she paused. "Is that highway robbery? I actually have no concept of money."

"It's more than I make in a month, three months when it's slow."

She waved me forward before turning and walking out onto the patio. "All right. Come in, come in. You don't have mud on your shoes, do you?"

I took a few steps. "No. Your son's place is nasty, but it's not got any mud that I saw."

"Then his living situation must have improved since last time," she called out to me. "Well, don't dawdle, dear."

The patio ran the length of the room, like a wraparound porch for super ritzy folk. I didn't know how much it cost to stay in this place for even one night, but I was quite sure that it was more than the $5,000 that I thought a kingly sum. From the edge of the balcony, all of Los Angeles stretched out in front of me.

"It's beautiful," I said, taking a breath.

"Is it?" Lilith said, walking over to me. "Here you go." She held a wad of cash in her hand and thrust it toward me. "There's extra for my son's troubles. Tell him to get a maid."

I took the money. "Seriously, why are you helping me? There's nothing in it for you."

"This girl. Kimberly says she can stop the Apocalypse. Is that true?"

"It is."

"Then there's something in it for everyone. I have no interest in seeing my terrible children again, or their awful father, in this life or the next." She brushed a stray hair from my forehead. "Besides, I like you, and you've been done dirty by fate. I don't like that." She cocked her head. "Have you ever had caviar, my dear? Foie Gras? Oysters straight from the sea so fresh it's like you plucked them out of the ocean yourself?"

"Well, I've picked oysters myself but not the other two things."

"When are you supposed to meet this person tonight for the exchange?"

"Not for a few hours yet," I replied.

She wrapped her arm around me. "Then let us feast and fill your belly with hope before Hell snatches it all from you."

I let her lead me. "I would like that very much."

CHAPTER 31

Lilith fed me a feast of tiny bites and massive plates, from steak to lobster, caviar to foie gras, and things I couldn't pronounce even if I tried. By the time night fell over the city and the lights flickered on like fireflies, I was stuffed. Right next to the satisfaction of a full belly, there was an emptiness in the pit of my stomach, too, and as I finally put my fork down, the disquiet on my face was blatant enough to draw Lilith's attention.

"I've never seen somebody eat so well and look so sad," she said.

"It's not—I'm very grateful for the food." I sighed. "It's just…I thought maybe I would have a chance to say goodbye to Kimberly. She's been such a big part of my life, and I didn't like the way we ended it."

A small smirk rose on her face. "Oh, you sweet, naïve child. That's Kimberly's way. She never says goodbye if she can avoid it. Hard conversations, uncomfortable emotions, that's not her bag." She took a sip from the martini glass she had been nursing. "That doesn't mean she doesn't love you, though."

"Oh, I don't think she loves me or anything like that. She's a thorn in my side, if anything. Still, she was a big part of my life."

This time, Lilith laughed. "Silly girl. She is only a thorn in the side of people she cares about deeply." She finished the last of her martini and ate the olive off the toothpick left in the glass. "There's nothing you can say to her that she doesn't already know. Trust me on that."

"Thank you," I said, tilting my head toward the stack of money on the table. "There's no earthly reason why you would be nice to me, but thank you anyway."

"Demons," she replied. "We really aren't all bad. Some of us are just trying to get by any way we can. The others, well…most of them are misguided. They think they need to be mean and cruel—that that is their nature, but"—she shook her head— "I wanted you to understand that we are not really like that. I know what you'll see down in Hell. Just…remember back to this moment, okay?"

"I will."

"Good, good," she said, then looked at the pile of money. "Now, do you want a bag for that or something? Palming ten grand looks pretty conspicuous."

I thought about it for a second, then nodded. "Yes, that would probably be good."

She rummaged through her closet and pulled out an exquisite Prada bag that probably cost more than the GDP of a small nation, handing it over as if it were a plastic bag from under the kitchen sink. I stuffed the money into it, thanked her, and left.

It wasn't until I reached my car that I remembered I had parked it at a meter which had long since expired. I pulled a half dozen tickets off the front windshield and threw them in the front seat. I might have been worried about paying them if I didn't have a wad of cash in a very expensive handbag…and if I wasn't headed into Hell, of course.

It took me another hour to make it across the city, and by the time I made it to Venice, it was well before midnight. I decided to spend the time until I had to meet Ollie by sitting on the beach and walking the boardwalk. I rarely made it to the big cities. They were expensive and crowded. It was hard enough to make a living on the road, and cities made that nearly impossible.

Venice Beach, even at night, was filled with weird people doing weird things, from long-haired hippie troupes dancing complicated routines to people spray-painting themselves and rolling on canvases they sold for fifty bucks. I dodged roller skaters and skateboarders as they swerved near me on their way down to the beach.

I passed people working out at Muscle Beach and others smoking bowls as they baked along the grassy knolls that speckled the walking path. I got myself some ice cream and a hot dog as I meandered from Santa Monica down to Marina Del Rey, then made my way back toward Ollie's house.

By the time I was done wasting my evening, it was just about midnight, but the hustle and bustle wasn't gone from the beach. People crowded into bars and walked along the streets as if it was the middle of the day, and by that time, I was absolutely done with other humans. You would have been lucky to see as many people in a whole week in the towns I frequented, and it was just…too much for me.

Weirdly, when I finally picked up the car and drove to Ollie's, I was kind of ready for Hell. I parked the car and made my way down the canals. The houses were tucked in close, blaring their televisions, and when I got to Ollie's, it was no different. The blue glare from the TV lit her face when she opened the door.

"Five grand, as promised," I said, handing her half the wad.

She chuckled. "I would have put good money that you were pulling my pud, kid." She reached under the couch and handed me a paper bag. "Here you go."

I grabbed the bag. "You know, I'm not a kid. I'm like 26, almost 27."

She chuckled, sliding the door closed. "Yeah, okay, kid."

I didn't care what Ollie thought of me. I wasn't trying to impress her. I maneuvered back across the city with the paper bag strapped into the passenger's seat. I had taken the least optimized route, ping-ponging from Chateau Marmont in Hollywood up to the hills high above, down to Venice on the other side of the city, back up to Hollywood for dinner with Lilith, then back down to Venice to meet Ollie, and now finally, back up to the hills to meet with Xavier. The gas tank was nearly on empty when I pulled into a spot across from his house. The lights were off, but when I knocked on the door, they flicked on, and he came to get me. I showed him the bag, and he swiped it from me.

"This is everything, I guess," he grumbled, closely eyeing the contents of the bag. "Come on in. I have us set up."

I followed him through the house to the kitchen, where he had drawn a summoning circle out of blood on the tile floor.

"Oh," I said, reaching into the Prada bag on my shoulder. "Your mom says to get a maid."

He swiped the money. "I'll need it after tonight." He placed the brick of cash on the messy counter between a Styrofoam cup from In-N-Out and a takeout container of half-eaten lo mein. "I need a totem, something special to you. Should be something you have carried for a while, if possible."

I reached around my neck and touched my black opal necklace. "I've had this since I can remember. It's the only thing I have left of my old life."

"Good, it will have powerful magic then. When you find the girl and are ready to leave, grab it and say *domum.* That will make the necklace on your body glow, and I will bring you back. Otherwise, I'll send a blue light to ping your necklace when you're running out of time, and once more when I'm about to pull you out. The first ping means you have two hours left. The final one means you have five minutes. Got it?"

I nodded. "When I'm ready to leave, squeeze the necklace and say '*domum.*' If the necklace glows blue, it means I have two hours left, and when I have five minutes left, it will glow again."

He grunted. "Good. Lie down."

The stickiness of the blood wet my arms as I rested them inside the circle. With my body completely prone on the ground inside the circle, I closed my eyes and took a deep breath.

"When you get into Hell, you'll be in the merchant district of Dis. Find the main street and listen for a very, very, very annoying little girl screaming for you to buy her father's shoes. This is Beatrice. Her father is Clovis. They will be able to help you. If they can't, then nobody can. Tell her that R'il'ick sent you at the behest of Lilith."

"Got it. Merchant District. Shoes. Beatrice. Clovis. R'il'ick."

"Good luck to you. You're going to need it." Xavier added. "Ready?"

"Ready."

Xavier muttered something to himself, and the blood beneath me began to boil white-hot. He snapped his fingers, and I felt a familiar tug on my stomach as I fell into the ground. Instead of slipping gracefully into the void, it was more like I was drilling a hole deep down into it, against its will, and the more it fought me, the harder I pushed against it. Finally, with a pop, the void spat me out, and I slammed against a wall.

As I pushed myself to stand, I felt the oppressive heat against my body and the red-orange sky above me that flickered between towers of souls, and I knew I was in Hell.

CHAPTER 32

"Hot mead!" a giant toad shouted from a mud and stucco bar.

"Iron bracers!" a human-sized boar screamed as I turned toward the flood of monsters making their way down the tightly packed avenue.

Everywhere I turned, there were monsters: ogres, orcs, trolls, changelings, nymphs, wraiths, demons, trolls—every manner of being I had only ever read about in storybooks. Mom and Dad told me that magical creatures had been driven underground on Earth, many species even hunted to extinction if they didn't learn how to integrate into humanity. Here in Dis, they walked free.

The small side street spliced with a much larger thoroughfare where pedestrians mixed with oxen, horses, and beasts of burden pulled by monsters hauling clothing and armor.

Don't get distracted, I said to myself. What was it that Xavier said? *Merchant quarter, shoes, Beatrice and Clovis.* Right.

"Excuse me?" I shouted to a golem packing itself tightly with clay on the side of the road. "This is the merchant quarter, right?"

"Human?" he said.

I couldn't imagine humans were very welcome in Dis, so I shook my head. "No. My mother was a water nymph."

"Not a lot of good that will do you down here," the golem growled. "Yeah, this is the merchant quarter. Everything you see is for sale."

"Thanks," I replied. "I don't suppose you would humor me with one more question."

"This place is going to eat you up and spit you out, girlie, if you keep talking like that. Sure, what you got?"

"I'm looking for a shoe stand run by a little girl named Beatrice."

He chuckled. "I knew you were trouble. Make a left and keep going until you hear a shrill shout fill the air. You can't miss it, even if you try."

"Thanks," I replied.

I pushed my way left through the traffic and went down a hill. As I passed the vendors, I heard trolls, goblins, and satyrs selling ceramic bowls, clothes, and other various items throughout the corridor. At the bottom of the hill, a female voice drowned out all the others.

"Hey, ugly!" she shrieked. "You need new shoes. My dad's the best. Absolutely the best! He'll fix you up." After a moment's break, she continued. "Really? You are about to fall out of those things. Your death, I guess."

The stall was three times bigger than any around it, filled with all manner of shoes, from buffed loafers to delicate slippers. A young girl with pointed ears and two teeth gone from the front of her mouth stood atop the stall, while an older elf with round glasses sat inside the booth, cobbling a pair of boots.

The girl barked at a tiny halfling as I sidled up to the booth. "Are you Beatrice?"

She nodded with a half glance in my direction. "What's it to you?"

"R'il'ick sent me on Lilith's behalf. Said you could help me?"

The girl wheeled on me. "Are you crazy? You don't talk about that kind of stuff here, and you never, ever bring up her name in public." She leaped down from the stall as several eyes stared my way. "Are you trying to get me in trouble with the big man? We run an honest business here." She poked at my chest, forcing me to step back into the alley behind the stall. When we were clear of the street, she looked around to make sure we were alone. "Take this alley back three blocks until it dead-ends. There will be a house with a green door. Stay there, and we'll come back when it calms down."

"But you can help me, right?"

Instead of answering me, she pushed me backward. "If you don't want any shoes, then get out of here and quit wasting my time!"

The cobblestone alley was a far cry nicer than the mud caking the main road. The narrow street I found myself on, filled with metal gas lamps and tight brownstones, felt like Dickensian London.

I followed the alley down until it dead-ended. Everything was a drab black or brown affair, with a couple of dark maroon doors thrown in, but nestled between them was a bright, almost neon, green door. It stood out.

I hated waiting, but it was better than wandering around Dis alone, being caught and ripped to shreds—or worse, thrown in the pits and forced into torture for the rest of eternity. I didn't want that. Still, what I wouldn't do for a book to pass the time while I waited.

Later rather than sooner, the young girl and old man ambled down the road like they hadn't a care in the world. Beatrice was swinging a pair of loafers in her hand while the old man hobbled behind her.

"That was a good day, old man." When she saw me, her face fell flat. "Oh yeah, you're here. Well, maybe it's less good now."

"Be nice, Beatrice," the old man said. He held out his hand to me. "I'm Clovis. It would seem we keep similar company, unfortunately. How is R'il'ick? Still sloppy as ever?"

"You could say that." I shook his hand. "And it's nice to meet you."

"And Lilith. She still a cu—" Beatrice saw her father eyeing her and shaking his head. "Crummy jerk?"

"Something like that," I said. "I think she's kind of nice once you get to know her, actually."

"I'm not surprised," Beatrice said. "You're a pretty little magical thing. She loves those." She stopped in front of me. "So, what can we do for you?"

I looked around, making sure we were alone, then leaned in with a hoarse whisper, "I'm looking for the Time Being, and I hear there is someone in Hell who has earned its favor. I need to talk to them."

"Are you taking a piss?" Beatrice said.

"Beatrice! Language."

"Dad, I'm thousands of years old."

"To me, you'll always be my little girl, so zip it."

"Sorry, Dad." Beatrice sighed and hopped past me toward the door. "If you're serious, then we shouldn't talk about this out here. How about you come inside away from prying ears and loose lips."

"I'll even make some tea," Clovis said, pushing into the house after his daughter. "Yes, won't that be nice?"

"Very nice, thank you," I said, following them inside.

CHAPTER 33

Beatrice and Clovis led me up the stairs of their brownstone and into a sprawling kitchen made of black obsidian with oak floors. Clovis walked to the stove and lifted the metal teapot to fill it in the sink.

"Water?" I said. "You have water?"

"Of course," Beatrice grunted, lifting herself onto the island in the middle of the room. "We're not animals."

"Sorry, it's just that…isn't it too hot in Hell for water to, like, not boil?"

Clovis chuckled to himself. "You'll have to dissuade yourself of notions of logic while you're here, umm, what was your name again?"

"Lizzie," I answered. "You have a lovely house." And it really was. Not even the kind of thing that you said as a pleasantry. Anyone would be lucky to have an open, spacious house like it even on Earth, let alone in the pits of Hell. "It's homey."

"We like it," Clovis said, placing the kettle on to boil before turning to me. "Now, explain to me why you need to see Rosalie Louey. Pardon the irony, but do you have a death wish?"

"Absolutely not," I said, and then, I told them everything. I told them about the prophecy, dying, going to Heaven, and being tasked by God to find a way to reverse time and save Veronica. When I was done, Beatrice looked at me slack-jawed while Clovis stroked his chin.

"So you…met God?" Beatrice asked.

"That's right."

"But…you're a monster, aren't you? If there's one thing I know about God, it's that he hates monsters. That's why we're all trapped down here working as slaves to Lucifer. You must be made of luck."

I shrugged. "I don't know. I don't feel very lucky right now since I'm in Hell and all. Perhaps this is my special Hell, and he's torturing me, so he doesn't have to torture somebody that's full human. Either way, I need to find the Time Being, and this Rosalie is my best shot."

"She's mad as a rabid beast, you know." Clovis cleaned his glasses as he spoke. "Demons have been trying for decades to break her, but she speaks in riddles, strings of numbers, and fragments of words that don't seem to make sense by themselves, and the greatest brains in Hell have come up empty at trying to decipher it."

"So, I've been told," I said. "But she's the best chance I have. I'm not asking you to decipher her or anything. All I'm asking is for you to help me get to her. Can you do that?"

"HA!" Beatrice said. "We're a little girl and an old man. What part of us screams experts at stealth?"

"I'm afraid my daughter is right," Clovis said, scooping tea into little strainers and placing them in three different blue cups. "We are more…facilitators. We connect beings in mutually beneficial partnerships, and I happen to know the perfect fairy to help you—if the price is right."

"I—I don't have any money."

"Well, that's a problem then, isn't it?" Beatrice snapped. "This place ain't cheap. We can't eat good feelings."

"Sweetheart, please." The water boiled, and Clovis poured it into the blue cups. "Perhaps there is something she can do for us. We peddle, after all, in information." He handed me the tea. "You say you have met the mother of demons. Tell me, where is she staying these days?"

I took a sip of the tea, but it was already hot as balls in Hell. Sipping hot leaf juice wasn't an appealing proposition. "Are you going to hurt her?"

"We don't hurt people," Beatrice said. "We have people that do that."

"We aren't interested in hurting Lilith." Clovis put his teacup down. "There are several interested parties that would pay top dollar to obtain the location of Lilith. What they plan to do with that information is not for me to say. Perhaps they want to throw her a birthday party."

"Not likely."

"But possible," Beatrice said. "Information isn't good or bad. It just is. What people do with it is not our concern." She kicked her feet out from the table. "The question is, how much do you want to save the world? Because from where I'm standing, an everlasting Apocalypse on Earth is a far cry better than being stuck down here forever."

"She was nice to me," I said, dipping my head low.

"First betrayal's always the hardest, kid," Clovis said. "Trust me when I say that she would turn on you in a heartbeat if it furthered her ends."

"Besides," Beatrice said. "If you find the Time Being and get your wish, then none of this would have happened, right? So it's almost like you aren't betraying her at all."

I swallowed and took a long, deep breath. They were right. Just like the parking tickets on my car, if this all went my way and I succeeded, this wouldn't even be a distant memory. It would be a never was. Then again, if I failed—which was more likely than not—I would be condemning

Lilith to an unknown fate. I just hoped she was as resilient as she seemed.

"Chateau Marmont. Penthouse. Top floor. I didn't see any security while I was there."

"That was easy." Beatrice reached forward and grabbed my shoulder. "You did the right thing."

"Did I?"

Beatrice shrugged. "How the heck should I know? But you made it quickly and didn't waste our time. I like that about you."

"I'll make the call," Clovis added. "If I had to rely on any soul in Hell, it would be Akta. You're in good hands."

Akta. I had heard the name before. Kimberly talked about her sometimes when I was younger and asked how she got so good with a dagger.

"It was in my mentor's blood," she told me. "She was descended from the greatest monster hunter maybe to ever live—Akta of the Forest. Akta helped Julia close a rift that opened in her town, and she helped save me, too, when I was a kid. Later, when I was old enough, Julia taught me everything she knew before she left to join Akta in the hereafter."

I never thought I would have a chance to meet Akta in the flesh—in the soul, I guess—and the thought of it made my fingers and toes buzz with excitement. A real-life legend, right in front of me.

She entered the house silently a few minutes later, without knocking, and floated up toward the kitchen on blue wings that left a brilliant glow behind her. It was the only way to identify her in the darkness of the stairwell, as the rest of her seemed to move with it, like a second skin.

Akta stepped into the light of the kitchen, and her wings retracted, her deep green eyes staring into me. Her face was wide, and her dark skin and hair made her eyes pop all the more. She wore a green suit that made her look like Link, and on a brown belt with several snapped pouches, daggers hung on her hips.

"I just want you all to understand," she said, "this is the dumbest idea I have ever heard in my life."

"Good to see you too," Clovis said.

Akta stepped toward me. "Is this your idea, nymph?"

"No, it's God's idea," I said. "At least, in the big picture theory of it."

She laughed. "God, huh? I met him once."

"How did that go?" I asked.

"Well, I wound up down here, didn't I? So, not great."

"I'm sorry to hear that."

She took another step closer to me. "I would tell you not to believe a single word he says, but you're here, so it looks like you already did."

"We're well acquainted with your feelings about God," Clovis said.

"Yeah, and while we don't disagree or nothing," Beatrice added, "maybe this ain't the best time, ya know?"

"Fair enough," Akta said. "Well, then. Let's get this over with." She turned around toward the stairs. "Come on, then."

"Just like that?" I asked.

"Just like that, unless you'd like to waste even more of the precious time you have left in Hell. It doesn't matter to me."

"No, no," I said, following after her down the stairs. "Let's go. I'm ready if you are."

"My friend," Akta said, "you are not even a little bit ready for what's about to happen."

CHAPTER 34

"You do realize this is the most secure facility in Hell, right?" Akta asked as we stood atop a cliff, looking down at a glowing orange mound below us that rose into the sky like an anthill. "You're lucky that with the overflow of souls, they don't have enough demons to guard it properly."

"No offense, Akta, but nothing about this is lucky for me. I'm in Hell trying to find an interdimensional time traveler. I just wanted a simple life." As we spoke, the black opal around my neck glowed blue, and I gripped it tightly. I only had two hours left before Xavier woke me up, or I'd be stuck in the pits of Hell forever. "Now, can we please go? I'm running out of time."

"You're the boss."

She grabbed me and extended her wings behind her. Together, we floated down to the base of the hill. We used the shadows from the swaying piles of people to maneuver through across the cracked ground, avoiding the sentries that patrolled above. We reached the other side of the mound and found a trench dug deep into the clay. Akta leaped down into it, and I followed behind.

"This is how they bring supplies into the facility," she whispered. "That door there clicks open at exactly the same time every day and stays open for precisely thirteen minutes. If we miss that window, we're stuck inside until the next day."

She moved forward with the grace and elegance of a ballet dancer, snaking through the trenches until we came upon a metal door in the side of the mountain. It seemed out of place in a sea of clay and mud. As we waited for the door to open, I heard the sounds of grunts and moans behind us.

"What's that?" I asked.

"The delivery," she said. "Don't worry. They're always a few minutes late. Demons don't keep time well and are hard-headed enough that if you give them a schedule, they'll defy it out of spite."

Akta looked up for a moment and then grabbed the door. As if on cue, the door clicked open, and we slid inside. The cheap construction on the outside belied the sophistication of the facility's interior. This was no mud hut. The walls were made of thick metal, with lanterns every few feet to guide our way through the hallways. Akta led me through the smooth metal corridors. I expected the walls to be hot to the touch, molten even, but they defied expectation, as so much of Hell did.

"How do you know all this?" I whispered.

"The good lord Lucifer trusts me with a great many secrets, and I use them to my advantage, when advantageous."

I stopped in the middle of the corridor. "You work for the Devil?"

"Keep your voice down," she hissed, wheeling on me. "We all work at the pleasure of the Devil down here, in some capacity. He gives me more autonomy than most, which I use to do favors for my friends, and make sure Hell doesn't fall too deep into the muck."

"Well, you're not doing a very good job of it."

Hooves clomping on metal brought me back to my present reality. This wasn't the time to grow a conscience or question my guide. I could take the moral high ground later. Now, I had a job to do.

Akta pulled me by the arm, and we ducked behind a door. A demon wearing a black uniform stumbled past, muttering, "Where are they? Better not be hungover again. I'm not carrying that sodding crap again. It stunk like manure for a week last time."

Akta watched the demon pass and, when the coast was clear, led me out of the room across the hall. "This needs to be timed perfectly. If you mess me up again with your stupid questions, I'll leave you for the demons. Got it?"

"I'm sorry I—"

"Don't care," Akta snapped. "Shut up. Got it?"

I nodded and followed the pixie as she leaped across the hallway and landed without a sound on the other side. I was not as graceful, but I did my best to pick up my feet and land gently. Years of waitressing taught me to be nimble and step quietly enough not to make a racket on the metal grating.

Akta must have been right about us being lucky because we found very little resistance on our way through the facility. We passed dozens of empty rooms, clearly meant as sleeping quarters or abandoned offices. If this place had a full complement of soldiers, then we would have never been able to get to the spiral stairwell at its core, but that's just what we did, without incident.

At the bottom of a set of stairs, red orbs lit the darkness from every angle, revealing a metal box at the center of a cavernous expanse.

"She's inside that box," Akta said. "The magic inside the orbs keeps her contained to this plane of existence. Otherwise, her soul would be able to phase all over the place, and we wouldn't be able to restrain her."

I stepped closer to the small window inset in the metal door, and a blue glow pulsed from my necklace. *Five minutes.*

The red light from the orbs fell across the floor of the room inside the metal box. A small woman sat on a small bed pushed against the back wall. Long, black hair fell over her face. Her body twitched as she lifted her face. When her eyes found mine, her body phased out of existence, just for a fraction of a moment. She came back into view and strode toward me. Another shift, and she was at the window. Her eyes were glassy and hollow, and a shiver ran down my spine as I looked at her milky white flesh.

"Rosalie?"

"25, 15, 21, 1, 18, 5, 14, 5, 23."

"I don't—"

"She only speaks in numbers," Akta said, sighing. "It's very annoying. She just said you are new."

"How do you know?"

"I've spent countless hours here, trying to decipher her. I speak fluent Rosalie now."

The blue glow at my neck beat faster. I was running out of time. "I need your help."

"23, 8, 25, 19, 8, 15, 21, 12, 4, 9, 8, 5, 12, 16, 13, 25, 3, 2, 16, 20, 15, 18, 19."

"We're not your captors," Akta said. "We're trying to help you."

"I don't believe that for one second," I said to Akta. "You can lie to yourself all you want on your own time." I turned back to Rosalie. "The world is going to end. I'm trying to stop it. God sent me to stop it, but I need your help."

"7, 15, 4?"

Even I understood that one. "Yes, God. If you don't help me find the Time Being, he will be very cross with you, but if you help me…perhaps he can help you, too."

"8, 15, 13, 5."

"This is your home," Akta said.

"Shhh," I growled at Akta before turning back to Rosalie. "You want to go home? Is that where the Time Being is?" The woman nodded. "Is that home?"

"See, I told her she's a nutter," Akta said. "She was born and raised on Earth."

Rosalie leaned into the door. "294651 – 376 19 1."

I turned to Akta. "What does that mean?"

"It's gibberish," she said. "It means she doesn't want to talk to you anymore."

"No, that's not—" I turned back to the woman. "Please, you have to—" A shock shot through my body. "No, no, no. I need more—" Another shock. "Please!"

Rosalie pushed upon the glass frantically. "294651 – 376 19 1"

A third shock pulsed through my body, and I felt myself floating. On the fourth pulse, I shot through the air, boring through the ground until I smashed full force into my body and sat up with a violent heave. Xavier placed a bucket under my chin, and I threw up into it, purging violently until there was nothing left inside of me.

I fell back, sucking in wind as I tried to come to terms with what had just happened and how I had so royally failed everyone. *Now what am I going to do?*

CHAPTER 35

My head felt like it was squeezed in a vice when the first rays of the sun glinted on my face, and I finally sat up. My back seized up, and pain shot through my forehead as the sunshine fell into my eyes.

"Don't move too quickly," Xavier said, handing me a bottle of water.

"How long was I out?" I asked with a gravelly voice.

"About eight hours. I shouldn't have pushed it so hard. I was barely able to bring you back. Your body is all sorts of jacked up."

I rubbed the wound on my chest. "I know. Thank you for giving me as much time as you could."

"Did you talk to her?"

"I did, but I'm afraid all I got was gibberish. I just wasted another day that I don't have." As the pain shot through my head, I suddenly remembered that I sold Lilith out to Beatrice and Clovis to get into the facility. "I need to use your phone. Do you have a phone book?"

He pulled the Yellow Pages down from the top of the fridge, and I paged through it before punching numbers into the phone.

"Chateau Marmont," a heavenly cooed from the other line. "How may we help you?"

"Yes, can you call up for Mistress Westcott? Tell her that Lizzie is calling, and it's urgent."

After a moment, the girl on the other line sucked her teeth. "I'm sorry, but there's a do not disturb on her line and—"

"This is a matter of life and death."

"Be that as it may, she's asked not to be disturbed and—"

I hung up the phone, thanked Xavier, and rushed to my car, trying hard to avoid vomiting from the pain coursing through my head. Luckily, the Hills weren't far from the Chateau, and this time I didn't wait to find parking. I left the car with the valet and rushed through the lobby as fast as my nauseous body would allow. I already knew the way to Lilith's room.

When the elevator doors opened, I rushed out to see that her door was already open, and green ooze leaked into the hallway. *Lilith.*

I stormed into the room and breathed a sigh of relief, followed quickly by the desire to retch. The headless form of a demon lay on the ground. Further down the hallway was another one, and a third laid in the kitchen.

"Lilith?" I asked, walking through the room.

I found her outside, covered in demon blood, staring out into the morning sun, drinking a Bloody Mary, face serene.

"Lilith, I'm so sorry. I tried to call and tell you that—"

She held up her hand. "You had to barter your friendship with me for your own ends. It's perfectly okay. I would have done the same. I have done the same hundreds of times before." She slid a second Bloody Mary across the table. "Would you care for one? I believe we've both had a day, and it's barely half-past nine."

I sat down next to her and took the drink. "You're taking this very well."

She laughed. "Do you think this is the first time I've had to deal with my detractors? No, this isn't the first, and it won't be the last. They still underestimate me." She looked over at me. "That is your power as a woman. Strong men will always underestimate you, and you can use that to your advantage, to kill them."

"Good advice." I took a sip of my drink. "This isn't poisoned, is it?"

"No, my love. I have no need for a coward's weapon. I will stab you in the front if I wish to kill you." She took another sip of her drink. "Did you get what you needed, at least?"

I shook my head. "No."

"That's a pity. You always hope a good betrayal yields results. When it doesn't, it leaves a bitter taste in your mouth."

"I'm sor—"

She held up her hand again, and I stopped. We sat in silence for a moment. Finally, I asked, "Where will you go now?"

"Oh, darling. There is no shortage of marvelous places in the world. I've grown tired of Los Angeles anyway. Perhaps I will get away from it all and disappear to a small provincial town for a while to await the end of days."

"I'm not going to let that happen."

She chuckled. "You still think you have agency. That's good. You'll need it if you hope to change the world."

"I don't know where to go now," I replied.

Lilith slid a napkin across the table. "I thought you might say that."

I looked at the address on the napkin. "What is this?"

"Kimberly's house. She thinks she is quite clever, but any time you put down roots, you open yourself up to being found. That is why I never put down roots." She finished her glass and stood. "And now, I will take a shower and plan my next move. Please don't be here when I'm done." She reached into her purse and pulled out a stack of money. "That should get you a plane ticket. Splurge for first class, darling. It's worth it, and everybody should do it once in their lives."

"Who says I haven't been in first class?"

She chuckled. "I mean, look at you, darling."

"What about the bodies?" I asked as she strolled across the room.

"I'm sure I have no idea. I pay very good money so I don't have to worry about things like that."

Something told me that would be the last time I saw Lilith. There was a sadness to her when she looked at me. She might have said she was okay with betrayal, but it still stung. The stack of money she gave me was a kiss-off, a way to tell me goodbye without saying it to my face, and the message was received loud and clear.

I took Lilith's advice and booked a first-class ticket to San Francisco. Even after paying for a same-day ticket, there was plenty of money left over which I stuffed in the Prada purse. I bought some new clothing that wasn't sticky with residual blood and used the first-class lounge to shower and change, throwing my old clothes into a trash bin before gorging myself on whatever food I could find in the lounge.

I was as hungry as I had ever been and the unlimited hors d'oeuvres helped settle both my stomach and my head, but I still popped two Alka Seltzer and three aspirin to ease what discomfort remained. I also took the flight attendants up on their offer of champagne to help me forget my horrible time in Hell.

By the time I landed in San Francisco, I felt better than I had in a long time, especially after three glasses of champagne. There was no way I could drive in my state, so I took a cab from the airport to the address listed.

"Welcome to the Continental," a doorman said as I stepped onto the curb. His name was Gill, and he had a kind, if not overly polite, way about him, down to how he tipped his cap when I entered the building. While I had only seen the interior of the apartment on my last visit, the view of the bay from the lobby was similar to the one I had seen several stories up.

Gill followed behind me, inquiring, "Who are you here to see today?"

"Kimberly…I actually don't know her last name. She's living with Molly." I looked down at my paper. "Apartment 913."

He crinkled up his nose. "Not sure I should ring you up, as you don't even know their names."

I shrugged. "I mean, that's fair, but I'm very sure she'll want to see me. Maybe you should just tell them Lizzie is back from Hell and would very much like to see them, please."

"Is that…a joke?" he asked. "Not sure it's a very good or pleasant one."

"Just make the call, please," I said.

He did as he was asked and called up to the room. "Yes, I have a Lizzie here to see you. She's a bit crass if you ask me." A pause. "Yes, ma'am. Right away."

Gill placed the phone down and smiled at me. "They said they are expecting you. Head on up. Take the elevator on your right."

Moments later, the elevator let me out on the ninth floor, and I followed the hallway around to apartment 913. The door opened before I could knock, and Kimberly stood there smirking at me. "It's about time you showed up. Took you long enough to find the place."

"Sorry, I was delayed, what with going to Hell and all."

"Come on in. We made paella and sangria—though it sounds like we might need to make a second pitcher."

CHAPTER 36

Even though I stuffed myself before leaving Los Angeles, I was still able to pack away two plates of Molly's delicious paella and several glasses of sangria as I told the story of my time in Hell to a rapt audience.

"That sounds nothing like my time in Hell," Kimberly said. "Somehow, it's gone downhill. I honestly didn't think that was possible."

"If I've learned nothing else in my life, it's that no matter how bad things are, more awful can pile on."

Molly pulled a blueberry out of her sangria and popped it in her mouth. "You know what's funny? I've been racking my brain trying to remember where I've heard about the Time Being before, and it just hit me. This whole story sounds a lot like this book I read a few years ago. *The Astronaut's Midwife*. Ever heard of it?"

"No," I said, shaking my head.

"Molly reads a lot," Kimberly said, smiling over her glass. "If there's a book she doesn't love, I haven't found it yet."

"What's not to love about reading?" Molly said. "It's like being on a great drug trip, hallucinating, and being led by your favorite writers. But that's neither here nor there. *The Astronaut's Midwife* is about a woman whose husband dies, and she sets off to win a wish from the goddess of time. She solves all sorts of riddles and puzzles, traveling across the universe until, eventually, she finds the being, but she's a shell of herself, having lost her sanity in the process." Molly ate a piece of apple floating in her glass. "Weirdly, she also only spoke in numbers by the end of it, flickering in and out of existence until she died, unable to remember when or where she was from."

"That is weird." I turned to her. "Too weird to be a coincidence. Do you have a copy of it anywhere?"

"Oh, not anymore. It wasn't very good, in the end. Shouldn't be hard to find, though. You can probably get another copy off Amazon."

I tried to search the internet for a copy, but no matter where I looked, the book was either out of print or not available. With every dead end, my frustration grew along with my intrigue. By the end of my search, all I had was a name, Christopher Bencze, and a publisher, Schrodinger Press.

A Google search returned no information on Christopher Bencze. There wasn't even a single review of his book, but there was information on Schrodinger Books, a small press located right in the Mission District of San Francisco. It made sense, thinking about it, as anything with national, or even regional, distribution would have been nearly impossible to scrub from the internet. The only way that Molly could have gotten ahold of such a niche book was through a local press.

The publisher's name was Tina Harrison, and while I couldn't find her address, I did figure out she was a teacher at San Francisco City College, where she lectured on what else but English Composition. *Fitting.* Kimberly had no interest in coming with me to a college, but Molly couldn't wait to tag along. The college wasn't far from their apartment in the Embarcadero, so we decided to hoof it, hoping this Ms. Harrison would have office hours.

"So, favorite genre?" I asked as we walked down the hilly streets toward the college.

"Oooh, that's tough. They all have so much to offer. For a long time, I was a non-fiction girl, but life is hard, and I just want to escape it these days, so I have to say my favorite now is fantasy. I don't mean just JRR Tolkien, either. Have you read *Storm Front*? It's a new book by Jim Butcher, or *Good Omens,* or anything by Anne McCaffrey, Ursula Le Guin, or Jody Lynn Nye?"

"Is it really fantasy when you, like, really are a fairy? I mean, I've met some incredible monsters in Hell, and it feels like fantasy would be so much less interesting, knowing all these things really exist."

"Not to me," she said. "If anything, it makes it more interesting. I mean, people read romance novels and contemporary fiction about boring things happening to regular people, and they still sell. Why should fantasy be any different, just because the creatures are real?"

"Touché," I replied.

I didn't mind the walk to the college. It was nice, actually. I had spent so much of my life thinking about saving the world, I liked to see what I was saving. Humanity was kind of the worst, but they also created books, constructed buildings, and birthed adorable children. Those things had their good points, too.

Once we got to the campus, we stopped for coffee before making our way to the English building, then crossed the quad, where hippies and jocks sunned themselves in the late afternoon sun. At one end of the grassy knoll was a massive library with a black dome covering its roof, and at the other, a long reflecting pool laid in front of a long, sleek administration building with glass walls across the front of it—tradition on one end, modernity on the other.

The English building didn't know which way it wanted to swing between traditional and modern, so it chose a horrible fusion of both. Glass windows and sleek angles adorned the front of its face, but detailed marble pillars held up an intricately detailed overhang. It perfectly encapsulated a city that was stepping into the future with both feet while its fingers grasped tightly to the past.

The doors slid open for us as we approached. Offset from the concrete hallway on the left was a glass door with 'office' printed on it. I walked inside to find a woman with rosy cheeks and a bob cut too high for her thick head sitting behind a marble desk.

"Welcome," she said. "How can we help you?"

"Yes, we're looking for Professor Tina Harrison. Does she have class today?"

"You're not here to arrest her, are you?" She smiled when we didn't answer and then started pumping her hands frantically. "Oh god, I was just kidding. She's the sweetest girl in the whole world. That's why it's so funny, but why would you know that? Stupid, Brenda. Stupid."

"Don't beat yourself up about it," Molly said. "If you could just point out her room."

"Of course," Brenda said, flipping through a binder. "Let's see. Tina's in room 231, and good news. Looks like her class is just about to get out. Lucky you."

I growled under my breath. "Yes, lucky me, indeed."

We took the stairs up to Tina's classroom and were met with a flood of people exiting down the hallway when we reached the top of them. I swam through them into room 231 to see a stout woman with frazzled salt and pepper hair and coke-bottle glasses wiping off the board.

"I'm sorry we ran long," she said. "It's just—" She turned and saw we weren't who she was expecting, and her shoulders slumped. "I'll just be a minute."

"Actually," I said. "We were looking for you."

"How interesting," she replied. "You aren't here to arrest me, are you?"

"Funny, that's not the first time we've heard that one today," Molly said. "But no, we're not. We're hoping you can help us. You were the publisher for Schrodinger Press, right?"

Tina sighed while she gathered up her things. "I can't seem to shake that monkey off my back. If you're from the IRS, I already told you I disintegrated that company years ago, and there is no money to speak of anymore."

"We're not from the IRS," I said. "Are you in contact with any of the authors? Specifically, Christopher Bencze, author of *The Astronaut's Midwife*?"

She laughed. "Well, I should hope so. He's me."

CHAPTER 37

"What do you mean you're Christopher Bencze?" I asked Professor Tina, confused. "You're a woman."

"Haven't you ever heard of a pen name?" She raised her eyebrows. "It's when somebody writes under a pseudonym to keep their identity hidden."

"And yet, you told us after like fifteen seconds," Molly interjected.

Tina laughed. "Yeah, it really, really was." She grabbed her leather satchel and slung it over her shoulder. "Would you like some coffee? If I'm going to go through this all again, then I'll need some of that sweet, sweet java." She stopped before she headed out the door. "You're buying, of course."

We'd already had coffee, but we followed Professor Tina from her classroom and back to the coffee shop at the entrance to the campus. She ordered a cranberry muffin and a large latte, and we sat outside around a grated metal table waiting for it. When I started to speak, she held up her finger and shook her head until the coffee came, and she took a sip.

"Thanks, Susan."

"Better now?" the barista asked.

"Much better," Tina said with a smile, ripping off a piece of the muffin and stuffing it in her mouth. "But who isn't, after a free meal on the government's tab?"

The barista pursed her lips and nodded before she walked away.

I rolled my eyes. "We're not part of the government."

Tina leaned toward me. "That's exactly what somebody from the government would say."

"I'm pretty sure we would have to identify ourselves," Molly said. "Otherwise, it's entrapment."

Tina held up her hands. "Fine, fine. For the sake of argument, I'll humor you. If you're not the government, then what could you possibly want with me?"

"If we *were* the government, what could we possibly want with you?" I asked.

"Well, let's see. I mortgaged my house three times to keep my publishing company afloat and haven't paid taxes in four years to try and crawl back above water, so…something about that, probably."

"I'm sorry to hear that," Molly said.

"Thank you," Tina said. "Of course, you also have a weird fascination with my book, even though it was such an abject failure that it bankrupted the company I formed to publish it, so maybe it's about that."

"Your book. Did you write it about Rosalie Louey?" I asked.

She took a long sip of coffee. "I see you've done your homework. It is so exhausting talking to spooks that don't know what they're talking about."

"How did you know her?" I said. "There's no information about her anywhere."

"Of course there isn't. She was a hermit who spoke in riddles and distrusted everyone." She sighed, poking at the muffin on her plate. "I know about her because she was my grandmother. She contracted Alzheimer's early in her life. After Mom died, I was supposed to take care of her but—"

"You didn't," Molly said.

"I was young and…mean, I guess, head stuck up my ass, for sure. I didn't take care of her. I came back to see her often enough, but it was hard. By the end, she was just talking in numbers, and she died a husk of herself. She left me everything she had, even after how I treated her. After she died, I couldn't stop thinking about her stories, and my fascination turned into an obsession." Tina sighed and leaned back into her chair. "I thought maybe my book would help shed some light on her journey and get it out of my head onto the page. I thought it might be her legacy. Maybe it was my guilt that drove me. But when it only sold a measly three copies—well, let's just say I failed her. I've been paying for it ever since, quite literally. I guess karma got back at me in the end."

"Where are the books now?" I asked. "The copies you didn't sell?"

"Gone. Somebody stole every copy in my warehouse a few years ago. That was the final nail in the coffin. I tried to take out another loan to print them again, but my credit was so terrible I couldn't even get a bank card."

"So the books are gone?"

"Every one of them." She took another bite of her muffin. "And then, a freak storm wiped out the hard drive the book was on, which means I would have to type it all out again, and I just don't have the energy."

Something smelled fishy to me.

"Did you keep any notes about the book or Rosalie's life that you can share with me? It could really get me out of a jam."

"She kept a diary, especially near the end. Well, it wasn't really a diary. More like a loose collection of papers, connected by a theme." Tina chuckled. "You really aren't spooks, are you?" She leaned forward, narrowing her eyes. "Your interest in the book is more personal. So, why do you want to meet the Time Being?"

The words slipped out of her mouth effortlessly, and the casual bluntness of her question threw me back, especially that she asked it in such an open forum like the campus cafe.

"To save the world."

"High ambitions," Tina said.

"I was sent by God," I added.

"Ah, you're one of those," Tina sighed.

"She's not lying," Molly said.

"Of course you would think that," Tina said. "She's your friend."

"She is my friend," Molly replied. "But that's not why I believe her. I believe her because I have seen some terrible things, the kind of stuff that would make the skin peel from your face if I talked about it, and through it all, the love of my life has been there, every step of the way, fighting back—and she believes in this girl. When I look into her eyes, I see that she's telling the truth." Molly's voice had fallen to a terse whisper. "Whether you believe her or not is irrelevant. If you can't help us, we'll find the information we need some other way."

After a long silence, I spoke again. "I met her, Rosalie."

"No, you didn't," Tina replied. "She's been dead a long time, and she was a hermit when she did live."

"I know that, and I did anyway." I leaned closer. "She spoke in gibberish and riddles."

Tina cupped her hand over her mouth. "You really did meet her."

"That's right, and every word out of her mouth was nonsense. That's why we're here."

"Well, it's not gibberish to me." Tina smirked. "Over time, you learn it like a second language."

"So what?" Molly said. "It's like a cipher?"

"Something like that. I could figure out what she wanted when she spoke, but her papers were harder to decode."

"Why?" I replied.

"She wrote in one long string of numbers, so you never knew if she meant a 1 and a 2 or a 12 or…well, you get the point."

"Do you still have those notes?"

She shook her head. "I sold them to a collector a year ago. The sale paid off one of my mortgages, and he was very insistent that I keep no copies." She paused. "He also had a worn copy of my book, which he asked me to sign."

"Can you please give me his name? I would like to have a chat with him."

"Sorry. He asked to remain anonymous."

Molly frowned, not looking at either of us. "How much would it cost to get you out of debt, right now, this minute?"

Tina sighed as though defeated even at the thought of it. "Like $500,000, give or take a few thousand."

"Done," Molly said without hesitation.

Tina scoffed. "You're kidding, right?"

Molly shook her head. "Half a million dollars for the name and an address. And another half a million to start a new life. A million dollars, right now, for five seconds of work."

Her eyes bounced back and forth between us for a long time, sizing us up. Then, she shook Molly's hand. "All right, you have yourself a deal."

CHAPTER 38

I knew that Kimberly and Molly were loaded, but I didn't know they had money like that—money they could use to get anything they wanted from somebody with just a few words—to waste on something that might not even bear fruit. *Must be nice.*

"I'm sorry," Molly said as we sat in the bank with Tina. "I didn't mean to take such unilateral action, but I was getting antsy, and I wanted to move it along. Maybe Kimberly has rubbed off on me."

"It's fine. I just didn't know you had 'screw you' money."

Molly smiled. "Honey, we have 'screw everyone' money."

A thin man with a neck too long for his body slinked back into the room holding a thick envelope. He straightened the lapel on his shiny black suit before he sat down behind his oak desk.

"Everything okay?" Molly asked.

The man nodded. "Everything is sorted and in order. There are protocols in place when somebody asks to take out so much money, that's all." He slid the envelope over to Tina. "I believe this is yours. If you need help setting up your own accounts, please let us know."

She shook her head. "I'm not gonna have this money for long, unfortunately."

She pulled two checks from the manila envelope. They were longer and wider than the personal checks I was used to and printed on thicker paper as well. The blue checks had a metallic sheen to them, and I caught a whiff of cardamom. One of the checks was made out, in calligraphy, to Tina's mortgage company, as requested. The other had her name on it, no less elegantly inscribed. As she looked at the two pieces of paper, her lip quivered, and she began to cry.

Molly didn't pause. "Now, I believe it's time for you to hold up your end of the bargain."

Tina nodded and pulled a sheet of paper out of her purse. "Here is the name and address of the man. He paid in cash, not fancy checks like these, but he gave me the address to send any other materials I might find in my possession. I never did, but I kept the address all the same."

I took the paper from her. The address was across the country, in Washington, D.C., and I wondered how somebody like that would even get their hands on one of her books. Perhaps Tina wasn't crazy to think the government was after her. Or maybe there was an eccentric collector out there with more money on his hands than he knew what to do with.

We said our goodbyes to Tina, who decided that perhaps she would need help opening a bank account after all, much to the delight of the banker.

"We should fill Kimmy in on what we found." Molly held out her hand. "Do you mind if we do this the easy way?"

I took her hand, and we ducked into a hidden crevice behind the bank. She closed her hand on mine, and we disappeared into the ether. There was the familiar sensation of my feet falling from the ground, and then my stomach shot into my throat just before we reappeared with a flash inside Molly's living room.

"Eventful day?" Kimberly asked, turning off the television. "I got a call from Gerald, so I assume you made some progress."

There wasn't a hint of surprise or anger in her voice about Molly spending a million dollars without consulting her. She was just stating a fact, inquiring as to a purchase, just like a husband might ask their spouse about an errant ten-dollar charge on their bank statement while reconciling finances.

"Yes. Sorry, dear. I got caught up in the moment and agreed to some things. I should have talked to you about it first, but the good news is we learned something vitally important."

"Well, at least there's a good reason for giving somebody a million dollars. That is good news." She glanced at me. "That's not always the case."

"HEY!" Molly said, putting her hands on her hips in playful exaggeration. "There's always a good reason, in my opinion. It's just that you don't always think it's a good one." She gestured to me. "Would you tell her what we found, so she stops giving me the third degree?"

"I mean, it's only a million dollars. What's to worry about?" Kimberly said. "What do you have to show me, Lizzie?"

I unfolded the paper and handed it to her. "Tina was Rosalie's granddaughter. She took care of her in her dying days when her mind was slipping and inherited her papers when she finally died. She used those to write *The Astronaut's Midwife* but then got into some financial trouble and sold the papers to this collector."

"I guess we're going to D.C.," Kimberly said after studying the paper.

"Not me, I'm afraid," Molly said, yawning with a stretch. "I've had quite enough excitement for one day. I'll leave this to you girls. I'm knackered." She kissed Kimberly on the cheek. "You be careful now."

Kimberly gave a sly grin. "You know I won't."

"I know, but it comforts me to say it anyway."

After they said goodbye, Kimberly took my hand in hers, and we flashed to the closest place in Washington, D.C. that Kimberly knew by heart—a small alcove behind the Jefferson Memorial. She peeked her head out to make sure the guards were nowhere to be found, and we made our way across the lawn. The entire structure was held by columns, and you could see Jefferson's statue from any angle. One side of the building had a rectangular portico, with steps leading up to the colonnade, which was also where the red and gray pavement met the waterline.

"I'm surprised you didn't flash us to the Lincoln Memorial or the Washington Monument," I said as we walked toward the water.

"Too crowded. Jefferson is farther from the others, and away from the Mall, so it's not as crowded, especially in the evening."

It might have been easier to conceal our abrupt, teleported appearance at the Jefferson Memorial, but it was also incredibly inconvenient to find a cab. When we eventually did find one, it was an exorbitant cost to bring us from the monument to Fairfax.

"Molly's nice," I said as the cab took a turn off the highway. "You chose well."

"Please," Kimberly said, "you think I chose her and not the other way around? I could never get somebody like her to do anything she didn't want to do, and I'm not much of a wooer, truth be told. No, she chased after me…thank the gods."

"Well, she chose well, too."

"We both know that's not true, but I appreciate you humoring me."

But I did think that she chose well. Kimberly was loyal, tenacious, and her moral compass always pointed true north. Even though she was a pain a lot of the time, she got the job done when almost nobody would even try, and I respected that about her. Really, I loved that about her.

I didn't say any of that. Instead, I just shook my head. "You're an idiot."

The cab slowed down after we'd gone through the forests of northern Virginia and stopped in front of a black gate emblazoned with a gilded "E" at its center.

"You want me to buzz the door?" the driver said.

"No, thanks," Kimberly said, exiting the car. "We got it."

She gave the cab driver a wad of money, and we watched him drive away. When he was out of sight, Kimberly flashed us both inside the gates to a fountain spouting water from a dolphin's mouth in the center of a round driveway.

"What's the plan?" I said as we walked up to the front door.

"I'm sure it will come to us in the moment."

Kimberly rang the bell, and an old man gingerly opened it wearing a tuxedo with tails. "Good evening, ma'am."

I glanced at the sheet of paper. "Yes, we're looking for Clifton Edington the third. Is that you?"

The man cocked his head. "No, ma'am. I'm just the butler. Do you have an appointment?"

"Does anyone, really?" Kimberly said.

"Mmmm…yes, they do. If you don't have one, I'll kindly ask you to leave before I call the dogs."

"Wait," I said as he started to close the door. "We're friends with Rosalie Louey."

It worked. The man paused. "Rosalie, you say? Well then, I believe my master will have a moment to spare for you after all."

CHAPTER 39

There were many words which could adequately describe Clifton's house—opulent sprung to mind first, then fastidious, but the one that best described it was probably *precise*. Everything felt placed for a purpose in its exact spot, turned to the correct angle to show it off perfectly. I had been in my share of rich houses and hotel rooms in the recent past, but this was something extra, even for them, which were extra compared to everything else that I had ever experienced in my life.

The white marble floors under us had been buffed to a mirror shine, and I felt a little guilty touching my grubbing shoes on them. Kimberly had no such reservations, but it was different because she was already rich and chose to eschew those conventions. I, on the other hand, had lived with nothing except a growing desire to be taken seriously.

"How do you know Ms. Louey?" the butler asked.

"We'll tell that directly to your master if he asks," Kimberly growled.

"I am just trying to be polite," the butler replied in a huff. "So that I may present you properly."

"I'm sure you'll do fine without it," Kimberly said. "It is your job, after all."

I didn't know why Kimberly was being so brusque with the poor, old man. He seemed nice enough to me, and as she herself had pointed out, the man was just trying to do his job. Still, I didn't ask questions. We needed to show a united front, and since I had no idea how to act in this sort of situation, I had to trust her.

We reached a pair of red doors, and the butler turned to us. "Wait here."

He walked inside the study and closed the door behind him, and I finally felt free to let out the breath I had been holding in since we walked into the door.

"Why were you being such a jerk to that butler?" I whispered.

"He is an extension of his master, and he is looking for any weakness. You were right to keep quiet and let me speak. If we didn't behave with authority, he would have turned us away, or at the very least, told his master that we were weak. He's in there right now, giving Clifton the rundown on us. He might say we are ill-mannered or downright jerks, but he won't say that we are weak. That puts us at an advantage."

Before I could ask anything else, the doors to the study flung open, and the butler gestured us inside. "The master will see you now."

A roaring fire crackled in the fireplace behind the leather chair where a cunningly handsome, older man swirled a brandy snifter in his hand. His salt and pepper hair was slicked back, and his mustache had been trimmed until it was little more than a thin line on his tanned face. He wore a red silk robe, a purple cravat with a tiepin in the center, and sheer white pants. Every bit of him looked manufactured, and I realized that he must have crafted his pose for our benefit, as no natural human would ever sit with such rigid posture if they weren't trying to purport a level of regality about them.

"Welcome to my home," he said with stilted enthusiasm. "I hear you were friends with my Rosalie."

"Your Rosalie, sir?" I asked.

"We didn't know each other intimately, but I have been fascinated with her story since I read about it many years ago."

"Is that why you tracked down her granddaughter and bought the papers?" Kimberly didn't take her eyes of Clifton, nor did he break his gaze on her. "Or was there some other reason?"

His forced laugh seemed more robotic than human. "You cut to the chase, and I love it. Yes, I did buy the papers from her granddaughter. A shrewd negotiator, let me tell you what. She knew what she had in her possession." He stroked the end of his pencil-thin mustache. "Of course, I'm no slouch myself in the negotiation department. Some might say I have a sixth sense for it, and I feel like we're heading into one right now. So, what can I do for you ladies?"

I glanced over at Kimberly. She shook her head and continued. "We would like to take a look at the papers if you wouldn't mind."

He chuckled. "Do you think you're the first, fifth, or hundredth person to come and ask for the keys to that particular kingdom? You are not. And I'm afraid if I gave access to every Jane, Jill, and Janet that walked through the door, well, how much value would the papers have to me then?"

"Why do you seek the Time Being?" I blurted out. The words just came—the same ones that Tina asked me earlier in the day.

Clifton looked me up and down and then turned up his nose. I had broken his concentration. "Excuse my frankness, but that is none of your damn business." He shifted in his seat and took a sip from his snifter. "Now, if this is a negotiation, you will have something to offer, yes?"

"I have money," Kimberly said. "Name your price."

Clifton scoffed. "Not interested."

"What, then?" Kimberly asked.

"Information." He leaned forward and looked from Kimberly to me. "The kind that unlocks the secrets of the universe and shows me its inner workings. Tell me, do you have anything like this?"

"I have a collection of books that would rival the library of Alexandria." Kimberly crossed her arms. "If you give me access to those files, I could bring you more information than you could consume in ten lifetimes. However, that would mean putting them in the hands of a demon, and that would be too dangerous."

Demon? Was this man a demon?

A dark smile grew on the edges of his mouth. "Very good, Kimberly. I was wondering if you would notice. True to form, you are every bit the legendary demon hunter they say you are."

"I have no quarrel with you," she said. "Until this moment, I had no idea you existed. You've kept your nose clean, which is more than I can say for your brethren. Give us the documents we seek, and I will leave you be…for now. Until your demon heart can't simply stand being polite, and you lash out in your truer nature and hurt my kind. Then, I'll be less polite."

He yawned. "Idle threats are so passe."

Kimberly placed her hands on her daggers. "Nothing I do is idle, demon."

Clifton's smile grew. "You really are delightful. However, even if I wanted to let you look at them. Sadly, I cannot. They have been stolen from me, you see, and despite my best efforts, I have been unable to retrieve them."

"Were you able to decipher any of the pages before they were taken from you?"

"Somewhat. Sadly, even those notes were taken from me. I have been searching for them for a long time." He took a sip of his brandy. "Perhaps I can offer you a trade."

"What do you have to offer me?" Kimberly asked.

"Find me the papers, and I will grant you access to them, and to sweeten the pot, I won't kill dear, sweet Professor Tina for welshing on our deal."

"You wouldn't!" I blurted out. "She's innocent."

"Of course he would." Kimberly didn't take her eyes off of Clifton. "He's probably already put a contract out on her head."

"I have, as a matter of fact, and I can cancel it just as quickly. But not if I'm to be insulted in my own house." He let out a short laugh. "She really is a sweet, dumb woman."

"Fine," Kimberly said. "What do I care? We were going to find it anyway." She turned to the door. "We'll find your stupid papers. Call off your dogs."

He snapped his fingers. "There, done. Now, wasn't that easy?"

CHAPTER 40

With all of Kimberly's resources, it surprised me that we ended up in front of the same Venice bungalow that Lilith's son had sent me to just a couple of days before. Kimberly rapped on the door, and Ollie slid the door open, holding a bottle of beer.

"Twice in one week, kid?" She looked at me through her sunglasses. "Did you miss me that much?" She took a swig of her beer before acknowledging Kimberly's dour expression. "I see you haven't lost your sense of humor."

"Can we come in?" Kimberly said. "Or are you going to be inhospitable, as always?"

"I mean, I haven't cleaned in a while." Ollie kicked open the sliding door and walked back to the kitchen. "But be my guest."

She wasn't kidding. Clothing hung from the old CTR television, and a blanket was balled up on the couch as if she slept there not too long ago. On the coffee table, a pile of old magazines tilted precariously, and many more of them were flung around the room, all with words and pictures cut out of them.

"Making a ransom note?" I asked.

"Yeah," Ollie replied. "What's it to you?"

I held up my hands, not knowing if she was joking or not. "Nothing."

"She's never seen the inside of a serial killer's house before," Kimberly said, staring right into Ollie's glasses. "Would you please take those off? I don't trust anyone whose eyes I can't see."

Ollie shook her head. "If I thought there was any way you would trust me, maybe I would consider it, but that's not the relationship we have, do we?" She pulled a wooden spoon from a drawer and stirred a boiling pot on her stove. "Can you hurry up? I'm making chili, and you're distracting me."

I noted the smell of pepper and tomatoes. "It smells good."

"Tastes better. Unfortunately, I don't break bread with clients. Now, what can I do for the two of you? Or did you just come to have a sewing circle? Cuz I can't sew."

"We're looking for a collection of papers," Kimberly said. "Written by Rosalie Louey."

"You and about a hundred other demons," Ollie called over her shoulder, still stirring. "Apparently, they think the Time Being can send them back to set the wheels in motion which will start the Apocalypse."

"Does that mean you don't know where it is?" I asked.

Ollie turned around and leaned on the counter. "I tracked down a shipment of books a couple of years ago, and the demons who bought them from me asked me to find the papers, too."

"Demons have Tina's book?" I said.

"I guess," Ollie replied. "Some of them can read, but the story is kind of terrible. It switches perspectives constantly, and the lead character is completely unlikeable. Plus, the ending is a complete bummer."

"Do you still have a copy of that book?" I asked. "We've been looking for it everywhere."

"I don't really keep things like that, or at all. I read the book and tossed it, but I doubt it had anything useful. If it did, the demons would have tracked down the Time Being already." She tasted the chili. "Needs more cumin."

"And smoked paprika," Kimberly added, sniffing the air. "Trust me on that one."

Ollie turned to her spice rack and pulled a couple of shakers from it. "Anyway, the real key is the papers, at least, that's what the demons believed. The book doesn't seem to matter much in the end."

"What demons did you work for?" Kimberly asked. "Maybe we can just ask them."

"You know I don't give out information on my clients, but I'm kind of surprised you have to ask me about that, since well—you know—"

"I don't understand." The words were out of my mouth, but then it connected in my brain. Of course, there was a reason why Lilith would help me. She was seeking the Time Being as well. By helping me, she helped herself at the same time. "You mean Lilith."

Ollie shrugged. "I'm not saying Lilith, but I'm not *not* saying Lilith either."

"Why would she want to meet the Time Being?" I asked.

"Maybe she wants to go back in time and fix a mistake, just like everyone else. I mean, she does have a big one hanging over her, what with pissing off God and being forced to roam the earth forever, with demons her only comfort. Maybe she wants to go back and make kissy-kissy with Adam."

"But that would undo everything," Kimberly said. "She wouldn't—no, no, she definitely would. That does sound like her."

"She doesn't have the papers," I said. "I'm sure of that."

"Are you best friends now?" Ollie asked. "My, you have been making the rounds."

"No, but there's no reason for her to jerk us around if she had it."

Kimberly laughed. "Actually, that sounds exactly like a thing she would do."

I shook my head. "I don't think so. But even if she does have it, she's not going to admit it. Not without proof. Isn't there anyone else who could help us besides her?"

"Maybe." Kimberly thought for a moment, then a pained look passed over her face. "When was the last time you talked to Charlie?"

Ollie grimaced at the name. "Let's see…last time he tried to screw me, and I nearly nailed him to a wall. I guess it's been a while."

"Maybe it's time I paid him a visit."

"I still think it's Lilith, but you do you." Ollie brought the wooden spoon up to her mouth. "I'm gonna stir my chili."

"Helpful as always." Kimberly placed her hand in mine. "Come on. Let's go to Scotland."

She dropped a pinch of pixie dust, and we disappeared into the ether. We reappeared in front of an old house. A purple orb pulsated around it, the energy rippling across its surface. After a few moments, the shimmer dimmed and then disappeared, leaving nothing but a nondescript house in its wake.

"Whatever you do, don't stop walking forward, no matter how much it hurts."

"What do you—"

But before I could finish, Kimberly dropped my hand and pushed through the forcefield. She drove her legs forward, and, after a few seconds, popped out on the other side. She turned and waved me forward.

I took a deep breath and drove my legs toward the bubble. As my flesh connected with it, every inch of my exposed skin began to tingle, crackle, and pinch, like a thousand little razor blades nicking my body. I followed Kimberly's advice and didn't stop churning my legs until I left the other side, where I lurched forward as if I had just leaped through a bowl of hummus.

"What was that?" I asked as Kimberly made her way to the door.

"It's the barrier, protecting The Bar from being found by people that shouldn't know about it."

"What's The Bar?"

Kimberly pushed open the door of the house. Inside were rows and rows of long, wooden benches. Demons and angels sat together, drinking pints of ale, laughing, and singing. In the back, a redhead, bearded mountain of a man stood behind a long, oak bar pouring drinks.

"It's a safe zone where demons and angels can drink together without killing each other. It's very popular with waylaid monsters from both sides of the divide, especially Charlie."

"Who's Charlie?"

"A demon who knows way too much about way too much. He's also a complete scuzzbucket. Do not trust him."

She pushed through the demons and imps sitting on either side of an aisle, and I followed behind, careful to avoid the splashing beer from the drunken beings sloshing their pints around. An imp slammed his head back into me and poked through my shirt with his horn, leaving a gash in my side.

"Sorry, love!" he screamed. "Want me to kiss it better?"

The demons and angels around him broke out in uproarious laughter. I kept moving forward, ignoring the blood trickling down my side until I stood with Kimberly near the bar.

"Let me see," Kimberly said. When I showed her the gash, she reached into her pocket and pulled out a pinch of pixie dust. She rubbed it on the gash, and it suctioned closed. "There you go."

"Wow," I replied, feeling my smooth skin. "That stuff is magic."

"Literally." She made her way up to the bar and held up her hand until the strapping bartender acknowledged her. "Have you seen Charlie?"

He shook his head. "Skipped out on his tab a while ago, and I told him not to come back 'til he can pay in full. Haven't seen him since. Why? What did he do now?"

"Nothing, at least not to me," Kimberly replied. "We're looking for information on Rosalie Louey's papers."

The gregarious bar got so quiet that you could hear a pin drop as the laughter died down and all eyes focused on Kimberly.

The bartender looked around and then back at us. "If I knew where the papers were, don't you think I would have used it by now to stop my grandfather from opening this place?"

She smiled and winked. "Just kidding, fellas! Next round's on the house!"

Cries of "Huzzah!" and uproarious laughter filled the room. The bartender went to pouring glasses, and a half dozen waitresses pushed through to deliver them to the tables. When he was done, he gestured me to the edge of the bar. "You need to go. Now, before you start trouble."

"Whatever you say."

Kimberly and I were heading toward the door when I felt a yank on my arm. I turned to see a dark-skinned, freckled waitress leaning toward me. She whispered into my ear. "Meet me out back."

I nodded, and she let me go. Kimberly and I walked outside, and I told her what had happened. We made our way to the back of the house, where the woman was waiting.

The waitress fumbled a pack of cigarettes in her hand. "I'm going to tell you this, Kimberly, but only because I don't like what would happen if these demons figured out how to find the Time Being. Charlie has nothing to do with it for once. I know who has it."

"How?" I asked.

The woman lit a cigarette. "Loose lips reveal a lot of things that should be kept hidden, and one of the things that I know is this—demons didn't steal it from Edington. An angel did."

"Who?" I asked.

"My boyfr—now he's my ex-boyfriend, Baraphel."

"Why would he steal it?" Kimberly asked.

She looked around her and then leaned forward, whispering harshly. "There's a group of angels that don't like the way God is handling this situation in Hell, and some of them have taken it into their own hands to try and fix the problem themselves."

"Are you saying there's a coup forming against God?"

"I don't know about all that," the waitress said. "But Baraphel sure hates God something fierce. I've never heard of an angel talking that way about the creator. That's something usually reserved for demons." She scribbled something on the pad of paper she used for taking orders and handed it to me. "This is where he lives. You have to be quick. I think he's close to figuring something out, and if he does…well, I don't know exactly what would happen, but it would be bad."

I took the sheet of paper. "Thank you. Seriously. What's your name?"

"Siobhan. And don't thank me. This is all screwed, and I dragged you into it."

"We're used to it by now, Siobhan," Kimberly said with a wink. "Now, get back before they notice you've been missing."

CHAPTER 41

The angel Baraphel lived in a crummy, walkup, third-floor apartment less than a mile away from The Bar. It was not becoming for an angel to live in such filth. I always assumed they would be pure, chaste, and definitely not slumming it with cocktail waitresses in a small town in Scotland.

Kimberly and I scouted the place for two days from an abandoned building across the street. Baraphel never seemed to leave, except to go to The Bar every night. Otherwise, he was hunched over a writing desk in his bedroom, poring over notes on his drawing table. He closed the windows when he was gone, so we couldn't get a good look at what he was writing, but it was a good bet that it was something to do with Rosalie's papers.

We made an ally in Siobhan, and she agreed to keep Baraphel busy at The Bar on the third night of our stakeout so we could break into the house and steal the papers. If he found out she was helping us, she would be in big trouble—the kind where someone wound up dead.

I wasn't much of a sneak, but luckily Kimberly was thief enough for the both of us. My job was to watch the street for Baraphel while she flashed in and flashed out with the papers. The whole thing would take less than five minutes. In, out, and on with our lives.

Kimberly spent the majority of that third day studying the room so she could blink in and out without being lost in the ether. While she worked, I dozed. I forgot how long it had been since I slept, and I needed it badly, even if it was on a floor filled with rotted wood and mouse droppings. I could have slept anywhere.

I didn't get up until Kimberly smacked my leg awake after the sun went down. "It's time. He's leaving."

I shot up and rubbed my eyes. They came back into focus just in time to see the lights turn off in the apartment. We waited for half an hour until we were sure that Baraphel had time to get to The Bar, sit down, and order his first pint.

"All right," Kimberly said. "I'm going."

"Good luck."

She threw a pinch of pixie dust on the ground and disappeared in a flash. A moment later, she reappeared in Baraphel's bedroom. She flipped on the light and began to rummage through things. I saw her jump up and down when she reached the writing table. She pulled a bunch of papers off the table and held them out toward me, holding out her thumbs.

As she looked at me, there was a blue flash into the room. Baraphel appeared behind her, and her face dropped. She didn't have time to react before the angel was on top of her. My eyes went wide in fear, and I lunged for the door. I was halfway across the street when a crash from above sent papers raining down on me along with bits of glass. Kimberly screamed as I rushed up the stairs.

"*Rigéscunt indutae!*" I yelled, and ice shot out of my hand, freezing the doorknob. I kicked it loose and smashed my way into the room.

"What are you doing here?" Baraphel hollered from the other room. "Are you working with those demons?"

"I'm no—" I ran toward the shouts and found Baraphel holding Kimberly in a headlock. She was running out of air, and her face was turning blue. "LIZZIE! RUN!" She barely got the words out through her choking.

"Glacies spica!"

An ice spike shot out from my hands and embedded in the angel's shoulder. He screamed and loosened his grip on Kimberly's throat. Her arms wriggled free and landed on her daggers. She pulled one out and stabbed it into Baraphel's side. The angel screamed again, and his grip loosened even more. Kimberly drove her other dagger into his chest. Blue blood oozed out onto the floor.

The blood loss caused the angel to crumble. Kimberly broke free and turned to him, stabbing him two more times in the chest before kicking him backward through the door, where he flipped over the railing and fell to the ground with a thud, splattering blue blood all over the asphalt.

"What have we done?" I said, leaning out to study the dead body of an angel. "I didn't know they could die."

"Demons are just corrupted angels. If you can kill one, you can kill the other." Kimberly looked down at the daggers. "Thank the gods that's true."

"We just killed an angel. God is going to be so pissed."

"We killed a scheming angel trying to go behind God's back. We're heroes." She said it with such confidence that I almost believed her. "Now come on, before somebody gets wind of this. We have to get all these pages out of here."

I was in shock. "I can't believe I killed an ang—"

"Hey!" Kimberly said, smacking me in the arm. "If we find the Time Being, you can go back, and it will be like none of this ever happened, remember?"

I hesitated. "Right, okay. You're right. You're right." And in that moment, I wanted so desperately for that to be true.

CHAPTER 42

294651 – 37 6 19 1.

Those were the numbers that Rosalie yelled at me before I disappeared from Hell. I hoped the notes from her diary would shine some light. Maybe they were gibberish, but she screamed them so emphatically that I couldn't shake the feeling they meant something.

Unfortunately, in scanning through her papers, the numbers still made no sense. None of it made any sense. It was all a bunch of scribbled drawings and numbers. Notes in different handwriting in the margins showed that more than one person had tried to decipher the letters, and often one set of handwriting scratched out the previous one.

Kimberly and I made copies of all the pages before bringing them back to Clifton Edington's manor. Kimberly had taken a long time studying the front of the mansion before we teleported away the last time so that we could appear again without taking a detour through the monuments of D.C.

We left the scanned pages with Molly to look over while we headed back to meet with Clifton. Before we could even knock on the door, the butler opened it from inside. The flash of pink and purple light must have signaled our arrival.

"The master is expecting you," he mumbled as he slid aside so we could enter. Although it hadn't been long since we were there last, the entirety of his house had changed. The marble floor and Greek statues had been replaced by black tile and Gothic statues of twisted demons that looked down at us with sneering hatred. Banners hung from the ceiling, the color of burgundy, and their movement mimicked blood trickling down the shadowy, pocked walls that seemed to undulate and ooze with every step we took.

The floor of the hallway squished under my shoes like a tongue pushing us further down an unseen throat. Gone were the red doors to the study, replaced by ones of bone and sinew. The butler dipped inside the room, and a shiver went down my back.

"What the—this is disgusting?" I whispered to Kimberly.

"Either this is an illusion to make us uncomfortable, or we are seeing the truth of this place. Whatever the reality, he's doing it to take us off our game and get into our heads. Nothing has changed since our last encounter. Project strength, no matter how you feel in your gut."

"That's probably good advice for any occasion."

"Words I live by, to be sure, but particularly apt in this moment."

The door to the study opened, and the butler gestured us inside. The room hadn't changed since our last meeting with Clifton, and I was thankful for that, but when my eyes met his, I stared into the black eyes of a demon. He who had foregone the formality of taking human form and instead sat on his leather chair with all the confidence of a demon lord, swirling a snifter of blood and viscera rather than brandy.

"Did you really kill an angel?" Clifton asked. His voice was deep and moist, and his words popped in my ears.

"We did what we had to do to get these," Kimberly held out the papers, and Clifton gestured for her to put them on a wooden table next to him. "We made copies, so we don't need your help anymore."

"Lovely," he said. "Then I suppose our business is concluded."

"Which handwriting is yours?" I asked.

He looked down at the paper. "The one scrawled in blood, of course."

I nodded. That was the third set, it seemed, after Rosalie and Tina, and before Baraphel's blue pen. "It seems like the angel thought you were wrong about a lot of your assumptions."

"He would." Clifton shrugged, taking a sip from his snifter. The thick blood coated the glass as he brought it to his lips. "He's only an angel, after all."

"And you are only a demon," I said. "How are you any better?"

He chuckled. "My dear, even to ask that question shows how utterly naïve you are. You should beg for us to rule over you. Should you be so lucky, I will be sure to make you my concubine."

"Hard pass," I said. "Did you find anything interesting on these pages? Or do we really have to dissect this all ourselves?"

"What fun would it be if I gave you the answers?"

"This isn't fun for us," Kimberly growled.

Clifton laughed. "Please, dear. You live for the hunt. Do not disrespect me with your lies. The thrill of the chase is the only fun you ever have." Clifton grinned, showing his spiked teeth. "And I include your bitch wife in that equation. There is nothing you love more than the chase, including her."

"I'll kill you!" Kimberly pulled the knife from her belt, and I caught her hand before she could slice Clifton in half. "Let me go!"

"I will," I said, with a meaningful look at Clifton, "if you don't tell me what you know. She's itching to kill a demon."

He scoffed. "I don't find your threats credible. But for the sake of decorum, fine. I'll tell you something, just one thing, and then you will leave."

I nodded to Kimberly, who dropped her dagger, and I let her go. "Deal."

"You may ask me one question."

I didn't want to tip them off about what I knew—about what Rosalie had said, but I needed a head start without studying a thousand pages of gibberish.

"294651 – 37 6 19 1," I said. "Do they mean anything to you?"

He scoffed. "You really haven't read the book, have you?" He didn't wait for an answer before he finished. "They are the celestial coordinates of the Time Being's lair. Of course, they are worthless now, as her palace never stays in one place for too long."

"Thank you," I replied.

"You're welcome," he growled. "Now, I believe it's time for you to go."

Clifton snapped his fingers, and we popped out of existence only to reappear on the front lawn of the property.

"I really, really hate demons."

Kimberly nodded. "Hard same. Sometimes, they are a means to an end, though. At least we got the papers out of it. Now, come on. Let's go find a telescope."

CHAPTER 43

"Clifton is an idiot," Molly said definitively.

"Okay," Kimberly said. "Care to elaborate on that?"

"Those numbers can't be celestial coordinates because that's not how you write celestial coordinates, at least not on Earth. Here we write celestial coordinates in terms of right ascension and declination." Molly shook her head. "I mean, do you think these demons have ever used a telescope before?"

She scoffed and then snorted before looking at us for agreement, but there were only blank stares from both Kimberly and me.

"I have no idea what you just said."

"Me either," Kimberly replied.

"Of course you don't." Molly sighed and scratched her head for a second. "Okay, so let's take the North star." She pulled out a piece of paper and wrote *right ascension 2h 41m 39s, declination + 89 degrees 15' 51*. "That's the celestial coordinates for Polaris. Do you understand now?"

I shook my head. "Absolutely not."

"I think I'm more lost than before," Kimberly added.

"Let's try this another way," Molly said in a huff. "Can you at least see that this"—she pointed to the coordinates before writing *294651 – 37 6 19 1* and pointing to it—"looks nothing like this?"

"Oh." My voice perked. "Yes. I can see how those two numbers are nothing alike."

"Thank Christ," Molly said. "And since these numbers are nothing alike, it means somebody mixed something up in translation." She spun back around to the scanned pages on her computer screen. "Which makes sense because Baraphel crossed out almost everything that both of the other translators wrote and started from scratch. He must have known they had gotten something or, more likely, everything wrong."

"Everything wrong?" I said. "But how could Tina get everything wrong? She wrote a book about it."

"Okay, maybe she didn't get everything wrong, but she definitely got a lot wrong." Molly clicked through the pages until landing on one of particular interest. "See, right here, the code is different than earlier in the book. If I had to guess, she was trying to throw people off the truth, and since it was all a mish-mash of numbers, nobody noticed." She twirled around again. "Then, when the demons stole the papers, they just assumed Tina was right all along."

"That would make sense," Kimberly growled. "They're sloppy and lazy and would look for any shortcut they could get."

"It's good news for us that we found this when we did because angels are not so sloppy." She leaned toward the computer, studying the screen. "It looks like he found a cipher in the document that was more complex than the simple letter replacement both Tina and the demons were using."

"So, do the numbers mean anything in this new cipher?" I asked.

Molly shrugged. "He was still working at it." She clicked her tongue. "I'll bet that with a few more days, he would have figured it out, though. He was clearly very smart."

"Lovely," Kimberly said. "What can you figure out from his work?"

Molly stood up and stretched. "Well, he translated a story about how Rosalie finally got to see the Time Being. Apparently, after finding the coordinates, she stared up at the sky and uttered a prayer. A bright light shot down from the Heavens, and a handmaiden came down to guide her to the Time Being." She tapped her pen on the desk. "Something is bothering me, though."

Kimberly gestured for her to continue.

"That's just not how telescopes work. Looking at something doesn't summon anything as far as I've ever heard, even if you do mutter a prayer while you do it. For that to be true, it would mean that handmaidens are staring out into the cosmos, waiting for somebody to find them in an infinite sky, and I have to believe even a god is not vain enough for that." She paused, seeming to gather her thoughts. "No, I think the numbers she shouted at you are not coordinates at all, but something else."

"What?" I asked.

"I think she found ingredients to summon the handmaiden, not coordinates."

"Ingredients?"

"Like, for a spell?" Kimberly asked, puzzled.

Molly clapped her hands together. "Exactly! For a spell, a summoning spell."

Kimberly smiled excitedly. "That's brilliant!"

"Oh, I know." She stopped to bask in the compliment before continuing. "If I graph these onto a periodic table, then 29 is the atomic number for copper; that makes sense. Palladium is 46. No, that can't be right. Maybe if I split the numbers up. Beryllium is 4, and carbon is 6. Yes, that's probably more accurate. That would leave 51, which is Antimony. All right. Now let's move on to the next set. …rubidium is 37—no, lithium and nitrogen make more sense, yes yes." She muttered to herself under her breath. "Next is—well, it can't be promethium, can it? That's 61, but it's very rare. Very, very rare. If it's not that, it would have to be…fluorine and hydrogen, and hydrogen is in most things. No, I don't like this at all. It's far too complex."

"I agree." I scratched my head. "You just said a lot of words that I don't understand."

"If we combine the right ingredients, I think it could be a formula for contacting the Time Being. Promethium is an incredibly rare element that's not found on Earth except as a byproduct of nuclear fission. If I were trying to make it hard for people to find me, then I would certainly add something like that to a compound." Molly paused and then frowned. "However, I don't know how we would get any without becoming international terrorists." She tapped her finger on the desk. "Something is upsetting to me. This dash—it's in the text of the book and the papers. Seems everyone just thought it was for emphasis, but I've found that nothing Rosalie wrote was just for emphasis. What if we treat it like a minus sign?"

"You've lost me again," I said.

"And you never had me to begin with," Kimberly said, then whispered to me, "Just let her work, hon. Let's get some food. She won't even know we're gone."

The promise of food overwhelmed my growling stomach, and I followed Kimberly to the kitchen. She pulled out some ham and turkey from the fridge and then went about cutting some lettuce and tomatoes.

"Turkey or ham?" she asked, laying out slices of rye bread on two yellow plates and slathering mustard on one side and mayo on the other.

"Why not both?"

She smiled. "A woman after my own heart."

"Dad always said that."

"I know."

I watched her assemble the sandwiches. "He wasn't right, you know?"

"Who?"

"The demon. I know you well enough to know there's nothing you love more than Molly."

"You barely just met her," Kimberly said, licking mustard off her thumb. "That should tell you something. You knew I was a monster hunter a decade before you knew about my girlfriend."

"But I only had to see you together for a second to know that you love that woman more than anything." I took a deep breath. "That demon was a big jerk."

"You don't have to tell me that," she said, cutting the sandwiches in half. "If you want to know the truth, I'm not sure he's wrong. I feel like I'm constantly called to help these people, and I can't resist, you know. It's like an addiction."

"Well, you don't have to convince me you're addicted to it, but you can be addicted to something and not love it."

She handed me one of the sandwiches on a plate. "True."

"You clearly love Molly more than anything, and that's the important part." I took a bite of the sandwich, and my taste buds sang. "Wow, this is really good."

"I know." She shrugged. "I don't have many skills, but I make a mean sandwich."

"EUREKA!" Molly screamed from the other room. She rushed into the kitchen. "Okay, this is too perfect to be a coincidence."

I took another bite of the sandwich and spoke with my mouth full. "What is?"

"I ran several equations and found that if you subtract certain numbers from each other, you're left with 7154."

"And how is that perfect?" Kimberly asked.

"Don't you see? What is 7 in Rosalie's code? Don't answer that? It's G. Then, 15 is an O, and 4 is D…and what does that spell? God. I'll bet this is it. If this really is a formula, then we just have to cross-reference that with the periodic table of elements." She pulled up another screen on her computer and stared at the periodic table of elements for a moment. "We need beryllium, phosphorus, and nitrogen. Simple and elegant."

"A little too simple," I said. "Don't you think?"

"No," Molly said. "I think it's an elegant and simple formula that anyone in the universe could find if they knew where to look. The exact kind of formula an immortal being would divine to contact them."

"How sure are you about this?" Kimberly asked.

"It's better than breaking into a nuclear facility. And if I'm wrong, we can try the complicated formula next. What do you think?"

I nodded. "Let's do it."

CHAPTER 44

Kimberly left Molly to discern how much of each element to use and the conjuring incantation necessary to summon the Time Being's handmaiden. Now that she had some semblance of a codex, she went to work figuring out how to decipher the rest of the text and get what we needed.

Meanwhile, Kimberly and I were on grunt duty, finding and hauling all the ingredients for the spell. The first required a drive out of the city. Phosphorous was a common ingredient in fertilizer. However, they were only 50–60 percent pure, which meant we needed to go to an actual fertilizer manufacturing plant to track down the pure stuff. Since white and yellow phosphorous were toxic and unpleasant, we hoped that the red phosphorus the factory used would be enough to summon the handmaiden.

There was one not far outside of San Francisco. People didn't often think of California as a highly agricultural state, but it produced almost all the almonds in the country, along with a bunch of other staple crops in its millions of acres of farmland. Heck, even wine is just high-class grape farming.

Cluster's Farm Feed was located ninety minutes north of the city, and it was easier just to drive than to have Kimberly flash us to the factory, as the only places she could fast travel to in Sonoma County were wineries.

A young woman with a curly bob and a bright smile met us at the reception desk. "Good morning. You must be Kimberly and Elizabeth," she said. "I'm Olivia. I hear you're interested in investing in our operation." She spun on her bright red heels toward a glass door leading into the manufacturing plant. "I'm here to answer any questions you might have."

"We're mostly just interested in seeing the operation for ourselves. As you see from my portfolio, my assets are vast and varied, but I like to have an intimate understanding of how everything works when I'm investing in a company."

"Follow me," Olivia said, pushing open the door. "This is our factory floor. We process ten percent of all the fertilizer used by corporate-owned farms in Sonoma County, and we have doubled every year since we started five years ago. We hope to expand to a new facility soon—investment willing, of course."

"Of course," Kimberly said. She had worn a blue power suit for the occasion and forced me into a scratchy pink skirt and jacket combo. I was supposed to take notes. "Did you get that, Elizabeth?"

I drew a penis on the paper. "Yup, I got it. Very impressive." I put my pen behind my ear. "If you don't mind, I'm just going to review your safety on the floor while you talk business. Safety is our number one concern."

"Umm…okay…"

"It's okay," Kimberly said. "She is very thorough. Perhaps we can continue, and you can tell me all about the machinery you are using to mix the fertilizer." She wrinkled her nose. "Does it always smell so bad here?"

Olivia offered an apologetic smile. "Always, unfortunately. That's the one downside."

I wandered away from them, toward a man in a red hardhat looking out over an assembly line where workers checked the bags of fertilizer for approval. "It smells awful in here. How do you stand it?"

The veins on his thick neck throbbed as he laughed. "You get used to it after a while."

"It smells like a dog took a dump inside my shoe, and then I wore it around for a week."

"It's a living, little lady. Not all of us can be...whatever you are." He looked me over briefly. "How can I help you?"

I pointed back to Kimberly and Olivia. "I'm here as a special guest of Miss Olivia. I'm trying to get a sense of your operation. Can I ask you a question?"

The foreman looked back to see Olivia wave at him. "Sure, I guess."

I flipped open my notebook. "Okay, so when we buy fertilizer at the store, you have mixed phosphorous into it, correct?"

"Often, yeah."

"But when I go to buy phosphorous from the store, even pure phosphorous, it's only 60 percent phosphorous. I understand you use 100 percent red phosphorous for your operation, one of the few in the country that does. Is that correct?"

He nodded. "It's true. More expensive for sure, but worth it for the plants, you know? We run a quality operation here."

"Of course. And where is the phosphorous added to the mixture?"

He pointed halfway down the assembly line, where a big metal monstrosity churned, mixing the raw fertilizer with a red powder. "Right over there. Why?"

"No reason," I replied. "I'm going to continue looking around if you don't mind."

He shrugged. "Do what you gotta do. Just don't touch anything."

Sorry, but that would be quite impossible, Mr. Man. I passed a half dozen workers moving between stations, bringing bags from one place to another. Reaching into my pocket, I pulled out a plastic bag. Next to the machine, a small concrete mixer took several different powders from funnels around its base and mixed them together. They were labeled with different letters, and one of them, containing a red powder, had a "P" outside of it, with "phosphorous" written in tape under it. Luckily, enough of the red mixture had dropped onto the floor that I could just kneel down and scoop it up into my bag without causing a fuss. When I was done, I looked down at the half-full bag. I hoped it would be enough.

I met up with the others and nodded my head to Kimberly. "Safety looks tip-top. I mean, I wasn't wearing a mask, goggles, or a hard hat, but everyone else was, so that's good. We'll work on your guest protocol if your financial projections work out."

Kimberly smiled. "If Elizabeth is happy, then I suppose those are all the questions I have right now. This was just a preliminary walkthrough, and things are looking very good. If you can shoot over the financials, I'll have my lawyers look them over. If it all checks out, I'm very excited to be in business with you."

They shook hands, and we left. On the way back to the car, Kimberly chuckled under her breath. "Never thought I would be investing in the fertilizer business."

"Wait, you're really investing with them?"

"Of course, if the numbers check out. Their five-year growth plan is aggressive, and I like it. It's important to be diversified, Lizzie."

I kept the bag of phosphorus far away from me in the car. Even though it wasn't supposed to be toxic, the fact that its sisters and brothers were didn't fill me with great confidence. On the way back to the city, Kimberly stopped at a custom auto repair shop. A young man walked out with a canister and handed it to her. Kimberly reached into the inside pocket of her jacket and pulled out a wad of money.

"Be careful with this stuff," the man said, pocketing the money.

Kimberly handed the canister to me. "We know how to handle liquid nitrogen. Thank you."

The man pulled his hand out of his pocket, holding a brittle piece of metal wrapped in a thick blanket. "I don't know what you're going to do with this stuff, but we found that other thing you wanted."

"What do I owe you?"

He shook his head. "You're doing us a favor getting it off our hands. It's just been sitting around for a couple of years. Be careful, it's murder on the skin."

We were quiet on the way back to Kimberly's place. Kimberly was usually contemplative, but I was quiet mostly because I was holding two items that I considered very dangerous, and also because the weight of what we were about to do laid heavy on my head.

By the time we got back, it was night. Molly had dimmed the lights on the balcony and set up a small summoning circle outside with a black cauldron at its center. She kissed Kimberly when we arrived and took the elements from my hands.

"I hope you have good news," Kimberly said.

"As good as news can be in this situation. I believe I've figured out the formula and the incantation."

"That's the best we can hope for," I said.

She pointed me to a small square drawn outside the circle. "Sit there." She indicated another one equidistant between us. "And you there, honey." When we were seated, she placed the ingredients down. "Okay, so once I place these all inside the cauldron, we have to chant '*virginem Talinda nos coget vos fundata est. Veni nobis et ne nos inducas in deam vestram.*"

Kimberly's eyes widened. "Do you have that written down somewhere? I'm never going to remember that."

"Give me a second." She ran back into the house. About five minutes later, she returned with the words written on a big piece of paper and placed it between the two of us. "Just reference that. Ready?"

"No," I said.

"It'll be fine," Molly smiled, her cadence almost giving me a shred of confidence. "You're going to do great."

She sat down in her square and used a tablespoon to scoop some red phosphorous into the caldron. Then, she took the beryllium and broke it in half. She took one of the pieces and continued to break it into smaller and smaller chunks until it was a coarse powder and shook it into the cauldron. Finally, she opened the canister of liquid nitrogen. Smoke plumed into the air, and as she poured it in, the contents of the cauldron began to pop and crackle.

When she was finished, she replaced the cap and grabbed our hands. "Now, recite."

"*Virginem Talinda nos coget vos fundata est. Veni nobis et ne nos inducas in deam vestram.*" I said. The second time, Kimberly joined in. "*Virginem Talinda nos coget vos fundata est. Veni nobis et ne nos inducas in deam vestram.*" We were slow, stumbling at first, but the third time we were more confident. "*Virginem Talinda nos coget vos fundata est. Veni nobis et ne nos inducas in deam vestram.*"

After the fourth repetition, there was a crack in the air, and a white light shot into the sky. For a moment, there was no movement, and then, a glowing white leg stepped from the light, followed by an arm, and finally a head. Long, ivory hair cascaded down the light being's shoulders.

The being floated in front of us and turned, extending its arms. It spoke in five voices at once, each layering in a different octave.

"I am a handmaiden of the goddess Talinda. Who has summoned me?"

I swallowed hard, then raised my hand. We had done it, and now…I had to live with the consequences, good or bad…for the time being.

BOOK 3

CHAPTER 45

An ethereal, glowing white being floated before us on the balcony of Kimberly and Molly's apartment, casting a glittering light. "Who calls upon the goddess Talinda?" the being spoke.

I raised my shaking hand and gave the creature a trembling smile. "Me. I do, ma'am."

"What is your name, child?" The thing's voice sang in harmony with itself.

"Lizzie, ma'am," I squeaked, as deferential as possible.

"Are you friend or foe to the flow of time, little one?"

"I believe I am a friend."

The glowing white being nodded. "Yes, I think so, too. Very well." She held her hand out to me. "If you wish to see my lady, I will lead you to her. If your heart is pure, she will grant your wish."

"And if it's not?" I said, finally regaining control of my tongue.

"Time is cruel, as is my mistress, at least to those who wish to do her harm. If your heart is indeed pure, you need not worry."

I looked over at Kimberly and Molly, and I realized then that they hadn't moved, not one iota since I raised my hand. Even the smoke that rose from the cauldron paused its danced through the air. Only the handmaiden, the light glimmering from the portal, and I were able to move.

I pushed myself to stand. "What will happen to them?"

"Everything will be fine. Once we are gone, they will continue as if none of this happened. There will be confusion, of course, but they will understand soon enough…and if your wish is granted, then it will be like this never happened."

"Yes," I replied, a hint of sorrow in my voice. "I've been told that before. Will I remember this moment if your lady grants my wish, even if they don't?"

"It will not matter, that much I can say for certain. Now, come."

I placed my hand into the maiden's hand. Her fingers clasped around mine, and she pulled me toward the light. As we neared the edge of the portal, she stood to one side, letting me go in front of her. "Take a breath, and walk forward, like you were strolling through a meadow. Let the light wash over you."

I took a deep breath and let it out. I let my left foot forward, cautiously, and it disappeared into the light. There was none of the harsh tug like when I disappeared with Kimberly. Simply the warmth of a warm summer day flooding over me as I disappeared, effortless and gentle.

As the final bit of me fell into the shimmering abyss, my life flashed before my eyes, slowly at first but gaining speed as it played out. The doctor at the hospital stared down at me, and I opened my eyes as they placed me in my mother's arms.

My birth mother was beautiful, even after the sweat and pain of childbirth. The vision lurched forward to my firsts: first steps, the first use of my powers, the first time I was introduced to Junebug and Carl—the first time in a long time I felt like I was home. From there, I saw myself getting my own room, meeting Anjelica, and hearing the prophecy. Then it was my life on the run, town to town trying to avoid my fate, running and running, a thousand towns flashed by, faster and faster until they were on top of each other—and then, home again. The death of my mother, the attack that took my father. Things went faster and faster until everything went white, and I realized I hadn't moved for a long while, enraptured by the visions in front of me.

I took a step forward, and the white light parted, revealing a green pasture under me and a red sun that fell over a blue barn. The white light dissipated until it formed into a huge, white, shimmering castle in the middle distance.

"Welcome," a voice said from behind me.

I turned to see an olive-skinned girl with long, black hair. Her outline was reminiscent of the vision from the roof, but she was far from a being of pure light. Her green eyes danced with the spark of creation in them.

"Who are you?" I asked.

"Viannah," she replied. "I'm sorry I had to use so much pageantry, but it is the theater my lady demands."

"That was you?" I said. "But…your voice…the light. You are so different than I imagined."

Though she no longer spoke in five octaves, her voice was just as lyrical. "What would the gods be without their theatrics? Now come, we have a long walk ahead of us if we are to reach the castle by sundown."

Her toga swished as she moved, which was the only way I knew she had feet under them. Otherwise, she still looked like she floated above the ground, gliding across the grass like a gazelle.

"Where are we?" I asked.

"We call it Tempus," she replied. "It is the planet my lady calls home and has for millions of years."

"And this planet moves with your lady?"

"Oh, the silly stories you mortals tell. The planet doesn't move, time moves around it, and with time, the galaxies, the planets, the entire cosmos rotates. Since we are not in the center of the universe, it seems like we move, but we are stationary, as it has been since her mother laid her here at the dawn of creation."

"Her mother?"

"Ananke, the great goddess of fate, first of her name. First of any name."

In an instant, the light dimmed over the horizon, and we were standing at a road not far from the shimmering castle. It was as if we had moved miles in a single step.

"How did we move so far so fast?"

"I simply pulled a loose thread closer to me and stepped onto it."

The castle was just beyond the dirt road we'd reached, and in another moment, we were standing within its courtyard. A hundred spires formed an enclosed circle around thatches of trees and bushes, and each bent toward the brightest white light centered in the starry sky above. The castle glittered in the moonlight, though the sun had been shining moments before when we began our journey.

Viannah pointed to a white marble bench in front of an ivory door. "Please take a seat, and I will check on my lady. It will only take a moment, for you at least."

CHAPTER 46

Viannah pulled the door open, and literally one second after it snapped closed, the door swung open again, and she smiled at me. Her dress was now purple, and her hair was up in braided buns on either side of her face, with a wreath of holly on top of her head.

"Come in," she said. "I'm sorry it took so long."

I followed her inside, passing through a stone hallway into an enormous antechamber. A thousand—no, tens of thousands—white silk threads hung taut across the room, zig-zagging across in every direction like it was home to an enormous spider. Entwined with them were thin strands of red thread.

"What's with the red threads?" I asked.

"Anomalies that must be dealt with, gods striking bargains they do not understand, demons fiddling with the laws of time for their own gain, maidens who—" she stopped. "Perhaps it is best for Talinda to tell you herself. She is wise beyond measure, and I am just a servant."

"You shouldn't talk about yourself that way. I'm sure you're every bit as important as her."

Viannah smiled. "That's kind of you to say, but wrong. Talinda holds the future and the past on her shoulders while I simply attend to her needs." We reached a large copper door. Dozens of threads weaved into a grate above us and the room beyond. Viannah pushed open the door and held it open for me. "This is where I leave you. As per my mistress's wish, I will be waiting for you upon the conclusion of your meeting."

I stepped through the doorway, expecting a grand throne room. What I found instead was a single loom on either side of a wooden spindle. Four women worked each loom, pulling thread as it fell from the top of the room. They weaved the white thread into the loom with no problem, but when they saw a red thread, they pointed up to it.

"Another one, mistress," a soft voice spoke.

A haggard woman rose from the wooden spindle in the middle of the room. For as perfect as the other maidens in the room were, clear of skin and smooth of face, she was the opposite. Every inch of her was covered in deeply grooved wrinkles, and her eyes sagged with the sadness of age. She walked with a hunch that caused her to hang over a cane as she stumbled forward.

"Again? Will it never end?" As the red thread fell to the loom, Talinda touched it with her hand and blinked out of existence. She returned a moment later, and the red thread turned white in her fingers. The loom accepted it. "There."

"Thank you, mistress," a baby-faced maiden curtsied, and then her big, brown eyes caught mine. "I think you have a visitor."

Talinda grunted and turned to me. "Ah, there you are. Right on time." She hobbled toward me. "So, what do you think of your Time Being, then?"

I stumbled over my words. "Uh—ah—umm…"

She held up a bony hand. "It's okay. I know what the gods say about me, and I know why you are here and that you mean no malice. Who, after all, do you think put that book on Molly's pile so long ago?"

"You?" I asked.

She shook her head. "Well, not me exactly, but also not, not me." She sighed. "Let me start again. You see, I have a problem, a dreadful one, that I can't seem to fix by myself, even with all my gifts. I'm afraid I need your help, which is why I arranged for you to find me."

I still couldn't believe she had been expecting me. "You need my help? Why me?"

"Do you believe in fate, child?"

I shrugged. "I don't know. Everything I hear about destiny seems to contradict itself, but it's hard not to believe in it, after all I've seen."

Talinda sucked her teeth for a moment, and her face twisted, like she had no interest in saying the next part but couldn't avoid doing so, either. "I can tell you destiny is real, and it was your fate to come here, at this precise moment, to do your part in saving the universe. You fought against it with every bone in your body, which is admirable, but this fate was too strong for you to avoid. I know. I spun the thread of it myself."

"Why?" I asked, rage boiling in my stomach. "Why would you do that to me?"

"It's not easy to—" She looked up at the red strings above her. "Do you see those hideous, abominable, red threads?"

"I do. They're not that hide—"

"The bane of my existence." She bit her lip. "They are anomalies in the timestream, cancerous, malevolent things that cannot be allowed to be woven into the tapestry of the universe."

"Viannah told me that they were from people messing with time."

"Exactly," Talinda said. "Not just people, but gods and monsters, too. Time is meant to flow in one direction. Once something happens, it has to happen that way, for all time. For better or worse, everything in existence only happens one time. It is an incontrovertible rule of the universe. Of course, sentience breeds arrogance, and beings of all types are all too eager to rail against that idea. It is why I am so detested because it is my job to maintain the status quo, as it were, so that the universe doesn't fall apart."

"It sounds like a hard and thankless job."

"It is. Whenever somebody disturbs that flow by changing something, good or bad, through magical means or technological ones—my job, above all, is to fix their arrogance, repair these threads, and keep the tapestry pristine. Most of the time, it's a minor nuisance to fix, but this time—" she stopped for a moment to gather herself. "This time, I cannot do it alone. I need you to help me stop the most menacing of these anomalies, one that has caused me consternation for many long years as I've watched the threads creep toward me, powerless to stop them."

"How can I stop something like that if you can't?" I asked. "I'm not a time witch. I'm not a god. I'm just a water nymph and not even a very good one."

"Unfortunately, I'm not sure how." She placed her fingers on a red string and jittered out of the universe, reappearing a moment later, and I watched as the red thread turned white. "A trillion possible timelines have flashed before my eyes, and they have confirmed a simple truth. I cannot stop this anomaly on my own. I have run every scenario possible, and each time we succeed, you…well, it turns out you are the only one who can save the universe from falling into chaos. It is a terrible burden."

"But I'm nobody!"

She shrugged. "Perhaps that is why only you can succeed, precisely because you are nobody."

It was an idiotic idea, but I still needed her help. She was still the only being in the universe who might be able to help me. "And if I do this for you, then you will send me back to save Veronica? To save my world?"

Talinda walked back to her spindle. "If you help me, I will give you a chance to save your world, yes, and the girl. In turn, you will have the honor of helping me save the universe."

"I don't care about that part at all. I don't like any of this, truth be told," I said to her. "I don't like being manipulated. I don't like having no choice in my own destiny."

"You always have a choice. It just might not be a good one." She beckoned me toward her as she hobbled around her spindle. "You can walk out that door, and Viannah will bring you back to Earth, but you will damn the universe in the process and abandon any hope of saving Veronica."

"Don't say her name," I growled. "Don't you ever say her name." I stepped forward. "Tell me, was she a part of this? Did you kill her to get to me? Because if you did—"

She held up her hand. "She was an unfortunate mistake. I promise, if you help me, I will allow you to rectify it, but only if you help me."

I didn't have a choice, no matter what Talinda or anyone else said. "Fine. I will help you. I will hate every minute of it, but I will help you."

"I can live with that." She smiled. "Come here then, my child." She reached under the spindle and pulled out a bracelet woven from red thread. "These are tiny pieces of the threads that have caused the trouble. Soon, they will all enter this room, ready for the loom, and I cannot stop them all. That job falls to you. If you can't prevent this by the time the threads reach us, then we will all be doomed." She leaned over her spindle toward me. "Hold out your hand."

"I don't get it." I did as I was asked and placed my hand out for her. "Can't you just stop time forever to figure out a good solution?"

She tied the silk bracelet of woven threads around my wrist. "If it were that easy, then we wouldn't need you."

"Fair enough, I guess," I replied. "Then can you at least tell me what it is that I'm doing exactly?"

Talinda eased herself down onto her stool. "A decade ago, by your measure of time at least, my greatest handmaiden abandoned us and began jumping through time, causing chaotic timeslips all over the universe. I need you to find her and get her to fix what she broke."

"And you really can't do it?"

She sighed. "She has shielded what she has done from me, somehow."

"I see," I replied. "Well, I'll do what I can. Don't know what I can do, but I'll give it a go."

"Lovely. But before we get to that, first things first. There is another matter we must attend to. Call it a training mission."

"Hit me with it," I said, relieved to be able to leave the castle again, even if it was on a stupid mission.

"You must go back to your world and burn the accursed papers that led you here so that nobody from your planet can find me again. When you've finished, one of the red threads on your wrist will turn white. Pull it, and you will end up back here."

"I can do that."

"I know you can. That's why you're here." Talinda snapped her fingers, and I disappeared, the taste of banana pudding on my lips.

CHAPTER 47

I reappeared in the darkness, jittering. I kicked my foot forward and found a bucket with a mop in it. I felt for a wall with my hands, and a light switch grazed across my hand. When I flipped the switch, I was surrounded by cleaning supplies.

Perfect. I'm in a supply closet.

The hint of banana pudding was gone from my lips, replaced with the tingly taste of metal like I'd touched my tongue to a 9-volt battery.

I turned the doorknob slowly and stepped out into an office building bustling with energy. Dozens of men and women in nice suits dotted the room, buried in phone calls. Several had removed their blazers and loosened their ties as they paced back and forth across their cubicles, faces on fire with blustering verve.

"Are you buying a thousand Cardin at $2.37 or not, Mister Zellin? It's now or never." One of the men shouted into the phone. "This is when you put your big boy pants on. Nobody ever retired to Fiji by playing it safe."

I had seen sleazy stock traders in movies, but I didn't think they actually spoke that way. Hearing it turned my already queasy stomach.

The man pumped his fist. "You're not going to regret this, buddy! Next time you're in New York, drinks are on you from all the money you'll be making from this deal. Let me connect you to my secretary." He pushed several buttons on his phone. "Tina, we have a live one."

He slammed the phone down and flailed his arms in excitement. His eyes found mine, and his mood tempered, likely from the angry, disgusted look I was giving him.

"Who are you?" he asked.

"Nobody," I said, turning toward the elevator.

"You're goddamn right. Remember that, bitch." He slammed his hands against his chest. Nobody else reacted as if it was the most normal thing in the world to say. "Nobody looks at me like that. Nobody. I'm the king around here!"

I balled up my fists, ready to fight. "Remind me never to visit your kingdom."

His face filled with rage, and he charged me. I wanted so badly to turn him to ice, but I doubted that would help fix the timeline. Still, when he put up his fists to meet mine, I had no choice but to lay him out on the floor with a left jab and right cross to the face. I was never much of a fighter, but you didn't make it ten years on the road without learning how to handle yourself.

There was an audible gasp as the jack-a-ninny hit the floor, and everybody rose to their feet. There, in the back of the room, hair just as wild as ever, was a much younger version of Tina, working the phones. She was considerably younger than when we first met, but it was unmistakably her trying to contain a giggle as she watched the proceedings.

Two burly security guards rushed toward me from either side of the room. I took one last look at the jerk, then at Tina, then at the guards screaming at me to stop. I panicked. The elevators dinged open, letting out two women in matching red dresses, and I rushed inside before security could follow.

When I got outside the building, I ran several blocks before I stopped to catch my breath in front of a newsstand, confident I was safe in the anonymity of the crowd. I assumed that Talinda had sent me back in time but didn't know exactly when I was until I picked up a paper. 1992.

In my original timeline, I had been on the run for a couple of years by '92. The time blurred together, but it was April, and if memory served, I was making my way across the Rust Belt—maybe Indiana or Ohio. I tried to make it that way in the spring once the snow had melted and before the heat of summer kicked into high gear.

This was clearly New York City, though. If it wasn't obvious from the *New York Times* that I held in my hand, all I had to do was crane my neck up at the mammoth buildings in every direction to know where I was, and the smell of piss and pizza only mixed like this in New York.

"You gonna buy that?" the newsstand vendor growled.

I shook my head and placed the paper back down. "Sorry."

"Frigging tourist," he snarled as I walked away. "Typical."

The good news about New York City was that it had a short memory. That vendor wouldn't remember me in five minutes, and the guards at Tina's office would forget me soon after. All that would be left was the story of the time a woman appeared out of nowhere and decked their colleague.

I spent the rest of the afternoon across the street from Tina's building, sipping coffee, eating bagels, and watching the front door for her to walk outside again. I only intended to have one cup and nurse it, but when I reached into my pocket to pay for my first cup of joe, I found a wad of money with a little note that said, "For your troubles –TB."

I spent the rest of the afternoon stuffing my face. There really was nothing like New York bagels, and I'd had bagels all over, in every small town and big city across the whole country.

It was half-past dark when Tina exited the building, her face lit by the subtle orange light from the lobby. I threw way too much money for what I had eaten on the table and rushed after her, crossing the street.

"Tina!" I shouted.

She turned around, adjusting her glasses as she went. "Are you talking to—oh, you're the lady who knocked out Thad this afternoon." She held out her hand and smiled. "I'm glad you found me. I very much wanted to shake your hand."

I shook her hand. "So, he really is that much of a jerk then?"

Tina's eyebrows went up. "This was actually one of his better days, and after you knocked him to the ground, it shut him up for a good three hours. When he did finally speak again, it was to complain about how he got blood on his favorite shirt. It was a very, very gratifying day."

"I'm glad you approved. Since you're in such a good mood, maybe you can help me. Can I take you to dinner? I just came into a bit of money."

She smiled. "Funny, me too. Lead the way. What are you in the mood for?"

"Pizza," I replied. "It's been too long since I had a slice."

"I know just the place," she said, walking in step with me. "Now, how exactly do you know my name?"

"Well, that, my new friend, is a funny story. Let's discuss it over food. It'll go down easier on a full stomach."

CHAPTER 48

We didn't have to go far to find a great slice of pizza, and soon enough, I was stuffing my face with a slice of sausage across from Tina, who was taking dainty bites from a pepperoni.

"How long have you been in New York?" I asked.

"I came here for school, and I just kind of stayed. My grandmother wanted me to move back home, but since she—died—and, well, she was the last family I had, so I don't see the point."

"Where's home for you?" I asked as if I didn't know already.

"San Francisco born and bred."

"You're a long way from home," I said. "It's nice there."

"You've been, then?" She spoke through a mouthful of pizza. "Yeah, I mean…people think I'm crazy for going away to school when San Francisco has everything, but it also doesn't. I mean, it doesn't have New York City, right?"

I took a big bite of folded pizza. "Oh man, this pizza."

"Best in the city." She sighed. "My grandmother left me her place in the will, along with, well, basically everything she had left, which wasn't much. She was a weird woman. I loved her, but she was really weird. By the end, she was talking in little more than strings of numbers."

"I'm sorry," I said. "That must have been hard."

"I was going back home once a month, trying to convince her that—well, that she had issues." Tina took a sad bite of pizza and looked out the window.

"What…kind of issues?" I asked softly

She looked back and forth around the shop and then leaned in toward me. "She thought she was unstuck in time. She said she met a god once, who granted her a wish, but it came with a terrible price. Alzheimer's…it's just awful."

"Totally," I said, putting down my crust. "She's actually the reason I wanted to talk to you, Tina." I chuckled to myself, trying to decrease the tension I suddenly felt between us. "You see, it turns out your grandmother might not be as crazy as you think."

She bit her lip. "You're mocking me."

"I'm not." I looked into her eyes. "But if I told you the truth, then I'm very sure you would think I was crazy, and I need you to believe me."

"Try me," she replied. "You might be surprised what I'm willing to believe."

"All right, don't say I didn't warn you." I could see her trust in me failing. Any second, she would run out the door. "Did your grandmother keep any papers or notes about her life?"

She bolted upright, then settled down again. "I mean, yes, but that's not all that uncommon."

"It's nothing but a string of numbers, right? And weird drawings?"

"Okay, this is getting freaky." She grabbed her coat and went to stand.

I latched onto her wrist. "Have you started decoding it yet?"

"I—" Her eyes narrowed. "I just started. Her lawyer gave me a stack of papers at the will reading…said it would help me understand her better, but when I opened it— nothing. Just numbers and drawings, like you said." She sat back down. "I thought if I could figure out her code, maybe I could write her story or something."

I nodded solemnly, still holding her wrist. "That's a noble, but terrible, idea. I need those papers. I need them before they can cause any more damage."

"Damage? I don't—what are you talking about?"

I released her and sat back. "I know what you're thinking about doing. You'll move back to San Francisco, write the book, and when no publisher buys it, you'll start a publishing company to do it yourself. It will ruin you. Please believe me when I tell you that those papers will cause you nothing but heartache. We need to destroy them now before they destroy your life."

"I—can't—" Tina didn't fully believe me yet, but she was close. She gave me a searching look. "Who are you? How do you know my grandmother?"

"I didn't know her, only her work—your work." I took a deep breath. "You're a really good writer, Tina. You don't need to tell your grandmother's story. You should tell your own."

"But…" she trailed off.

"I'll pay if that's what it takes. Tell me what it's worth to you, and I'll pay."

"You're asking me to put a value on my grandmother's life."

"No," I replied. "I'm asking you to put a value on the fate of the universe."

She studied me for a long moment. "And you're not messing with me."

"You don't know me well, and I get that, but please believe me when I say that I hate pranks and people that play them on people. If this wasn't a matter of life or death, I would not ask this of you."

"Okay," she said. "I believe you."

She believed me enough to lead me back to her apartment, a fifth-floor walkup in Hell's Kitchen, with walls thin enough that I could hear a baby across the hall and two people arguing next door. The place itself was small, with a mini kitchenette with a hot plate, a bed, and a tiny TV in the corner. Tina reached under her bed and pulled out a box, handing it to me. I removed the top and found the papers.

In the years since this moment, it had been pawed over and handled by multiple people, but now, it was a pristine collection of papers not yet yellowed by the ravages of time.

"How much do you want for them?" I asked.

She shook her head. "If they are as bad as you say, I just want them out of my life."

"You're a good person, Tina." I smiled. "Invest in Amazon, Apple, and Google. As much as you can, as often as you can."

"I only know what one of those things are," she replied. "And Apple is a disaster right now."

"It won't be forever," I said. "Trust me."

I probably wasn't supposed to give her stock tips, but she had been so helpful and basically turned down over a million dollars for these stupid papers. The least I could do was give her a little something. She might have just saved the universe, for all I knew.

Tina grabbed a metal trash can and led me up to the roof, where I could see all of New York City sprawling out in front of me. There, I lit the first page and tossed it into the bin, followed by the others, and we watched them burn in the night, the city sparkling beneath us.

When it was done, I looked down at my wrist, and sure enough, one of the red strands had turned to white.

"Can I use your bathroom?" I asked.

"Sure, it's just inside—well, you can't miss it. My apartment is so small."

"I'll find it." I held up my hand. "Be right back."

It was a lie. The first one I told her. As the door closed, I pulled the white string and vanished into the ether.

CHAPTER 49

I didn't reappear inside Talinda's time castle. Instead, I showed up on a barren wasteland with nothing but cracked clay and large rocks for as far as the eye could see. The sky was dark, but heat swirled from the ground, causing waves to form in the air that distorted my vision.

As I tried to find my bearings, footsteps crackled on the broken ground, coming closer. I readied my hands for an attack, but none came. Instead, a waifish woman, gaunt-faced, with sunken, wounded violet eyes, stumbled from the haze. Her arms were thin, uncovered by the simple white dress she wore. A red blood stain trickled down her neck, blossoming in a thick mess on her abdomen. Her feet were bare, and they sizzled upon the hot clay under them.

"Hello, Elizabeth. It's nice to finally meet you." She winced as she spoke. "Or, perhaps I should say that it is nice you have finally met me. I have met you countless times before."

"Who are you? What have you done to Talinda?"

"My name is Doretha." She gasped and clutched her stomach. "I have done nothing to Talinda or her castle. I simply brought you to a waystation along our journey." Blood dripped from her nose and fell to the ground beneath her. "Every moment I keep you here drains me further, and I have precious little left." She coughed. "The great tragedy of my life is that I made so many mistakes, some for selfish reasons, but the worst ones, by far, were the ones I made for selfless reasons." She began to shake violently. "I was wrong…about everything. I know that now, only too late. I didn't believe you…but you were right." She fell to the ground. "You were kind to me, and I will never forget that kindness."

Before I could help the poor woman, the last of her life fell from her eyes, and a flash of white light blasted me backward into a hard stone wall. When my eyes focused, I was in Talinda's castle, in the spindle and loom room with all the strands of silk thread. I pushed myself to my feet as Viannah rushed over.

"There you are!" she shouted with excitement. "We thought we had lost you."

I shook my head. "No. I'm here. Just got a little sidetracked, that's all. I'm back now." I felt the back of my head, where a welt had formed. "Also, ow."

Viannah helped me to my feet. "You're quite safe now, I promise you." She turned me toward the door to the loom room. "And our mistress has been worried sick about you. Come, come. She will be thrilled you have survived your journey through the timestream."

We walked forward, her legs moving faster than my wobbly ones could manage, but we reached the door and pushed it open. The maidens worked the loom just as when I left, with Talinda furiously peddling on the wooden spindle in the middle. Her eyes lit up when she saw me.

"You're back!" She clapped her hands together and hurried toward me. "That is lovely. I don't know what would have happened if we lost you in the timestream. So, tell me, hero, how was your first trip through time?"

"I hated it," I started with a wry smile. I told her about the rest of my trip, how I burned the book. "I don't understand, though. How did that save the anomaly since I couldn't be here without reading that book?"

She smiled. "You see, the fact that it turned white is a very good sign. It means that when you went back, you never came here in the first place. Problem solved. Understand?"

"No?" I replied, frowning.

Viannah squeezed my arm. "It took me centuries to understand even a fraction of it. It's best just to let it wash over you and accept it without question."

"Not ideal, I admit," Talinda said. "Especially for one as inquisitive as you, but she isn't wrong, either. I only understand it because I was created to understand it, understand?"

A sharp pain cut across my head. "No, but I'll just go with it." The moment I said that the pain in my head dissipated. "That's better."

"You have told us about your journey, yes, but how did you get lost?"

"I wasn't lost," I said. "At least I don't think I was. The woman who I met there said she had invaded the timestream to send me a message."

"My, my. That is very interesting. What did this woman look like?" Talinda seemed expectant and positive, but as I gave my account of the strange woman, the eagerness drained from her face. "Yes, that is Doretha. She has grown more powerful than I could possibly imagine." She paused. "Do you know what time you were in when she took you?"

"No," I replied. "But I think she died whenever time it was, so maybe it's all going to be okay?"

Viannah shook her head. "Even if she is dead, the chaos that she caused in the timestream hasn't been fixed."

Talinda grabbed my arm and held up my wrist, showing the red threads entangled on it. "All of this, all of this is her fault, and it is still red. You fixed one small piece of it, but there is still more to untangle."

"Oh," I replied. "I thought all these were from Rosalie's papers?"

Talinda laughed. "That is a very small inconvenience compared to what Doretha has done and what I need you to fix."

"Care to elaborate on that or…"

"All will be made clear in time."

"That's a very god thing to say." I laughed. "Then let's get to it, I guess. No more side quests or training missions."

"Very well. The job is a simple as it is complicated," Talinda said. "Prevent Doretha from infecting the timestream, then kill her. Once that's done, pull on the white threads, and you will be brought back here."

"I'm not an assassin," I said.

"I never said you were. But even heroes have to get their hands dirty every now and then. And I believe you are a great hero. Perhaps the greatest in the whole universe." She pointed to my chest. "But only you can make that true through your actions. Heroes do not make easy choices. They make the right ones."

"How will I know what is right?" I asked. "Everything I do seems to make things worse."

Talinda shook her head and indicated a white thread directly over us. "You see that thread? It was red, and you turned it white. If you need a guide to your actions, just look at your wrist."

"I guess I can do that."

Talinda nodded. "Then you are already a hero."

"I don't know about that, but if you say so." I stopped for a moment. My chest burned, and my head ached. I couldn't remember the last time I'd slept. "Do you think I could get a nap before I go? I haven't slept in forever."

Talinda smiled. "I suppose a good rest won't kill us—yet."

CHAPTER 50

I slept like the dead, and when I brushed the sleep from my eyes after waking, I felt as if I had shed every ounce of tiredness from my life. Refreshed, I flung my legs over the edge of the bed when there was a knock on the door.

"Come in," I said.

Viannah walked in with a towel and two blankets. "Oh, you are up. We didn't know if you would ever awaken."

"How long was I out?"

"A week and a second all at the same time. When you walk out that door, it will be mere moments since you entered, but your body has been asleep in this room for seven days. Talinda thought the least she could do was make sure you were rested and healed before you took on the world."

"That's very kind of her," I said, stretching. "And that towel is for—"

"A shower," Viannah replied. "If you haven't slept in a long time, I thought you perhaps hadn't showered in a long time, either." She crinkled her nose as if she knew very well that I stank but was too polite to say anything. "If you don't want it, though—"

"No, no," I replied, taking the towel. "You can never be too clean, right?"

"My thoughts exactly."

I showered and found that my clothing had been washed, folded, and restored to like-new conditions while I was in the bathroom. *God bless time witches.* When I was finally clean and changed, I met Viannah outside. Sure enough, I opened the door in the middle of night, though it was midday when I walked out of the room.

"Ready?" she said.

"Absolutely not. This is the least prepared I've ever been for anything, and I was on the run for a decade. I wish you could give me any indication of what I'm supposed to do."

"We do as well," Viannah said. "Unfortunately, Doretha has learned how to keep her machinations a secret to us. Like mother like dau—" She clapped a hand to her mouth. "Oh, bother. There I am talking out of turn again."

"Daughter? You mean Doretha is Talinda's daughter?"

"Yes, but you can't say anything to anyone, even me, as you might be seeing a past version of me next time we meet. My loose lips have revealed a deep secret, but I suppose you were bound to learn sooner or later since you know now."

"Exactly. I wouldn't think about it too much."

"Good advice," Viannah said. "I find it's best not to think about anything too much. Before I was made a handmaiden, I was desperate to learn the secrets of the universe. Now, I understand that it is better just to accept."

"Sounds horrible."

We made our way into the thread room as she shook her head emphatically. "No, there is a great relief in accepting the world as it is, and not striving for answers. Ignorance, as they say, is bliss."

"I don't think they say it as a positive, though."

"Really?" she replied. "That's a shame. I very much like that expression."

"Is there anything you can tell me about where I'm going?"

"I have already said too much. Talinda believes the less you know, the less likely Doretha will know you are coming and thus unable to stop you. That is our hope at least."

"I don't know if I should take comfort in the fact that gods don't even know what they're doing or worry that humanity's fate is in the hands of beings that know so little."

She laughed. "Oh no, silly. Fate is not in the hands of gods. It's in the hands of you humans."

"Okay, now I'm officially petrified."

We continued through the thread room into the loom room, where Talinda sat up from her spindle and called me over to her. "I trust you are rested now, child. Are you ready to go?"

"I'm ready."

"Oh, goodie." She placed her hands on my temples when I approached. "About time." A pinprick of pain shot through my mind and I let out a whimper. "I've given you the power to understand any language, on any planet you land on, at any time in history. It's not much, but communication is the key to understanding."

"Thank you," I said, rubbing my raw temples.

"It's the least I can do. Now I bid you farewell. Good luck." She snapped her fingers.

I vanished with the taste of banana pudding on my tongue again and fell into the darkness. This time, I didn't appear inside of a storage closet but behind a shed, inches from falling back into a ravine and tumbling to my death. The steep mud embankment fed into a babbling brook filled with jagged rocks perfect for neck-snapping. Maybe Talinda didn't care about dying since she could control the stream of time, but I had already died once and had no interest in doing it a second time.

I stepped out of the thick thatch behind the shed and spent several minutes picking burrs from my legs and butt. When I was brushed clean, I set off to figure out where— and when—I was, and how to find Doretha.

A black rottweiler barked as I cut into the front lawn, leaping at me until a thick metal chain took exception to its excitement and yanked it back to the ground. That didn't deter the dog from rushing me again, furiously, as I stepped onto the sidewalk, nor the chain from once again slamming it to the ground.

The street was nice. Quaint, even. The air was crisp in late fall, and the trees had turned into a hundred different colors of autumn. Leaves crunched as I walked just enough so that the white noise of it reminded me of raking leaves with Junebug and Carl and falling into them after the great piles had been stacked high into the air.

I could have seen them if I had put off destroying the papers. I could have told them that I loved them. I could have lived with them until the time a god decided to strike me down for causing an anomaly in her precious timeline. But if I did that, I would have been as much an enemy of Talinda as Doretha.

I was lost in my thoughts when I saw her. She wasn't nearly as gaunt or bruised as our previous encounter, and blood didn't stain her shirt, but it was her all the same. Her eyes were determined as she stomped through the street and turned up a driveway. That's when I saw the gun in her hand, gripped so tight her knuckles were white.

Now came the hard part, stopping her.

CHAPTER 51

No worries, Lizzie. All you have to do is stop a deranged demigod who has dominion over time-space…and a gun. How hard could it be?

Doretha didn't knock on the door. Instead, she touched the doorknob, and as she did, her hand vibrated faster than I could follow until her wrist disappeared through the door. A moment later, the door clicked open, and she stepped inside. There was a look of determination on her face that scared me.

I needed time to stop and think, but that was a luxury I didn't have. Funny how just minutes ago, I was in a place that expanded and collapsed time at its will, and now, when I needed it, I couldn't call on any of that for help.

I balled my fists and felt the cold of my powers flow through them, numbing my fingers with the pain of a thousand needles. I gathered my strength and rushed inside the house. For holding the fate of the known universe in its precious clutches, the house was remarkably normal, save for the fact that every surface was trimmed with oak and maple, like a hunting lodge in the middle of a suburb. The heads of beasts I didn't recognize hung on the walls.

I wasn't a zoologist or anything, but I knew enough to recognize bears, moose, and deer, among other creatures that hunters prized for trophies. There was nothing familiar about three-eyed blue beasts, six-foot-tall insects, and other strange creatures decorating the walls.

"Don't take another step!" I heard from upstairs. An open railing showed Doretha in a doorway, pointing her revolver into a room. I rushed up the steps to where she stood with shaky palms. The gun wobbled in her hands, and tears streaked down her face. All the resolve on her face from moments ago fell away in the cold reality of the terrible act she was about to commit.

"You don't have to do this," I said, inching closer to her.

The sound of my voice startled her, and the gun blasted into the air. From inside the room, a man screamed, but it wasn't the scream of somebody who had been shot. Just very, very frightened.

"Who the hell are you?" Doretha screamed as she whipped around to face me, the gun now pointed at me. The blue eyes that had been so dim on our last meeting were icy blue and vibrant as the Arctic sea. Her trembling hand found my heart with the tip of the gun, but I did not feel afraid. There was no menace to her words, just alarm and surprise.

"I'm a friend, I think."

"I don't know who you are," she replied, trying to regain her composure. "Don't lie to me. My mother sent you, didn't she?"

"She did, but before she did, you and I met. Somewhere in the future, and you told me I was right all along. So, I'm telling you, please, for your own sake. Don't do this. You'll thank me later."

Doretha lifted the gun away from my chest and pointed it again toward the unknown man in the next room. "I can't…you don't understand. If you knew—"

"Then tell me. Put the gun down and tell me."

She gritted her teeth. The scared girl vanished, and the stalwart resolve of a cold, calculating killer returned. "No."

"*Rigéscunt indutae!*" A bolt of ice shot from my hand and covered hers in ice. Her finger was on the trigger, and the gun went off, shattering the ice around it, causing the man to scream again— another yelp borne of fear, not pain.

I couldn't let her get off another shot. I rushed forward and slammed into her chest, knocking her backward. The banister behind us snapped and sent us falling to the living room below, smashing hard into a coffee table.

It took a moment for the world to come back into focus, and when it did, a fist connected with my face. Doretha kicked and flailed at my chest until she was able to forcibly push me off of her.

She made for the stairs, but I dragged her back to the ground by the waist of her pants, and she spun back toward me, ready to fire her pistol. I kicked her gun arm, and the revolver flew across the room.

"Get out of here!" I screamed up the stairs. Footsteps clattered above, and a wiry man, his long face locked in a look of terror, peered out from the stairwell.

"Let go of me!" Doretha screamed, socking me in the chest. I lost my grip on her. Free of my grasp, she rushed across the room toward the gun. The man ran to the door as she unloaded three bullets behind him, missing her target each time.

The man scuttled out the door, and Doretha gave chase. I was winded, and my chest ached from the fight, but I followed after them both into the street. My lungs burned like fire as I leaped onto the front lawn toward the driveway where the man was having trouble turning over the ignition to start his car and escape.

Doretha reared back the gun and smashed through the window, dragging the man out through the broken glass.

"Glacies spica!"

The ice spear I'd formed shot from my hand, connecting with Doretha's leg. She screamed out in pain and let go of the man, then fell to the ground.

"You idiot!" she roared. "You can't stop me! I'll just keep coming back again and again!"

"I won't let you kill him! You'll destroy everything!"

The man disappeared into his car and turned the key again. This time it fired up, and he started to back up out of the driveway. Doretha howled out in frustration and pain, then started scrambling in her pocket. She pulled out a golden pocket watch encrusted with rubies and sapphires. With a glare, she said, "I'll see you next time."

"*Rigéscunt indutae!*" I yelled as she went to press the top of the clock, and ice encased her hand for the second time.

"Get this off me!" She smashed at the ice with her gun, but no matter what she did, this time, nothing would break the crystal. In the distance, I heard sirens. In moments, the police had swarmed her, knocking her to the ground.

"She almost killed that man, offi—"

But they swarmed me, too, bowling me over before I could explain anything. As I lay prone on the ground, I heard Doretha's laughing. When I finally looked up at her, she smiled at me.

"What does it matter? Soon, this will be a distant memory, and I'll be able to return to finish what I started."

CHAPTER 52

"What am I doing here?" I growled to a constable sitting across from me at a metal table. They hadn't been kind when they arrested me or when they threw me in a cell next to Doretha, and I felt no need to be polite to them just because they happened to have a badge.

"You trespassed into a residence and threw somebody off a second-story balcony."

"To save that guy's life! Does your stupid report say that?"

I twirled the red twine on my wrist. I expected that by now, it would have turned white. I stopped the murder, didn't I? Shouldn't I be back in Talinda's palace reaping the rewards of my success? I really didn't want to talk to the chode cop across from me. His noxious cologne made my stomach turn as much as his dumb face made me want to punch it.

"We're still trying to figure out what happened, and nobody is going anywhere until we do." He looked down at his clipboard. "Do you even know whose house you broke into?"

"I didn't break in! The door was open…and no."

He opened his mouth to speak but then thought better of himself. "Perhaps it's best that way."

"Are you kidding me?" I said. "I saved that guy's life. I'm a good Samaritan."

"Then you have nothing to worry about."

He shrugged on his way out. In his wake, two officers wearing red uniforms and derby hats stormed into the room and carried me back to my cell. They weren't gentle. They tossed me inside like rotten meat and slammed the door.

"See what you get for being a hero?" Doretha said through the bars of her cell. She held her hand up. The ice still remained, but she had chipped off the edges of it. "How long does this take to melt? What is it…super ice?"

"As long as I have the will to keep it going, I guess. I don't know. I've never been in a fight long enough to watch it melt before."

"Brilliant," she said with a sigh.

"I'm surprised you're not just vibrating it off. I saw how you opened the door to that guy's house."

"That guy's name is Matias Newton. He is on the verge of a breakthrough in perpetual motion which will change the course of history. He'll become famous for it."

"Then why are you trying to kill him?"

"Because that same technology will destroy this world." She let out a disgusted huff. "What do you care, anyway? You're working for her."

"I'm not working for her," I said before thinking better of myself. "Well, okay. I am working for her, but not in the way you think."

"I think she is dangling a slip in time to you for your service," she said, not waiting for me to confirm her suspicion. "My mother's not very original, and you're not the first."

I held up my hands, pleading. "Has anybody told you about the chaos you're causing in the timestream? If you don't stop, you're going to destroy the universe."

She chuckled. "That's funny. How long have you known Talinda? A couple of days? A week maybe?"

It was hard to know for sure. I slipped in and out of time in her castle from one moment to the next. "That's irrelevant."

This made her spin toward me with fire in her ice-blue eyes. "No, it means everything. I served her for eons, and in those eons, the lies she told were incalculable—but the absolute worst was that she made us stand by while people suffered." She shook her head. "Any universe that won't let me save people isn't one that deserves to exist." When her eyes found mine, the look of self-determination returned. "What would you do to save a world?"

"I wouldn't destroy the universe, for starters."

She pushed back onto her knees and took a deep breath. "Do you know how many worlds I watched burn for her? Justifying that it was for the greater good? How many lives erased for the good of the timestream?"

"I don—"

"Thousands, and every time it got harder until one day, I couldn't stand it. I just couldn't." Tears fell from her eyes. "I'm not going to let this world die. I'm not going to let any of them die, not anymore."

"If I don't stop you, then my world will be ravaged by an Apocalypse. What do you say to that? You're damning my planet to save this one and destroying the universe in the process."

Her eyes met mine. "Have you ever watched it happen? Have you ever seen lives vaporized in front of you?"

I choked my tears. "I watched my father burned to death by demons."

"That's terrible. Nobody should have to see that. Now imagine it happening a million more times, in a thousand different ways. Humans are so fragile, and the gods should be protecting them—guiding them. They should be caring for their creation at all costs." She wiped the tears from her eyes. "Did you know she doesn't even know what will happen if a red thread enters the loom? She's too scared to risk it, so she stops them. But what if adding red, or even blue, green, and yellow to the loom wouldn't doom the cosmos? Maybe it would just make it more interesting."

"I sympathize with you, I do." I slid to the floor and leaned against the bars. "I'm doing all of this to save one girl—a girl I care about—so I have to ask, who do you care about enough to destroy the universe?"

Doretha slid down to the ground. "His name is Tobias. I met him fifty years from now, days before the end. I tried to save him, but it was no use. I begged Talinda to let me fix it, but she refused. And that's when I realized that I didn't need her approval. I just needed her power."

I placed my hand on her shoulder. I don't know what possessed me to do it, but at that moment, she seemed so…human. "He must have been some man for you to be willing to destroy everything for him."

I felt her hand on top of mine, and then she yanked me toward the bars. The power drained from my body, and I let out a shriek. After a moment, she dropped my hand and smashed her hand against the bars. This time, the ice around her shattered, and she laughed—a horrible, hysterical laugh. She took out her watch and reached for one of its buttons.

The watch clicked, and a white light enveloped her. I couldn't let her leave without me, or I would never find her again. There was only one choice. I had to grab for her and hope that the aura would ensnare me as well.

When the light reached my hand, it latched onto it as well, coating my body in a white cloud. The world faded from my sight as gravity lost its hold on me. I slipped into the timestream and vanished.

CHAPTER 53

The hot white light of the pocket watch spat us out into a dirty alleyway. I fell prone onto the mucky asphalt, and Doretha landed with all her weight on top of me, vomiting the air from my lungs with great violence and force.

"Can you get off me?" I grumbled weakly. My ribs already felt broken from our last fight, and now they felt like they were stabbing into my lungs.

It took her great effort to roll off me. "Why would you do that? Do you have any idea how stupid that was?"

"You might not believe this, but my barometer for stupid is pretty low."

"Oh, I believe it." She sat up against a brick wall. "I haven't known you for very long but can confirm you are a moron."

I leaned against the opposite wall, my body seized with the throes of a massive migraine. "Why do I feel so terrible?"

"You just slipped through time." Her voice was hoarse, and she rubbed her throat. "There are side effects."

"Talinda sent me through time with no problem."

"Yeah, well, her powers are greater than mine. It's enough for me to just slip into the stream. I can't really control it much when I get there." She looked down at her watch with a grimace. "Great. You realize that we can't jump for a few days now, right?"

"I don't understand any of this, Doretha. Not even a little bit of it. All I know is that to get my ticket back in time, I have to stop you so I can turn these" —I held up my wrist and showed the red threads tied to it— "white. So that's what I'm going to do."

"Wait." She crawled over toward me. "Why haven't they turned white yet? You stopped me."

"That's what I thought, too. I must have screwed something up in the process."

Doretha's eyes went wild. "That means I did it still. Somehow, I saved—" She stood up too fast, and her feet wobbled until she crashed against the side of the building. "Ow."

"You're really selfish, did you know that?" I said, glaring at her. "I just told you the universe was screwed, and all you can think about is your boyfriend, who might or might not have been born wherever and whenever the hell we are."

Doretha wasn't listening. She continued her slow march onto the busy street in front of her. I couldn't let her out of my sight. If she slipped from my view, I might never find her again and would be stuck wherever I was for who knew how long.

"Wait!" I shouted. The vibrations of my voice quaked against my aching head, and a shooting pain traveled from the base of my neck to my forehead.

I stepped out of the alley, stumbling and shuffling like an old woman, sure that she had evaded me, but when I reached the street, she was in front of a newsstand, gripping a paper tightly and shaking. Tears streamed down her face.

"No, no, no, no, no," she said, sobbing softly. "I can't—" She spun to me and shoved the paper in my face. "Do you have any idea what you've done?"

The headline on the paper read, *Jasmine Blossom Festival Brings Thousands to City.*

"I…don't understand what you have against jasmine…or what I could have done…"

She slammed her finger down in the top right corner of the paper. "You don't understand. The date. It's two days from the end of the world, and this is the exact headline. The *exact* headline from every other time the world ended." She collapsed onto the ground, crying. "How could it—I don't understand."

I couldn't help it, I pitied her. I knelt beside her. "Because fate is a bitch, and that's one thing I know for sure. You can try to outrun, outlast, or outthink your destiny, but it will catch up with you."

"I don't believe that." She threw the newspaper away. "I can't do anything right. Screw destiny."

"You have all the time in the world to fix this and save the world."

Doretha let out a shuddering sigh. "You don't get it. In two days, they turn on an interconnected network of reactors that are supposed to power the world for free in perpetuity. Small-scale tests were promising, but they couldn't test it at scale until it went live. The machine relied on the rotation of the planets, which means it needed to connect through almost every major city on the planet to work, and when they turn it on…when they turn it on, all of this gets destroyed. All of it." She swallowed hard. "There is nowhere for people to hide. Everything, down to the smallest microbe, dies. In a matter of days, this planet is a desolate wasteland. I can't let that go. But even if I could, it wouldn't matter." She held up her pocket watch. "Because this needs three days to recharge, which means this is my last trip. We'll all be dead before I have a chance to slip again."

Her words took a moment to register. They worked their way from my ears, to my gut, to my heart, and finally to my head, causing every muscle along the way to seize up. My fists formed into tight balls and my jaw clenched as my stomach bubbled.

"What?" I shouted. "You're telling me that we're going to die here!"

"There's no other way."

"Maybe not for you. I'm outta here." I grabbed onto my wrist and yanked the red threads. Nothing happened. I gripped the red threads tightly in my hand, but they just laid there, limp.

This caused Doretha to let out a slight chuckle. "You don't understand time at all. The white thread is a marker. It lets Talinda know that something has changed back, and that's how she pulls you out of the timestream. Without it, those red threads are useless."

I grabbed her around her throat and began to squeeze tightly. If I killed her, then this would be done. She didn't resist, not like last time. Whatever had happened, the jump had taken the last of her will to live. I felt the breath leaving her. It would only take a couple more seconds before she…

My mind flashed to Veronica's dead eyes and how Doretha's glassy eyes matched hers. I couldn't do it. I unclenched my hands, and Doretha fell to the ground, gasping for air.

She grabbed her throat, rubbing it tenderly. "You could save the whole universe by killing one person and look at you. You can't even do that. How could I let an entire world vanish when I had the power to try and save it?"

I fell back onto my butt. She was right, after all. It was one thing to tell her to end the world, that there were plenty of other planets—but to see people walk by us, gawk at us, wondering what two grown women were doing sitting on the ground of a grubby street—that was different. It was different from knowing you can do something and do nothing.

"Then," I said, with the courage of conviction that only came when there were no good options left. "I guess we're going to save the world."

CHAPTER 54

Doretha cocked her head. "You can't possibly be serious. You were just arguing that we should let them all die, right before you tried to kill me." She rubbed her neck. "And now, because you are suddenly at risk, you're willing to save all these people. Who's the selfish one?"

"I've been called that by better people than you." I stood up. "I'm a hypocrite. I admit it. Maybe this is all about self-preservation, or maybe it's because I've been so far up my own ass this whole time that I forgot to realize these are people. I mean, I know it's completely stupid, but looking at them, and even you as the light left your eyes, I just can't…I've seen too much death." I held out my hand to help her up. "I don't want to be part of more."

She brushed herself off once she was standing, then looked me dead in the eye. "Even if it means destroying the universe in the process?"

"One thing at a time," I said. "Let's save this world first and worry about the universe later."

We heard a cough behind us and turned to see an older man sitting behind the newsstand. He had been staring at us, clearly, for a long time. "Not to get in the middle of your thing, but are you going to buy that paper?" He shook his head. "You know what? Never mind. You're clearly going through some something…just take it."

"Seriously?" Doretha asked, holding the crumpled, tear-soaked paper in her hand.

"Yeah, it's no good to me anyway, not now." He leaned forward. "Hey, were you serious about the world ending, because I have some things I need to make right if that's true."

"You should make those things right anyway." I placed my hand on Doretha's back, and we began to walk away. "How about some food?"

She shook her head. "No, there's something I have to do first."

It didn't take a genius to know that she wanted to see her boyfriend since we probably only had two more days left to live. Hopefully, we could find a way to save this planet, but realistically, there wasn't much two people could do to stop the Apocalypse, even if one was a nymph and the other was a demigod.

Tobias was a doctor who worked at a big hospital downtown. It was the kind of building that towered over everything else, its magnitude swallowing up every bit of your attention. When we reached the grassy park across from the hospital, I thought we would go inside, but instead, Doretha took a seat on the bench across from the main entrance.

"What are we doing?" I said. "Don't you want to, like, go inside?"

She looked down at her pocket watch. "I can't. It's almost time."

Before I could ask why, a doctor walked out of the door with a younger Doretha on his arm. She was wide-eyed, beautiful really, with none of the lines etched in her face as she had now. Her smile said she hadn't a care in the world.

"That's Tobias," Doretha said with wistful longing on her breath.

Tobias was tall and broad and dreamy. His hair shimmered in the light, and his chin was sharp enough to cut glass. They laughed together as the younger Doretha wrapped herself tighter around his thick arm.

"How many times have you come here to watch them?"

She glanced at a tall tree behind us. "I usually sit up there. When I did, I would watch me down here, looking at me, watching them. We must somehow have come before all of that." She chuckled. "I'll be honest, I have no idea how any of this works, even after all this time."

"Well, that's definitely what you want to hear from our only hope to get out of this Apocalypse alive."

"Oh god, that's a horrifying thought." She stood up. "Come on, now that I've seen him for the last time, let's go. You're right, food is a good idea."

"Why does this look so much like my Earth?" I asked as we walked away from the hospital, down the street of what could have easily been San Francisco, or Seattle, except that the advertising was for brands I had never heard of before. A soda brand name *Vizzit*, a razor named *Florbi*, a new TV series called *Tom*.

"Gods. They can create something from nothing, but they have no imagination. Everywhere, all over the universe, is pretty much the same. The languages are different, and sometimes the technology differs a little bit, but generally, humans evolve the same way everywhere and have access to the same tools and same basic building blocks, which leads to kind of the same thing happening all over the cosmos—though that depends on which god they leave in charge and which cultures they choose to shepherd."

"There are different gods in charge of each different planet?"

"The habitable ones, at least. When the gods make a habitable world, they all show up to guide it along—think about this, you know how there used to be all sorts of stories about gods meeting with people on your planet?"

"Yes, we have a couple of books about it."

"But not so much anymore. Why? Because the other gods headed to another planet, leaving just one of them in charge. Some gods are good managers, others are terrible, and almost all of them are vain, giving an edge to the people that look like them, talk like them, and think like them. If I had to guess, this planet was controlled by one of the Norse gods. Man, they are going to be pissed their world is about to end."

Suddenly a lightbulb went off. "That's it. That's what we'll do. We'll find an angel, contact the god that controls this place, and tell them what's about to happen. There's no way they'll be okay with a whole planet dying, right?"

Doretha shrugged. "It would look pretty bad to the other gods, and they have very fragile egos." She stopped in front of something like a hot dog stand. "You know it's not like looking up a number in the phone book, right? Gods tend to be hard to contact."

"Well, in the past couple of weeks, I've met two—three, if you count yourself. Besides, maybe if a god stops this Apocalypse somehow, it won't cause a rift in space-time or something."

She thought for a second. "You know, in all my time here, I never thought of asking for help from the pantheon. It's just crazy enough to work."

CHAPTER 55

There were temples to many gods in the city, from Bragi to Thor, and Odin to Hel, but the grandest temple was devoted to Loki, the trickster god of Norse mythology. Doretha had asked a half dozen priestesses at a temple we visited, and they all agreed that Loki was the regent in charge of Astadell, the planet we currently occupied, and his temple was the most influential in Terdan, the city where we found ourselves.

"This is not going to go well." Doretha ground her teeth as she looked up at the green banners hanging from Loki's golden temple. It looked more like a house than a cathedral, except whoever built it decided to keep layering on rooms on top of each other, and it rose into the air, each section smaller and smaller until the silver spire pointed toward the sky high above.

"Why not?" I replied. "I know that he's a trickster god, but—"

"Don't!" Doretha hissed. "He does not like being called that. He is the mother of monsters, or 'Your Grace,' but do not call him a trickster. I don't know much about Loki, but Talinda told me that much."

Mother of monsters? Yes. Now that I looked closer to the façade of the intricately carved temple, I saw all manner of monsters perching on ledges and poking out from the building itself, swiping at the sky and howling.

"Then why do you think this will be so hard?" I said.

"Because he's a trickster," she replied with a smile. "On top of that, Odin's line hates Zeus's, and you have his kin's stench all over you."

"Odin's line? Zeus's line? What are you talking about?" I asked.

"Gods have kin, just like humans. Odin's line, including Loki, Thor, Sif, among others, once helped Zeus's line create planets, but there was a great schism eons ago, which caused a war between them and sent them careening off in different directions, splitting the universe like you would cut a pie."

"And I smell like Zeus's line?"

She nodded. "Every god's magic has a tinge to it, and Zeus's is no different. It infects everything he creates. You reek of it, as did your whole planet."

I hesitated. "Then I should wait outside, right? I don't want to piss off a god."

"You'll be fine." She started up the concrete stairs toward the wooden pillars which held up the temple's roof. "The druids that protect this temple won't be able to tell. Besides, it's not like we'll manage to summon a god anyway. They are notoriously temperamental and hate being disturbed. In all my time on this planet, I've never heard of one speaking to a human, not for thousands of years."

I followed behind her. "If you don't believe it could work, then why are we even trying it?"

"Might as well. I've tried everything else," she said. "It's probably our only hope left…and yes, I do understand how sad that thought is, but it doesn't make it any less true."

She pushed open the tall jade doors where more monsters were carved, biting and clawing at us in permanent stony relief. Inside, a wooden lacquered finish stained the entire church, causing it to glow against the lights that hung from the ceiling. Incense spread through the air. We followed the red carpet that carved a path down the center of the room. Painted wooden reliefs of a thin, waifish god surrounded by different monsters hung above and below the wooden beams encircling the walls.

"That's Loki." Doretha pointed to the god, clad in emerald and gold, in each painting. In some, he was a man, and in others, a woman, but his figure remained similar regardless.

"Duh," I replied. "I'm not from here, but I'm not an idiot, either."

"Could've fooled me."

Monsters etched onto the wooden pillars held up the ceiling, screaming at us in eternal, frozen silence as we moved toward the altar. On either side of the pews that lined the church, golden statues of Loki mixed with jade, obsidian, and silver ones. We passed one showing him birthing a kraken, and a second where she was surrounded by four huge deer. Another depicted him naked, with a massive wolf curled around his back, while a fourth displayed her flying atop a giant bird, shouting into eternity. A silver statue near the front of the church had Loki marveling into the sky as a huge lindworm dragon erupted out of the ground, and in another, she sat on the shoulder of a hairy, pointy-eared giant as he loped across the golden ground. In each, Loki was in control, sometimes in dominating fashion, but mostly the expression on his face was loving. He cared for those monsters he had birthed into the world.

A gray-haired man with a long beard stepped out from a door in the back of the church, carrying a wooden bucket. His green robes had different monsters sewn onto them and matched the flowing banners hanging on the walls. He made his way to an enormous ivory statue of Loki, the god standing with his arms open, looking down at his worshippers from the altar. When the man saw us, he dropped his bucket in alarm. He quickly recovered, and a gracious smile rose on his face.

"Good morrow to you. Welcome to the temple of the mother of monsters. How can I help you grow closer to the great god Loki this fine day?"

Doretha stepped toward the altar, and I followed behind. Food and drink had been placed upon a cedar table as offerings, and the smell of pungent, rotting fruit overtook the subtle smell of incense as we neared the man.

"We have been told it is the great god Loki that looks over this planet for his kin. Is that true?"

"It is," the old man nodded. "Loki welcomes the worship we bestow on him and reigns his countenance down upon us when he is able." He waved his arm at the altar. "Have you brought an offering for the great god?"

Doretha shook her head. "We did not know what to bring, druid. We are not from around here."

"Loki is not picky. Whatever you can spare, he will take."

"Has any of this worked to summon Loki before?" I asked from behind Doretha.

"One does not simply summon the goddess of monsters," the man replied. "To demand his counsel unceremoniously is to bring his ire. No, we ask and beg for his guidance, and when he deems us worthy, he deems us worthy."

"How often is that?"

The druid looked up at the statue. "I cannot say."

"Does that mean he hasn't made an appearance in a while?" Doretha asked.

"He shows himself with every flower that blooms, every blade of grass, and in the love that fills our heart, but if you're asking if he has graced us with his presence on this planet…we have not seen him in an age."

"But I'm guessing you have access to some way to summon him if the situation was dire enough, right?"

His brow furrowed, and he began to shake, visibly flustered by the question. "We…have our ways—but that is beyond my ability, I'm afraid. Only the Archdruid has access to that kind of knowledge, and she has kept it hidden for our protection."

"Gotcha." I looked around the temple. "And how do we find this Archdruid?"

"She roams between our temples at his leisure and keeps an office in the rectory. That's where she is now. I can assure you she doesn't have time to talk with you this fine day."

Doretha smiled. "We'll see about that."

The druid stepped forward, and I held up my hand, clad in blue frost at him. "You do not want to stop us, priest. Step out of the way."

"It would be my honor to die protecting the inner sanctum."

Doretha growled, shoving him into the altar with a hard push to the shoulder. One of the table's legs snapped, and the rotten fruit tumbled down on the priest's head.

"I am sorry about that," she said. "But we don't have time for this."

"Stop!" the druid shouted, but his voice was lost under the sound of our footsteps echoing against the wood. Doretha rushed to the door where he had entered, and we both disappeared behind it, toward the inner sanctum.

CHAPTER 56

"Excuse me?" I asked a woman wearing a green tunic similar to the one worn by the priest we had assaulted on the altar. "Do you know where the Archdruid's office is?"

Behind the altar door was like a different world from the rest of the temple. Wood paneling was still the decorative choice, but the walls were narrow, and offices lined either side of the hallway. It was as homely as it was homey.

The woman looked frail as she wrung her hands, trying to avoid our gaze. "End of the hall, make a right and then a left. Her door's the last one. You can't miss it."

We thanked the woman and edged past her, following her directions until we reached a double door at the end of the circuitous hallway. It was beautifully ornate, with a symbol of two snakes circling each other to form a golden S etched on each green door.

"No sense going back now," Doretha said, placing her hand on one of the doors.

I placed my hand on the other, and we pushed them open to find a large office, larger than any we passed in the rest of the building, with a bright, smiling woman sitting at a stone desk that clashed against the wood around it. She guarded a green door with another S symbol etched onto it.

"Welcome to Archdruid Margorie's office," she said, glancing at her computer screen. "Do you have an appointment?"

Doretha closed the doors behind her, locking them as discretely as she could, while I walked up to the black desk.

"Hi, we would like to see the Archdruid, please," I said.

"Of course you would. She's very popular. Everyone wants her to bless them with a moment of her time…however, I can't help you if you don't have an appointment. So, do you, or don't you?"

"That's a heady question," I asked. The phone rang, and when she went to answer it, I placed my hand on it and froze the base without a word. As the chill rose up the cord toward the receiver, I smashed the phone into a thousand pieces. "But the truth of it is that no, we don't have an appointment. Can you please help us anyway, though?"

"Absolutely not. Now, I'm going to have to ask you to leave," the woman said, calm and courteous. There was a force to her words that told me she wouldn't be intimidated.

The doors to the room began to slam thunderously. It had taken a moment for the guards to find us, but between the woman who we spoke to in the hallway and the druid we'd nearly knocked unconscious, I was surprised it took so long. Luckily, the doors were thick, and the lock to bolt them heavy.

Doretha pushed a bookcase over and leaned it against the door before rushing over to us. "We're not here to hurt you, but we need to see the Archdruid, and we need to do it now." Guards slammed on the doors. "We don't have a lot of time."

The assistant smiled sweetly. "I understand, but I simply can't help you without an appointment."

"Screw this," I said, rushing past the woman toward the door. When I touched the door handle, a spark shot through my body and sent me flying backward.

She looked down at me. "As I said, I can't help you without an appointment."

"Then make us a goddamn appointment!" Doretha slammed her hands on the desk, sending papers flying everywhere.

"You don't have to be rude about it." The polite girl disappeared, and the face of the woman changed to resolute and fearsome. "Though, admittedly, even if you asked nicely, I simply can't do that."

"Then we're going to have to hurt you," Doretha growled.

The woman kicked out of her chair and rose into the air. Her mousey demeanor melted away, and she removed her green headband to reveal a plume of red hair that fell past her shoulders, which were broad and strong. Her shirt ripped when she flexed her powerful muscles. She clapped her hands together, and a huge flaming sword appeared in her hand.

"You can certainly try." Enormous white wings plumed from her back.

"You're a frigging angel," I said, spinning away from her and crawling around the table toward Doretha.

The woman let out a mirthless laugh. "Please. Angels are pussies. I'm a Valkyrie. And now, you will both die."

She swung her sword. I leaped through the air and tackled Doretha before the blade could lop her in half.

"*Crepitus glacies*!" I shouted, turning to the Valkyrie stomping toward us. A ball of ice shot from my hand, but the Valkyrie cut clean through the sphere before it could even explode. She reared up and swung again, this time straight down. I rolled right, and Doretha rolled left to avoid the attack.

"*Rigéscunt!*" I placed my hand on the floor, and a sheet of ice rose from the ground and coated the Valkyrie's boots, freezing them to the ground. "Keep her busy!"

I had an idea. It was a stupid idea, but it was an idea. I rushed over toward the desk as the Valkyrie hacked at the ice on the floor with her sword. I slid into the chair and hit a few keys to wake up the computer. Perhaps if I just put an appointment into the Archdruid's planner, it would force this whole thing to stop.

They used a simple calendar that was already up on the screen when the computer flickered on. My eyes darted to the skirmish. The Valkyrie had freed one boot and lunged at Doretha, who barely avoided the raging woman's sword. With two good feet, the Valkyrie would end this battle in a matter of seconds.

I had to work fast.

The Archdruid didn't have anything in her calendar for the current time block, and so I placed something right atop where we were in the day that said "meeting with Doretha and Elizabeth." I didn't like using my god-given name, but it sounded more official than Lizzie.

"There!" I shouted. "We have an appointment."

The Valkyrie smashed through the ice and turned to me. "That's not how it works. Now, I'm going to slaughter you, and I'll enjoy it, too. The streets will run red with your blood toni—"

As she spoke, the door behind me creaked open, and a tall, statuesque woman with long, black hair and a perfect, pewter face walked out. Her lips were tinged a bright red, and she cocked her head wistfully at the scene in front of her, though she didn't seem bothered or alarmed by it.

"Theoreal," the woman said in a sweet voice. "Who are Doretha and Elizabeth? I've never heard of them before."

"Don't worry about that, Your Grace," Theoreal hissed. "It was a mistake, and they'll be going now—straight to the underworld."

"No, we're not! We have to speak with you…Loki." With a Valkyrie protecting her, it wasn't hard to deduce that this woman was more than an Archdruid. "It's a matter of life and death. Literally, this planet is on the line if you don't take this meeting."

"Well spotted." The woman smiled at me. "Hmm. I suppose I can clear some time for you. As you can see, my schedule is very flexible today." She moved into her office. "Come now, I've seen that look on Theoreal's face before. Move swiftly, or she'll lop off your head for sport, and even I won't be able to stop her."

Doretha was already making a beeline toward the opened door. Theoreal looked as angry as I had ever seen anyone in my whole life, but I couldn't stop myself from giving her a quick smile before we disappeared into the office and the door shut behind us.

CHAPTER 57

The minute I passed the threshold to Loki's office, I felt the familiar drop in the pit of my stomach that always presented itself when I traveled through the ether with Kimberly, except that instead of rebounding into my throat, the feeling settled in my knees, weighing down my feet as I moved toward the sleek black desk set up in front of a raging fireplace.

His room was full of books—no, not books—ledgers. Some of them sat open, and I noticed the script notating a series of numbers and letters I didn't understand. Most of them, though, sat in tall stacks, unnumbered with little but the color of the leather to distinguish them.

"You'll have to forgive the mess," Loki said, sliding cross-legged onto a backless stool. "I usually mask this kind of thing for commoners, but, well, you know my little secret, don't you?"

I weaved through the maze of books toward him. "How long have you been the Archdruid of your own church?"

"Who can tell. I came down one day, some time ago, when Margorie was still alive. When she died, I agreed to take over for a short time to name her successor, and then…I kind of enjoyed it." He waited for a response, but we were both digesting the last few minutes. "I didn't believe it at first, but being down among the people, seeing how they live…well, it gave me perspective, didn't it?"

"I…guess so," Doretha said. "It's more than I can say for most gods, at least, who never come down from Moun—Asgard."

"Yes, yes. They do enjoy being away from their flock. They believe that since we made these creatures—

humans—that they are little more than our playthings." He sneered. "I don't agree. I believe once you make something, it's your responsibility to grow it, nurture it, and make sure it doesn't destroy itself." He let out a deep sigh. "Which brings me to you, and specifically the statement you made about the world ending. Please, tell me more."

Doretha hesitated for a moment. "I am a handmaiden of Talinda—many of you call her the Time Being, I believe."

"I know of Talinda, though I have never had the pleasure of meeting her."

"I'm aware. If I'm not mistaken, you were instrumental in that deplorable nickname sticking for eternity."

He smirked proudly. "Please, I came up with one expression, and then 'for the time being' was manipulated into something I didn't intend."

"It still grates on her."

Loki chuckled dismissively. "If she was more malleable, then perhaps she wouldn't be seen as such a heinous wench."

"Don't mistake me, I have no love for my former master. She is rigid and cold, and she would let this world die, which is why we are here." Doretha cleared her throat. "In two days' time, your planet will turn on a perpetual motion machine. I'm sure you have heard about it."

"Heard about it?" Loki laughed. "I'm to bless it, child. Nothing happens on this planet without me, hands deep in it, these days."

"Then you must know it's doomed to fail," I said, sick of the smug look on the god's face.

"Piffle," Loki spat. "If I had a nickel for every time somebody told me the world was going to end—well, perhaps I do, actually. I am a very rich god, after all."

"You arrogant son of a—" I shouted. "Doretha is a handmaiden of time. She has seen it happen over and over again."

Doretha's eyes dropped to the floor. "It's true. I've tried in every conceivable way to end this accursed Apocalypse, except for petitioning the gods for help."

"And why haven't you come to me before?"

"Because I don't believe you will help me, even if you can." Doretha's eyes now found Loki's. "You gods are all the same—my mother, your mother, the whole lot—and frankly, I didn't want anyone tattling on me back to Talinda about where she could find me."

Loki smiled. "So instead of groveling to me, you decided to relive the death of my planet, again and again?"

She shook her head. "No, I only lived fully through the death of your planet once. Every other time I managed to jump away." She took the stopwatch out of her pocket. "Using this watch to travel backward to stop the Apocalypse…except I can't stop it."

"I recognize that watch. From Talinda's collection, right?"

"Yes, I stole it from her," Doretha replied. "After I watched this planet die at her insistence, I stole it and came back here to fix it, no matter the cost."

"Stealing from the Time Being? Now you have my attention." Loki stood up and walked to the fireplace. "How much time do we have?"

"Two days tops," I said.

"Not a lot of time." He stared deeply into the flames. "Very well. I will help you, but first, you must do something for me."

"I wouldn't expect anything for free," Doretha said. "What can I do for you, mother of monsters?"

"You're malleable, too," Loki caressed Doretha's cheek. "Talinda taught you well. Perhaps you would make a good concubine when all of this is said and done."

"Don't touch her!" I snapped, placing myself between them.

"No," Doretha said, her voice even and calm. "It's okay. If that is your wish, my grace, and you save this world, then I will serve you in any way you deem fit."

"I'll hold you to that." Loki walked to his desk and pulled out a blue vial, a deck of playing cards, and a jade coin the size of a quarter. He placed them on his table. "My price is simple. I wish to return to Asgard, but I have been barred there for my hand in killing Odin's son, Balder. The problem is, it never happened. The blind god Höd lied about my involvement. I never wished Balder dead. We were close—close in a way gods shouldn't be, and Höd hated Balder. They were rivals for the hand of Nanna, a battle that Balder won, so Höd slipped a vial of pureed mistletoe into my friend's drink." He held up the vial. "This is a vial of Thökk's tears. It is the only thing that can bring my love back to life. Travel to Asgard, where Balder lays in state for eternity, feed him these tears, and return him to me."

"We will do it," I said.

Loki shook his head. "Oh no, I can't let you both go. What kind of leverage would I have then?"

I gestured around me. "How about this whole frigging world?"

"No." He pointed at me. "You go. Save my love, bring him here, and I will do my part. Meanwhile, my pet and I will have some fun." He sniffed Doretha's hair, and she stifled a whimper. He leaned closer to her and spoke softly. "What do you think of that? Will you willingly put your life in this one's hands?"

"But—" I said.

"Yes," Doretha crowed. "I will trust her with my life."

"Excellent," Loki growled, his lustful eyes turning to me. "And will you save this one's life?"

Just days ago, I had not known Doretha. Yesterday I was supposed to kill her, and yet, now, I wanted nothing more than to protect her and the world she loved. "I will do this, but you must promise not to touch her until I return."

Loki inhaled loudly through his nose. "That is a tall order, but you have less than two days. I suppose I can wait that long." He handed me the vial then spun the coin in the air. "When you have him, place this coin on your lips, and it will bring you back to me."

"What about the cards?" I asked.

He smiled. "Something to while away the time. Now, have fun in Asgard."

He flicked his wrist and snapped his fingers. I was gone in an instant, with the taste of bitter chocolate on my lips.

CHAPTER 58

Stalagmites of crystal and sleek metal rose from the shimmering ground, and the lights from the buildings twinkled as beautifully as the stars in the inky black night sky of Asgard. The great structures rose high into the air, cutting it with their jagged edges, but the sky did not break or bleed at the incursion of the buildings; they wove together in beautiful symmetry.

The Asgardians eyed me suspiciously. I was quite a bit darker than any of the other citizens of the city, and while I wore jeans and a simple shirt, their flawless bodies were draped with finely hemmed silk tunics that danced in a hundred different colors.

"You don't belong here," a squirrely voice squeaked behind me.

I turned to see an olive-skinned boy with black hair leaning against the side of a glassy building. His tunic was dark purple mixed with periwinkle and lilac, and the bottoms of his feet were covered with golden sandals.

"Of course I do," I lied, but even a kid could tell I stood out like a sore thumb. "Why? What do you know about it?"

The boy kicked off the building. "I know that outsiders aren't welcome here. You shouldn't have even been able to get in, and yet—here you are. So, are you a spy or a groupie?"

"Excuse me?"

"Do you wanna bang a god or kill one?" He stepped forward. "Because if you're here to kill a god, I have to turn you in…but if you're a groupie, and all you want to do is sleep with a god—then I can be persuaded." He wiggled his eyebrows. "Know what I mean?"

"Gross," my face contorted in disgust. "You're a kid."

"I'll bet I'm older than you," he said with a wink.

"Yuck. I'm not a groupie. And I'm not a spy." I brushed my hair out of my eyes. "I'm looking for Balder's tomb. Do you know where it is?"

"Of course," the boy said. "There's a whole building downtown dedicated to him, but you're not going to get in looking like that, or smelling like that putrid malcontent, either."

My stench. Doretha said I smelled like the Greek gods, though Loki hadn't said anything about it—or maybe that's why he sent me here. He knew I would be found out immediately, and then he could move his plans forward without a hitch.

Seemed like a long way to go when he could have just killed me with the snap of his fingers. Then again, I had quickly learned that nothing the gods did made a lick of sense. They seemed to be both simultaneously the most powerful and least capable beings in the whole galaxy.

"I could help you, for a price."

"I'm not sleeping with you." I dry-heaved to indicate my disgust. "What is it with you gods and your libidos?"

"That's not what I want—I mean, don't get me wrong, I'll take it. But you smell…like pain and suffering, too much for one so young. I want to know your stories. I have never left Asgard, and I have spoken at length with everyone in this city, even Odin, and heard their tales a thousand times. Tell me something new and exciting. When I'm satisfied, I will help you."

"What do you want to know?"

"Let's start with your name, and don't lie. We'll go from there."

It wasn't a trade I was happy to make, letting myself be known by this ancient child, but if I wanted to survive Asgard, I needed allies, and I needed them quickly.

"My name is Lizzie—Elizabeth. What's yours?"

"Forseti," he replied. He took a long moment. "You aren't lying. That's a good start. Usually, people have lied to me twice by now."

"I'm not a liar."

His eyes narrowed. "Well, that wasn't a total lie. You might not lie to others, but you often lie to yourself, don't you?"

The hair on the back of my neck stood on edge. "What is this, a psychology session?"

"No, I just have a sixth sense for truth and justice. Now, come with me and tell me your story, the whole of it, from the beginning, and I will judge your worth."

"I don't know how I feel about a child judging me."

He laughed and slid into an alley behind the building. "Silly mortal, children are the only ones pure enough to have any business judging anything. Come, speak the truth of your life."

There was nothing else to do, so as he led me into the mazes of buildings, I spoke. I told him about my childhood and my adopted parents. I told him about the prophecy, how I ran away from home, along with what happened when I returned home—that both my parents died, and I blamed myself for it. The death of Veronica. I talked about my quest for the Time Being, then meeting Talinda, how I've broken my promises to Talinda already, to everyone, and now I'm helping Doretha save a planet by working with Loki, who had been banished from Asgard.

Forseti asked a lot of questions and listened silently as I answered. When I was finished, he nodded. "We will see how truthful you were being. If your heart is true, when we exit this alley, we will be in front of Balder's memorial, and I will help you enter it. However, if you have lied to me, we will be in front of the guard's station, and I will turn you in."

"What? That wasn't the deal. You said you would help me."

"And I told you to tell the truth. Did you?"

"Of course I did."

He grinned. "Then you have nothing to worry about."

"You know if I was truthful, don't you?"

He shook his head. "If I focused on the truth of your words, I would not be able to hear your story. I have enchanted the alley to act as my proxy so that I might engross myself in your tale, which was truly quite fascinating. I do hope it was true."

We exited the alley and an enormous spire, twirling like a corkscrew high into the air, rose before us, its prismatic light bathing my face.

"It seems as though you were telling the truth, or enough of it, at least." Forseti smiled. "I like the part about you and Veronica best. All right, let's get you inside so you can save the world."

He didn't turn to the spire. Instead, he turned back into the alley.

"Wait!" I called after him. "Where are you going? I thought we were going inside."

"We are." He nodded. "But you can't go looking like that. I have a tailor on retainer. Come, come. Let's get you out of those dreadful clothes. No time to spare. If you're to be believed, then a world hangs on the tip of a needle."

CHAPTER 59

Forseti's tailor dressed me in layers of red and white, intermixed with sparkling, sheer lace. When we were done, my tunic moved like lava bubbling out of a volcano, with reds, whites, oranges, and yellows blending into each other like I controlled the very element of fire itself.

"What do you think?" Forseti said. "It's pretty great, right? As if it were made by the fingers of Frigg herself."

"It's lovely." I turned so I could watch the lava wrap around my back and down my leg. "It's a lot, though. I mean, I feel like I'm going to stick out like a sore thumb in this thing."

"Nonsense. Drab is what sticks out on Asgard. If you want to blend in, you have to stand out." He spun around, and the white on his tunic blended with the purple to create the feeling of dusk, with white clouds shifting over the ground as the sun set in the distance. "I think you look perfect."

Forseti left coin on the counter, and we left the store. Instead of turning toward Balder's keep, we moved away from it, crossing the street toward a perfumery on the other side.

"Where are we going now?" I asked.

"We've fixed your look. It's time to fix your smell." He opened the door to the shop, and a thousand scents accosted my nose at once, each outdoing the last. "Hulder, we have special need of you today."

The woman at the counter had wild hair that stuck up from her head in a thousand different ways, and yet, none seemed to be out of place. She wore a mauve and taupe tunic, and her sagging shoulders stood at attention as we moved closer.

"Oh, thank god, Forseti." She rushed toward him and kissed his rosy cheeks. "What a dreadfully boring day." She sniffed the air. "And you have brought me—my, you do smell like Zeus, don't you? I was hoping for some hot gossip, but this is even more delicious." She grabbed my face, much darker than hers by a dozen tones or more. "And your color, dear. How did you get here?"

I looked over at Forseti. I knew how much he hated lying, and his curt nod was my cue to tell the truth. "Loki sent me to free Balder from his slumber."

Hulder's lip twitched, and then she laughed. "That's literally too wonderful for words." She beckoned with a single finger for me to follow her. "Come along, let's see what we can do to spruce you up a bit. Can't go visit our sleeping heir smelling like that, can you?"

We must have tried three dozen perfumes before she landed on one that she thought properly masked my stench. The smell of mint, oak, and smoke made me want to wretch, but something about it caused both Forseti and Hulder to smile.

"Yes," Forseti said. "I think that will do it."

Hulder held up her finger and turned from me, picking up a tin case from one of the glass shelves. "Not quite yet." She dabbed her finger into the container and rubbed it under my eyes. "There, now you look like a proper goddess."

When I looked at myself in the mirror, my face shimmered slightly. I hadn't noticed before then, but both Forseti and Hulder's faces glowed in a similar fashion. Forseti flashed a big smile and spun me toward the door, leaving some coin on the counter to pay for Hulder's services.

"Why are you helping me?" I asked as we walked down the street. "Won't you get in trouble?"

His stubby legs moved fast, and I had to break into a half jog to keep pace. "The truth is always trouble, but it is also worth spreading," he said. "I believe you have told me the truth. Our little game proved that. But can you be sure that Loki told you the truth? He is a trickster, after all."

"I have been told never to trust a god. However, they do stick by their word, and I am sure that if I bring Balder to him, then I will help save millions, billions of lives, and that is worth it for me, even if his true intentions may be opaque."

Forseti shrugged. "I suppose that all you can ask from the gods is to keep their word, even if they hide their intentions."

We reached the front of the tall corkscrew spire, where two burly guards in silver and green plate armor stood, their lips downturned in a permanent scowl.

"It's time. Let's hope the magic of the gods can get you inside. Step quick, and don't look at the guards. They are beneath you, understand?"

"That's a terrible way to think."

"Gods are terrible." His words were passionless and straightforward. "Look forward. Nowhere else."

I nodded and followed him toward the doors, keeping my eyes trained forward. I could feel the guards' stares burn into my skin, but I did not falter. I did not look at them, despite every bone in my body wanting to flinch at their imposing demeanor. From the edge of my sight, one of their wrists flinched, but even that did not avert my gaze.

Soon enough, we were through the entrance and standing in the atrium. It felt like it took an hour, but it must have taken no longer than a few seconds to cross the threshold into the airy space. A huge statue of a smiling Balder, dressed in a golden chest plate and skirt to cover the top of his legs, begged for admiration. Long, blond hair blew behind him in the wind, and his eyes smoldered intensity. Along the jade walls were twenty-foot-high paintings of Balder engaged in battle and other feats of bravery.

I wanted to crane my neck up to see the tip of the spire from the inside, but Forseti grabbed my tunic and pulled me toward him. "Do not stare in awe at this place. You will give yourself away. We have lived millennia with this spire, and though it is impressive, the sheer magnificence has become banal."

He released me and shuffled off to the ticket counter, where a Valkyrie with a forced smile sat behind glass. "Forseti! How are you?"

"Good, good, Val," he answered. "My friend is visiting from the outer world and wishes to pay her respects to Balder." He placed a coin on the counter, followed by three more. "I understand the exhibit is closed, but I thought you might be able to allow us access as a favor to an old friend."

"I…couldn't." She shook her head. "The royal family is preparing him for—"

"No, no. I know all of that." He waved off her words. "Who was the one that told you of your true parentage, the one that freed you from working as a slaver to that brutal—"

"You, it was you—and you will never let me forget it, will you?"

Forseti held up his hands. "I don't ask much. Just a favor here, a consideration there. In the grand scheme, what I ask is nothing in comparison to what I have given you." He pointed to the coin. "And I always pay handsomely, do I not?"

She nodded and pulled two tickets off the carousel and handed them to Forseti while pocketing the money in one swoop. "Yes, you are very kind," she grumbled.

He smiled, but there was a malevolence to it that I hadn't seen before. "Please don't forget it, unlike you will forget that we have come, yes?"

"Who are you?" Val said with a playful wink. "I don't think we've ever met."

"Very good." Forseti turned from the counter and handed me a ticket.

"So, that's what you do? Use truths against people?"

"Of course," Forseti said without skipping a beat. "We all get along as we see fit. Truth is a very powerful weapon. It is also a deadly one. Many don't wish to hear the truth, and others want nothing more than to keep theirs concealed. I do both—hide and reveal, given the circumstances…and the price to be paid."

We walked toward a glass elevator opposite the entrance.

"And what price will you ask of me when this is done?"

He chuckled as he inserted his ticket into a turnstile, and it stamped his ticket, allowing him to enter. "You, a mortal? There is nothing that you can do for me. But there is a truth buried below the lies of Balder's death, and I wish to see it exposed."

I placed my ticket into the turnstile, and it clicked for me just as it had for Forseti. I followed him toward the elevator. He placed the ticket into a small slot on the wall beside it, and a green light dinged above before the glass doors opened, and we stepped inside.

CHAPTER 60

"When we reach the top of this spire, we will enter a chamber. Inside of it, Balder lays perfectly preserved under glass. As one of Odin's sons, he was once considered the true heir to the kingdom before his unfortunate accident. My grandfather has never recovered."

"Grandfather?" I asked.

"Yes, Balder—he was my father. I am his only son." Forseti looked down at his hands. "That is my truth. It has destroyed my family and sent them to the brink of madness. I have searched for the truth behind his death for eons, and now…now, I may finally have found it." He wiped a tear from his eye. "I am sorry for keeping this from you. You smelled of death and Zeus's magic, and I needed to be sure you were true of heart before I told you. While I do seek the truth, it is not only for the sake of truth itself. I wish to learn what happened to my father."

I nodded. "That is understandable, I suppose. I don't like being jerked around, though, Forseti, and while I can't do anything to you, I can certainly ask you to be forthright with me in the future."

"And now that I know you are worthy, I will trust you with the truth."

The elevator rose high into the air, and the enormous statue that took up half the entryway shrunk like an ant as we reached the tip of the spire. The sparkling lights from the stars were replaced by the sterile orange ones from the elevator, lighting our path forward.

The elevator came to a stop, and the doors opened to reveal a sterile white room lit by an orb as brilliant as the sun. Windows cut into the roof of the spire allowed the light of the stars to rain down on the glass coffin in the middle of the room. The door closed behind us, and our feet on the golden tiles echoed against the walls.

Candles glowed on either side of the entrance, and along the wall, there was a small padded wooden ledge to kneel and pray. Forseti knelt on the left of the room, and I followed on the right. The only prayers I knew were the ones I learned in Sunday school as a child, but something told me the Norse gods would not appreciate my Christian prayers. Still, I took a small piece of wood and used the fire from one candle to light another.

"What was he the god of?" I asked. Even at a whisper, my words echoed.

"Light," Forseti said, irritation dripping from his voice. Understandably so, as I had just broken the silence of a sacred place for him. "They say he was the purest among us and that his joy knew no bounds."

I bowed my head. "I am lost, Balder, at a crossroads between the destruction of a world and the annihilation of time itself. I have no idea what to do next. I hope that when you wake, I can find clarity of purpose." I held tight to the vial of tears in my pocket. "If for some reason this doesn't do what Loki said it will, then I'm sorry. At least know I'll probably be paying for it the rest of my life."

I stopped myself from making the sign of the cross and stood. Forseti was already standing over Balder's coffin. I walked over to it, trying my best to step softly to avoid the cavernous echoes of the solemn place.

"I have waited my whole life to hear him speak to me again," Forseti said, tears in his eyes. "I admit, my hope has blinded me to what might happen if this doesn't work."

I took the vial from my tunic. "It has blinded the both of us."

He touched the glass atop the coffin. "When I remove this glass, it will sound an alarm, and there will be no turning back for either of us. Are you sure you are ready to invoke the wrath of the gods should you fail?"

I shrugged. "I don't feel like I have a lot of choice in the matter."

"There is always a choice. It just might not be a good one."

"Talinda said that, too," I said to him.

"I'm not surprised," Forseti replied. "It is a truth the gods have known for eons. One of the only truths we can all agree on."

"That's kind of sad."

"The truth often is." Forseti sighed. "The gods are very powerful, but we still have to make difficult choices like this every day. As much as I want this more than anything, opening this coffin is not my choice to make. You must decide how we proceed."

I thought for a minute. "Let's do it, then."

"Very well."

Forseti closed his eyes and placed his hands on the container. It vibrated for an instant but then flickered out of existence. The moment the case was gone, a high-pitched alarm shot through the room. Above us, thick metal cascaded down from the spire, covering the windows and locking us off from the elevator.

"Do it now!" Forseti shouted.

I pulled the stopper from the vial and opened Balder's mouth, pouring the liquid down his throat. Nothing happened. His skin was just as gray as it had been when—and then, his whole body heaved, and he lurched up.

"What happened?" Balder said, rubbing his head.

I grabbed the coin out of my pocket and touched Balder's arm. "Welcome back. Now, I'm sorry about this but—"

I touched the coin to my lips just as I felt Forsetti grab my tunic, and then, the sinking feeling came again. We fell into the ether, the taste of bitter black chocolate on my tongue.

CHAPTER 61

We were pulled out of the ether onto a fluffy white cloud, just like when I entered Earth's Heaven, but this wasn't just a golden gate and endless fields of nothing. This cloud city contained dozens of white marble structures that looked more like Ancient Greece than anywhere in Scandinavia and bustled with activity from hundreds of Valkyries. This wasn't Loki's office.

"Ow, my head," Balder said, his voice gravelly but smooth. "What happened?"

"Dad!" Forseti lunged on top of him. "You were killed by Höd—poisoned. For generations, we believed that Loki deceived Höd, and Odin banished him for it. But now Loki has given you a means to save you and prove his innocence." Forseti wrapped his arms around Balder's broad chest. "Isn't that amazing, Papa?"

Balder was still lost in thought, but Forseti's last word jogged something inside of him. "Papa? Wait…are you Forseti? My boy?" When Forseti nodded, tears dripping down his face, Balder smiled a great smile and squeezed him tightly. "By the gods. I missed you. You have no idea the torture of being caught between the living and the dead."

"You're here now, Papa," Forseti said. Even though he was ancient, he sounded like a tiny child. "We're together."

Balder looked past him to me. "Are you the one I should thank for saving my life?"

"Just the messenger." I waved. "All thanks should go to Loki."

Balder stood with Forseti still wrapped around him. It didn't seem likely the kid would ever let go again for the rest of eternity. "Where in the nine realms are we? Mount Olympus? Helheim?"

I looked around and shrugged. "I really don't know."

From the center of the street, a Valkyrie flew toward us. As it neared, I recognized the red hair of the receptionist from Loki's office. She landed gracefully in front of us and held out her arms to welcome us.

"Welcome, esteemed guests," Theoreal spoke solemnly. "Loki is very pleased that you have returned. He has prepared a feast for you. Follow me." She glanced at me. "It's easier if you bounce."

I already knew that from my experience in Heaven and bounced easily next to Balder and Forseti. We followed Theoreal through the streets of the cloud city until we reached a castle high on a mound of clouds with several dozen stairs carved into the plush ground leading up to it. Neither Balder nor Theoreal needed to use them, but I did, and I stepped two at a time until I reached the front door, which had been thrown open in greeting. Doretha stood in a white tunic and golden leaf tiara, smiling at us as we entered the castle.

"I can't believe it's really you," she said to me as I approached. "And not a moment too soon. The world is set to end in hours."

"I'm sorry it took so long." I hugged her tightly, and her warmth made me feel like everything I had experienced on Asgard was worth it.

"Loki didn't think you would come at all. He teased me mercilessly about it, and yet here you are." Doretha pulled away from me and smiled at Balder. "We have prepared a feast for you, given that you haven't eaten in eons." She leaned closer to me with a smirk. "It was really nothing since Loki can conjure things out of thin air, but he's very proud of it, so make a big deal, okay?"

The ground of the palace was hard tile, mercifully, which meant I didn't have to bounce. I simply followed Theoreal and Doretha as they led us to an enormous banquet hall. The table was filled with more food than I could ever imagine from as many cuisines as I could name, in every size, shape, and color. Loki stood at the far end of the magnificent table, carving a turkey with an ivory knife.

"Good friends," he said. "It's so lovely to see you again." He smiled at Balder. "How was your nap?"

Balder stretched. "I feel a bit stiff, but otherwise, it wasn't half bad. Always nice to get away from the machinations of Asgard for a time."

"Isn't it, though?" Loki pointed the knife at an empty chair next to him. "Please sit down." He chuckled as he carved. "It's funny you say that about getting away. Did you know I have been banished from Asgard for my part in your death?"

Balder placed Forseti in a chair and sat down beside him. Doretha sat across from them, at Loki's right hand, and I took the chair next to her.

"It's a tragedy," Balder said. "Forseti told me that the old crone Höd implicated you in my death. Preposterous. You don't have the cunning to do something like that." He laughed. "Or the courage of your conviction to murder me."

I could see Balder's comment slap across Loki's face. The mother of monsters bit his lip. "You always knew just what to say to—well, I hope this is a way to bury the hatchet, as they say, for any bad blood between us. I do hope that you can help me reenter the glory of your father."

Balder grabbed a turkey leg and ripped off a large bite. "This is delicious, old chap. You've really outdone yourself." He took another bite and talked with his mouth full. "Once I get back to Asgard, I will tell my father you are too cowardly to ever try to kill me, and all will be forgiven. The fact they could believe a scrawny thing like you"—he punched Loki in the arm— "could take down a virile god like myself." He punched his own chest. "Frankly, it's insulting."

Loki took a breath and studied the ivory knife in his hand. "You don't know this knife, do you?"

"I can't say that I do." Balder leaned closer. "It's a fine blade, though, minus the turkey juice."

Loki wiped the dagger with a napkin. "It has few equals in the entire universe. You see, once you were poisoned but didn't die, I realized that no poison could kill a god. I studied every book I could to find a way. It turns out there are only a finite number of weapons to do the trick. They're called godkiller weapons." He turned the dagger in his hand, admiring it. "I searched the whole universe for one, and it led me to this planet, which is where Odin caught up to me and banished me. I found this weapon and vowed that if I ever got a second chance, I would not fail to kill you again."

Without another word, Loki buried the knife deep into Balder's chest. The color drained from the god's face as he screamed out in pain and fell to the ground, dead.

"Father!" Forseti shouted, but that was his last word because the knife cut through Forseti's throat as quickly as it had his father's, and a moment later, they were both lying dead and bloody on the floor.

Loki simply smiled as he pulled a napkin from the table and dried the knife off. "It appears you've fulfilled your part of the bargain, and as you can see…this knife will certainly kill a god. Now, it's time to fulfill my end."

A smile rose on Doretha's face. "It's about time. I couldn't listen to him say another word."

CHAPTER 62

"What is he talking about, Doretha?" I asked as my eyes scanned the maniacal look on her face. Her smile wasn't one of joy but of psychotic menace, and her beady eyes glowed with the wild look of a woman who had finally gotten everything she ever wanted.

"You really are naïve." She stood up. "I have to admit, I've been looking forward to this for so long I thought it would fail to meet my expectations, but it has exceeded even my wildest dreams. Watching your heartbreak was truly delicious. Do you know how long it took for me to line everything up just so? How much testing and failing? A hundred timelines, a thousand attempts to get you to trust me just the right amount." She smiled. "That burning world, though—where I 'died' to deliver you a final message that you were right? That was the final flourish I needed. It really made you trust me, didn't it? I thought it might be too over the top, but it worked like a charm. Your ego truly knows no bounds."

It was all a trick. Some plot to get me to turn on Talinda—and it worked.

She sucked her teeth. "Of course, Loki had a part to play, and he played it so well."

Loki bowed. "Thank you."

Doretha held out her hand. "And now I'll take the knife and the watch."

He placed the knife into her hand and pulled the glowing stopwatch from his pocket. "Here. It's been endowed with my magic, which should be enough to get you back to her, as promised."

"What are the two of you talking about?" I snapped. "I want some answers."

Doretha placed the pocket watch in her pocket. "Oh, you'll love this."

She stabbed Loki in the throat with his own knife. The poor trickster god never even saw it coming. Some part of that was fitting, in its way. Tricked by a trickster trickier than you. He fell to the ground, bleeding from the throat, with a look on his face so piteous that I almost felt sorry for him.

Doretha didn't seem phased at all by the blood around her. She washed off the knife for the third time and sat down across from me, picking a grape from a cornucopia on the table.

"Was any of it true?" I asked, defeated. "Did you love Tobias? Did you care about saving this world?"

"At some point, it was true. I did love that poor Tobias, for a time at least. After watching the flesh flay off his bones for the thousandth time, I grew numb to it, and my only thoughts turned to revenge against my creator, the one who caused me so much misery."

"Talinda," I said.

She nodded. "I've never been able to return, you see. I have not seen her since I left. Her planet moves with the time, and if she doesn't want to be found, she can't be found. But I realized some time ago that I knew exactly where to find her because I had been with her in the past." She popped another grape in her mouth. "All I needed was a way to kill her…and a gullible sap to help me."

"Me," I breathed.

"It was wonderful. You performed brilliantly. Tell me, do you remember how many times we've played this game before, now that the veil has been lifted on my deception?"

"Before?"

She clapped her hands. "Brilliant. Yes, we have been at this for a long while, resetting things, trying different combinations, making you believe me a little more each time, failing and resetting things, until finally, at last, we have reached the endgame."

"How long was Loki in on it?"

"Honestly, I don't even remember." She took a pewter pendant from her shirt. "He gave me this pendant, which allowed him and I both to remember. I think it was maybe sixty or so rotations ago I told him I could give him revenge on Balder. It blinded him to everything else and allowed me to bring him deeper into my trap each time I returned."

"What the hell happened here?" Theoreal shouted. She stood at the entrance of the room, glaring.

"Freedom," Doretha answered. "You are no longer bound to look after this fool. You are free to live your life—but just know, the world is going to explode in a couple of minutes, so don't be on this planet by then."

The Valkyrie put her hand on her sword.

"He's not worth fighting over, and you know it."

Theoreal thought for a moment longer and must have realized she agreed because she bowed and then ran away.

Dorothea stifled a giggle. "It really is sad how much everyone hates him."

"You're not going to save them?" I said. "This world?"

"They can't be saved. Don't you understand anything about fate, even after all this time?" She pointed to my wrist. "You should thank me. I did you a favor."

I looked down at my wrist before remembering I had pulled off the bracelet. I dug into my pocket and pulled it out, only to see every red thread had turned white. "It's over?"

"For you, but not for me." She smiled. "Or maybe not either of us. Tie those strings and pull them again. Maybe I'll see you on the other side."

Before I could say anything else, she grabbed the pocket watch from her pocket and clicked it. She vanished in a flash, and at the same second, I heard a rumbling under me.

It was the planet, collapsing into itself. I had failed, even in my success.

I didn't have the stomach to stick around. I wrapped the threads around my wrist and pulled them, vanishing into the white light. I reappeared in the room of the loom and spindle. Every single one of the white strings was red, and sitting at the spindle was not Talinda, but Doretha, with the same mad smile on her face I had seen on her face in Loki's banquet hall.

CHAPTER 63

The threads flowed like streams of blood toward the front of the room where gaunt, piteous women with thin hair, dark bags under their eyes, and pasty skin weaved the red silk into their looms. The joy had gone from their eyes since Talinda's keep; the room's previous warmth had been replaced by a cold, merciless wind that whipped through me.

"So nice of you to join us," Doretha said, her voice breathless and scratchy. "I have been waiting a long time for this meeting."

"What happened to Talinda?"

"She's dead, my dear. Thanks to you."

"How could—" Tears flowed down my face. "You killed your own mother!"

"It was the only way." She stepped down the stone steps from the spindle. "Now, I have taken her place and remade the universe in my image. Here, there is no death, no pain, and everybody gets a happily ever after."

"You bitch! You can't do that. Look at these threads! It's all wrong!"

"Wrong to who?" She growled. "Wrong to the fates that made the universe? Wrong to my mother?" She swaggered forward, and the ivory dagger shone at her side. "Who are they to decide right and wrong?"

I stood my ground, even though every instinct in my body was to run. "So now you're the judge of right and wrong?"

Doretha smirked like a magician who had just performed her greatest trick. "That's right."

"What makes you better than the gods? You simply replaced your judgment for theirs."

"No! You don't understand!" She lurched forward, screaming at me just inches from my face.

"I understand everything. You're not the first person to think that just because they didn't like something, it was wrong. I've met plenty of people like that before, hundreds of times on my travels. It's nothing but arrogance and ignorance. Your way isn't the right way just because you believe it is."

She slapped me across the face, and I fell hard. Her hands had absorbed the power of a god, and she relished showing her newfound strength. People could say what they wanted about Talinda. I preferred her to the frazzled maniac standing before me.

Doretha snapped her fingers, and two shadows emerged from the darkness. "Take her to the dungeon."

There was no use fighting. Even if I could escape them, there was nowhere to go. I had no way back to my planet, and no way to know what I would find there even if I could return. With all the damage that Doretha had done, it was amazing I was still alive.

The shadows tossed me in a stone cell with nothing but a wooden plank suspended from the wall for comfort. Water dripped down the walls and formed into puddles on the uneven floor. The thin bedding did little to stem the cold that nestled in my bones.

It was impossible to know how long I laid there, shivering, before I heard the rattle of metal on metal as the lock clicked and the door creaked open. The mousey form of Viannah snuck into the cell. Far from the regal, clean handmaiden I'd summoned from the deck of Kimberly's apartment, a thick layer of grime covered her face, and rags had replaced her white tunic. Still, I recognized her immediately.

"Viannah!" I jumped up and wrapped her in a hug. "It's so good to see you."

She tapped my arms, and I released her. "There is no time for reunions now. We must move swiftly and silently."

She took my hand and led me out of the cell. We moved quickly through the dungeon and up into the castle proper, where she slipped behind a hidden stone door in the rock face. Inside was a small room with far too many trinkets and baubles stacked around as if somebody had been collecting them for a long time.

"Do you know why the red threads are so dangerous to the cosmos?"

I shook my head. "I really don't."

"Because they are weaker than the white ones, warped and twisted because they've been wrenched to fit someone's ends, frayed by the careless hopes of an unwitting traveler. The tapestry we build is the fabric of the universe. When we weave a red thread in with the white, it weakens the fabric and allows for tears—between dimensions, between realities…it threatens everything. One thread is bad enough, but Doretha has been weaving red threads into the tapestry for thousands of years. The universe can't hold together for much longer. Soon, it will unravel, like cutting a tight thread, rebounding on itself, and destroying everything. We cannot let that happen."

"No, we can't. We have to stop her, but how?"

"Listen to me carefully," Viannah said, taking my hands in hers. "There is only one chance to save Talinda.

The pocket watch that Doretha used to kill her mother. She always keeps it on her person, a memento of her great victory over time itself. I have tried to take it from her a thousand ways and died every time. This room was blessed long ago as a sort of panic room against the ravages of time."

"Why are you telling me this?" I said.

She squeezed my hands. "Talinda believed you were the only person who could end this, and I still believe that now. My lady had faith in you. I do, too."

"How do you remember that? It happened in a whole different timeline."

"This palace," Viannah said, looking around us. "It's the same reason that though everything has changed, you still exist. This palace is outside of time. I have not left this palace in so long, but you must. You need to take the pocket watch and go back to the moment when Doretha killed Talinda. That will save us all." She shuddered. "Over the last decades, I have told the other handmaidens to await your arrival. We will work as one to buy you time."

"How will I know when to return?"

"I've been able to get my hands on the watch once or twice. I am almost certain that she keeps it set to the same moment she disappeared last. Take the watch when she is at rest, but do not let her touch you when you disappear, or she will go with you and destroy the timeline just by being there." She looked at me deeply in the eyes, her hands gripping my shoulders. "Do you understand?"

I frowned. "No, but I'm just going to go with it."

"All of the universe is relying on you." She pushed open the door and looked down at the entrance to Doretha's keep. "I will go first. When you hear me scream, do not hesitate. You will have ten seconds to rush in while we contain her. After that, she will have control again, and all of this will be forfeit."

I watched her disappear behind the door to Doretha's lair. I followed behind, listening for her cue.

"You again?" I heard Doretha hollering. "Aren't you sick of—"

"NOW!" Viannah screamed.

Just as I'd been instructed, I didn't hesitate. I pushed open the door just as the handmaidens grabbed Doretha's hands, restraining her and preventing her from even snapping her fingers. Viannah kicked Doretha in the chest, and the jolt caused her to fall forward, exposing the watch hung around her chest.

I slid under Viannah's legs, and Doretha's eyes went wide at the sight of me. She screamed as she realized what we had planned, but it was too late. I pulled the watch off her neck and leaped toward the spindle, out of her reach. When I was clear of her, I clicked the top of the watch and vanished.

CHAPTER 64

I reappeared from the white light, lying in some dewy grass. Looking up, I saw Talinda's castle glistening in the evening sun. The ground looked as windswept and pastoral as when I had first visited. The sky was slightly different, though, and the castle—though timeless—looked younger, brighter, and more vibrant than in my memory. *I made it.*

"Are you okay?" I heard a familiar voice behind me. I turned to see Doretha staring at me with a bright smile. I braced to attack but reminded myself that this was not the same girl I knew. The mania in her eyes was gone, replaced with kindness, love, and humility. She wore a pink flower tunic, and a white rose hung on her ear. "Let me help you up."

"No…" I said, scooting backward. I didn't know if I had destroyed the timeline already, but I certainly didn't want to ruin anything by touching my worst enemy. I stood up and brushed myself off. "I mean, I can do it myself. Thank you."

"Of course," she replied. She pulled a piece of red fruit that I didn't recognize from a woven basket at her side and held it out to me. "Would you like a komilo? They're perfectly ripe." I shook my head, and she shrugged and took a bite herself. Juice dripped down her chin, but she didn't seem to mind. "Your loss."

I glanced at the castle. "I should be going."

"Are you headed to the castle?" Her eyes brightened. "I'll walk with you."

"I think I can find the way."

"Are you sure? It might look close, but without a handmaiden, you will find it quite impossible to get any closer to it."

"Seems I don't have a choice in the matter."

She gave a little laugh. "Maybe you like impossible tasks. I don't know."

"You have no idea. I do need to see Lady Talinda as quickly as possible, so I will go with you."

"Wonderful."

Doretha was so much different now than when I'd met her. In the future, she was weighed down with the importance of her task, beaten down by failure, and wounded by the uncaring universe pressing down upon her. This Doretha had none of those worries. She nearly skipped through the fields and even sang to the birds as they passed. I found myself liking this version of her and wished she could stay this way forever.

"What is your wish?" Doretha asked as if she'd read my mind.

I froze. "My wish?"

"Nobody ever goes to see my mother without a wish." She smiled brightly as if this were the most obvious thing.

"Oh," I replied. "Right. Well, I want to save a little girl's life."

"Noble. Foolish, but noble."

"How do you figure?"

She slowed her steps and walked beside me. "Everything in the universe happens for a reason, doesn't it? If you believe that, then you have to be okay with bad things happening to good people, even if you don't like it."

I sighed, thinking about my fate. Thinking about Veronica.

We were getting closer to the castle. Doretha continued. "I get it. We all want to believe that everything is in our control—that we have agency over our actions. But the universe is kind of like a big, old clock. Every piece in it makes the others function in perfect harmony. If you take a piece out, move it around, and start messing with the mechanism, well, the whole thing starts to break down. Independently, each of those pieces has agency, but together, they are part of a big whole."

I chuckled. "I wouldn't care to live if I thought that."

"Most wouldn't," she said, and with a final step we were on the bridge into the castle proper. "I hope you get your wish, though I have found that people get what they need inside of these walls, even if it's not what they want."

"I hope you never change," I said. "The world is hard, but please, stay as soft as you are now, as long as possible."

She gave me a queer look and said, "I'll try."

Out of the corner of my eye, a heavier, bulkier, older Doretha moving with the weight of the world on her shoulders, slid into the castle at the far end of the hall.

"I have to go."

"It was nice to—"

I was gone before she could finish, rushing toward the door. When I was out of sight of the younger girl, I broke out into a sprint. I didn't bother to hide myself. The older Doretha moved carefully through the thread room.

"Don't move," I shouted, lunging toward her from the hallway.

Doretha turned. "Hello, Lizzie. Long time no see."

"You don't seem surprised to see me." I frowned. "Why not?"

"I have known you for a long time, longer than you've known me. In fact, it was something you told me long ago that stuck in my head and helped me decide to save that pathetic world." She smiled. "You might say that you made me, Lizzie."

"How is that possible?" I looked back to see Doretha's younger self turning down the hallway. "I told you to be soft—to stay soft. How could you use that to destroy the world?"

"That's not what I remember." She shook her head and continued wandering around, studying the threads. "No, before that, you told me you wouldn't care to live in a world that didn't give you agency over your choices. That ate at me for a long time, over the centuries, as I watched my mother do her work, as I watched all the planets she allowed to vaporize into nothingness, as I watched quadrillions hang out in pain. How could I live with myself when there was so much pain in the world?" She smiled. "If you really think about it, this is as much your fault as mine."

I faced her, crossing my arms over my chest. "No. If you want your own agency, you can't pawn off your mistakes on somebody else. That's not how personal responsibility works. You own the good, and you own the bad." Tears welled in my eyes, and I held up my hands. Cold blue magic wafted from them. "Now, don't move."

"You do what you have to do," Doretha said. "I won't live in a world without agency."

She spun to the door just as it opened, and Talinda stepped out. Doretha moved toward her mother, and I took a deep breath. *You own the good, you own the bad.* I had created this monster; it was my job to kill it.

"*Glacies spica!*" A perfect spike of ice grew from my hand and shot across the room, embedding itself in Doretha's back as she raised her hand to strike. Blood spat from her mouth as she turned to me, surprised, and then fell to the ground.

Talinda gave me a cold, sad, painful smile. "I knew you could do it."

CHAPTER 65

Talinda snapped her fingers, and Doretha's body disintegrated back into the universe just as the younger version of her daughter appeared around a corner.

"Oh good," the younger Doretha said. "You found her."

"I did, sweetie." Talinda's voice broke as she spoke, trying hard to keep her composure. "Can you go make Mommy's friend and me some tea?"

She nodded. "Sure thing."

Doretha wandered away toward the kitchen. When she was gone, I sidled up to Talinda. "You knew…this whole time?"

"I did. I had no idea how you got here or what you had done to save me, so I had to keep you in the dark lest I ruin it all." Her hands were trembling, but she kept herself composed. "In an eternal life, this is the hardest thing I have ever done, allowing my own child to die at your hand." She looked up into the air, and a red thread evaporated into whiteness. "For the sake of the timeline, it had to be done."

"How can you do it? Make such sacrifice for the sake of the universe?"

"Oh, you get used to it." She swallowed and sighed heavily. "And now, I must ask you to make an impossible choice, too."

"Why am I not surprised?"

She pointed to another red thread snaking across the room. "The girl you mentioned, your Veronica. She was not supposed to die. Some demon mucked with the timeline, so sending you back to her is not a problem for me. It will right a great wrong."

"Awesome," I replied with a smile. "That sounds like good news. Wait…why isn't that good news?"

"You," she said. "You were supposed to die. You were supposed to learn of your prophecy and leave home, only to return at the last moment. You led a tragic life with a tragic end. Not fair, but it was supposed to end the way it did in that warehouse. I can give you back the decade, as your god promised you, but it will cause a rift in time-space, a rift you tried so hard to fix for me." Her eyes seared into mine. "Or you can embrace your destiny."

"So, it really was always my destiny to die?"

"Unfortunately, yes. And now your destiny has been written, and it will stay written for all time. If I used magic to change that—well, you would become one of the red threads." She leaned forward and wiped the tears from my cheek. "It's not fair, but the rules of the universe are immutable. Maybe next time, they'll write a different rule."

Doretha appeared in the doorway. "Tea's ready."

"Thank you, honey. Can you put out some biscuits, too? And jam?"

"Of course." Doretha disappeared back into the doorway.

Talinda turned to me. "Would you like to spend a little more time with my daughter? She is a lovely girl."

"Until she kills you." I shook my head.

"Yes, but I never knew the woman she becomes. That burden is borne by a future me." She stared into the middle distance for a moment before turning to catch my gaze. "You must make your choice. Will you embrace your destiny or rebel against it?"

"And become like your daughter?" I said.

"You are given a choice to change your future. It is a choice not given to many. I would seriously consider it."

"But the girl will die if I choose that path?"

"She will, but you will live."

I wanted desperately to make the selfish choice, but if I did that, then what was all this for? "If this is my destiny, so be it. I promised I would die to save that girl, and I stand by it. If she lives, then I'll die for her."

"I thought you would say that." Talinda smiled. "You really are the most remarkable human."

She snapped her fingers, and I was gone. This time I did not disappear into the ether but shot across the universe like a ray of light. I zipped across time and space, watching the cosmos flash across my face until I could see Earth in the distance. I watched the planet spin forward faster than I could track, finally slowing slightly when I entered the atmosphere. Europe shot toward me at blinding speed, and then I was in Prague, on top of the building next to Kimberly and Zachary, who had already leaped into the air. A moment later, Kimberly handed me the switchblade and I stuffed it into my pocket. We followed through the skylight, and as we fell to the ground, I reentered my body, and time returned to normal.

I knew my cue and didn't hesitate. *"Glacies spica!"* I shot ice spikes into the demons guarding the conveyor belt and leaped onto it as chaos erupted around me. Zachary and Kimberly fought against the tides of the demons while I rushed toward Veronica's bound body.

I felt the beating of my heart, how the blood rushed through my body, and the feel of the rubber under my shoes. I wanted to remember every single moment, but this was not about me. I had a girl to save.

When I reached her, I pulled out the switchblade and cut off the rope that bound her. Veronica leaped into my arms, and for an extra moment, I treasured the smell of her, the feel of her arms around my neck. Too quickly I had to come back to reality as the battle raged behind me. I had a job to do.

"Got her!" I shouted on my way toward the door. A single thought rushed through my brain: *I'm going to miss this*. Perhaps I could defy fate yet again. I thought of Lilith, then. I had agency. I could still say no. I could stay alive if I wanted. My fate was in my hands, after all. What was one red thread weighed against eternity?

No. Talinda was right. I would not be selfish, could not be. I had worked so hard to save the timeline, I couldn't imagine destroying it for one pathetic, little life, even if that life was mine.

When we made it past the mass of demons, I dropped Veronica to the ground. "Run outside."

"Aren't you coming with me?" she cried.

"I'll be right behind you," I spun to face the demons. "Now go!"

The little girl didn't hesitate. I heard her tiny feet pumping toward the door. Five demons rushed toward me, and I laid spikes in their skulls. I fought bravely, brave enough to make sure she was safe, but it was not enough to save myself. I felt the rebar rush my body, cutting through my insides, and I fell to the ground. Kimberly screamed, and Zachary cut a path toward me.

It was too late. They grabbed me and rushed me outside, where I took one last look at the sky. My head listed backward to find Veronica's face filled with tears. I smiled a weak smile at her, then fell into darkness for the last time.

CHAPTER 66

When I opened my eyes, I was enveloped in a dewy cloud. Gabriel knelt next to me and the gates of Heaven behind me.

"Letting me cut the line?"

Gabriel put his fingers to his mouth. "Don't tell anyone. You're a very important person. You might have just saved the whole world."

He helped me stand, and I chuckled. "Oh, I saved quite a bit more than that." I was lost in thought for a moment. "Is she going to be okay?"

"You did well." Gabriel nodded. "Come on. I have something to show you."

I bounced along across the floor of Heaven. In the distance, the pillar where I had met God loomed over the fields, but we weren't heading in that direction. We stopped in the middle of the clouds, in a place as sparse and nondescript as any other in Heaven.

"This is nice," I said with a smirk. "A bit barren, but…nice all the same."

He didn't say anything but closed his eyes and pushed his hands together, then back apart. As he did, a hole opened in the floor of Heaven. At first, I saw the United States, soaring from thousands of feet above, and as I watched the view narrowed to Oregon, then the northwestern tip of the state to a little town called Overbrook, and finally, it settled on a townhouse.

"Kimberly found Veronica's father," Gabriel said. "He's a hard man, a preacher, but she'll be safe there until the time comes. His tough love will make her strong and prepare her for what is to come. Her life will not be easy, but she will be prepared."

As I watched, Kimberly walked into the picture holding Veronica by the hand. The door opened, and a stern-looking man in a stained T-shirt ambled out onto the porch. An older boy with curly hair ran past him down the stairs.

"You Veronica?" the boy asked.

"Nice to m-meet you."

"I'm Barry." He held out his hand. "Come on. Let me show you your room."

Kimberly gave Veronica a hug and then stood behind her as the little girl I saved took the boy's hand and walked inside.

"So it'll all be all right?" I asked, hopefully, to Gabriel.

"No," he said. "But it will be okay…for the time being."

***

You have just finished *Time*. Keep reading after the author's note for a sneak preview of the team-up book, *Heaven,* which features the leads from this book along with Ollie from *Magic,* Anjelica from *Evil,* and Kimberly!

AUTHOR'S NOTE

The whole idea for this book came from a meme. In it, somebody said something along the lines of "for the time being," and the other person responded. "You can see the time being, too?" I have thought of that every day for more than a year, and each time I say that phrase, I do so with reverence.

In planning for this book, I knew a couple of things. I wanted to tell a different story than anything else in the series; I needed to use Lizzie, and I wanted it to tie in with *Death.*

I've now written twenty-five novels, and this was the first one that dealt with time as a central component of the story. Playing with time terrifies me as a writer, and that it became the central focus of this book freaked me out. I worry about talking about time because it's such an easy crutch for people to fall back on when things get bad. That's why I developed the white and red threads and the turning back of time. I figured that gives us all a reason NOT to mess with the timeline, but it also gave Lizzie a reason to take on the mantle of helper human…er, fae.

I didn't know Lizzie would be the main character until I sat down to parse things out. Originally, I planned that she would die a lot sooner, but she ended up being the perfect main character for this book because I kind of abandoned Anjelica's family after the first book of *Evil* and thought that Lizzie, Junebug, and Carl deserved more story. I'm glad I was able to give it to them.

Now that you've met all these characters, it's time for the big finale. Are you ready for a team-up book between

Lizzie, Ollie, Anjelica, and Kimberly? Because that's what you'll get in *Heaven*.

***

Now, here is a sneak peek of *Heaven*.

HEAVEN

Book 4 of The Godsverse Chronicles

By:
Russell Nohelty

Edited by:
Leah Lederman

Proofread by:
Katrina Roets & Toni Cox

Cover by:
Psycat Covers

Planet chart and timeline design by:
Andrea Rosales

CHAPTER 1

Kimberly

I'd finished picking the lock to the door and stepped inside the demon's apartment. The brimstone smell immediately overpowered me. Demons moved often, usually following the night as it moved across the world, taking their scent with them. But this one, Ch'ri'yl, had stayed put long enough that every surface of her apartment reeked of battery acid and sulfur.

"Be on your guard," I told Molly as she followed behind me.

Molly was my wife. We married the first day it was legal, in a big ceremony at San Francisco city hall with hundreds of other gays who had waited to marry the loves of their lives for years—or, in our case, decades. We had lived together since the 90s, so marrying her didn't change much, except that it changed everything.

"It stinks in here," Molly said as she broke away from me, moving toward the kitchen to make sure there weren't any body parts in the refrigerator. She opened the door, and another scent crashed into the brimstone: rancid food and spoiled milk. "Holy good god. That is foul."

"Rotten meat?" I asked, turning my attention to her.

"Some maggots, too." She slammed the fridge closed. "Don't think it's human."

"Well, that's good, at least. Means he's probably not dead yet." I said. "Anything else?"

She held up a blue post-It note. "Just this stuck to the fridge. Mean anything to you?"

I walked over and looked down at the note. Ten numbers and a name. *Horace Carlson.* "You don't see that name often."

"I'll run it through our database," Molly said.

I bit the inside of my cheek. "I don't think you'll find anything. I'm going to stay here and keep looking for a clue."

She kissed me on the cheek, and I swerved to connect with her lips. "Okay. Love you."

"Love you, too."

It was good she left. She distracted me. We worked well together, but I felt myself always looking over my shoulder to protect her. One day she would die, and I was going to have to learn how to exist without her. She would never have that problem. The years were showing on her face even as mine stayed as youthful as the day we met. Her reflexes diminished exponentially with every birthday. I much preferred her back at the apartment, where I knew she was safe.

Besides, I thought better alone, and I needed every bit of my faculties to find out where Ch'ri'yl had taken Geordi. His mother came to me yesterday after taking a flight from Vancouver down to San Francisco, scared out of her mind because he hadn't come home in a week. He was an eleven-year-old with a rebellious streak, but he had never stayed out all night before. It had been three weeks since she had seen her son. If I found him, I had a feeling he wouldn't be doing it again.

I had a special affinity for protecting magical creatures, and while his mother didn't have an ounce of magical blood in her, she assured me that her son was touched by the gods. If this was true, it made him a very rare breed indeed. I took the case, which led me across the country up to Canada, and finally to Fresno, where I caught the trail of the demon named Ch'ri'yl. She had stayed hidden for a quarter of a century.

I followed a hallway to a locked door at the end of it. I knocked, hearing the ting of metal. The door was thick. It wouldn't give, even when I pressed my weight against it. It was possible for me to use my powers and teleport into the room, but without having seen within its walls to direct my coordinates, I risked losing myself into the abyss forever.

There was no need for something so drastic. People who spent a lot of money on metal doors often conveniently forgot that their walls were made of flimsy drywall. I drummed my knuckles on the wall next to the door, and sure enough, it was hollow. I tapped around some more, looking for studs. Confident that I wouldn't hit anything solid, I took a running start and smashed my shoulder against the wall, tumbling through to the other side.

I hopped up and brushed myself off before flicking on the light in the dark, dank room. What the red light showed me was disappointing. It wasn't a prison to store the boy; there were no chains, no bed, no boy. Just dozens of trays filled with chemicals and pictures hanging on clotheslines to dry.

The front door creaked open. Instinctively, I went for the pair of daggers on my belt and crept to the hole in the wall. A tall brunette woman with olive skin walked into the kitchen and put down two duffel bags with a huff.

"Gross," she said, opening the fridge and pulling out the maggoty meat. "Check your fridge before you leave for the weekend, Cheryl." She tossed the meat into the trash as her face changed into an onyx demon with long, fire-red hair and two long orange horns coming out of her head. She stepped into the hallway, and I got a look at her blood-red eyes just as she caught me peering through from the hole in her wall.

"What the hell?" She marched toward me, inspecting the damaged wall. "You know I have to pay for that, right?"

I stepped out of the room, leveling my daggers at her. "Where is Geordi?"

She held up her hands. "Are you kidding me? Who is Geordi, and who are you?"

"I'm here to find Geordi. I know you have him. Where have you taken him?"

"Are you crazy? I don't know any Geordi. I was on a trip to Napa for the weekend…with my boyfriend…and also, you're in my house pointing frigging daggers at me!" She pulled a phone out of her pocket. "I'm calling the cops."

"I don't think you want to do that, demon. Not unless you want them to know what you're doing in that room back there."

"You mean my darkroom? Where I process film? For my job, as a photographer!" She dialed. "Yes, I would like to report an invas—"

I sliced the phone in half as she spoke. "No cops. Not until you tell me where Geordi is."

She glared. "Okay, so this is bananas. If I had Geordi, whoever that is, why would I call the cops on you? Jesus, you are stupid." She smacked her forehead. "Think for two seconds. Just because I'm a demon doesn't mean I'm evil."

"It doesn't mean you're good."

She scoffed, placing her hands on her hips. "That's racist. I have been up here twenty years and haven't caused one single problem, and yet, you guys can't stop harassing me for every little damn thing."

I opened my mouth to speak, but I couldn't find the words. *Had I made a mistake?* Just then, my phone rang. It was Molly. I put one of my daggers away and kept the other one pointed at Cheryl. "Don't move."

"I know the drill," Cheryl said, crossing her arms across her chest. "This is bull, though."

"What is it?" I said into the phone. "I'm in the middle of something."

"That number was for a bed and breakfast in Napa," Molly replied. "Apparently, they rented a room there this weekend to a Horace Carlson."

"Hang on," I said, putting the phone against my chest. "What's your boyfriend's name?"

"Like I have to tell you!"

"Please," I said.

She sighed. "Horace Carlson."

"Shit," I said to Molly. "I think we made a big mistake."

* * *

I wrote Ch'ri'yl a check for $50,000 to repair her wall and pay for the photographs I'd ruined, which got her to calm down. She even offered me tea after I told her I was a bit of an art collector.

"I don't like that name, you know," she said. "Ch'ri'yl is my slave name. I like Cheryl better."

"I like Cheryl better, too," I said, sipping the cup of black tea.

"Me too," she said, taking her own sip. "I know some of us are awful, but most demons are just trying to get along in the world. It sucks that people are trying to scapegoat us for their awful crimes. Don't mistake me, this is horrible. It sucks that this kid is missing. People that steal children are the worst kind of people."

"I agree."

She smiled. "It's funny what we could agree on if you looked past the horns on my head."

"I don't want to seem indelicate, but is there anyone else you could think of that might want to—"

She shook her head in a snit. "You just can't do it, can you? You can't comprehend that I'm not a criminal, and I don't know criminals."

"Everybody knows criminals," I said. "That's one thing I've learned in my life."

"Well, I am very glad I don't have your life because I have no interest in being around, or associating with, criminals." She drained her cup. "I think you should go."

I slid the check over to her. "My number is on the check. If you think of anything, please give me a call."

"If I do, I will, but I won't, so I shan't."

I took my leave of her with a rock of guilt swirling in my stomach. She was right, of course. By the most aggressive standards, most demons I met weren't a danger to themselves or others. Even if they came up to Earth with evil intentions, that bloodlust left them over time, and they ended up working jobs as taxi drivers or accountants. They became upstanding citizens and productive members of society.

***

I slammed Atticus's head into the table of the very nice Embarcadero restaurant where I'd asked to meet him. It wasn't my intention to slam his face into the table, but his face was so slammable, smiling at me so smug.

Blood smeared the white table cloth as he slid to the floor. "What was that for?"

"You fed me bum information, Atticus. I should rip your face off. Getting your head smashed is a courtesy because we're old friends, or at least we used to be."

"It's not my faaaaault!"

He situation himself in his chair once more, ignoring the other patrons who stared at us unabashedly. I turned to the waiter who stood two tables away, an aghast expression on his face.

"Sorry about that. Can you tell all these nice people their meal is on me? Thanks." That seemed to settle everyone in the restaurant, and I handed the waiter my credit card with a curt smile. "Add a nice tip for yourself as well."

"You gonna pay for my meal, too, Kimmy?" Atticus held a napkin to the cut on his forehead. "Least you can do."

"Who are you protecting, Atticus?" I said, ignoring his request. "And don't lie to me, not again."

He looked around, then whispered, "You don't want to mess with these guys. They are no joke."

"I literally hunt demons for a living. It takes a lot to scare me."

"I know it does, so believe me when I tell you that you have reason to be scared of these people. I was trying to protect you."

"By sending me to harass an innocent demon?"

"Better her than me!"

"Who took Geordi? Give me a name," I snapped. "I'm a big girl and can handle myself."

"Not against these guys you can't. They are bad news."

"Ten seconds." I sat in silence, refusing to budge and staring daggers at him. Atticus squirmed in his chair, refusing to catch my eyes. "Three, two, one."

"Okay!" he shouted. The restaurant patrons all turned their attention to us for a second time. "You're gonna get me killed."

I leaned toward him. "Better than me killing you, which is what will happen if you don't tell me what you know right now." I grabbed him around the throat. "The only reason I allow you to keep your awful operation going is because you feed me the information I need, no questions asked."

"Okay, okay, okay," he squeaked as I crushed his larynx. "They're called the Blue Trident."

He gasped for air after I released him. "That sounds like a healthcare plan," I murmured.

"They aren't. They are bad news, and they're planning something big."

"You're not lying to me, are you, Atticus?" The threat in my tone was obvious.

"Of course not," he replied. "Though you should hope that I was lying, because if there's one group you don't want to mess with, it's the Blue Trident."

"What do they want with Geordi?"

"I don't know!" His voice cracked. "But they're being real secretive about a lot of things these days."

"Thanks, Atticus," I said. "Find out everything you can on where they took the kid, and call me when you have something."

"Are you serious? Do you think I have a death wish?"

"No, I think you very much want to live, which is why you'll help me." I stood up as the waiter brought the bill to my table. He had given himself a $1,000 tip. "I thought I told you to be generous," I said to him, smirking. I added a zero to it, making it $10,000, and signed it. "Thank you for your service."

CHAPTER 2

Angelica

Standing before a thousand staring faces used to cause my entire body to tremble, but now I could address the general assembly of Forche like I was singing to myself in the shower. It had taken a long time to win their respect, and the ones that didn't, at least tolerated my presence due to my connection with Queen Margaret.

"And in the next quarter, we expect to open up relations to Nuralia and Endosp, increasing exports by thirty percent and cementing our trade routes for generations to come."

Neither Margaret nor I were from Onmiri, but we had done the hard work of integrating ourselves into the world when Margaret's uncle opened a portal with her blood and sent us here. It didn't hurt that she was a member of the royal family and the only one left to ascend to the throne after we killed her father and imprisoned her brother for crimes against the people.

"I look forward to working with all of you on the next budget proposal." There was a boisterous laugh across the chamber. "I know it's never fun to discuss our fiscal solvency, but what is the parliament for, if not to make sure we live within our means?"

It had been a shaky proposition, moving Forche from a monarchy to a constitutional democracy, and I was just a kid when we started the process. It ended up pretty good in the end, I thought. There were still people loyal to the old king even now, 25 years after his demise, but we worked hard to rebalance his power back to the people. Other countries took notice. Where once we ruled with an iron fist, now we did so with a white glove.

Most days, I wished we could just jam through whatever crazy proposal we had without having to fight tooth and nail for it. Even then, though, I have never thought about reinstalling the monarchy. The people deserve a voice, even if it was a pain in the ass to give it to them.

"Thank you," I said. "And may the gods shine on Forche for many years to come."

There was thunderous applause when I walked out of the chamber. My assistant, Gible, was waiting for me just outside.

"Great speech, ma'am," she said, pounding her tiny legs along the floor to keep up with me. I walked briskly to avoid the throng of reporters descending on us. "The delegates seem to have really loved it."

"Did they? Or were they just excited I was finally done?"

"I do—"

It was a rhetorical question, so I didn't bother listening to her response. "Tell the communications team I don't want to do any more speeches over thirty minutes long for at least another year."

"I told them already, miss. I told them last time, too."

I let out an exasperated sigh. "Then why do they insist on making me drone on and on for hours?"

"Miss Anjelica!" A bubble-faced reporter hollered as the flashbulbs started going. "What do you have to say about your missile strikes on the Forchean settlements?"

"No comment," Gible yelled over her shoulder. We rushed down the stairs of the grand parliament building toward my car waiting outside. "We'll be available for press questions in the conference room in an hour back at the residence."

The settlements. The bane of my existence. We had given them freedom after the king's passing and allowed them to self-govern, but that wasn't enough for them. They wanted to break off from Forche to form their own government, and they had taken to bombing government buildings to show their dissatisfaction with the current structure. *How could they expect us not to bomb them back?*

"Perhaps we should prepare a statement," Gible suggested when we were safely in the limo back to the palace.

I placed my hands on my head. "There is nothing else to say. Peace talks are ongoing, but the settlements are being intransigent. They have no leverage except blind faith in their cause, and yet they refuse to yield."

The black divider between the driver and the back of the limo rolled down, and I heard a familiar voice. "Were you any different when you came here?"

Director Frente smiled at me from the front of the limo. She had grooved wrinkles on either side of her mouth, and thick bags hung from her eyes to the tip of her nose. Gray hairs overtook the brown in the mod cut she had kept since we met nearly three decades ago, but she was still the same optimistic do-gooder that she had been when we wrested power from the king.

"Director." I was not pleased to see her. "I thought I told your office I wasn't available today."

"Today, yesterday, this week, this month, this year. Every time I contact you it's always the same."

"Because I am always busy."

She chuckled. "There was a time you would rely on me to make every decision."

"Before I learned you were unreliable."

"Because I side with the colonies?"

"Because you side against Margaret and the crown, yes."

"Listen to yourself!" Director Frente threw her hands in the air. "You sound just like the previous king."

"Don't you dare," I growled. "I am still the Grand Advisor. Insulting me is to insult Queen Margaret herself. Remember that, Director."

"Oh, I remember it. You'll never let me forget it."

I snapped my fingers. "Gible, make a note that the director isn't to have access to me for any reason until further notice. If she violates this order or gets within thirty feet of me after this ride, see that she's arrested."

"You can't avoid this fight forever!" Director Frente was still shouting as I pushed up the separator and locked it into place.

When I turned back to Gible, her mouth was pursed shut.

"Anything to add?" I spat.

She shook her head but didn't speak, which I appreciated. Even if she disagreed with me, she kept quiet until the appropriate time, and this was not the appropriate time to discuss such nasty business as succession. If we allowed that, we would seem weak at a time when we needed to be strong. Democracy still rested on the head of a needle, threatening to tumble if we didn't keep a firm grasp on it.

***

"How was your speech today?" Queen Margaret asked at dinner. No matter what else was going on with our lives, we always ate together at least once a day, usually dinner. The banquet table was set for thirty, but tonight it was just us. We sat next to each other, sloughing off our responsibilities and sitting like old friends instead of queen and advisor.

"You didn't watch?" I asked.

She laughed. "Oh god, no. It's all so dry. I mean, I don't have to tell you that, right? You were there."

I took a sip of my tomato soup. It wasn't exactly tomatoes, but it was close enough on this foreign world. They called it *visuri* here on Onmiri. "I've begged them to cut my speeches down to thirty minutes. There is so much bluster in them. But my team insists every word is vital to the effort." I made a slurp. "What did you do today?"

"Met with the generals about the unpleasantness in the colonies, like every other day. They think it will lead to civil war across all Forche soon if we don't squash it in the coming weeks."

"How can we squash it without destroying the colonies completely?"

"I'm not sure we can. But if they get the support of Uyin, there could be trouble."

I furrowed my brow, thinking about our tenuous allies to the north. I had negotiated a peace treaty with them a decade ago, but it was always on the verge of falling apart.

"You can't possibly think we should annihilate own our people."

"Of course I don't!" Margaret said, setting her cup down loudly. "But in a democracy, it's not what I want, it's what the people want, and we're starting to lose the public's patience. If it were up to me, I would cut them off like a bad limb. If they're so sure they could exist on their own, then I'd like them to prove it. They'll be back in six months begging for our help."

I downed the last of my soup and gave her a hard look. "We can't do that either. Half the world thinks we're going to crumble any second, and the other half is waiting to pick over the remains when we do."

Margaret sighed. "Remember how we thought we were going to change everything?"

I nodded. "And we did."

"Maybe. but the more things change, the more they stay the same." She took a long drink from her wine glass. "At least there's wine."

"*Bicho*," I replied, tilting my glass to hers before the exhaustion of the day hit me. They didn't have grapes in Onmiri, and what they made wasn't wine exactly, but it did the job. I finished what was left of my wine before standing. "On that note...I have a busy day of being yelled at by bureaucrats tomorrow."

She sighed. "And I have a long day of pretending people aren't talking about me behind my back. Until tomorrow, tomorrow."

I kissed her hand. "Goodnight, my love."

She pulled me close to her and kissed me full on the mouth. "Goodnight."

We had kept our relationship secret for a decade, even as we worked to give all people the right to marry who they loved. Not because we were ashamed, but because the idea of Queen Margaret's chastity and virtue was the one thing we could count on for positive public opinion.

Even if she could marry or date, it wouldn't be with me. I was one of the most hated figures in Onmiri, the punching bag for the entirety of the government. Every bad decision was luffed off on me. It might look powerful from the outside, but my position was little more than a scapegoat for everything people felt was wrong with the world.

I slid into bed after washing my face and brushing my teeth. I took one deep sigh and turned off the light. Nights like these I wished I could lay my head on Margaret's chest and listen to her sleep. We had to be careful, though. Our enemies were everywhere, especially with tensions so high, and were looking for anything to tip the delicate balance into anarchy.

"Good evening, lady Anjelica," a voice from my past spoke from the dark room. "I'm sorry to come to you like this."

I wasn't surprised to see Araphael, god of death, emerge from the shadows. In fact, I was almost glad that perhaps my long life would be finally over.

"Please tell me you're here to kill me, Araphael."

He shook the hood from his head, his bright eyes staring out blankly. "It is not your time, I'm afraid."

"Then why are you here?" I propped myself up on my elbows. "It can't be good."

He sighed deeply. "I'm afraid your mother has passed. As her friend, I promised to deliver this message to you. Her funeral will be held tomorrow on Earth, and she requested your attendance."

I stared back at him for a long moment before finally saying, "Of course. Let me get my things."

***

I hadn't seen my mother in decades, not since the day I was kidnapped by demons in order to sacrifice my body to open a portal to Hell. Luckily, it didn't work. To protect her, though, I had no choice but to go into hiding. Kimberly took me to a safe house after she and Ollie saved my life, or at least they thought it was safe. Little did they know I would befriend a witch from another planet or that she'd open a portal back to her world that sucked me through along with it.

There was one moment, in the abyss of death, that Araphael brought my mother and me together to say a sort of goodbye before I decided to stay on Onmiri and build a better world for the future. I often wondered if I had made the wrong choice. Yes, I would have been a nobody on Earth, but I would have been a happy nobody. I wouldn't have Margaret, and yet maybe I could have found somebody to be happy enough with most of the time instead of blissfully happy in tiny, hidden moments.

I would have been closer to my mother, that was for sure. Maybe not immediately, but eventually, the heat would have died down on me, and I could have seen her again. Now, I would never have that chance again.

It surprised me how emotional I was when Araphael led me into the funeral home, and I saw the body. I had negotiated deals with princes and held my own against generals without breaking, but taking one look at my mother's peaceful, dead face was enough to send me to my knees, wailing an ugly cry that turned my face a beet red.

A kindly old man in a black coat rushed in, but when he saw my condition, he didn't say anything. He simply dropped a handkerchief at my side and walked off. It was a full half-hour that I bawled my eyes out before I could pull myself up to see my mother's face serene face one last time.

Funny, I never thought of her as a peaceful person. Her body was never at rest. Part of the reason she worked so much was because of the nervous energy she bottled up. Another shift was eight more hours she didn't have to confront the darkness within her. That darkness was all she would have for the rest of eternity.

"Was she happy?" I asked the shadows, knowing Araphael was inside of them.

"I will not lie to you," he replied. "She never found true happiness. There were moments when the guilt of her past didn't crash upon her when I think she found peace or the closest a ship at sea can find."

"Ah," a voice behind me said. I turned to see the old man shuffling up to me. "It is a dreadful thing to lose the ones we love. Were you close with the deceased?"

"I was her daughter."

"Oh," he said. "I wasn't sure you would be coming. Will you be saying something at the service?"

"I…I don't think I knew her enough to speak at her funeral." The words crushed me when I spoke them out loud, sinking my stomach down into my feet. It didn't make them any less true.

"I understand. Well, the viewing will begin in an hour. You are welcome to be alone with her until then. If you change your mind and wish to speak, let me know."

I had spoken in front of friends and enemies alike, thousands at a time, but the thought of speaking at my mother's funeral filled me with a dread I hadn't felt in decades.

"I won't, but thank you." I turned back to the casket as the old man left and looked down at my mother's face. "I want to see her again."

"You are seeing her, right here and right now," Araphael replied.

"No, I mean I need to go into the underworld and say a proper goodbye to her. I need to make my peace."

"That's not advisable," Araphael said, emerging again from the darkness.

"I don't care if it's advisable. Bring me to Hell. I know you have the power."

"You will not like what you find there."

"I don't care. I need to see her again. Make it happen."

Araphael was silent for a long moment. "No."

"Fine," I snapped, spinning away from the coffin. "Then I'll do it myself. Thanks for nothing."

CHAPTER 3

Lizzie

Heaven was boring. Not just a little boring, either, like watching a nature documentary about tortoise migration boring. Wait, actually, that wasn't not boring at all. I would kill to get the nature channel here. No, this was more like C-SPAN, all day, every day.

Not only were there very few people in Heaven, but they were all duller than dishwater. Apparently only super boring people could fit through the eye of the needle. I met plenty of people in my travels across the country to know there were plenty of amazing, interesting, fun churchgoers. Clearly, none of them got into Heaven.

I had checked. I knocked on every door to every apartment in Cloud City and really tried with these people, from the ancient to the…well, slightly less ancient. Perhaps it would be easier to make friends with them if we had literally just one single thing in common. And there hadn't been a new person in Heaven for several hundred years.

Even the ones who would have been interesting hundreds of years ago, like Joan of Arc, ended up having all the fun sucked out of them in the droll doldrum and repetition of Heaven. On Earth, at least you had to eat, sleep, and poop, which chewed up most of even the most banal day. We didn't have to do any of that in Heaven, which meant there was nothing to look forward to or dread.

I ended up spending most of my time parting the clouds to watch people on Earth. I tried to keep the privacy of people I knew and instead chose to watch philandering husbands and felonious women all day. Even the most interesting life was boring most of the time.

It was hard not to turn my attention to Veronica. She was growing up so fast. I watched her join the volleyball team, get her black belt, graduate high school, and start working at a delivery company in town. She had friends, and even a nice boyfriend, Dennis. I couldn't help thinking he was holding her back, keeping her chained to Overbrook instead of traveling the world and having incredible adventures.

It was hard to fault her decision to remain in one place, though. That was all I had ever wanted: a quiet life on the farm with my parents. My life had been the opposite, having run away at sixteen and traveling the country for a decade. I regretted it still. I had been trying to avoid my destiny…a destiny that caught up with me anyway and left me dead, swallowing my parents along with me before the end.

"I found them." Gabriel blinked into existence in front of me as I watched a cruise liner move over the ocean, hoping for some bit of intrigue that never came.

I popped my head up. "My parents?"

For the price of embracing my destiny to save the world, God promised that my parents would be able to get into Heaven along with me. I had been waiting fifteen years for the angelic guard to follow through on that promise and return them to me. It had been almost twenty years, and they still weren't with me.

I kept pestering, and they kept responding with placations and platitudes. Eventually, I gave up, assuming that it would never happen and trying to make my peace with being lied to by an all-powerful being. I wasn't the only one.

"Yes," Gabriel responded. "They should be here any time now. Come with me."

I followed Gabriel toward the Golden Gates of Ascension at the entrance to Heaven. I had been waiting for this moment for so long that butterflies bounced in my stomach as I hopped along the clouds. With the magnitude of the situation, I wished that I could do something more than bounce along like a child on a trampoline, but it was the most efficient way to move across Heaven, especially since only archangels received wings. Bouncing was fun for the first ten minutes, but after that, it just got annoying.

"Where were they?" I asked as I tried to keep up with Gabriel. "And why did it take you so long to find them?"

"I'm not sure if you've looked in on Hell recently, but it's nothing if not unorganized."

"And whose fault is it that they were sent to Hell in the first place?"

"I didn't have anything to do with it," Gabriel grumbled. "Since they were dead before you came to us, I couldn't put in the necessary paperwork to make sure they ended up here. If you recall, I even had to traverse Hell to find you the first time you died."

Oh, I remembered. The first time I died, I wound up in a huge line, hundreds of miles from the Gates of Abnegation, where millions upon millions waited to be judged. It was a complete mess down there.

"Seems like something God could have figured it out, what with being all-powerful and all-knowing."

"God doesn't sully his attention on such matters. Besides, he and Lucifer have an accord. If Lucifer needs his help, he needs to come to him. Otherwise, God has agreed to stay out of the management of the underworld."

We reached the gates, and after a moment, they creaked open. Gabriel and Peter gave each other a thick, side-long glance as we moved past. They didn't get along very well.

"It took us a while to get the necessary paperwork together and for God to sign off on it, especially seeing as he has a whole planet to run," Gabriel continued once he broke off his gaze from Saint Peter. "When we eventually did, it was a matter of searching millions of souls to find the right ones."

"But you found them. You really found them?" I hadn't dared to hope for a long time, but I found that it tugged on me, and I wanted so badly to let it in again.

"We did." He snapped his fingers, and two puffs of clouds exploded in front of me, causing me to jump back. Nothing so surprising had happened to me in many years. "I present you your parents, Carl and Junebug."

The dust cloud dissipated, and my heart dropped. The man and woman standing there before me looked nothing like my mother and father. They were younger, for one, but even in their youth, my father had darker skin and my mother lighter. Even if I wiped the soot and dirt from their faces and squinted, they barely held a passing resemblance to my parents.

"These people are not my parents." I wasn't even angry, just disappointed.

"Don't say that, honey." The woman smiled, but her eyes filled with panic. "Of course I'm your mother. Don't you remember that house in"—her eyes darted back and forth, trying to summon the right answer—"Missouri, where you were born…?"

I sighed. "I was adopted by Carl and Junebug. And I was born in Wisconsin."

"Umm," the man chimed in. "That's what she meant. We're your biological parents."

I looked over at Gabriel. "Then why did he say you were Carl and Junebug?"

The man and woman looked at each other, flushed with dread before the woman turned to me. "Come on, kid. Don't make us go back there. Please. I'm begging you."

"I want these two in Heaven as well," I said to Gabriel.

There was a stern look in the angel's eyes. "You know I can't do that."

"This is your screw-up, and I'm not going to have these two people's eternal torture on my hands."

"You won't," he snapped his fingers, and the two souls went away. "It's on mine. I'm very sorry about this. I really thought we had found them that time."

I stepped forward on wobbly legs. "If you let me go into Hell, I could find them myself."

He shook his head. "Only archangels are allowed to leave Heaven."

"Then make me an archangel!"

Again, he shook his head, more vehemently this time. "You have to do something truly incredible to become one of us."

"Oh, and saving the whole world, maybe the whole universe, isn't enough?" I raised an eyebrow. "What did you do that was so deserving?"

"I have been an archangel as far back as I can remember. On this planet alone, I protected the first humans as they searched for meaning, appeared to Daniel to save him from the lions, and appeared to the Virgin Mary to announce the birth of Jesus."

"So, you're a messenger? I could deliver messages if that's all it takes."

"It's impossible right now."

I was so close to him now that I could smell the brimstone left over from his trip to Hell. "You owe me. Figure out how to fix it—and quickly. I'm sick of waiting. This is supposed to be paradise, but it's so boring, and I'm so filled with worry, every day is a nightmare."

"There is a way. Show me how to get to the Time Being. I can go back and—"

"No." This was a tactic he had used before, many times. I was one of only two people on Earth that had ever met Talinda, the goddess of time, who controlled the flow of the universe. The other was trapped in Hell, her mind warped and twisted to uselessness.

Gabriel told me that if I helped him find Talinda, he could simply go back and make sure he put in the proper paperwork to get Carl and Junebug sent to Heaven, but time didn't work like that.

I explained it once again. "She doesn't want to see anyone else. She doesn't want to help anyone else. If she did, she would show you how to find her yourself." I crossed my arms across my chest. "If you want my help, make me an archangel. Otherwise, figure this out. Leave me alone until you do."

This was Heaven. I shouldn't be constantly disappointed. If there was one place in the universe where I should be able to count on things going my way, it was in frigging Heaven. And yet, more often than not, it felt like Hell, just a different kind of Hell.

***

I had mapped out several interesting storylines down on Earth. There was a mother in Minneapolis desperately trying to keep her child from turning into a right-wing internet troll. There was a cop in Rio De Janeiro attempting to hide the fact that he was corrupt from his partner. Meanwhile, the prime minister of Italy was doing his best to convince people he wasn't a womanizer. There were a half dozen others that I flipped between like TV channels when I was feeling bad about myself.

However, I didn't go to any of those after I left Gabriel and reentered the golden gates. Instead, I made my way to the cloud cover over Oregon to spy on Veronica. She was calling herself Connie now, something her dad insisted on after he took her in. Kimberly wasn't wrong about him being a hard man, but I don't think anyone would have predicted how much bitterness he held against his ex-wife, or how much Veronica would have reminded him of her. There was very little love in his heart for his daughter, and eventually, it made Connie strong. Powerful, too. It pushed her to be better and taught her to see the flaws in manipulative people.

"I'm sorry," Gabriel said behind me.

I don't know how long I had watched Connie on her route, biking away without a care in the world, but it was long enough for day to turn into night down on Earth.

"Go away," I said. "I don't want to see you."

"I know," he said, walking toward me anyway. "There's something you should know, though. God isn't omniscient. Neither am I. We're old, so we've seen a lot, but God is also prideful. He had the Metatron spin a tale bigger than he is." Gabriel sat down next to me. "I know that doesn't make it better. I just thought maybe if you knew that you would be a little more understanding of our mistakes, maybe cut us some slack."

I leaped to my feet. "Cut you some slack? It's been fifteen years, and you haven't done anything at all to find my parents. I mean, even the sun shines on a dog's ass some days, but it's never shone on mine. Have you actually tried to find my family? Do you even care how unhappy I am here?"

"Of course we do!" Gabriel said, his hands held out. "What kind of Heaven is this if we can't provide for the people here?"

"Not much of one," I spat back. "Go away. I don't want to see you."

"Fine," he said, deflated. "But just remember—"

I bounced away from him before he could finish and didn't stop again until I was behind a cover of clouds several hundred yards away. He flew away, and I wiped the tears from my eyes. No matter what, I would never let him see me cry.

"Aw, pet…what's wrong?"

A hulking, soot-covered man in tattered clothes stood nearby. His hair was messy, and he grinned at me with malice on his face. The smell of brimstone and sulfur permeated off him even stronger than it had from Gabriel.

"What—what do you want?" I stepped back, trepidation in my voice.

I looked down at his hand, where he held a crooked knife with a big gem on the end. "Just to have a chat," he said.

I turned away to run, but he grabbed my arm. The heat from his hand burned into my skin, and I whimpered in pain. When he pulled me to him, I balled up my fist, using the momentum to clock him across the face. He barked in pain and let go.

He recovered quickly, though, and yanked my hair as I tried to flee, pulling me down to the ground. He could have ended me there with the knife, but he held back, instead smashing me in the face with his other hand, again and again, until I bled. I hadn't tasted the acrid tinge of blood since I was on Earth.

"Surprised you could still bleed, pet?"

I was wobbly on my feet. "Everything bleeds."

"Tell me what I want to know, and you can go."

"Eat sh—seersucker suits." I really hated that you couldn't curse in Heaven.

The ugly man pulled back his upper lip, revealing a row of baked bean teeth. "Oh, you already have." He charged me with the knife.

"*Flagellum aqua*," I shouted. I hadn't used my water nymph powers since I died and wasn't sure they would work now that I didn't have a body. Fortunately, water leached from the air and formed into a whip in my hand. I snapped my wrist, wrapping it around his knife. I yanked hard, but he was stronger than me and instead pulled me toward him.

I slid my body under his hulking frame and grabbed his forearm, slamming it hard against my knee until his arm bent in the wrong direction. He gave up trying to stab me and howled in pain, dropping the knife.

I kicked him off me and went for the blade. He charged again, this time barehanded, and I had just enough time to spin toward him as he lunged. When we made eye contact, he let out a small scream. I felt something wet against my skin. The knife had embedded in his stomach, and green blood oozed from his mouth.

"That's not how this was—" he started, coughing green blood onto my face and looking down at his hands. They disappeared into dust. I was able to make out a blue trident on my attacker's arm before he disappeared in a million particles of dust, like the embers of a fire, leaving me with nothing but his blood on my white toga and the gnarled knife, as proof of the attack.

***

If you enjoyed that preview, make sure to pick up *Heaven* today.

ALSO BY RUSSELL NOHELTY

NOVELS
My Father Didn't Kill Himself
Sorry for Existing
Gumshoes: The Case of Madison's Father
Invasion
The Vessel
The Void Calls Us Home
Worst Thing in the Universe
Anna and the Dark Place
The Marked Ones
The Dragon Scourge
The Dragon Champion
The Dragon Goddess
The Obsidian Spindle Saga

COMICS and OTHER ILLUSTRATED WORK
The Little Bird and the Little Worm
Ichabod Jones: Monster Hunter
Gherkin Boy
How NOT to Invade Earth

www.russellnohelty.com

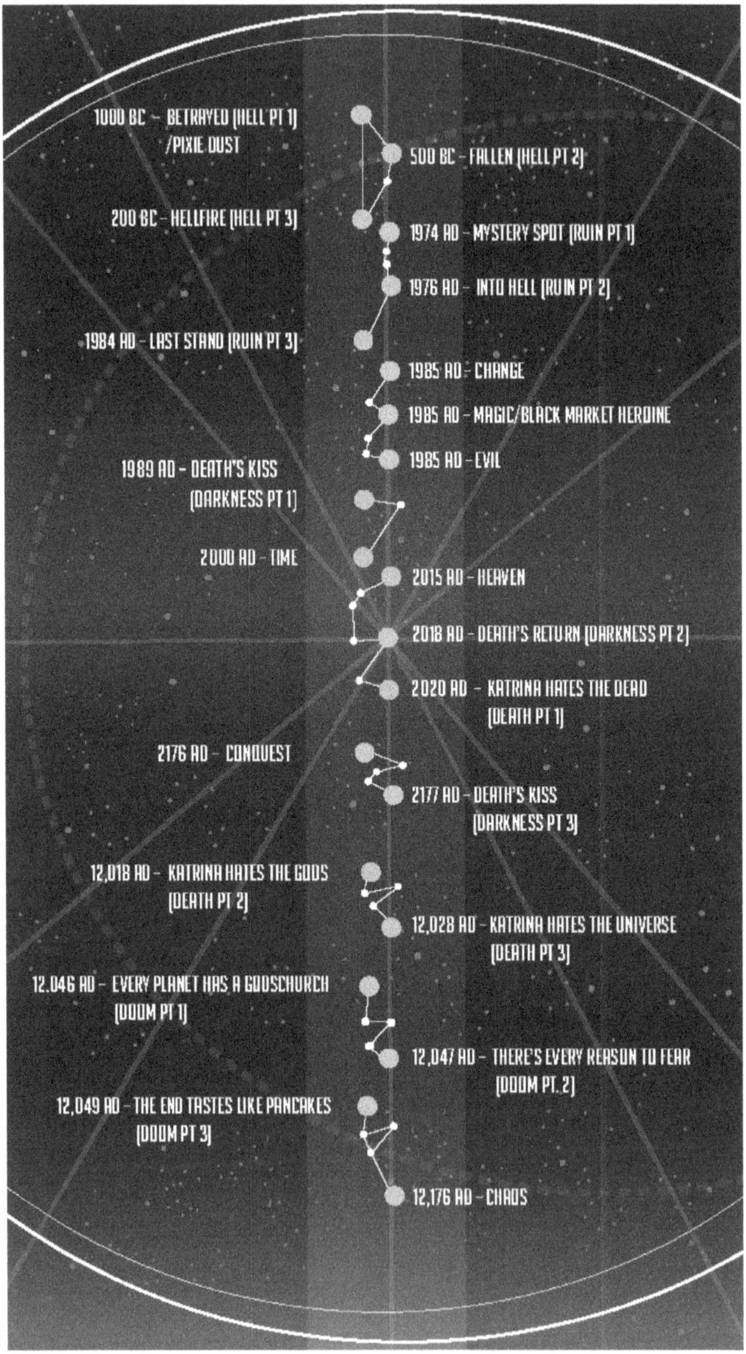

1000 BC – BETRAYED (HELL PT 1)
/PIXIE DUST
500 BC – FALLEN (HELL PT 2)
200 BC – HELLFIRE (HELL PT 3)
1974 AD – MYSTERY SPOT (RUIN PT 1)
1976 AD – INTO HELL (RUIN PT 2)
1984 AD – LAST STAND (RUIN PT 3)
1985 AD – CHANGE
1985 AD – MAGIC/BLACK MARKET HEROINE
1985 AD – EVIL
1989 AD – DEATH'S KISS
(DARKNESS PT 1)
2000 AD – TIME
2015 AD – HEAVEN
2018 AD – DEATH'S RETURN (DARKNESS PT 2)
2020 AD – KATRINA HATES THE DEAD
(DEATH PT 1)
2176 AD – CONQUEST
2177 AD – DEATH'S KISS
(DARKNESS PT 3)
12,018 AD – KATRINA HATES THE GODS
(DEATH PT 2)
12,028 AD – KATRINA HATES THE UNIVERSE
(DEATH PT 3)
12,046 AD – EVERY PLANET HAS A GODSCHURCH
(DOOM PT 1)
12,047 AD – THERE'S EVERY REASON TO FEAR
(DOOM PT. 2)
12,049 AD – THE END TASTES LIKE PANCAKES
(DOOM PT 3)
12,176 AD – CHAOS

www.ingramcontent.com/pod-product-compliance
Lightning Source LLC
Chambersburg PA
CBHW051002180726
48291CB00006B/1941